Finding Me

The Music Within – Book 3

Faith Gibson

Copyright © 2017 Bramblerose Press LLC

Published by: Faith Gibson

Editor: Jagged Rose Wordsmithing

First print edition: February 2017

Cover design by: Simply Defined Art

Photography: Randy Sewell - RLS Model Photography

Model: Jason Estes

ISBN: 978-1542830737

This book is intended for mature audiences only.

Dedication

To everyone in the world who has ever doubted yourself for whatever reason. The heart knows what it wants usually before the brain does, and sometimes it takes a while for the two to catch up with the other.

Acknowledgements

To my writing posse – your feedback, ideas, critique, and support is the most important part of my writing. Without you ladies, I'd lose my mind.

I've had the photo of "Andy" for months. As soon as I saw Randy Sewell's post with this amazing picture of Jason, I knew it was the one I had to have. After months of waiting, the photo is finally on the cover, and it couldn't be more perfect.

Christina Johnson: You are without a doubt one of the best at what you do. From you video reviews to your feedback, you are such a doll, and your words help shape my books into something better. Love you.

To all the readers who love my "boys" as much as I do. This genre is so near and dear to my heart, and I thank every single one of you who understands that love is love.

To the man who gives me my quiet time when it's supposed to be our time. For understanding this isn't only a job to me, but my passion. And maybe, just maybe, an obsession.

Chapter One

Andy

Andy slammed his phone on the counter. This was bullshit. Why the fuck could he not find a job? Andy'd served his country for the last eight years. Fought so the bastards telling him *no* could tell him no. Motherfuckers. He picked his phone back up, praying he hadn't shattered the screen. No job meant no money, which meant no new phone. He had some cash saved up from his two tours, but he needed to save it for hard times. *Harder* times. Andy had been home from the sand for going on six months, and he was starting to panic. That was something he couldn't afford, either. Nightmares were bad enough, but panic attacks were a whole 'nother ball game. Dreams were contained to night time when he was alone. Panic attacks could cripple him anytime, anywhere.

Maybe Andy needed to talk to someone. He had opted out of psychiatric therapy when he returned home because everything had been fine up to that point. Andy had been one of the lucky ones, coming home with all his body parts intact. He had seen a fair bit of trauma while serving, but again, it could have been worse. Not wanting to wait until things got completely out of control, Andy headed for the VA Center. Maybe they could help him find a job. He should have called for an appointment, but he didn't have anything better to do with the rest of his day.

Andy angled his large frame out of his piece of shit car and locked it. Not that he had anything someone would want to steal, but he'd hate to come back and find his vehicle gone. As he strode toward the door, a good-looking

1

man and his dog exited the building. Andy loved dogs. He'd always wanted one growing up, but his mother wouldn't allow a *mutt* inside their fancy house, yet she had two meaner-than-fuck cats hissing at everyone. The lab trotted to Andy and stopped in front of him, sitting at his feet, tail wagging. Andy knelt down and gave the animal a good rubbing. "Hello there," he greeted the dog as he scratched behind his ears.

"You keep that up and he'll never let you go." The owner had caught up to his canine companion. "I'm Erik, and this is Duke."

"Hello, Duke," Andy said before standing. He reached a hand out to the man. "Andy Holcomb. Nice to meet you."

"Same here. Duke and I visit the patients every Friday. He has a way about him that's therapeutic to some of the veterans."

"Maybe I should borrow him," Andy admitted aloud.

"I can arrange that, if you think he'd help. I'm not a psychologist, but I have a special place in my heart for those of you who are trying to get readjusted to life back home," Erik stated as if he could read Andy's mind.

Andy didn't know this man from Adam, and even though he admitted he wasn't a doctor, Andy felt comfortable talking to him. "I appreciate the offer. I think I need a job more than a dog. I never thought it would be so tough finding work after I got out."

"What kind of work are you looking for? I might be able to help," Erik offered.

"At this point, I'll take anything. It's been almost six months, and my savings is shrinking instead of growing."

"It just so happens I know someone who needs workers. I spoke to another veteran inside in pretty much the same predicament as you. He's taken me up on the offer, and if you agree, it will help out a great deal. I don't mean to be rude, but we'll need to get a copy of your psych evaluation before I can give you all the information. The job is working on a farm, helping with cattle and odd jobs. You would have your own bedroom and would be living with the foreman and the other veteran I mentioned. Does that sound like something you'd be interested in?"

"Hell yeah. I love the outdoors, and manual labor is right up my alley."

"Excellent. Let's go inside so we can discuss it further. We'll get the paperwork we need, and I'll introduce you to Bryan, the other veteran."

Andy couldn't believe the stroke of good luck. Here he'd come to whine about his problems, and the answer presented itself before he stepped into the building. As they walked together, Erik said, "I need to ask you something else before we proceed. How do you feel about gays?"

Andy's hackles went up. Was Erik a homophobe? He didn't give off that kind of vibe, but you never knew with some people. What if they wouldn't hire him because he was gay? His hesitation caused Erik to frown. "I need to know because the foreman is gay. If you're homophobic, this job isn't for you. I should have mentioned it sooner."

Andy breathed a sigh of relief. A grin tugged at his mouth for the first time in months. "No, I'm not homophobic. I'm actually gay myself."

Erik broke out into a large smile. "Excellent. I think having another gay man around will be good for Malcolm. Come on." Erik and Duke led Andy through the center to the administrative offices. Erik must be someone important, because there was no waiting around for hours. That was the main reason Andy had stayed away for so long. His impatience got the better of him, and he would get frustrated when he had to sit. He was a doer, so this job sounded perfect.

By the time Andy walked out the door thirty minutes later, he had met the other Marine who was also going to be working on the farm. The guy was relatively quiet; then again, Andy hadn't shut up since meeting him. Bryan Moore was a couple inches shorter than Andy. His ethnicity was impossible to pinpoint with his smooth, darker skin. And those eyes. Fuck! Andy had never seen eyes that color, sort of an aqua blue-green. Andy didn't know all the colors of the rainbow, but he did know beautiful when he saw it. And Bryan Moore was beautiful, in a built like a brick shithouse, chew you up and spit you out kind of way.

After saying goodbye to Erik and thanking him for finding them jobs, Andy and Bryan decided to go have lunch and get acquainted. "So, are you gay too?" Andy blurted as soon as they were seated.

"Why would you think that? Do I look gay?" Bryan's eyebrows were dipped low.

Oh, shit. Andy couldn't pull his foot out of his mouth fast enough. "No, you don't look gay. It's just that Erik mentioned our new boss is gay."

"Again, not sure what that has to do with me."

Andy slid down a little in his seat. The waitress chose that opportunity to arrive at their table, and for that, Andy was grateful. It figured the first man Andy had a reaction to in a long damn time was his exact type. And straight. Before Andy joined the Marines, his one and only boyfriend had been built just like Bryan was. The only difference was their coloring. The ex was fair-skinned and red-headed. When their relationship turned violent and ended badly, Andy swore he'd never fall for another man who was large enough to man-handle him. It was probably a good thing Bryan was straight. It would save Andy a lot of heartache and pain.

"Where'd you go?" Andy looked down at the hand covering his. His eyes found Bryan's, who pulled back when he had Andy's attention. "You okay?"

"Yeah, just got lost in a thought's all. So, Bryan, tell

me a little about yourself. If we're gonna be living together and working side by side, we should probably spill our guts."

Bryan laughed, a deep, throaty sound that made Andy's dick twitch. "Spill our guts, huh? Not much to tell, really. Grew up in the projects. Mom did the best she could to raise four kids while our father was sitting in prison, so it was up to me, being the oldest boy, to help out around the house. I have two brothers and an older sister. I managed to stay out of trouble while helping keep food on the table. As soon as I was old enough and saw they were all gonna be okay, I enlisted. It was sure money, and being provided everything I needed twenty-four seven, I sent all my money home to help my mom feed my siblings. Now, how about you?"

"Wow, that's... I was born into a very wealthy family. You ever hear of Holcomb Oil Company?" When Bryan nodded, Andy continued. "That's my grandfather's company. Old money and old values. Good old boys with Southern Baptist roots so deep they probably come out in China. Anyway, when I was dropped off on my parents' front doorstep all battered from the boyfriend who was supposed to love me, I was too incoherent to realize I outed myself. If it had just been my parents, they might have covered it up. Swept that shit under the rug. But my grandparents were visiting to celebrate some award my father had won.

"My grandfather didn't give me a chance to recover before he disowned me. He tossed me out of my father's home. My home. Cut me out of my inheritance and left me to fend for myself. With a body full of bruises and a back slashed wide open, I was put out on the side of the road like a dog with the mange. My mother tossed a bag out the front door, where she'd put a few of my clothes and forty bucks. If my grandfather knew my mother slipped me the money, he'd probably have cut her out of the will, too."

5

Andy waited for the waitress to drop their food off. He took a long drink of the sweet tea he'd ordered. After baring his soul to Bryan, he wished he'd ordered a beer. Or tequila.

"Wow, man. That sucks. So what'd you do?"

Andy had already told him the worst of it, leaving out the harsh details of what exactly Patrick did to him. He might as well tell the rest. "I went to my best friend's house and begged her to hide me. I only had a couple of months left until I graduated high school. When her parents got a look at the condition I was in, they were pissed, especially her mom, Carol. She couldn't believe my own parents would toss me out needing medical attention. They called in a family friend to look at my wounds, something my own family hadn't even done.

"When my father came around asking if they'd seen me, Christy's mom lied for me. Said I had come by, but she didn't know where I'd gotten off to. Things seemed like they were gonna be okay until I got to school that next week. As soon as I walked in, the first period teacher told me to go see the principal. When I got to his office, he informed me my tuition had been cut off, and unless I could come up with the money, I'd have to finish my last two months at the public school. I had no way of coming up with the cash, so I said 'fuck it' and went straight to the recruiter's office. When I got there, they informed me I needed my diploma, so I had no choice but to go to the local school and graduate. Carol knew someone who let me in with her signing for me instead of my own mother. I graduated and went back to the recruiter. Been out almost six months, and here we are."

Bryan hadn't moved while Andy was telling about his past. Now he looked like he wanted to hit someone. His beautiful eyes had darkened, and his nostrils were flaring. "That's bullshit," he seethed. "Parents are supposed to love their kids unconditionally. Fucking grandparents, too. I'm really sorry you had to go through all that. I've never had money, so I wouldn't know what it would be like to lose everything. We didn't have a lot, but our mom kept us fed, and we had decent clothes. Besides that, she loved us like nothing else. Even when my youngest brother blurted out he was gay, my mom smiled and said, 'As long as he treats you good, I don't care if he's purple.' Since she was white and my father was not, we learned early on that people discriminated because of one reason or another. My beautiful mom was the only white woman in our projects, but she didn't let anyone bully her or her kids."

Andy could tell by the anguish in Bryan's eyes there was more to the story, and he knew better than to pry, but he had to know. "What happened to her?"

"Cervical cancer. I got a call from my sister when Mom was already too far gone. She hid it from all of us. The doctor's appointments. The treatments. Even with the money I sent home, it wasn't enough. Since all the kids were grown and making it on their own, she decided it was okay to forgo the treatment instead of struggling the rest of her life to make payments on something that may or may not have worked. That was two years ago."

"I'm so sorry, Bryan." Andy wanted so badly to be able to comfort the man sitting across from him, but they weren't friends. Not yet. "So, what made you want to work on a farm?"

"Like you, I've been stateside for about six months. I've been struggling with PTSD and can't seem to keep a job. Everywhere I go is so fucking loud, and the least little thing triggers my panic attacks. Erik assured me the loudest thing on the farm would be a tractor, and I would know when it was going to start up. Malcolm sounds like a great guy who needs a little help. I figure being out on a farm in the middle of nowhere will be perfect. I'm not opposed to manual labor. I actually prefer it."

Andy let the last comment go. He wasn't going to insult the guy by feeding him a line of bullshit when he didn't know the truth about Bryan's education. Instead, he kept the subject safe. "Did you complete two tours?"

"Yeah. It was all I could do, though. Physically, it was no problem. But mentally? I just couldn't handle seeing the shit we saw day in and day out any more, you know?"

Andy did know. "I feel the same way. I went in to learn a skill I could use on the outside. Growing up, I thought I'd go on to college, study business, and work for my family. I never had plans outside of that. When the rug was pulled out from under me, I did the only thing I could think of besides becoming a stripper."

Bryan laughed again, his eyes crinkling at the corners. God, he was beautiful, and it was all Andy could do not to stare. Schooling his features, Andy scoffed at him. "What? You don't think I could have made my way dancing?"

Bryan didn't lose his grin. He slung his beefy, tatted arm across the back of his chair. "You in a G-string is not an image I care to think about."

"Oh, come on. Admit it. You'd love to see me shaking my lily-white ass on the dance floor." Andy squatted over his chair, shaking his ass back and forth.

Bryan tossed his head back and laughed louder. Smiling, he said, "You're a crazy sonofabitch; I'll give you that." Some of the other patrons were checking out Andy, but most couldn't keep their eyes off Bryan. Andy knew how they felt. He wasn't sure working with the gorgeous man was going to be possible. How in the hell was he going to keep his dick under control?

The two of them made small talk about their time in the Marines while finishing their meal. When they were done, they exchanged phone numbers.

"Unless you're completely bat-shit crazy, I'm betting Erik will recommend you to Mr. Wilson," Bryan said as they walked toward their vehicles.

"When are you moving to the farm?" Andy asked,

since Bryan had already been approved.

"I was going to go in a couple of days after I get all my shit packed, but I can wait to see if you get to go. That way we can drive up together. That is, if you want to."

"I'd really like that, but don't wait too long. I don't want the new boss getting pissed at you for putting him off."

"From what Erik said, Malcolm is just a down-to-earth guy who needs help running cattle. Do you know anything about working on a farm?"

"Can't say that I do." Andy had grown up in the south, but his family's money was in oil. "All I know about cows is they taste really good on a grill."

Bryan flashed his beautiful, slightly crooked smile, and said, "Yeah, that's about the extent of my knowledge, too. I thought about researching the subject at the library. I don't want to look like a complete idiot when I get there."

"I should probably do the same. I haven't studied anything in quite a while. It wouldn't hurt my stagnant brain to read something besides sports magazines."

"Do you like baseball? I happen to have two tickets to the Sounds game, and I have no one to go with me."

Andy was practically bouncing. "Are you kidding me? I fucking love baseball. When's the game?"

"Tomorrow night. If you want, I can pick you up so we both don't have to pay for parking," Bryan offered.

"Careful, or I might think you're asking me out on a date. That ass wiggle got to you, didn't it?" Andy teased.

Bryan blushed but took Andy's joking in stride. "Yeah, fool, I'm all about your pasty, white ass. I'll pick you up at five and we can grab supper, or would you rather get a hotdog at the park?"

"Hot dogs! Gotta have 'em when you go to a game. If you want to grab a beer first, you can still come around at five."

"Beer sounds good. I guess we need to exchange

9

phone numbers, since I don't know where you live."

Andy grinned. "Yeah, that might help."

After swapping information, Bryan said, "I guess I'll be going. It's been great meeting you, and I'm looking forward to getting to know you. I really hope you get the job, Andy."

"Me too. I think we'd make a good team." Andy meant it in more ways than one. "I'll see you tomorrow."

Bryan held his hand out, and Andy shook it. "Tomorrow."

Chapter Two

Bryan

Three days after the ball game, Bryan parked in front of Andy's apartment building. He had thoroughly enjoyed spending time with the blond. Andy was loud and constantly cracking jokes, where Bryan was quiet and reserved. Andy was gay, and Bryan was straight. Andy liked country music and had a beautiful voice. Bryan preferred loud rock music and couldn't carry a tune in a bucket. Their backgrounds were completely opposite, but somehow they meshed together better than anyone Bryan had ever been around in his life. He found himself looking forward to living and working with Andy.

He climbed the steps leading to Andy's second floor apartment, and when he knocked, Andy yelled from inside for him to come on in. Bryan turned the knob and entered the small living room. A boxer brief-clad Andy met Bryan just as he closed the front door.

"Sorry, man. I'm almost ready." Andy turned his back, and Bryan couldn't help but stare at the broad, muscled back of his friend. It wasn't just all that skin grabbing his attention; several scars marred the otherwise pristine flesh. Strangely, Bryan wanted to reach out and touch the shiny marks.

"No, it's okay. I'm early." Bryan looked away just as Andy looked over his shoulder, grinning.

"Couldn't wait to get over here, could you?" Andy asked, wiggling his ass as he pulled his T-shirt over his head. Now Bryan's eyes were drawn to Andy's bubble butt. Why couldn't the man have gotten dressed in his bedroom?

Not being able to control himself, Bryan slapped Andy on the ass as he walked past him to get to the kitchen. When Andy yelped, Bryan laughed. "You know it. That pale skin of yours has turned me to the other team." Bryan averted his eyes, *again*, wondering why the hell he'd been ogling a man's ass in the first place. *Because you need to get laid, that's why.* It had been far too long since Bryan had been with a woman. He was a rare breed when it came to fucking. He wasn't the kind of man to hook up with a woman just to have sex. It was why he'd only been with a handful of women in his twenty-six years. Even in high school, when his hormones had taken over both heads, he had been too busy working and helping his mother raise his siblings to spend time fucking around. When he had taken the time, he hadn't found it fulfilling, thus thinking sex wasn't special unless it was with *the one*.

Bryan helped himself to a cup of coffee. He'd only known Andy a few days, it didn't take Bryan long to figure out the man was a diva when it came to getting dressed. His clothes had to be ironed, and his short hair had to be styled perfectly. Bryan ran a towel over his own short hair and called it done. Not Andy. He had more styling products than a hair salon. When they went to watch the ball game, Bryan had been wearing a ball cap. He asked Andy if he had one, and the look on the blond's face had been priceless.

"And mess up all my hard work?" he'd admonished. Bryan rolled his eyes and settled in for the thirty minute wait.

Since they were moving into Malcolm's house that was already furnished, everything they were taking with them would fit into the bed of Bryan's truck. "Where's your shit? I'll go ahead and start loading the truck." Bryan wasn't one to sit around and do nothing. For the last six months, he'd worked out more than he had in his entire life just to have something to do. He was in better shape now than he'd been in the Marines. Andy must have been just as bored, because his body was as solid as Bryan's. Bryan knew that because Andy loved walking around in his underwear, giving Bryan ample opportunity to study the tattoos on his chest and arms.

"All the boxes in my bedroom are ready to go, but you don't have to carry them all. It's my stuff."

"I don't mind. Besides, if I wait on you to primp, we'll be here all damn day, and I'm ready to get on the road." Bryan started down the hallway to the bedroom, but Andy stepped out of the bathroom, hands on his hips.

"I don't primp."

"Do so. Now move, Lily, so I can get your shit." Bryan had adopted the nickname for Andy when he kept talking about being a stripper. He tousled a hand through Andy's gelled spikes, knowing it would only cause them to be delayed longer.

"You ass. I had it just right. Now I have to redo it." Andy retreated into the small bathroom and proceeded to start the process all over, singing random songs. Bryan smiled to himself. He loved ruffling Andy's feathers. By the time his buddy was out of the bathroom, Bryan had all the boxes loaded and had finished another cup of coffee.

"How do I look?" Andy wasn't digging for a compliment. He was truly concerned with his appearance. Years in the military and having to look a certain way were ingrained in them both, but where Andy couldn't let go of the need for perfection, Bryan had tossed that shit out the door as soon as he was back stateside.

"Like a wet dream. Now can we go?" Bryan loved yanking Andy's chain. He really shouldn't kid around in such a flirtatious way. One day, Andy was going to take him seriously, and then what would he do? Run for the nearest set of tits he could find? Maybe.

Andy looked around the small apartment, and Bryan waited patiently. He'd already said goodbye to his own home. Bryan had only lived there for six months, but it had been his, and he was going to miss the solitude. Bryan had bunked with others during his last eight years, but that had been a requirement. Now, it was his choice to share a house with two other men. One he didn't know at all and one he was only getting to know. The little time he'd spent with Andy he had enjoyed and already considered him a friend. He hoped Malcolm was as laid back as he'd been described. If things got too hectic, there were over a thousand acres he could roam around on to be alone.

"Are we doing the right thing?" Andy asked, pacing around the living room as he bit his bottom lip. When Andy's movements became more frantic, Bryan stepped in front of him, stopping his progress.

With his hands on Andy's upper arms, he assured him, "Yes. We need a job, and this one is perfect for both of us. At least on paper it is. If we get there and you don't like it, you can always look for something else. This isn't permanent if you don't want it to be."

Andy chewing his lip drew Bryan's attention to his teeth. It was something Andy did when he was nervous, which was often. Every time it happened, Bryan caught himself staring at Andy's teeth as they cut into the pink flesh of his lip. Bryan felt Andy's insecurities within himself. You give your life to your country for eight years, and when you return home, you expect to be able to assimilate back into society fairly easily, even though you've heard the stories of other Marines who are having a hard time doing so. You just never expect it to happen to you. Bryan squeezed Andy's thick biceps. "Hey, look at me." When Andy met his eyes, Bryan continued, "You've got this, Buddy. I'm right there with you every step of the way. If you don't like it, we'll fix it. Okay?"

Andy nodded and let out his breath. His minty coffee breath. Bryan inhaled, drawing the scent in. He released the grip he had on Andy, not understanding his sudden infatuation with his friend's breath. "Okay, let's get a move on. I want to get there before lunch time."

Andy left his key on the end table and locked the door behind him. They had discussed moving over beer before the ball game, and since they would be spending all their time on the farm, Bryan offered the use of his truck if Andy needed to go anywhere. Agreeing, Andy sold his car to a neighbor for a few hundred bucks. Now they loaded up into Bryan's truck and headed north to a little town in Kentucky. When Erik mentioned where the job was, Bryan had been concerned for Andy. Arlo, Kentucky, was the epitome of small town, redneck living. Erik explained that Malcolm was gay, but he stayed away from the locals. They didn't care that it was the twenty-first century. They were still as homophobic as they were racist. Bryan wasn't worried about himself. He'd lived with name calling and hatred his whole life. His father was a mixture of Nigerian and Italian, and his mother had been a blonde with blue eyes. Bryan was an odd scramble of all the above. He had started and ended many fist fights over harsh words, but his mother was the one who showed him words didn't matter.

Bryan had also gone to bat for his youngest brother, Brett. When Brett came out as gay, Bryan had punched more than one homophobe's face for their nasty words. Brett eventually grew into his large frame and was now bigger than Bryan. His little brother could more than take care of himself. Bryan wouldn't hesitate to have Andy's and Malcolm's back should anyone have something nasty to say to either of them.

Traffic was light, and Andy filled the hour-long drive with his rendition of country music. The radio was playing, but his beautiful voice carried over whoever was singing on the radio. Bryan hated country music, but somehow when Andy sang it, it wasn't so bad.

When they arrived at their new home, Bryan breathed a sigh of relief as he pulled into the driveway. He had called ahead and told their new boss what time to

15

expect them. A handsome man who appeared to be around his and Andy's age was waiting by the gate on a four-wheeler. He waved at them as he got off the ATV, opened the gate, and motioned them on through. Bryan drove down the driveway and parked beside an old farmhouse that had seen better days. He put the truck in park and turned off the ignition. Looking over at Andy, he asked, "You ready?"

"Yeah. Now that we're here, I feel better." Andy gave him a smile, but it didn't meet his eyes. If Malcolm hadn't been waiting for them, Bryan would have tried to offer Andy some reassurances, but he honestly didn't know if this was going to work out for either one of them. They were both here on a trial basis, but knowing they would be together every day somehow made Bryan feel better. He was quickly becoming comfortable around Andy.

They angled out of the truck as their new boss was shutting off the ATV. "Hey there. I'm Malcolm Wilson, and this is my home. Please, call me Mal. I sure do appreciate y'all comin' to help me out." Malcolm held out his hand, and Bryan and Andy took turns shaking with the boss. Bryan already felt better about the situation with the easy way Mal welcomed them. "My ma's in the house, so why don't you come on in and meet her then we'll get your stuff unpacked."

Bryan and Andy followed Mal to the back of the house. Two dogs were sitting by the small back porch, guarding the steps. Bryan had never had a dog in his life and had only been around a couple. He wasn't sure how to approach them, but Andy dropped to his knees and allowed the animals to greet him properly. They sniffed him over before licking both sides of his face.

"Moe, Curly, leave the poor man some skin," Mal chastised. The dogs immediately stopped licking Andy, but their tails never stopped wagging. At that point, Bryan felt it was safe enough to at least pet them, so he held out his hand and let them sniff. He gave them both a rub on the head and ran his hands through their thick fur.

"What kind of dogs are these?" Bryan asked.

"Australian Cattle dogs. I had Larry as well, but he died. Now it's just these two. Moe is the one with the black colorin' over his left eye. Once they get to know you, they'll protect you as fiercely as they would me. Stay," Mal commanded, and the dogs sat back down on the ground. Mal led Bryan and Andy inside to a country kitchen, where an older woman was sitting at the table. "Ma, I'd like you to meet Andy and Bryan. This is my ma, Suzette."

Suzette stood from her place at the table and held out her hands. "It's a pleasure to meet you both. I hope you don't mind a little hard work. My Malcolm's been busting his hump trying to keep this place up all by his self."

The first thing Bryan noticed was that Suzette was pretty. The second thing was she appeared to be blind. Bryan stepped into her space and took her hands in his. "I'm Bryan Moore, Mrs. Wilson."

"Please, call me Suzette. May I feel your face so I can see what you look like?"

"Of course." Bryan stood still while Suzette ran her fingers along his forehead, his cheeks, nose, and chin.

"Thank you, Bryan. I can see outlines, but nothing's really clear. Feeling helps me get a better picture."

"No problem, ma'am." Bryan stepped out of the way, and Suzette repeated the process with Andy.

"Boy, Malcolm. You've got yourself two very handsome helpers. First Cade, and now these two? I don't know if my old ticker can take all these fine-looking fellas," Suzette gushed. Bryan had no idea who Cade was. Maybe he was another worker.

"Ma, behave. If you're finished oglin' the help, I'll show 'em to their rooms."

Suzette laughed and waved her hand, motioning for them to carry on. "Welcome to our home, Bryan and Andy."

"Thank you," they said in unison. With Malcolm's

help, they had the truck unloaded and their things in their respective bedrooms in no time. Since the bedrooms were the same size, Bryan gave Andy the choice of which one he preferred. Andy chose the one across from the bathroom, so Bryan put his stuff in the one closest to the kitchen. Mal gave them time to put their clothes away before showing them around the house. There was a large living room with a fireplace. Suzette was sitting in a den with the television on. Her bedroom was down the hall past the den. Mal's room was upstairs where another bathroom was. The house was much larger on the inside than it appeared from the outside. After they'd taken the short tour, Mal took them to show them around the farm.

"We'll start with the barn," Mal said, once they were outside again. "I've already been workin' on it some, but it needs a lot more work to get it back to proper. I have two horses bein' delivered this week, and I'll need your help gettin' their stalls ready. Do either of you ride?"

Bryan had never been on a horse. Actually, he'd never even seen one in person, so he shook his head no. Andy spoke up. "I rode a pony at a birthday party once."

Mal didn't ask questions about either of their pasts. As it had been explained by the man who hired them, a Mr. Matheson, Mal was the foreman. The farm had originally been in his family for many years but now belonged to a corporation that had purchased the land from the bank. They all technically worked for the company, but for all intents and purposes, the farm was still Mal's, and he had the final say on everything.

"This four wheeler here belongs to my boyfriend, Cade. I still feel weird callin' him that. We've only been together a short while, and he lives in California. Anyway, you'll eventually meet him. Feel free to ride either ATV when you're out on the property if you don't want to ride one of the horses after they get here. There's lots to be done, like fixin' up the barn and the house, but with the company buyin' up the land around us, we'll need help with the cattle. I know neither one of you have worked a farm before, but there's not much to it, really. Let's get in the truck, and I'll show you the land."

Mal gave a short whistle, and Moe and Curly jumped into the bed of a new-looking Chevy dually. The three men got into the cab where a shotgun hung on a rack behind them, and Mal took off through an open gate. Andy was sitting in the middle, and since the three of them filled up the front seat, they were pretty much wedged in. It shouldn't feel strange, but something about sitting so close to Andy had Bryan heating up.

Mal pointed out the different parts of the farm where the cattle were grazing, explaining which ones were to be bred. He drove them by a pond, where he said they were welcome to fish on the weekends. He showed them the fence line and explained that part of their job was to make sure the fence was always in good repair.

"Just a few months ago, coyotes got in and took out a few cows. Had to get Walt's backhoe over here and bury 'em. Speakin' of Walt, you'll meet him later. He's been a good friend of the family for as long as I've been alive, and now he and my ma are seein' each other. He's a good man. If I'm not around, you can listen to whatever he says. Think of him as my assistant foreman." If Walt didn't have a problem with Mal being gay, then Andy should be okay, but Bryan had to wonder if he'd be looked at differently because of his skin tone. He would find out later when he met the older man.

After they were finished with the tour of the land, Malcolm put them to work on the barn. Since they had horses coming in the next day, getting the stalls repaired was priority. Hammering boards wasn't hard work, and Bryan enjoyed being outside. June in Kentucky wasn't nearly as hot as the desert had been, but the humidity was high, and that made the air thick. Bryan took off his T-shirt and wiped the sweat from his forehead. When he tossed it aside, he caught Andy staring at his chest. Bryan waited until Andy turned back to hammering a piece of wood in place and looked down. Had Andy been staring at his tattoos or his body? Bryan knew he was ripped, but he wondered how someone else viewed him. He had a deep pit between his pecs, and his six-pack had recently become an eight. Bryan had been around gay men in the Marines, so having someone stare wasn't new, and it didn't bother him. If anything, it was a boost to his ego that others found him attractive. Well, at least his body was being admired. With him being mixed, he'd often had to endure the ridicule of being a mutt.

Andy was the epitome of the handsome, blond-haired, blue-eyed boy next door. There was no way he would have ever been made fun of for his heritage. He had the same coloring Bryan's mom had. He was just as fit as Bryan was, and the man was stunning. And again, why was Bryan checking him out? Thinking he should probably do something to stave off his sudden odd thoughts, he asked Malcolm, "Hey, Boss, where do the pretty girls hang out around here?" He wasn't going to go get laid for the sake of busting a nut, but if he was going to live in Arlo, he needed to find out where he could start looking for a girl to at least hang out with. He wasn't interested in a relationship. Not yet, anyway. He wanted to make sure the job on the farm was going to work out for him and Andy. For some reason, Bryan didn't think he would stay with Malcolm if it didn't work out for his new friend. The man was slowly becoming important to him.

Mal laughed. "Not that I keep up with the women, but most of the girls I went to high school with are already married. Those who aren't hang out at the bar. It's filled with girls lookin' for a good time every Friday night. If you're lookin' for someone more reserved, you can visit the bank. I think Addison Miller works there, and she's really pretty."

"Do you think she'd have a problem with the way I look?"

Mal stared at Bryan for a beat, frowning. "From where I'm standin', there's absolutely nothin' wrong with the way you look."

Andy coughed, and Bryan looked his way. "You got something to say, Lily?"

Andy started laughing and shaking his ass at Bryan. "You sure do have an unhealthy fixation with my money-maker to be a straight dude, you know that? Boss man's gonna think we're sweet on each other if you keep calling me Lily."

Bryan looked at the ceiling and prayed for mercy.

Mal asked, "Why do you call him Lily?"

"That's his stripper name. Lily – as in lily-white ass."

Mal frowned at Andy. "You strip?"

Andy laughed and slapped Bryan on the shoulder. "No, but I thought about it for a hot minute. Bryan just wishes I would."

"Right. Like I want to see your hairy ass and legs wrapped around a pole."

"I'd wrap 'em around your pole," Andy joked, wiggling his eyebrows.

Malcolm grinned at their antics, and Bryan shoved Andy playfully. This was the type of camaraderie he'd been missing for the last few months, even if Andy's words made him feel funny inside.

Chapter Three

Andy

Bryan pushed Andy and scowled. "In your dreams, Holcomb. I'll be making a trip into town as soon as we get paid. I need to open a new checking account anyway."

Andy couldn't help himself. Messing with Bryan was too much fun, and Mal didn't seem to mind. As a matter of fact, he was smiling at the interaction between his new workers. It was the first smile Andy had seen on the man. Malcolm Wilson was a good-looking cowboy, but surprisingly, he did nothing for Andy. Andy had a suspicion it was because both his brain and his dick were fixated on Bryan. Something about the other man called to him on a level he'd never felt. Not even with Patrick. Andy had kept his sexual orientation hidden while in the Marines. He'd been afraid to have the occasional hook-up when he was on leave, and he never sought out anyone in his unit for fear of retribution if they were caught.

Andy wondered if fraternization between coworkers would be frowned upon by Malcolm. Not that he was expecting for anything to happen with Bryan since the man was straight, but he could certainly dream. Hell, he'd already had a couple of dreams about Bryan giving him head, and he'd used the image of Bryan on his knees as jack-off fodder ever since he met the man. Maybe working with Bryan had been a bad idea. Andy needed to get over his infatuation with his fellow Marine.

They got back to work on the barn. The company they worked for, AAW, was delivering two horses the next day, and the stalls were almost complete. Andy was excited at the thought of getting to ride again. Back before his drunken confession, his life had been as close to perfect as one could be. He had parents who loved him, or so he thought, a bright future with the family business, and more friends than he could shake a stick at. Being in the closet had been hard, but Andy had been the golden boy at his prep school. He hadn't felt the need to rock that boat. He never dated anyone seriously, and he took girls out once in a blue moon to keep up appearances. He did hook-up with boys from other schools, but until Patrick, Andy had kept his personal business to himself and away from his school and family.

As far as grades went, Andy had been top in his class. He played baseball in the spring, and during the other months, he studied classical piano. Andy was an only child, so he had no siblings to back him up when things went to shit. The task of being the heir apparent had fallen to him and only him where his family was concerned. They had groomed Andy to be a leader from the time he was born. When they kicked him to the curb at seventeen, he had been lost. Everything he'd ever known had been ripped out from under him, leaving him to fend for himself. Joining the Marines had seemed like the right thing to do at the time. He'd planned to have Uncle Sam foot the bill while he tried to find himself. He was going to do four years, get out, and get his business degree.

If Andy had been straight, that plan might have worked like a charm. Being gay, he was constantly hiding his true self while trying to fit in with the regime and structure of the military. It was worse than hiding his sexuality from his parents. There had been other gay men in his unit, but like Andy, they were afraid of the consequences of being found out. When his first tour was up, Andy thought long and hard about whether or not he wanted to spend four more years hiding who he was, but his CO had come to him, specifically asking him to stay. Andy really liked the man. He'd treated Andy like a son, and that was something Andy had clung to. He had no contact with his family once they kicked him out, and Andy had missed that terribly. Not the people, but the closeness that came with having loved ones around all the time.

His team had become his family, but being in the closet, Andy still didn't let anyone get too close. When he opted out after his second tour, he was no closer to having figured out who he was or who he wanted to be. The one thing he knew was he wanted nothing to do with a business degree. For eight years, Andy's heart fell apart piece by piece as his former life drifted further away. The longer he was in the military, the harder it was to see his future clearly. The fact that he was gay made it that much harder.

If he'd been straight, he would never have enlisted. He would have gone to school, found a nice girl to marry, and he'd have taken over the family business. Now, here he was, working on a cattle farm doing manual labor. Blue collar work wasn't beneath him; it just wasn't where he thought he'd be at twenty-six. As Bryan had told him, he could use this time to figure out what he wanted to do with the rest of his life. Working on the farm was just a job. A temporary means to an end. He and Bryan had only been there a few short hours, yet Andy felt freer than he could remember ever feeling. He had a boss who was also gay, so he didn't have to hide anything — other than his infatuation for the straight guy slinging a hammer next to him.

Andy had no idea what the future held for him. Did he see himself working a cattle farm the rest of his life? Probably not, but since he had no formal education, he couldn't get a desk job even if he wanted to. Looking around at the wide-open space of the farm and the two handsome men he was working side-by-side with, Andy found he wasn't in such a hurry to figure things out. There was a peacefulness in being where he was.

"Y'all ready to call it a day and get cleaned up for

supper?" Mal asked.

"Sure thing, Boss," Andy said, realizing he was hungry. The day had passed quickly, and since he and Bryan had arrived right after lunch, he hadn't had anything other than coffee and a couple bottles of water. He wasn't tired, but he was ready for a home-cooked meal. "How does your mom cook if she can't see?"

"She doesn't. I do all the cookin'. That's somethin' I was gonna ask you both about. Do either one of you know how to cook?"

Bryan shook his head. "You don't want me in the kitchen. I burn toast, but I can grill a mean steak."

Andy had loved to cook when he'd been at home. He didn't have much time to spend in the kitchen with their cook, but when he had, he'd paid attention. "I'm not too bad. If you give me a recipe, I can cook most anything."

"Good. I'd like for us all to take turns. Bryan, you can make sandwiches on the night it's your turn. You can make a sandwich, can't you?" Mal joked.

"Yeah, I can handle that as long as it isn't grilled cheese."

Andy would love to see Bryan in the kitchen wearing nothing but an apron. The man was so fucking sexy. He'd only seen him without a shirt, but he had imagined what the gorgeous man looked like completely naked. "I'll teach you how to cook," Andy offered. He knew spending more time around Bryan would be torture, but for some reason, he was drawn to the straight man. Maybe it was because Andy knew Bryan was safe. Or maybe it was the challenge of wanting something unobtainable. Either way, he would have to work on keeping his dick in check around his new friend.

"You're going to need patience, but if you're willing, so am I." Bryan grabbed his T-shirt and pulled it back on before the three of them made their way inside.

Mal stopped at the sink and washed his hands.

"Good. I don't have a grill, but we can see about gettin' one."

"You don't have a grill?" Andy asked before he thought better of it.

"I had an old one, but it finally rusted through. If I want burgers, I fry 'em up."

"Do you fry steaks, too?"

"Nah. I usually broil those, but it's been a while since I had one. Back when we had more cattle, we used to fatten one up and slaughter it for the meat. It would last us most of the year, but when the farm started dwindlin', I had to sell off all the calves for money. Now, if y'all wanna go ahead and shower, I'll get supper started."

Andy felt bad for Mal, so instead of putting his other foot in his already full mouth, he asked Bryan, "Do you wanna go first?"

"Sure. I won't be long." Bryan headed toward his bedroom, and Andy stayed in the kitchen with Mal.

"I just wanted to say thanks for the opportunity, Mal. I don't know anything about cattle, but I'm a quick learner and a hard worker."

"I appreciate the help. It wasn't that long ago that I had no idea what I was goin' to do. If AAW hadn't come along and bought the place, both Ma and me would have been out on our ears."

"Wow. I didn't know." Andy washed his hands before asking, "Is it okay if I get some water?"

"Make yourself at home. Glasses are in the cabinet over the counter next to the fridge. I make sweet tea every mornin', so if you'd rather have that, help yourself." Mal grinned. Obviously, he found the thought of making tea humorous. Andy had already overstepped, so he didn't ask.

"Thanks. I'll stick with water for now and have some tea with supper. So, what are you making?"

"Meatloaf. It's easy and doesn't take much to put it together. While it's cookin', I can put vegetables on the stove. By the time we've all showered, it'll be ready. I'm not gonna brag and say it's all that, but my cookin' is edible." Mal slapped his flat stomach. "I do like to eat."

Andy smiled at his new boss. So far, Mal had been nothing but nice and laid-back. Andy prayed he stayed that way. "Does your boyfriend come by often?"

"Nah. He lives in California. He's a drummer for a rock band, and we don't see each other much."

"What's the name of the band?" Bryan asked as he returned from his shower.

"Damn, you're quick." Andy loved taking showers. Stood under the spray letting the water run down his back until the hot water was all but gone. He'd have to remember he was sharing with three other people.

"He was in 7's Mistress, but he just took a job with Divining the Dark."

"Your boyfriend is Cade Anderson?" Bryan asked, his eyebrows shooting north. Andy had never heard of either band, but the way Bryan had reacted, they must be big time.

"Yep." Mal blushed and turned back to the stove.

"Damn, Boss. How'd you snag someone like him?" When Mal turned and frowned at Bryan, he caught his mistake. "I didn't mean it that way. You're a good-looking man, but you're a cattle farmer in a small town, and he's a rock star. How did you meet?"

"He came in the bar one night. Sat there 'til closin' time, and when he needed a ride back to his hotel, I offered, not knowin' he was stayin' in downtown Nashville. When he was lookin' to drink, he wanted somethin' out of the way and ended up in Arlo. Long story short, he spent the night here, and the rest is history."

Mal had already told them about the bar he owned. He had recently found someone to take it off his hands, and now he could devote all his time to the farm. Andy was looking forward to visiting the watering hole even if it didn't belong to Mal any longer. Ever since he'd gotten out of the Marines, he preferred the smaller taverns to big, noisy bars. They weren't as conducive to finding someone to take home for the night, but they were easier on his nerves. Now that he had a job, he hoped his nerves would calm the fuck down and he could feel like his old self again.

Andy excused himself to the shower. While he washed off, he wondered what it would be like to have a famous rock star as a boyfriend. The long distance had to be hard as hell to handle. The trust Mal put in Cade's fidelity… Andy didn't know if he could do it. He'd already had his trust abused once, and Patrick hadn't been famous. He cringed thinking of the last time he'd been with Patrick. Shaking that image away, Andy hurried and finished bathing so he could get back to the kitchen. He didn't want to miss out on any conversations between Mal and Bryan. Yeah, he was nosy.

When he walked back into the large room, Mal was pulling a bag of potatoes out from under the cabinet. Andy asked, "Do you want me to peel those while you take a shower?"

"Yeah, that'd be great. Thanks." Mal handed over the spuds and the knife.

Andy got busy peeling and cubing the potatoes, putting them in the pot to boil. "You cook a lot?" Bryan asked, coming to stand next to Andy at the counter. The scent of Bryan's body wash accosted Andy. He hadn't seen it in the shower, so Bryan must have taken it back to his room. If they were going to share the bathroom, they might want to discuss where they put their things.

"Not as much as I'd like. It's hard to cook for one person without having a lot of leftovers. Not that I'm opposed to leftovers. I've eaten my fair share of them over the last six months. Cooking feels a little tedious with no one else there to appreciate the trouble."

"I don't think that'll be a problem here. I know I'll

appreciate the trouble, especially since I've been living on take-out and frozen dinners. I used to try to help my mom out, but I just never could get the hang of it," Bryan told him.

Bryan was watching Andy's hands as he slid the knife under the brown peeling. Andy looked away from the distracting man and returned his attention to what he was doing. He didn't need to cut himself the first day on the job. Andy had peeled his share of vegetables when he was younger. His family dinners were big to-dos, but he preferred helping Francine in the kitchen over making small talk with his parents' friends. He had always been scared someone would ask about a girlfriend, and he'd have to lie. Whenever he had to go to a function for the family business, Christy would accompany him. His best friend loved dressing up and attending the fancy parties, so it wasn't a hardship for her. She loved Andy more than life itself and did whatever she could to help keep his secret. They stayed in touch while he was in the Marines, and she begged him to come back home to Irving when he got out. She was the only one who ever wrote him. The only person left in the world who loved him. Still, Andy had no desire to return to the city where he'd been beaten then kicked out of his home.

He would never forgive his parents for turning their backs on him. He did miss his best friend and promised to go see her once he got his feet under him. When she asked him why he was settling in Nashville, he explained to her that it was both country and big city living all rolled into one, sort of like Irving. What he didn't tell her was for a brief moment, he'd considered trying to make a go of a music career. Andy could play the shit out of a piano, and country bands employed keyboard players. What he hadn't counted on was the loud noises and the elbow-to-asshole crowds giving him anxiety attacks.

Bryan's movement brought him back to the task at hand. As soon as the last potato cube was in the pot, Andy washed his hands and looked around the kitchen. It had a warm, homey feel to it, the very opposite of the one he grew up with. Nothing was new. As a matter of fact, everything was old and worn, but gave the room character. Andy would bet there was a lot of history in the house. He was eager to add to that history. Turning to Bryan, he said, "Like I said earlier, I'll be glad to teach you. If nothing else, you can help cut up vegetables. I'm sure you're handy with a knife."

"I sure am, and I appreciate the offer. I'm willing to pull my weight around here however I need to, even if you do double duty cooking and I do extra laundry."

Andy slid a sideways glance at Bryan. The man was doing a number on Andy, and all he was doing was standing there. Whatever body wash he'd used in the shower was stronger than Andy remembered. Or maybe it was because Bryan was closer than he'd been since they sat shoulder-to-shoulder in the truck earlier. That had been torture. *Straight, remember?* Maybe that was the reason Andy was so infatuated with his new friend. Besides the fact Bryan was handsome enough to be on a magazine cover, he was safe. Other than the probability of blue balls, Andy wasn't worried about getting hurt. Physically or emotionally.

"I'm not sure what else we'll do to occupy our time at the end of the day, so we might as well put that time to good use. Besides, I love a good challenge," Andy said as he stirred the beans and corn. He added a little salt to the potatoes before turning to face Bryan.

"Between the two of us, we have enough DVDs to last a while. Besides, didn't you tell me you can play the piano? You could always serenade Mal and me after dinner," Bryan said with a wink. Andy was glad Bryan felt secure enough in his straightness to flirt with Andy, but Andy's dick didn't know the difference between a hot gay guy and a straight one, and this straight one was going to kill him. Andy's stash of toys was definitely going to get a workout. He prayed the walls weren't thin.

Chapter Four

Andy

Mal returned from upstairs, his dark hair damp from his shower. He was wearing a clean pair of jeans and a T-shirt with some band Andy had never heard of on the front. While Mal got the food ready, Andy and Bryan set the table and fixed their drinks. Mal left all the food on the stove, and once they'd all dished out a plate, they sat down and enjoyed their first meal together. Bryan and Andy took turns telling Mal a little about themselves. Bryan's story wasn't any less painful the second time Andy heard it. The hurt from losing his parents wasn't anywhere near what it must be for Bryan to have completely lost his mother. At least Andy's mom was still living, and although the chances of them reconciling were slim to none, there was a chance.

"Where'd your mom get off to?" Andy asked.

"She's over at Walt's. She has been spendin' a lot of time with him, plus she wanted to give y'all some space on your first night."

Leaving out why Andy found himself on his parents' front porch, he shared his story with Mal. "I have to admit, it feels good to be around another gay man," Andy said after he talked a little about the last eight years.

"I'm not exactly out and proud," Mal admitted.

"But you're dating Cade Anderson. If you're not out, how does that work?" Bryan asked.

"I need to tell you my story, but I'd rather do that after we eat. Once you hear what I have to say, I think you'll understand why I don't fly a rainbow flag."

Andy was certainly curious about Mal still being in

the closet, especially since he was dating such a high-profile person. As soon as they'd finished eating, Andy and Bryan did the dishes while Mal excused himself to his office. His phone had pinged several times during dinner, but he'd refused to look at it while they were eating. His face was flushed when he returned, and Andy had to wonder exactly what his new boss had been doing.

Mal grabbed a six pack out of the fridge and said, "Let's go outside." Andy and Bryan followed Mal to where a circle of large stones was on the ground. Wood had already been stacked up, and Mal lit the kindling he placed strategically around the larger pieces. Once he had it going, he handed them a beer before taking a seat on the ground against a hay bale. Andy thought it was dangerous to have hay so close to a large fire, but Mal obviously didn't see anything wrong with it. Andy and Bryan also sat down, stretching out and getting comfortable. Moe stretched out between Andy and Mal, with Curly taking the spot next to Bryan.

"My pa tried to kill me," Mal said, shocking the shit out of Andy. Both he and Bryan were staring, mouths open, and Mal continued. "He came home early from work one day and caught me with my best friend, Tyler. Me and Ty had become much more than friends, and we were always careful. But my pa had gotten laid off from his job, and when he got home that day, he caught us." Mal rubbed a hand over his chest and took a long pull from his beer.

"He tried to kill me. Almost succeeded, too. He left me for dead in the barn and went after Ma. If Tyler hadn't called the cops, I would have bled out. That's what's wrong with Ma's eyes. He beat her so bad she nearly went blind. Blamed her for spittin' out a faggot. I've been pretendin' to like girls ever since. It's just easier than puttin' myself out there for another bigot to come after me. Now that I've been seein' Cade, things are kinda confusin'. He does visit here, but we meet up in Nashville for the most part." Mal removed his ever-present baseball cap only to reset it, still not looking at either man.

"I can understand you hiding. I imagine small town minds are much like Marine mentality. I've hid who I am all my life. As much as I'd like a husband and kids, I don't see me ever getting either," Andy admitted. It hurt his heart, because he absolutely loved kids. Had always thought he'd have a houseful of his own one day.

Bryan nudged Andy's boot with his own. "Don't give up, Lily. My brother and his husband are trying to have a baby." Andy's stomach fluttered at the nickname. He'd love nothing more than for Bryan to grab hold of his ass and . . . *Don't fucking go there.* Bryan was trying to make him feel better. When he looked over at Bryan, the sincerity he found in the gorgeous man's eyes made Andy long for something he couldn't have. He assumed Bryan's brother was just as good looking, and Andy knew any child that came from their genes would be beyond beautiful.

"Yes, but they live in an area where being gay isn't grounds for attempted murder." Andy wished he could take the words back. "Sorry, Mal."

"Don't be. You're just speakin' the truth."

"Where's your dad now?"

"He's in the state prison over in Eddyville. Anyway, I wanted you to know my situation and why I'm not a big fan of going to town, even if I've tried to convince everyone I'm straight."

"But you tend bar. Isn't that hard? And what does Cade think about you flirting with girls?" Andy asked.

"Who says I flirt?" Mal responded before tipping back his bottle. He tossed the empty in the fire and pulled another bottle out of the small cooler. "Beer?" he offered.

Bryan

Bryan had missed the simplicity of sitting around shooting the shit with others. Even in the middle of war-torn countries, there had been plenty of peaceful nights spent relaxing while swapping stories and listening to music. Sitting there on the ground with Mal and Andy brought back the fond memories from his time in uniform. Mal's story was horrific. Bryan's life hadn't been a cake walk, but it hadn't been that bad either. Yes, he'd lost his mother, but he'd had her love until the day she died, and that was worth more than all the money in the world. Bryan couldn't imagine what it would be like to have grown up having everything you could want handed to you without working for it. Not only had Andy had the privilege taken away, he'd lost his whole family. Mal still had his mom, and now a boyfriend, even if he was a high profile one, so maybe Andy's past was worse than Mal's.

Mal was a reserved man, quiet in much the same way Bryan was. His eyes spoke the words his mouth wouldn't. The new boss was a tortured soul. He rarely smiled, so when Andy said something amusing, it was nice to see Mal's lip turn up on one side. Now that they had laid their pasts out to each other, the conversations turned back to happier things. Mal bragged on his nieces, and Bryan could feel the love from where he was sitting. He couldn't wait to meet the little girls. He missed being around his own family, but he hadn't wanted to subject them to his dark moods ever since he left the Corps. Brett had begged him to stay with him and David, and their sister Brianna had also offered him a place to stay. She and her husband had their hands full with their twin boys. Bryan had visited them over Christmas, but the boys were loud like little boys could be, and Bryan's nerves just couldn't handle the stress. His middle brother, Bryce, was off in California. They only spoke about once a year, and they weren't as close as Bryan was with Brett and Brianna.

Before joining the military, Bryan often thought about getting out, finding a nice girl to settle down with, and starting his own family. Now, he'd be lucky to find someone to put up with his mood swings. Working alongside Andy on a daily basis would help with that since Andy was also in the same boat. Hopefully, though, their bad moods wouldn't come on at the same time.

"I'm gonna turn in. Y'all are welcome to stay out here for a bit, if you like. I want you both to make yourselves at home, since this is your home now. It's not much, but the company's agreed to fixin' it up, so it won't be so run down soon." Mal headed into the house, and instead of following their master, the dogs continued to guard the fire pit. Or maybe it was the two men they were guarding.

Bryan and Andy bid Mal a goodnight, but neither one of them moved to get up. Andy pulled another beer out of the cooler and offered it to Bryan. They sat in companionable silence watching the flames in the pit flicker and dance. Andy hadn't stopped rubbing Moe's fur the whole time he'd been sitting there. Bryan had tentatively petted Curly. When the dog sighed and placed his snout on his paws, Bryan felt he'd made a friend. It was comforting rubbing over his fur. Maybe that's why Andy had latched onto Moe.

After a while, Andy shifted on his ass and turned toward Bryan. "So, you gonna go to town and meet some girls?" His question was innocent enough, but the way he wouldn't look at Bryan made him wonder what was really going through the other man's head.

"I want to get settled in first. Besides, I've never really had a girlfriend. I don't see what waiting a while longer will hurt. I don't have anything to offer a woman, you know? I have my savings, but I'm living in a house with two other men, and I'm not exactly steady as far as my moods go."

Andy seemed to be deep in thought when he muttered, "That's okay. You have me."

Bryan wasn't sure how to take the comment, so he let it go. Andy had already told Bryan how lonely his life had been. Maybe he was looking forward to spending time with someone who could understand him. The two of them had fun hanging out, and Bryan didn't see that changing. Other than Andy taking for-fucking-ever to get ready to go somewhere, he was a great guy, and Bryan already thought of him as a friend. If he was honest, he was looking forward to spending more time getting to know Andy better. He liked the same sports and the same movies Bryan did. He was funny, and he could sing well, even if it was country. So yeah, he was glad he had Andy. "You have me, too," he admitted.

Not giving Andy time to comment, Bryan stood and brushed the grass off his jeans. "I'm going to head on in. I doubt I get much sleep, being in a new place and all, but I need to try. We have horses coming in tomorrow, and it'll probably be a full day." He wasn't lying, but he also wanted a little alone time.

"I'll give you a head start to do whatever you need to in the bathroom. See ya in the morning." Andy's eyes shone brightly from the fire casting light across his face.

"Goodnight," Bryan said and left Andy where he sat. He stopped off in his bedroom and grabbed his toothbrush and toothpaste. When he passed by Andy's room, Bryan noticed the door was cracked. Mal had mentioned it not latching right. Bryan was tempted to peak in, but that would be invading Andy's privacy. He continued on to the bathroom to get ready for bed.

Bryan had meant to ask about setting his toiletries up, but forgot. He didn't have that much crap, not anywhere close to what Andy had, so he only needed a small space on the counter. After he brushed, he took a piss, washed his hands, and made his way back to the bedroom, leaving his things on one end of the counter. His new room was larger than what he'd had in his apartment. The bed was queen-sized, and that, too, was larger than what he'd left behind. The inside of the house wasn't all that warm, and Bryan wondered if Mal kept the heat turned down to save money or if the old house wasn't insulated very well.

He changed out of his clothes, and once he was down to his underwear, he pulled on a pair of thin sleeping pants. Instead of putting his pistol under the pillow like he normally did, Bryan left it in the bedside drawer on the far side of the room. He'd already removed the clip and made sure there wasn't one left in the chamber. He was in a new place. A strange place. He didn't want to run the risk of being woken up and shoving his gun into someone's face accidentally.

Bryan slid beneath the covers, leaving the comforter turned down. Even though the room was cool, the sheet would be enough to keep him comfortable as well as not make him feel smothered. He was almost afraid to go sleep. When he first moved into his apartment, he often woke up disoriented with the bedding wrapped around his legs. Bryan panicked more than once trying to untangle himself. Still, he closed his eyes and took several deep breaths trying to relax. The back door opened and closed. Bryan knew it was Andy because he was singing. Bryan didn't think Andy realized how often he sang.

The floor in the hallway creaked with every step Andy took. It was oddly comforting having his friend and fellow Marine sleeping across the hall. If Bryan happened to have one of his nightmares, Andy would know what to do and would know to keep Malcolm out of his room until the worst of it subsided. Bryan concentrated on the noises Andy made while getting ready for bed. He assumed Andy was brushing his teeth when the water turned on and off. The toilet flushed, and the water sounded again. The bathroom door opened, and Bryan waited for Andy to close his bedroom door. The sound never came. At least not the snick of it closing completely. Bryan did his best not to imagine Andy removing his clothes. He didn't understand his sudden infatuation with the other man's body. Maybe his brother had been wrong, and gay *could* actually rub off on you.

The smell of bacon met Bryan's nose the moment he woke up. His stomach growled, and he pushed the covers back, swinging his legs over the side of the bed. Bryan stretched his arms overhead and closed his eyes. He'd had a peaceful night's sleep, even if it had taken him an hour to wind down. He stood and padded barefoot down the hall to the bathroom. The door was closed, so he turned to go back to his room to wait, but before he could take a step, the door opened. He turned back around to find Andy in his tight boxer briefs and nothing else. Bryan's eyes traveled down the length of Andy's body and back up. He knew Andy had caught him staring, but when he braved a look at Andy's face, the other man's eyes were glued to Bryan's chest. He unconsciously rubbed a hand where Andy was staring.

"Sorry," Andy muttered. In his attempt to hurry around Bryan, Andy's nearly naked body brushed against Bryan's. The feel of the other man's bare skin pressed against him did seriously crazy things to Bryan's head as well as his body. His dick stirred, and not for the first time from being around the blond.

Fuck. If they were going to be living in such close quarters, seeing each other in various stages of undress was more than likely going to be a common occurrence. It wasn't like Bryan wasn't used to seeing other men naked. Being in the military meant you lived, slept, showered, and did everything else with others all around. Hell, he'd even seen a few guys going at it when they thought no one was looking. Watching two fellow Marines sucking each other off always got him hard, but he had chalked it up to not

39

getting any action himself. Seeing Andy in his underwear shouldn't matter. Feeling Andy's body against his shouldn't cause such a stir.

Bryan stepped into the bathroom and closed the door. His morning wood had been noticeably absent ever since returning to the States and the doctor put him on anxiety meds. Now that he'd come in contact with Andy's body, his erection decided to make its return, the same way it had when Andy opened his door dressed in only his briefs the previous morning. *I definitely need to find a girl and soon.*

Ignoring his aching dick, Bryan rushed through his morning routine and returned to his bedroom to get dressed. He found Andy and Mal in the kitchen tag-teaming breakfast. Bryan called out, "Good morning," and asked if he could help. Mal told him to grab the plates and some glasses for juice. Andy poured an extra cup of coffee and handed it over, not looking him in the eyes when he did.

"Thanks, Lily," he said, hoping to lighten the mood. It wasn't Andy's fault he was gay or that he stared at Bryan's body. If anything, Bryan was honored his new friend found him attractive. Andy snapped his head up, smiling.

The three men made quick work of their meal and headed outside to get busy. Having a few hours before the horses were supposed to be delivered, Mal showed them his morning routine, and by the time they'd unloaded the last hay bale in the back pasture, it was time to head back to the barn. Mal let them out while he went to unlock the gate by the road. "That wasn't so bad," Bryan said. Andy had been unusually quiet, and Bryan hated to think he was the cause. When Andy merely nodded, Bryan continued, "Did you sleep okay?"

Andy, running the toe of his boot over the dirt, said, "Yeah, as good as could be expected on my first night. You?"

"I didn't wake up screaming, so yeah." Andy looked

at him, the skin crinkled in between his eyes. "What?" Bryan asked.

"I thought I was the only one who did that," Andy admitted.

"Nah. It's better now that I'm taking something for it, but it still happens every now and then. I guess it's a good thing you sleep across the hall from me instead of Mal. I won't feel like a complete loser if you're the one who has to deal with me freaking out."

"Same here, except I don't have meds keeping my nightmares at bay."

The sound of truck tires crunching on the gravel interrupted their conversation. Mal parked behind the barn so the other truck had plenty of room to maneuver the two-horse trailer. Bryan stayed back out of the way since he'd never been around horses. He'd leave that task to the cowboys. Andy, on the other hand, didn't hesitate to offer his assistance.

It didn't take long to offload the two large animals. Mal and the man who'd driven the truck led the horses to a small enclosure off the side of the barn. Neither animal tried to get free. They both followed the men, and once inside the fence, turned their heads to the grass at their feet. Moe and Curly didn't hesitate to scoot under the bottom rail to check out the strangers. The horses had either been around dogs or just didn't mind the smaller creatures sniffing around their legs. One of the horses, the one with the big spots, leaned his head down, sniffing Moe in return. A snort escaped its nostrils, and Moe yipped his response. Bryan had no idea if animals could speak to each other, but watching these animals together, it seemed like they were communicating.

Mal and the other man spoke quietly, and Andy stood at the fence talking to the horses. Bryan made his way to where Andy stood. "Aren't they magnificent?" Andy asked. When Bryan didn't answer immediately, Andy turned his gaze to Bryan. "I know they can be intimidating, but once you get the hang of riding, it can be fun. I'll teach you, if you want."

"I didn't think you'd ever ridden."

Andy shrugged. "It was a long time ago, and only a few times at that. I didn't want to make it sound like I'm an expert or anything."

First cooking, and now riding horses. Bryan couldn't think of anyone he'd rather have as a teacher than Andy.

Chapter Five

Andy

Andy was trying his damnedest to keep his eyes off Bryan. He was failing. Miserably. After their run-in outside the bathroom, Andy had thought of nothing except Bryan's chest. And the V that dipped into his thin sleeping pants. And the dick that was hidden beneath those pants. They'd been together on the farm for less than twenty-four hours, and Andy was already ruining things. He was trying to make up for it by offering to help Bryan with the things he didn't know how to do like cooking and riding horses. He thought he'd screwed up again until Bryan grinned.

"As much as I would enjoy the four wheelers, I'd really like to learn to ride a horse. You know, play the part of cowboy since we are working on a farm. Maybe I'll even get me a cowboy hat and boots to look the part."

Andy squinted his eyes as he tried to imagine Bryan with pointed boots peeking out from the hems of a pair of Wranglers. The man's ass would certainly fill the jeans up nicely. His dick twitched at the thought of Bryan's ass, and Andy turned back toward the horses, praying Bryan couldn't see the effect he was having on Andy. Gravel crunched again, and Andy turned as the truck and trailer pulled away from the barn. Mal met them at the fence and said, "The Paint is Cochise, and the Quarter Horse is Calculus."

"What kind of name is that for a horse?" Andy asked.

"The owner said she's smart and calculating. Good with a herd. Besides, his daughter called her Callie instead."

Mal let out a low whistle, and both horses ambled over to where the three men were propped against the fence. Callie stood directly in front of Andy, and he rubbed the area between her ears. She nodded her head at him before stepping closer to sniff his face. Her breath puffed out of her nostrils, tickling his skin. Andy wiped his face, and Bryan laughed.

"Looks like you have a new girlfriend," Bryan said. Just then, Cochise nipped at Bryan's shoulder when he wasn't looking. He yelped and jumped backwards.

Andy was the one laughing then. "Yeah, so do you. Yours is a biter. Kinda kinky."

"Shut-up, Lily." Bryan stayed where he was instead of coming closer to the big animal. Mal let himself into the pen with the horses and got right between both of them.

After a few minutes of letting the animals get acquainted with him, Mal led Cochise out of the enclosure into the barn. "I'm gonna saddle him up and see how he rides. One of y'all wanna ride Callie?"

Andy asked Bryan, "Do you want the honors?"

"Uh, no thanks. I'll watch you two from right here."

"Okay, but you can help me put the saddle on her. No better time than the present to start learning."

"Yeah, I can do that. I think."

Andy hated the doubt in Bryan's voice. Horses were big and intimidating, even for someone like a Marine. Andy entered the pen and grabbed the lead, directing Callie to the barn where Mal had disappeared with Cochise. Two new saddles were waiting for them along with blankets and tack. It had been quite a few years since Andy had fitted a horse, but once he got started, it all came rushing back. His grandmother would have been mortified if she knew he'd ever done such a mundane task. The bridle was already on Callie's head, and as he moved about the horse, he explained everything he was doing to Bryan. When Bryan kept a good distance between him and the big animal, Andy grabbed his hand and pulled him closer. The current he felt from their skin touching had his dick coming to life inside his jeans. Still, he didn't release Bryan's hand. Instead, he placed both their hands on Callie's back.

"Just like any animal, she's going to sense your fear. You have to let her know who's in charge, or you'll never be able to control her."

"I'm not sure I will ever get to that point. She's so... big." Bryan didn't remove his hand. He rubbed over the soft swell of Callie's flank.

"Size doesn't matter when it comes to dominance. Attitude does."

Bryan raised his eyebrows, one side of his mouth twitching.

Andy realized what he said. "Mind out of the gutter, Marine. We all know size matters, usually. But like I said, not when it comes to being dominant. Haven't you ever . . . Never mind. I don't want to know. Anyway, if you're scared, she'll know it. You need to be around her and get used to her before you ride her. When you're comfortable, then we'll put you in the saddle."

As Andy pushed thoughts of Bryan dominating him in the bedroom out of his mind, he tightened the flank cinch and pulled on the saddle to make certain it was good and snug. His combat boots were going to be a tight fit in the stirrups. Maybe he and Bryan could go into town and both of them could get some cowboy boots. He'd had several pair growing up, but he had no doubt they, along with all his other stuff, had been burned by his grandfather within minutes of his being kicked to the curb.

Andy did his best not to think about his family. No, they weren't his family. Not since they turned their backs on him. Christy was the only family he had, even if they weren't related by blood. Maybe Bryan and Mal would keep him around, and they'd also become his family. Andy's chest tightened at the longing to belong somewhere. It had been over eight years since he felt wanted. Loved.

"Lily, you okay?" Bryan's voice brought him out of his maudlin thoughts.

"Fine."

"You sure? I called your name several times."

"Yeah, just remembering riding a long time ago. You ready, Mal?" Andy didn't look at Bryan. He didn't want him to see the half-truth that was probably written on his face. He knew his face was expressive. He'd lost his ass at poker more than once because of it.

"Yep. Just waitin' on you. Bryan, you wanna follow along on the four wheeler?"

"Yes. I want to see you two riding." Mal had shown them where the keys were kept for the ATVs and how to start them the day before. Bryan found the key to Cade's and loaded up while Andy and Mal mounted the horses. Mal inserted the shotgun into some kind of holder on the side of the horse before he softly touched his heels to Cochise's sides to get the horse moving. Andy did the same to Callie, and she followed the other horse out of the barn. The dogs trotted alongside the horses, not getting too close to be underfoot. Bryan kept a safe distance behind them on the ATV, and the three men set out across the fields.

The feeling of the powerful animal beneath his body brought a sense of nostalgia to Andy. One he didn't want. He wanted no reminders of his time before Patrick. He needed to get over the longing for what could have been that he still clung to subconsciously. The farm was so different from the land he'd grown up on. Where in Texas it was wide open spaces with a monstrosity of a house, here the land was nestled in between hills, and the home he was living in was old and in need of repair. But the biggest difference Andy found in the twenty-four hours that he'd been there was this place was a home. The love between Mal and Suzette was tangible. Hell, he'd felt her love for Bryan and him in just the way she touched their faces. The woman

46

was a true mother. Instead of helping to kick Mal out of the house when she knew he was gay, she'd almost given her life for her son.

After stopping several times to check on the fencing, Mal directed them back to the barn. Whoever chose these two horses for Mal had done well in Andy's opinion. He only needed to nudge Callie with his knee and she'd turn the direction he wanted her to go. Not once did she try to take the lead away from him. It allowed him the opportunity to breathe in the fresh air and take in his surroundings. They had traveled over more of the land today, and Andy was thinking he would enjoy his time spent working on the farm. His gaze found Bryan several times, and his fellow Marine was enjoying himself too, if the smile on his face was any indication.

As much as he'd enjoyed the ride, Andy was glad to slide down from the saddle, because his ass and thighs were already sore — and not in the way he longed for. If Callie hadn't been so docile, Andy's legs would have gotten even more of a workout. He led her inside the barn, where he and Mal removed the saddles and stored them in the tack room they had finished repairing the day before. When he'd ridden as a teen, he'd had someone in the stable to take over at that point, so he wasn't sure what needed to be done. "Do we need to brush them down?" he asked Mal, embarrassed that he didn't know what to do.

"We didn't run 'em, so they'll be okay for now. I wanna get 'em set up in their stalls with feed so they get used to their new home. We need some supplies, and I'd really appreciate if one of you would go into town. Or you can both go, if you'd like. That way you can drive around and see where it is you're gonna be livin'," Mal said.

"I want to get some new boots. Is there a clothing store?" Andy asked.

Mal removed his baseball cap, ran a hand through his dark hair then put it back on. "Depends on the kind of boots. There's a Tractor Supply down the street from the feed store that carries western boots, if that's what you're lookin' for."

"Yes. I prefer to wear something besides my combat boots while I'm riding. I also want to grab a couple pairs of gloves."

"I need some things as well, so I'll ride with you," Bryan said.

"Come on in the house. I'll give you the list of what I need. I'll call ahead so they can get everything ready. That way you can drive around the back of the store, and they'll load you up. Here's the company credit card. Use it for the feed and for your gloves and boots."

"I have some money to buy my stuff." Andy hadn't expected the company to pay for his boots, and he told Mal as much.

"If they're for work, you can expense them. If you're buyin' clothes to hit the town on, you can pay for those yourself," Mal explained.

"Fair enough." Andy didn't think he'd need a new wardrobe since the town was small. The way Mal had explained it, his former bar was one of the few in Arlo, and it was a redneck joint. Andy figured he'd fit right in with a pair of jeans and T-shirt. He'd just have to keep his eyes averted from any of the men. If Bryan went with him, he'd need to remember to keep his eyes away from him, too. Andy had pretended to be straight for the last eight years. Hopefully, he could keep up the charade long enough for him and Bryan to throw back a few beers on Friday nights.

After they washed up, Mal handed Bryan the list of items they were to pick up at the feed store. "Take your time lookin' around town. I've got some paperwork I need to do. I'll have supper ready by five." It was only two o'clock then. That gave them three hours to drive the short distance into town, get what they needed, and shop around a little. Instead of taking Bryan's truck, Mal insisted they take the company dually. It was larger and had more room for what they were picking up.

The dogs followed them toward the truck, and Andy pointed at them, saying "Stay." They both sat where they were. Andy gave them each a rub on the head and told them what good boys they were. He wondered if Mal ever let them inside. Andy would love to be able to pet one or the other while he was watching movies.

Bryan didn't offer to hand over the keys, so Andy jumped up into the passenger seat. When Bryan started the big engine, the radio came to life with sounds of hard rock coming through the speakers. It surprised Andy that Mal would listen to something other than country music, but he remembered Mal's boyfriend was a major rock star. "What do you know about Cade?" Andy asked Bryan.

"Not much. He was in 7's Mistress until they broke up last year around Christmas. The lead singer's daughter was kidnapped right after their last show. I had just gotten out of the Corps and went to that show. I had no idea any of the madness was going on until the next day when it was all over the news. Tag, the singer, ended up marrying his boyfriend. It was rumored that Cade and Tag had been lovers a long time ago, and if you believe the tabloids, Cade was a horn dog fucking both men and women wherever they went. Other than that..."

Andy barked out a laugh. "Other than that? That's a lot. I can't imagine dating someone that high profile, especially someone whose reputation is what you mentioned. Can you?"

Bryan tapped out a rhythm on the steering wheel as he maneuvered the big truck like he'd driven it his whole life. "I can't imagine dating anyone at all, much less someone like Cade."

"You don't want a relationship?"

"It's not that. I just don't see myself finding someone to put up with my issues."

49

"You just have to find the right person," Andy said. He emphasized person instead of saying woman. He knew he was setting himself up for a big ole letdown, but dammit if he didn't want to be the one to put up with Bryan's issues. Why the fuck did he have to want his straight friend so bad? They'd only known each other less than a week, but in that week, he'd had more fun than he could remember ever having. Bryan was not only easy on the eyes, but he was kind and funny, even if he was quiet.

"Did you date much before you enlisted?" Andy had already admitted his one boyfriend and the way that turned out.

"Not really. I spent most of my time working and helping my mom with my brothers and sister. I mean, I went out a few times, but nothing serious." Andy had to wonder at Bryan's sex life, or lack thereof. He wasn't about to ask though.

The drive to town was a short one. They decided to hit the Tractor Supply store first so the feed wouldn't be sitting in the back of the truck for anyone to come along and take. A bell on the front door sounded as they entered. The cashier called out a welcome. When she looked up from the items she was ringing in, her mouth fell open. The man who was checking out was also staring at both of them. Bryan turned toward the clothing without another glance, but Andy threw up a hand and said hello. If they were going to be around the town folks, it wouldn't hurt to be friendly.

Bryan was trying on a cowboy hat when Andy found him. "What do you think?" he asked. Andy thought he wanted to drop to his knees right there in the middle of the store and blow Bryan. He was beyond good-looking. The hat did something to make his already sparkling eyes stand out more.

"That bad, huh?" Bryan said, frowning.

"Uh... No, uh..." Andy cleared his throat and turned toward the boots. "Not bad at all. As a matter of fact, if you don't buy it, I will. Cowboy's a good look on you," Andy said, barely above a whisper. Bryan hadn't moved, so Andy chanced a glance over at him. He couldn't tell if Bryan was pissed or flattered.

"Can I help you fellas find anything?" The cashier, a pretty girl who looked like she might still be in her teens, asked as she walked toward them. Her eyes flitted between the two of them like she couldn't decide who she wanted to look at more. Andy laughed to himself. If she only knew. "I'm Janene, by the way. I don't think I've seen you around these parts. Just passing through?"

"Are these all the boots you have in stock? I like this black pair, but you don't have my size," Andy said instead of introducing themselves to the girl.

"Oh, yeah, we have more in the back. What size do you need?"

"An eleven if you have it."

"Sure, just let me go check. What about you, Sugar? You a larger size, too?" she asked Bryan. When his eyebrows shot up, Andy laughed out loud.

"I'm good," Bryan muttered. The blush on his cheeks was adorable in an *I can kill you with my bare hands* kind of way. Adorable was not a word Andy would have associated with the bulky Marine until that moment.

As soon as Janene was out of earshot, Andy winked and asked, "You sure about that, *Sugar*?"

"Suck it, Lily," Bryan shot back, but blushed even harder when he realized what he said.

Andy leaned in close and whispered, "Anytime." He turned his back on Bryan, because now Andy was blushing. Hopefully Bryan would think he was joking and not get pissed. Janene was back with the box and directed Andy to a chair where he could remove his own boots. Bryan began humming while looking through the different styles of boots. Andy didn't recognize the tune, but he didn't normally listen to the kind of music Bryan did.

Bryan pulled a box from the bottom of the stack, and instead of sitting next to Andy, he chose to try them on in the middle of the aisle. Andy stood when he had both boots on and walked down the aisle toward Bryan. Right as he got within arm's reach, Bryan was hopping on one foot as he tried to keep his balance pulling the boot on. Without thinking, Andy grabbed his arms to hold him steady.

"Thanks. I didn't realize how tight these would be."

"They'll stretch out when you wear them a few times. Once they're broken in, you'll find yourself wearing them all the time. Much easier to slip into than dealing with laces." Andy didn't want to think about tight places and loosening them up. The boots he was trying on were tight, too, but his toes weren't scrunched. He'd chosen a pair with square toes instead of the pointier ones. He noticed Bryan had chosen a similar style but in brown instead of black. When Andy walked back toward the seat, he caught sight of the box Bryan's boots came out of. Size twelve. He wondered if the rest of his body was in proportion with his shoe size. Having seen Bryan's hands, Andy had a feeling he would be thinking of nothing else later on when he tried to go to sleep.

"He's right. They'll stretch out. You never did say if you were just passing through or..." Janene was fishing. Bryan looked over at Andy for help. The man was obviously shy around women. No wonder he hadn't dated much.

"We both just moved here for a job. Our second day, actually. These will work fine for me. Those boots gonna work for you, B?" Andy didn't want to give out Bryan's name since he hadn't offered it. If he wanted Janene to know his name, he could tell her himself.

"Yeah, these should do okay." Bryan tried to toe the boots off, but they were too tight, so he leaned against the shelving and pulled them off, replacing them in the box.

"Don't forget the hat," Andy said. Bryan had put the cowboy hat back on the rack. When Bryan rolled his eyes,

Andy reached around him and grabbed it, placing it on top of the box on the floor while he finished lacing his combat boots. "If you'll take these to the counter for us, we need to look at the gloves." Andy wasn't trying to be rude, but he didn't like the way the girl kept eyeing Bryan. Jealousy wasn't a good look on anyone, so he plastered on his best smile.

The girl actually batted her lashes at Andy, and he bit his tongue to keep from laughing at her. Bryan followed Andy to where a rack of gloves was, and they pulled several pair off, trying them on for size. When Bryan selected the extra-large, Andy did his best not to groan. They needed to get out of there and go somewhere that didn't require trying things on. Bryan was quiet normally, but he was being unusually so. Andy figured he'd pissed the guy off, so he kept his mouth shut until they got to the register. He handed Janene the credit card Mal gave him, but Bryan pulled the hat off the pile and stalked away. When he returned, he was empty handed.

Chapter Six

Bryan

Bryan was flattered Janene was flirting with them. She was cute enough, but she was young. And not his type. While he was returning the cowboy hat to the rack, he tried to imagine what his type actually was. The girls he'd been with were all different. There was nothing about them he could pinpoint that drew him to them other than they'd come on to him first. He hadn't sought them out for sex or for any type of companionship. It had been so long since he'd jacked off that he couldn't remember what it was he thought about when doing so.

By the time he returned to the front of the store, Andy was already outside. As he walked past, Janene twirled a strand of hair around her finger and waved. "Bye. I hope to see you around." Bryan threw his hand up but didn't speak. He pulled the keys out of his pocket and pressed the remote lock. Andy put their boots in the backseat before climbing inside.

As soon as Bryan was seated, Andy mumbled, "Sorry about that."

Bryan had stuck the key in the ignition, but he paused and looked over at Andy. "For what?"

"I don't know. Making you uncomfortable?"

Andy wouldn't look at him, so he reached out and placed his hand on top of Andy's. "Hey, I'm not sure what you think you did, but you weren't the one who made me uncomfortable." Bryan squeezed Andy's hand before letting go. The touch was meant to be reassuring, but for some reason, it made Bryan want to reach back over and not let go this time. This whole thinking about sex thing was wearing on him. Why else would he want to hold his friend's hand?

Andy turned his way and asked, "What *did* make you uncomfortable?"

"Janene. She was sweet, but she's just a kid."

"Oh. Well . . . okay." Andy nodded once like it all made sense. Bryan hoped he came across as sounding truthful. It wasn't that Andy's attentiveness or playfulness was uncomfortable. It was the reaction Bryan was having to his attention. He was becoming more and more confused the longer he was around Andy. Bryan couldn't wait until the next night when they could go to the bar and he could be around women his age. He wanted to see if there was any type of attraction there or if his body had somehow changed teams and forgot to tell him.

Bryan started the truck and put it in gear. He placed his hand on the back of the seat behind Andy when he turned to look behind him. With the truck being as large as it was, he didn't trust using only the rearview mirror. His thumb brushed Andy's shoulder when he pulled his arm back, and Bryan's cock twitched at that small connection. Yeah, he was fucked if that's all it took. Instead of driving straight to the feed store, Bryan decided to drive around the small town and see what was what. They passed a Dairy Barn that advertised the best burger in town. "We'll have to check that out," he said, pointing it out to Andy. From previous conversations, he knew Andy loved chocolate milkshakes with his burgers.

On the left was a small grocery store. Several churches and a strip mall were on the right. Bryan turned down the next street and found the bar Mal had recently sold. DW's was smaller than Bryan had imagined by the way Mal described it. He'd also never referred to it by name, just *the bar*. The D must have stood for Dwight, his father. Bryan probably wouldn't refer to it by name either if his father had tried to kill him. "You wanna get out tomorrow night? See what the inside of the bar looks like?"

"Yeah. I could use a drink," Andy said. When Bryan caught his tone, he waited until he rolled to the stop sign to look over. Andy was chewing on his bottom lip while staring out the side window, but there was nothing to be seen other than an empty parking lot. Bryan wanted to ask him what was wrong, but he didn't want to pry. Maybe Bryan was the one making Andy uncomfortable when he touched him. Or maybe he was giving off mixed signals. He didn't mean to. When he grabbed Andy's hand earlier, he'd done it out of friendship. Dammit. This was going to be hard.

Needing to end the silence, Bryan drove to the feed store, pulling around back. Andy got out of the other side and met him at the front of the truck. They didn't have to wait on someone to help them. The back door opened, and a man that dwarfed them both stepped outside. He wore overalls that were unbuttoned at the sides. Bryan doubted he could have buttoned them if he wanted to. The man spit tobacco juice on the ground, not bothering to wipe the leftover from the corner of his mouth. "Y'all here for Wilson's stuff?" he asked.

"Yes. Do you need me to back the truck in?" Bryan asked. The man narrowed his eyes at Bryan, obviously trying to figure out if he was black or a mixture of something.

"Nope." The man spit again and walked over to a forklift. The wheels squatted when the man sat in the seat. Bryan fully expected the tires to pop under the weight. Not looking behind him when he backed up, the man drove the forklift like he was on a racetrack. Balls to the wall. He lowered the forks, sliding them underneath a pallet that was stacked high with bags and shrink-wrapped to keep them in place. He pulled up to the back of the truck and sat there. Andy was the one who went to the back of the truck and lowered the tailgate. Bryan was thankful Andy was able to move, because Bryan was frozen where he stood. The hair on his arms stood on end when the man spit again, never taking his eyes off Bryan. He wished he'd remembered to put his pistol in the truck. After today, he'd never go anywhere without it.

Once the pallet was loaded, the man parked the forklift and jumped down, as agile as if he was a gymnast. He walked over to a desk that was located under the large metal overhang and grabbed a clipboard. "Sign here," he said to Andy. Yep, the guy didn't like the way Bryan looked. He mentally rolled his eyes. If that fucker thought he was intimidating, he had another thing coming. Bryan might not be as tall as others, but he'd been fighting his whole life. Men like this one didn't scare him. If anything, they got his blood pumping. It had been a while since Bryan had used his fists, in more ways than one. He wasn't opposed to a good brawl, but this was his first day on the job. He didn't want it to be his last.

He ignored the sneer from the man and pulled himself into the cab of the truck, leaving Andy to deal with the asshole. It was probably a good thing the man didn't know Andy was gay or he might have given them both nasty looks. Andy took the receipt and said something Bryan couldn't hear. When he got in on his side, he asked, "Are you okay?"

"Yep. I've been getting looks from assholes my whole life. Not anything new." He started the truck and headed toward the farm. When he glanced in the side mirror, the jackass was watching them drive away. *Motherfucker.*

It was Andy's turn to put his hand on Bryan. Since both Bryan's hands were white-knuckling the steering wheel, Andy placed reached out for his shoulder. "Next time, I'll come by myself," Andy offered. The spot where Andy's hand touched Bryan was like a brand through his T-shirt. If he wasn't driving, he would close his eyes and enjoy the feeling. *Shit.* Bryan swung the truck into the parking lot of the grocery store, braking a little harder than necessary, both their bodies catching on the seatbelts.

"Sorry," he muttered before getting out of the truck. Bryan stalked into the small building and looked around. Most stores like this didn't carry liquor, but he could at least get some beer for later on that night. When he got their juice earlier that morning, he noticed there was less than a six pack in the fridge. Instead of asking for directions, Bryan started on one end and walked the length of the store, reading the signs over each aisle. When he found the beer aisle, he turned down it and ran into a girl. Reaching out to keep her from falling, Bryan grabbed hold of her biceps. "I'm so sorry," he told her. When she looked up, the girl gasped. Only this girl wasn't a girl. She was all woman.

Instead of finding fault with the way Bryan looked, her face slid from the startled look to a sexy grin as she blatantly checked out his arms that were attached to the hands still holding onto her. "Sorry," he said again.

"I don't think I've seen you around here. I'm Laurel." She held out her hand, and Bryan took it, shaking firmly but gently.

"Bryan," he returned. Her hand was soft, where Andy's was rough. Her eyes were green, where Andy's were bright blue. Her hair was blonde, but not natural like... *Seriously?*

"It's my pleasure, Bryan. So, are you new to the area? I could maybe show you around, you know, as a welcome to the community?"

This was it. A beautiful woman wanted to spend time with him, and he was stalling. Why? Fuck it. "I'd like that."

"How about tomorrow night?"

"I have plans tomorrow, but maybe Saturday instead?"

Laurel paused and narrowed her eyes. "That works,

too. Do you have a cell phone? I'll text you my address." Bryan pulled his phone from his back pocket and entered her number. "Now, call me so I'll have your number." Bryan did as instructed. Laurel's phone rang, and she grinned. "Got you now. I'll see you Saturday." Laurel leaned in and kissed Bryan on the cheek before walking off. He heard her say, "Excuse me," as she rounded the corner. Bryan finally found his feet and continued down the beer aisle until he found what he was looking for, all the while wondering what the fuck just happened.

Bryan grabbed two cases of beer — one he liked and one Andy liked. He didn't stop to think about what that meant. Instead, he thought about going on a date with Laurel on Saturday. Bryan should be excited. Instead, he was nervous. He hadn't been on a date in... damn.

When he got to the truck, he loaded the beer in the back seat. When he climbed in, Andy was staring at him. For some reason, Andy looked like he was ready to blow a gasket. "What?" Bryan asked.

"Just checking your mood. Seeing if I need to drive."

"Nope. I'm good now." And he was. Sort of. He'd been pissed because the jackass at the feed store didn't like his looks. Now, a good-looking woman had appreciated his looks, so yeah. He was better. Still, he didn't know why he wasn't more excited about the possibility of spending time with her. He felt Andy's gaze on him, but he focused on the drive back to the farm.

Bryan waited in the truck while Andy pushed open the gate. As soon as he was through, Andy waved him on, yelling he'd walk. By the time Bryan got the truck backed up to the barn door, Mal was waiting on him. "Everything go okay?" he asked.

Bryan climbed out of the truck and handed Mal the keys. "Other than the big fucker at the feed store giving me the stink-eye, yeah."

"That'd be Roland. Sorry, I should've warned you."

"Warned him about what?" Andy asked as he rounded the truck.

"About Roland. Him and his brother, Randy, are dickheads. Remember when I told you how Cade and me met? It was those two who were tryin' to pick a fight with Cade outside the bar."

"That explains a lot. Anyway, we got some boots, and I got some more beer for tonight."

"Good. Let's get this unloaded, and we'll get ready for supper," Mal said, climbing up into the back of the truck. He pulled a knife off his belt and carefully slit the plastic. "There's an empty pallet in the tack room. We'll stack the feed in there." He grabbed the first bag and tossed it down to Bryan. He grabbed another and tossed it to Andy.

"Hand me that one," Bryan said to Andy. The bags weren't that heavy, and it'd go a lot quicker if they didn't take them one at a time. Andy passed by with his arms full, but he didn't look Bryan's way. Andy had been quiet on the ride home. Bryan thought he was giving him space after what happened at the feed store. Now he wasn't so sure. Within ten minutes, the truck was unloaded. The horses had been watching them with their heads hanging over the stall doors. Andy stopped to pet them both. Bryan stepped up next to him and did the same. Instead of talking to Bryan, Andy mumbled silly words to the animals. Feeling like a wall had been erected, Bryan left Andy in the barn and headed inside.

Mal was already at the sink washing his hands. Bryan went about putting some of the beer in the fridge. The rest of it he put in the small pantry. "Thanks for pickin' up the beer. I don't usually drink every night, but it's nice knowin' it's there if I want it." Bryan wondered if Mal was hinting that he didn't want Andy and him to drink if he didn't. Like he'd read his mind, Mal added, "I don't care how much you drink as long as it doesn't interfere with you crawlin' outta bed every mornin'. I can't imagine what you and Andy went through overseas." He looked like he wanted to say something else, but he stopped talking when Andy walked through the door. "So, did anything else excitin' happen while you were in town?"

Andy gave Bryan a funny look and said, "Excuse me. I'm going to wash up."

Bryan watched him walk away before he said, "I met a woman in the grocery store. Her name's Laurel."

Mal's eyebrows shot up. "Tall blonde with lots of hair?"

"Yeah. I take it you know her."

"If she's the same one that comes in the bar, then yeah."

"I'm supposed to go out with her Saturday. Do you think that's a good idea?"

Mal grinned. "If you wanna get laid, then it's a good idea."

"You make it sound like she sleeps around."

Mal shrugged his shoulders. "I've seen her leave the bar with different men on occasion. Maybe they were goin' for coffee."

"Or maybe she's a real slut," Andy said when he returned. He stuck his head in the fridge and pulled out a beer. Popping the top, he sucked half of it down without stopping. Bryan wanted to get him alone and ask him what was bothering him. He'd been acting funny ever since the grocery store. Totally ignoring the surprised look Bryan was shooting his way, Andy asked, "Say, Mal, do you ever let the dogs in?"

"No. They've always stayed outside. They guard the place."

"But you have an alarm."

"And?" Mal asked, frowning. "What's your point?"

"I just... never mind." Andy downed the rest of his beer. While he was tossing the empty in the garbage, Mal cocked his eyebrow at Bryan, who shrugged. He didn't know what was going on with Andy. But he sure as shit was going to find out before they went to bed.

Supper was strained with Andy not making his small talk, so Mal filled in the silence by telling them more about his three nieces. The love Mal had for the little girls was evident in the way he described each one, but it was also evident he was partial to Mattie, the five-year-old. "I can't wait for you to meet her. She's a pistol." Bryan was looking forward to it as well. As rambunctious as his nephews were, he missed being around them. Something about seeing the world through a child's eyes made everything better. Less stressful.

Once the dishes were washed and put away, Bryan grabbed the cooler Mal had used the night before and filled it with beer. Mal had told them the night time was theirs to do as they pleased as long as they were up and ready to go the next morning after breakfast. This was so different than being in the military, and Bryan had a feeling he was going to enjoy his time on the farm. Mal had plenty of firewood and kindling stacked up by the pit, so it didn't take Bryan long to get it going. He didn't expect Andy to join him with his sour mood, and that had been okay with Bryan. He was going to drink a few beers to loosen up before he found Andy to talk to him.

Andy found him instead. "Mind if I join you?" he asked sheepishly.

"Not at all." Bryan opened the cooler and pulled out one of Andy's beers he'd packed, just in case. "Here you go."

"Thanks." Andy popped the top and swallowed several long sips before sitting on the ground close to Bryan. Moe and Curly took the same spots they had the night before, and Bryan didn't hesitate to run his hands through the soft fur. "So, you going out with that girl tomorrow night?"

"No. You and I already talked about going to the bar

tomorrow. I'm meeting her Saturday instead."

Andy nodded, but didn't respond.

"Does that bother you?" Bryan asked.

"Why would it? You're a good-looking, straight man who has needs like the rest of us."

Like the rest of us. Andy had needs too, but who was he going to find to fulfill them? Bryan didn't want to think about that.

Chapter Seven

Andy

Andy needed to apologize for acting like a dick, but what was he going to say? 'Please don't go out with the blonde bimbo and let me suck your dick instead?' Before he could make things any more awkward than he already had, Andy said, "Tell me more about your family." He dug his fingers into Moe's thick fur and let the animal soothe him in a way nothing else could. Andy thought back to Duke and how Erik took the dog to visit the veterans. He understood why now.

Bryan's voice was deep, and it lulled Andy with its soft cadence. "I already told you I'm the oldest boy. Brianna's a couple years older than me. Bryce came next, and finally Brett. We're all two years apart, almost to the day. It was like my mom planned on when to get pregnant," Bryan said, grinning.

"What's up with all the Br names? What was your mom's name?"

"Connie. She hated her name, said it was so boring. It was actually Constance Ann, but she'd been Connie her whole life. When my sister was born, Mom thought Brianna was going to be a boy, and she'd chosen the name Bryan after a singer she had the hots for when she was younger. When Bree came out as a girl, Mom changed Bryan to Brianna. She saved Bryan for me."

"And your dad was okay with that?"

"Yeah, he was. He'd have given her the moon and stars if he could. To hear her tell it, they were so in love that nothing and nobody else mattered. It's why she was so strong living in the projects. My dad got so caught up in trying to give her everything he thought she wanted that he made some really bad choices. He went to prison soon after Brett was born."

"Do you ever talk to him?" Andy didn't know how he would feel if he were in Bryan's shoes.

"I went to see him a few months ago. He's not the same man I remember. My father was larger than life. He was stern when I was little, but everything he did was with love. Losing my mom took its toll on him, even if they were separated by bars. She never stopped loving him. Now... Now, he's sitting in a cell, waiting to join her."

"Is he not eligible for parole? You didn't say what he did that landed him in jail. If he's been there this long, it must have been bad."

Bryan swallowed down his beer and tossed the empty can in the fire. "It was." Bryan didn't elaborate on what his father had done, and Andy changed the subject. Sort of.

"Since you had to help out, did you get to do anything fun in school? Like play sports?"

Bryan shook his head. "Since my mom had to work two jobs, I came home and helped Bree out with our brothers. A neighbor watched Brett until he was old enough to go to school. As much as I wanted to play football, it just wasn't in the cards. What about you?"

"I played baseball, but my grandmother insisted I learn to play piano, too. Not only was I groomed to take over the family business, I was given lessons so I could entertain their guests during parties."

"I'd love to hear you play sometime."

"I doubt you'd like the kind of music I play. Besides, it's been so long, I've probably forgotten how."

"I doubt that. Why don't we go test that theory?"

"Now?"

"Why not? It's starting to sprinkle, so we're going to

65

have to go inside soon anyway. Unless you're chicken. Are you chicken, Lily?" Bryan teased.

"Now you're just being mean. And, no, I'm not chicken. It's your ears, so don't say I didn't warn you." Andy stood from the ground, finished his beer, and chucked the can in the pit. The dogs followed Andy and Bryan to the back door but sat down at the top of the steps. Andy wished they could come in the house. He'd love to have Moe sleep with him. Once inside, Bryan took the remaining beers out of the cooler and returned them to the refrigerator while Andy headed to the den.

Maybe he wasn't chicken, but he was nervous as shit. It had been over eight years since he'd touched a piano. He sat down on the bench and ran his fingers over the keys in a warm-up exercise. To be so old, the piano was in tune. Andy did his best to shut out Bryan from his thoughts as he let muscle memory kick in. He missed a couple of notes in the beginning, but after that, he closed his eyes and allowed himself to feel. When the song he was playing ended, he segued into another without missing a beat.

Music had played such an important part in Andy's earlier life. He didn't mind learning the instrument, but he didn't like being paraded for his grandparents' and parents' friends. His grandfather told him it would build character. Whatever. The music Andy enjoyed, though, was the country music he listened to on his radio. Living in Texas meant country and southern rock was played by everyone. Andy was more of a cry in your beer kind of listener. With having to hide who he was, he connected with the sad lyrics in more ways than one. Still, there were upbeat songs that kept him going on the days he wanted to give up.

Andy didn't realize he'd started playing one of those old songs, or that he'd started singing. Not until he got to the chorus and his voice choked. A single tear rolled from the corner of his eye, and he quickly began playing something fast and upbeat. Bryan must think him a fool.

Why the fuck did he have to choose that song to sing for Bryan? Movement out of the corner of his eye stalled his fingers. Andy took a deep breath, wiped his face on his shoulder, and pushed back from the piano. "I think that's enough for one night," he said, not looking at the other man.

Before he could get out of the room, Bryan snagged Andy's wrist, halting his progress. He still didn't look at Bryan. "You have a beautiful voice, Lily," Bryan ghosted against his ear.

"Thank you," he whispered, pulling away. Andy couldn't get to his bedroom quick enough. *Fuck!* Why did Patrick still make him hurt? And why did the soft voice of his straight friend make him hard? Andy closed his door as far as it would go. He really needed to fix it so it would shut all the way. He would worry about that tomorrow. Right then, he wished he had a bottle of whiskey to drown his blues in. Or a hot ass to stick his hard dick in. Either one would give him relief. Andy opened the closet and pulled out the box of toys he'd brought with him. He might not have a hot ass available to him, but he did have somewhere to stick his cock. Andy stripped out of his clothes and fell back onto the bed. He shifted his body until he was leaning against the headboard. He groaned at the ache in his inner thighs from riding Callie.

Dripping lube into his palm, he fisted his erection, slicking it enough to glide into the jelly stroker. He pretended it was a nice, tight ass instead of something from between a woman's legs. It was the perfect fit over his cock, so it worked for him as long as he didn't look at it. Andy bent his knees, pulling them as close to his ass as his muscled thighs would allow, spreading them so he could get at his hole with his lubed fingers. He had toys for that, too, but right now he needed to get off and in a hurry. Andy slipped the toy over his aching dick and closed his eyes. Andy allowed himself to imagine Bryan – his beautiful eyes gazing longingly, lustfully at Andy while he rode Andy's dick. Pumping the sheath up and down, Andy reached between his legs with his other hand and inserted two slick fingers.

Andy alternated stroking his cock and pumping in and out of his ass. It hadn't been that long since he'd had an orgasm. He'd jacked himself in the shower before Bryan showed up at his apartment the day before. He figured that would hold him for a while. It wasn't like he got off every day, at least not before he met Bryan. Since he met the Marine, Andy had been jacking off more frequently. A lot more frequently. He didn't understand why the straight man did it for him. But he did. Just the touch of Bryan's hand sent the blood rushing south, and Andy didn't get it. He'd been around lots of guys in the military and never had trouble keeping his dick in check.

One touch, one soft breath on his ear from Bryan, and Andy was gone. When he felt the pressure in his balls, Andy dug his heels into the bed, pumping his hips into the toy faster. He removed the fake hole from his dick and grabbed the T-shirt he'd removed earlier. As his orgasm slammed through him, Andy hissed out Bryan's name before biting his bottom lip hard enough to draw blood. He couldn't make the mistake of letting his new friend know how much he desired him. That would surely have Bryan leaving the farm without so much as a goodbye or a fuck you. Andy molded his back to the bed but continued to stroke his dick with his fist until the last spike of heat left his body.

Andy opened his eyes and lay there motionless while allowing his breathing to return to normal. He wiped his hand on his shirt before wadding the toy up inside and tossing both to the floor. He should get up and clean it right away, but he was too spent, both mentally and physically. Wanting what you couldn't have was tiresome. Andy slid down the bed until his head hit the pillows and pulled the covers up over his naked body.

The rain that had started off as sprinkles was now pelting the window. Andy didn't mind the rain, but he wondered if it would prohibit them from getting outside the next day and working. He knew the animals were used to bad weather, but he wasn't sure he could handle being inside all day. Not after what just happened. Trying not to think about Bryan, Andy closed his eyes and prayed for sleep.

Bryan

Bryan followed Andy down the hallway to their bedrooms, but Andy closed his door before Bryan could get to him. He didn't understand what happened. Andy had been playing such a beautiful piece of classical music before he started in on a country love song. The words were haunting and no doubt reminded Andy of someone. At least that's what it felt like to Bryan. Andy's voice could rival anyone on the radio. It was soulful, and Bryan could listen to him sing all day and night. After Andy's reaction, Bryan doubted he'd ever get Andy to sing for him again.

He'd tried to lighten the mood by calling him Lily, but he'd made the mistake of grabbing hold of Andy's arm. That one touch had scared his friend off, and Bryan wanted to apologize. Bryan went in his room and sat down on the side of the bed, not bothering to turn on the light. He liked the dark; it helped him think better. He ran a hand across his short hair, trying to figure out if he should say something or let it go. Thinking Andy probably wanted to be alone, Bryan decided to leave him be and get ready for bed. He padded out of his room and had just passed Andy's door when he heard moaning coming from inside. Not hesitating, Bryan turned back but paused outside the door, listening.

There was no mistaking the sounds coming from Andy. The moans. The heavy breathing. The soft curses. Bryan should turn away. The door not closing properly wasn't Andy's fault, and if Bryan looked, it would be invading his friend's privacy. The fact that his dick was getting harder the longer he stood there should have had Bryan running back to his room, but his feet wouldn't move. The hallway was dark, and since it was raining, there wasn't light in Andy's room, but Bryan didn't need light. He closed his eyes, and palmed his dick over his jeans. Bryan knew what it was like to try to hand fuck your demons away. It had been a long time since he'd needed to do it, but when the pain, the loneliness, the memories, when they hit, sometimes getting off was the only thing to take your mind off your troubles. Just listening to Andy masturbate caused Bryan to need relief of his own. Just as he decided to take go care of his hard-on, Andy gasped and called out Bryan's name.

He knew he was well hidden from sight. There was no way Andy could see him. The only other explanation was Andy had been thinking of Bryan while he was fisting himself. Goddammit. That wasn't helping his situation. Bryan went as quietly as possible into the bathroom and closed the door before turning on the light. Leaning his back against the door, Bryan unbuttoned his jeans and lowered the zipper. He slid his hands inside his underwear and palmed his aching cock. Bryan couldn't remember ever being so hard, and it was because he'd listened to Andy getting off. Calling out his name. *Fuck!* Bryan pushed his pants down his thighs so he could stroke his dick. He didn't have lube, so he spit in his hand, mixing the saliva with the moisture leaking from the tip. Bryan closed his eyes tight and jacked his dick slowly. He wasn't in a hurry to bust a nut for the first time in nearly six months. In case this was a fluke, he wanted to enjoy the rush.

Bryan thought of Laurel and the way she smiled. He let his mind wander to her large tits she didn't mind showing off with the low-cut shirt she'd been wearing. He imagined the woman on her knees, the red lipstick smearing on her face as she wrapped her mouth around his dick. Bryan gripped his erection tighter as he mentally pushed her blouse over to suck on her nipple. A flat chest with small nubs flashed through his mind. He brought Laurel's large breasts back to the forefront, but Andy kept intruding. Bryan's mind wouldn't cooperate.

When he couldn't keep Andy from popping in his head, Bryan tried a different tactic. He imagined one of the girl's he'd slept with before joining the military. She'd been beautiful and had ridden Bryan's cock like she owned it. When his dick began deflating, he thought of Andy's moans and the way his breath hitched earlier when he was chasing his own orgasm. At the remembrance of Bryan's name coming off Andy's lips when he blew his load, Bryan felt the heat at the base of his spine. His balls tightened, and with just a few hard strokes, his own release spilled over his hand. Fuck, but that felt amazing.

Breathing hard, Bryan did his best not to think about what it meant that visions of Andy had him shooting harder than he ever had inside a girl. He wasn't going to freak out. Not yet. He would go out with Laurel Saturday. See if there was a spark. Bryan wasn't a one-night stand kinda guy, but he might have to try it this weekend to prove to himself he was still attracted to women. Until then, he would not let things between him and Andy get weird. He couldn't. Andy was one of the only friends Bryan had in the world other than Brett and maybe Mal. Bryan could see Mal becoming important, even more than as a boss. The guy was already proving to be a great person.

After cleaning up the mess on his hand, Bryan brushed his teeth and took his pill. He decided to go ahead and take a quick shower so he wouldn't have to in the morning. He didn't slow down at Andy's door as he made his way to his bedroom. Crawling under the covers, Bryan willed himself to go to sleep. The rain beating against the windows wasn't helping. As much as he liked the dark, Bryan hated storms. He pulled the extra pillow over his head and began humming, doing his best to block out the noise.

His sleep was restless with all the thunder and lightning, but somewhere around three, Bryan finally drifted off. Even with four hours of sleep, Bryan's body woke up at seven on the dot. It was like he had an internal alarm clock. He pulled his clothes on and made his way to the kitchen. The rain had stopped, but it was muddy as fuck outside. "Good morning, Boss," he said to Mal.

"Mornin'. Coffee's ready." Mal was putting a pan of biscuits in the oven.

"Do you make biscuits every morning?" Bryan asked while putting sugar in his coffee.

"Yep. Ma really likes 'em, so I got in the habit of makin' 'em every day. They don't take much time, really."

Bryan wasn't going to complain. He loved breakfast food almost as much as he loved a good steak. Andy entered the kitchen whistling. Bryan pulled down an extra mug, poured coffee in it, and handed it over. He wanted to keep things peaceful between them.

When he took the mug, Andy smiled and said, "Thanks, B."

Andy's smile was beautiful. His teeth were white and perfectly straight, and Bryan wondered if he'd worn braces. His own teeth were crooked, but there was nothing he could do about it now. "You're welcome. How are you this morning?"

"If I was any better, I'd be triplets," Andy replied, pulling a chuckle from both Bryan and Mal.

"Did I hear someone playin' the piano last night?"

Mal asked.

Andy looked at Bryan, his eyes wide. "Yeah, I asked Lily to play me a song. I hope we didn't wake you up."

"Nah, nothin' like that. I was on the phone with Cade, so I was still awake. From the sounds of it, you sure know what you're doin', Andy."

Andy's cheeks turned a light red. Bryan thought it was adorable to see such a big man blushing. Andy had to be at least six two, because he was taller than Bryan. "He does know what he's doing. And he can sing, too." Bryan turned to Andy and asked, "Have you ever thought about cutting a record?"

"I'm not that good."

"Uh, yeah. You are."

Andy bit his bottom lip, so Bryan decided to change the subject. "I know that animals are used to being outside, but if the rain hadn't let up, what would we be doing today?"

Mal cracked several eggs in the skillet while he talked. "Same thing we're goin' to do today. Take most of the day off. I have a little more paperwork to catch up on, but now that y'all helped get the barn in good shape, we're good to go. I've already fed the horses. I thought we'd talk a little bit about the cattle and calvin' season so y'all will know what to expect. Walt usually helps out, but seein' as we have a whole lot more to look after than we have in the past, I'll need y'all to help keep an eye out while you're makin' the rounds."

"What about the dogs?" Andy asked.

"What about 'em?"

"Where do they sleep when it's raining?"

"In the barn."

"You never let them come in the house?"

"You really like 'em, don't ya?"

"I do. They're calming."

Bryan was watching the conversation like a tennis

match. He wouldn't be opposed to the dogs coming inside either, but he was going to let Andy fight this battle.

"You know, you could always get a doggie door so they could come in when they wanted."

Mal stirred the eggs and turned the eye down so he could pay attention to Andy. "Yeah? And who's gonna clean up after 'em when they track mud on the floor?"

"I will. I'll even do extra cleaning days so you won't have to worry about it."

They had agreed to split the cleaning duties between them just like they were alternating cooking days. Fridays were "fend for yourself" days as far as Mal was concerned since he expected Andy and Bryan to go to the bar and get out of the house.

"I'll think about it. Now, what are y'all gonna do today?"

Bryan said, "We have lots of movies we could watch."

"I'm okay with that," Andy said.

Bryan was glad to see Andy in a better mood than when he'd gone to bed the night before. Maybe he'd just needed to blow off some steam. Or jack off in his bedroom. Either way, things seemed to be okay between them.

Chapter Eight

Andy

When Andy woke, he was disoriented and sweating to the point of an almost panic attack. After he jerked off to thoughts of Bryan, he'd fallen into a fitful sleep. Normally storms didn't bother him, but they'd somehow conjured a nightmare where Bryan was yelling at Andy, telling him he was straight and to keep his faggot hands off him. He made a decision to keep his thoughts and his feelings to himself. There was no way he would lose Bryan as a friend. Even if it had been a bad dream, it made Andy see how important Bryan had become to him. Important enough for Andy to stop thinking about things he could never have.

When he entered the kitchen a few minutes before, he'd done so whistling, hoping to hide the way his heart was still beating a little too fast. He had been running his new mantra through his head – just friends. Then Bryan smiled at him. And after that, Bryan went and complimented him on his piano playing and singing. *Just friends. Just friends.*

Thankfully, Bryan changed the subject, and they eventually got on the topic of the dogs. Andy wasn't trying to be pushy, but he really wanted Moe and Curly to be able to come inside. If they'd been in the house the night before, Andy probably wouldn't have freaked out during the storm. He was willing to do just about anything to get Mal to relent, including doubling up on cleaning the house. Andy didn't mind cleaning. To him, it was therapeutic.

While they were eating, Mal explained the calving process. Most farms calved in the spring, but with the way things had been for Mal and his expecting to sell, he had missed the opportunity, even with the small herd he had. They were settling in for a late spring calving, so they didn't have a lot of time to learn the process. Walt was going to help separate the cattle into heifers and cows, cows being those that had already produced a calf. He told them about the different vaccinations and vitamins they would have to inject during the pregnancy as well as the tagging process once the calves were born. Mal and Walt had already been making sure the cattle had their vitamins, but with Bryan and Andy on board, it was going to make their lives a lot easier. Mal made it seem like a simple process, but Bryan knew every step was important to the well-being of both mother and calf as well as the success of the farm.

While they were cleaning the breakfast dishes, Andy asked Mal about Cade. He hadn't said much about his boyfriend, but once Andy asked, Mal became a whole new person. He told them as much as he knew about the new album, about Cade falling in love with Megan, Mal's middle niece, and about their daily talks on the phone. He left out the sexy parts, but Andy was okay with that. He didn't need any more reminders of what he wasn't getting.

Mal told Andy and Bryan to make themselves at home, and he left them alone to disappear into his office. "Wanna watch a movie?" Andy asked.

"Sure. You pick." Bryan let Andy choose more often than not.

Together, they made their way into the living room where they'd already unloaded all their DVDs. Bryan had offered to put his flat screen in place of the smaller, older box-type version Mal had. Mal had readily agreed, saying he didn't watch a lot of television.

Andy didn't have to worry about picking the wrong kind of movie to watch since he already knew Bryan liked the same movies he did and steered clear of the same types. Andy chose the first "Expendables" movie. He was a big

Sylvester Stallone fan. His love for the actor started with Rambo, and he had almost every movie the man ever made. He hadn't watched any of the Rambo films since leaving the Marines, afraid it would hit too close to home.

Andy popped the DVD into the player and sat on the opposite end of the couch from Bryan. They'd watched movies together before they moved to Arlo, so this felt like they were getting back to the way their friendship had been before Andy started getting all weird over his buddy. When the credits began scrolling, Andy told Bryan to choose the next one, so he chose to keep the action going with the second movie in the series. Once it ended, they stopped long enough to make some sandwiches. Mal hadn't come up for air from his paperwork, so Andy made him a sandwich as well. He took the plate down the hall and knocked on the door.

"Come in."

Andy entered the room to find Mal kicked back with his cell phone in hand. "Sorry, I thought you might be hungry." He put the plate on the desk and turned to leave.

"Thanks, Andy," Mal called out before Andy closed the door behind him.

He and Bryan took their plates to the living room and ate while watching the last show in the franchise. The tension from the night before was gone, and Andy enjoyed spending the day relaxing with Bryan. He'd been able to keep his thoughts on the movie for the most part. After the third film ended, Andy felt happier than he had since they arrived at the farm. They were going to DW's later, so while Andy was putting the DVD back in its case, he said, "I'm going to rest for a little bit before we head to town." He didn't want Bryan to get tired of being around him.

"Do you want to eat before we go, or do you want to grab a burger and shake at the Dairy Barn?" Bryan asked.

"Burgers sound great. I'd like to get to the bar before it gets too crowded, if that's okay."

"Perfect. Wanna leave here around six?"

"Sounds good." Andy headed down the hall to his bedroom. He was tired from not getting a good night's sleep, so he set the alarm on his phone for five. That would give him plenty of time for a shower and to get ready. He pulled the covers back and slid into bed. It was still dreary outside, so the little bit of daylight coming through the window didn't bother him. Within a few minutes, he was out.

Bryan

Bryan had thoroughly enjoyed his day with Andy. It had been a long time since he'd felt comfortable just being with someone and not having to talk. Their friendship was easy as long as they weren't talking about personal shit or touching one another. It was hard to concentrate on the movies with Andy so close. Bryan couldn't stop thinking about hearing his name when Andy was coming. It flattered him that Andy chose to use thoughts of him for spank material. He should have been freaking the fuck out, but the more he thought about it, the more he liked it.

When Andy said he was going to rest before they went to the bar, Bryan took the opportunity to call go Brianna and Brett and to let them know where he was and how he was doing. He'd told them both he had a new job, but he didn't elaborate on the details. He'd wanted to get settled and make sure the farm was going to be a good fit for him before he got their hopes up. Bryan knew they worried about him with his PTSD, but he had a good feeling about his current situation.

The sky was overcast, making the June day comfortable outside. Bryan took his cellphone out to the front porch where he sat on the swing. He'd just sat down

78

when Moe and Curly came bounding up the steps. Moe sat down, but Curly came to Bryan and sat at his feet. Bryan gave the dog a good rubbing. When Curly was satisfied, he went and took his spot beside Moe. Pushing back and forth with his foot, Bryan let the rocking lull him. He'd never sat in a porch swing, and now he knew what the appeal was. The motion was soothing. It must be how a baby felt to be rocked.

Bryan took a good look around the front yard. There were several large trees surrounding the house. The little bit of grass had recently been mowed. The area between the trees and the road was more than likely cut down with a tractor, and he could see himself sitting atop one, riding over the property cutting hay. It was another thing he had no idea how to do, but he was willing to learn. If someone had asked him a year ago if he ever saw himself in a small town on a farm, he'd have laughed. Growing up in the suburbs of Chicago was nothing like what he found in Kentucky. When Bryan left the Marines, he wanted somewhere quiet to start over, and here, he'd found it.

Unlike Andy, Bryan had joined the Marines for nothing more than a steady paycheck and to defend his country. He had his high school education, but with helping his mom, Bryan had never thought about life after the military. He'd planned on staying in until he found a woman he wanted to settle down with and start a family of his own. When he enlisted, he never thought about all the shit he would see. The things he would have to do. The lives lost on both sides. That kind of shit stuck with you, no matter who you were. When his CO mentioned Bryan training in the Special Ops Command division, Bryan knew it was time to opt out. There was no way he could get in deeper than he already was.

When he made the decision to leave the Corps, Bryan pulled out a map, closed his eyes, and pointed. His finger was on top of Tennessee, so that's where he ended up. If that didn't work out, he would move on. Now that he didn't have to take care of his family, he had nothing but time. Since he didn't have a college education and no training other than how to shoot a gun, his choices in jobs had been limited. He thanked God that he'd run into Erik at the VA Center. While he didn't know for sure what the future held, life on this cattle farm didn't seem so bad. The only exception was the wife and kids.

After the way Mal described Laurel, Bryan wasn't putting too much hope in their date Saturday, but at least it was a start. He wasn't in that big of a rush to find a woman since he'd just started this job. After he was settled in, he might find someone he wanted to spend his life with. The pay was good, and he had his savings. He could always move off the farm but come back to work there every day. That way, he'd still get to see Andy.

Not wanting to revisit thoughts of the previous night, Bryan punched in his sister's number.

"Bryan? Is everything okay?" Brianna asked when she picked up.

"Hello to you, too," he said, laughing. "Everything's fine. That's why I'm calling."

"Oh, good. You scared me."

"Why would I scare you? It's not like I never call."

"No, but you usually wait until bedtime. Hang on a second." Brianna fussed at the twins in the background before returning. "Do you want two boys? I swear, they're going to be the death of me. School's only been out a week, and I'm ready for August to get here, like now."

"I thought you had the summer off, being a teacher."

"I do, but I'm still trying to get my classroom cleaned out. I had found a local woman to watch the boys after school since they only went half days, but she kindly asked me to find somewhere else for them to stay when Noah tried to flush her kitten down the toilet," Brianna huffed. It wasn't funny, but Bryan still chuckled, because he could see his nephew clearly. Jonah was just as bad.

"How much longer do you have?"

"I finished up today. Now I have them to myself all day every day. You sure you don't want to come visit? Take them camping for like a month?"

Bryan couldn't hold back the laughter. "Gee, Bree, if I hadn't started this new job, I'd totally do that for you." *Not.* "That's why I was calling." Bryan told his sister all about meeting Erik then meeting Andy and how things were going so far, leaving out the part about being attracted to his friend. "I think I've finally found a place I can be myself and not have to worry about the panic attacks. Andy and I have so much in common with that regards. He was in for eight years, and he has some of the same triggers I do."

"Sounds like you've found your perfect match. Is he cute?"

"Why would you ask me that?"

"Because the way you're going on about him, sounds like you like him."

"I do like him. We're already good friends. He's funny, kind, and he has these crazy southern sayings I've never heard before in my life, but when he comes out with them, they sound normal somehow."

"Bry…" Brianna paused to yell at the twins again.

He realized he'd said too much about Andy, so he cut their call short. "Listen, I gotta go get ready. We're going to grab some burgers before we hit the local bar. I just wanted you to know I'm doing good."

"I'm really glad to hear it. You sound happy."

"I am happy. Now, don't let the twins run you ragged. Find one of those mother's day out places before they drive you to do something crazy."

"I will. Take care."

"You, too." Bryan disconnected and put his phone in his pocket. Just listening to his sister on the phone was exhausting. He didn't know how she did it. Her husband was a good partner and father who helped out when he got off work. Jared was a quiet man. Bryan had never seen him raise his voice, but even with his quiet tone, the boys listened to him. For some reason, they obeyed his easy instructions much better than they did Brianna's. She didn't yell, but sometimes she lost her temper and raised her voice. Being around them when they wouldn't mind often had Bryan rethinking wanting kids in the future.

He had planned on calling Brett, but he wouldn't be off work yet. Instead, he shot off a quick text telling him he'd found a job and was loving it so far. He'd call him over the weekend when they could talk. Brett was the baby of the family. Having graduated college with honors, he was making a good living as an accountant and had a good head on his shoulders. David was a few years older. He was an investment specialist and had done well for himself at an early age and helped put Brett through college. Brett had wanted to wait until he graduated before they got married, but David talked Brett into it the year before. Now, they were looking for a surrogate so they could have a baby. Bryan prayed the good Lord would see fit to give them what they wanted.

Bryan continued to rock back and forth in the swing, enjoying being outside where it was quiet. He had a feeling this was going to be a favorite spot for him. A little while later, the front door opened, and Mal came outside. "There you are. I'm gettin' ready to head over to Walt's to sit for a spell with him and my ma. Andy's still holed up in his room, and I didn't wanna leave without tellin' someone where I was goin'. Y'all have fun at the bar. Call me if you need a ride home."

"Thanks, Mal. Tell your mom hello for me, and I'm sure we'll be fine. I don't plan on drinking that much."

"Sounds good. See you later." Mal petted both dogs before walking down the steps. He disappeared around the corner of the house, and the deep rumble of the dually's engine fired up. Bryan stood from the swing and made his way inside to get something to drink. He opted for a glass of water and took it to his room. He glanced over at Andy's door just as the alarm on Andy's phone went off. Bryan ducked into his own room so Andy wouldn't catch him looking. Not that he was doing anything wrong. He didn't want Andy to get the wrong idea.

Bryan went to the closet and pulled out a newer pair of jeans along with a blue button-up shirt. He'd been told that blue was a good color on him. Something about it made his eyes pop. He didn't think popping eyes sounded too appealing, but what the hell did he know? He changed clothes and pulled on his new boots. They were a bit snug, but he trusted Andy when he said they would stretch out. He took a final once-over at his reflection in the mirror and hoped he wouldn't have to put up with any bullshit tonight because of his looks.

The bathroom door closed, and the shower turned on. Before Bryan could even begin to think about a naked Andy, he went in the living room and turned the television on. He knew he had a good hour to wait on Andy, so he settled in for the duration. In almost exactly an hour, Andy came strolling into the room. "How do I look?"

"Like you were born to be a cowboy," Bryan said, keeping his comment friendly. The way Andy's jeans hugged his thick thighs was distracting. Like Bryan, Andy had put on a button-up shirt and had also rolled his sleeves up, showing off his toned forearms.

"You don't look so shabby yourself. You ready to ride?"

"Yep. Let me grab my keys and wallet." Bryan turned the TV off. When he passed by Andy, he caught a whiff of cologne. It smelled like nothing he'd ever encountered before, and it had Bryan wanting to bathe in it. Or bathe with Andy while he was wearing it. *Seriously?*

The ride to the Dairy Barn was done with Bryan

keeping his mouth shut and Andy singing at the top of his lungs. When he didn't know the words, which wasn't often, he made them up. By the time they got to the little hamburger place, Bryan was laughing at the other man's antics. As soon as he laughed once, Andy started ad-libbing most of the lyrics. It was like the one time Bryan and Brianna had made up the words to a Latino soap opera. Bryan parked his truck, and they both got out. Andy held the door for Bryan, and somehow it felt intimate. Bryan didn't mind, though. As soon as they entered the building, all eyes were on them. Bryan felt like turning around and going back home, but Andy strode right up to the counter, smiling. What was it he'd said about the horses? Size didn't matter when it came to dominance. Attitude did. Bryan decided Andy had the right attitude, and he copied the friendly smile and joined his friend at the counter.

They ordered practically the same thing with Bryan's shake being strawberry instead of chocolate. While they waited on their double cheeseburgers and fries, Andy filled about a dozen little white paper cups with ketchup. He then grabbed napkins for both of them and found a booth toward the front of the room. Bryan was glad he hadn't chosen to sit in the back. He didn't like being in new places where he couldn't see the door.

They ate in companionable silence, with everyone who came and went staring at them. Andy smiled at anyone who happened to walk by the table, but Bryan kept his focus on his food. "This is really good," he said around a mouthful of beef. "I haven't had a burger this good since the last time I grilled one."

"Yeah? When was that?"

Bryan swallowed his food before answering. "Before I enlisted. We had this little charcoal grill we kept on the back stoop. It barely held four burgers, but I used it all the time. I've never eaten off a gas grill, but I'm pretty sure I would still prefer charcoal over gas."

"I've never eaten off a charcoal grill. The gas one back home was this monstrosity on our back patio. But if charcoal's as good as you make it sound, maybe we can get one. Summer's here, and I'd like to have a good steak or rack of ribs every once in a while."

"Mal said he'd get us a grill. Let's hope it's sooner rather than later. I don't want my turn feeding everyone sending y'all to the ER with food poisoning."

"I already told you I'll teach you. Now, are you done?" Andy asked, pointing at the empty tray. "I'm ready to have a beer or five."

"I'm done." Bryan let Andy take the tray to the garbage bin while he thought about Andy getting drunk. Bryan would need to be the responsible one and take it easy. As he drove the short distance to the bar, Bryan prayed for an uneventful night. He wasn't in the mood to go to jail.

Chapter Nine

Andy

It was early by bar standards when Andy and Bryan got to DW's. There were a couple of men sitting at the bar when they entered the building, but the tables were empty. They'd already discussed where to sit before they got out of the truck. Bryan wanted to be as far away from the dance floor as possible. Not that he was opposed to dancing, but that area tended to be more crowded. Andy pointed to a high top, and Bryan nodded. He looked around but didn't see a waitress. A few minutes later, a man walked up and introduced himself.

"I'm Kason. You must be Bryan and Andy." Kason held out his hand to shake.

"How'd you know?" Andy asked.

"Erik told me about you two moving here to help Mal. How's it going so far?" Kason was former military if the way he held himself was any indication. The short haircut was another.

"So far so good, but we've only been here two days. How about you? You buy the place or just the bartender?"

"Bartender slash manager. I've been out of the Corps a couple of years, but it took me quite a while to get my head out of my ass. Losing my leg had me really bummed for a long time." Kason thumped his prosthesis. Andy wouldn't have known if the man hadn't told him. "So, what can I get you men to drink?"

Andy and Bryan both ordered beer from the tap. Kason returned a few minutes later with their glasses and a bowl full of cashews. "Here you go. I've only been here about a week, but so far things are going well. I have a small apartment not too far from here. Most of the regulars seem nice. The women are pretty, and the beer's cold."

"This is our first night out, but if things go well tonight, we'll probably become regulars ourselves," Andy offered. He already liked Kason and figured the man could use some friends. Kason made sure the customers sitting at the bar had full drinks, but when he had downtime, he stayed with Andy and Bryan. They each told a little about their time overseas, and Andy felt like he and Bryan had someone else in their corner. Eventually, more patrons trickled in, and Kason had to stay behind the bar.

"He's nice," Andy said as Kason walked away.

"That he is," Bryan agreed. "I hate to break the seal after only two beers, but I'm going to hit the head."

Andy automatically thought about Bryan and head, but it had nothing to do with going to the restroom, unless it was for a quick blow job. *Just friends. Just friends.* Right as Bryan was returning to his seat, a couple of women came through the door. "Well, hell," Andy muttered. Bryan must have noticed them as well, because his ass hovered over the stool before he sat all the way down. Andy had hoped to have Bryan all to himself for the night, but it didn't look like that was going to be an option when Laurel headed their way.

"So, this is why you put me off until tomorrow?" she accused Bryan, but the expression on her face was anything but scornful. Her eyes were glued to Andy. "Can't say I blame you there. You're welcome to bring your friend tomorrow, you know, if you're into that sort of thing," she purred.

Ew. Just, no.

Bryan cleared his throat and said, "I appreciate the offer, but I don't share."

"Too bad. He's hot," she replied, running a long fingernail down Andy's arm. Did she think he and Bryan were together? When he thought about the way Bryan phrased his sentence, she could have taken it either way.

"We'll leave you two alone then." Laurel and her friend gave each other a knowing smile and leaned in, laughing.

"That was Laurel," Bryan explained.

"Yes, I know," Andy responded before thinking better of it. Bryan hadn't seen him come into the grocery store. He'd stayed hidden behind the endcap when Laurel was flirting with Bryan in the beer aisle.

"How did you know?" Bryan asked, his eyebrows dipping between his eyes. Andy hated when Bryan frowned. He wasn't nearly as handsome as when he smiled.

"By the description Mal gave and the fact she mentioned tomorrow. I assume she's the only one you have a date with tomorrow. Am I wrong?"

"No, you're not wrong." Bryan downed the last of his beer and looked around.

"I haven't seen a waitress, and Kason's pretty slammed. I'll go get the next round." Andy stood and headed to the bar, going to the opposite end from where Laurel and her friend were standing. When Kason noticed Andy, his face lit up. "Another round, please."

"Sure thing." When he returned with two full pints, Kason winked. "I see you've met Laurel and Trina."

"They come in here that often?" If the bartender had only been there a week and he already knew their names, they had to be regulars.

"Every night." Kason placed his arms on the bar and leaned in closer. "And every night, they've left with someone different."

"Thanks for the warning." Andy lifted his beer in mock salute and returned to their table. He wasn't sure whether to tell Bryan about Kason's warning or let him figure it out for himself. Bryan was a grown man, and hell, maybe he wanted a loose woman. She'd definitely know her way around a dick, but Andy halted those thoughts. He couldn't have Bryan, but that didn't mean he wanted to think about someone else having him.

The longer they sat there, the louder the place became. Someone put money in the jukebox, and a few couples got up to dance. Bryan was quieter and less attentive. His eyes never strayed over to where Laurel and Trina were sitting. When they got up to dance together, he didn't glance their way. He kept his focus on Andy and their conversation. Andy hadn't known Bryan long, but his body was tight, and his face was shutting down. Andy knew that look. It was the one he felt when he was close to having a panic attack. "You ready to get outta here?" he asked.

Bryan nodded. He pulled out his wallet, handed Andy a twenty, and said, "I'm going to wait by the truck."

"Yeah, I got this. I'll meet you outside." Andy grabbed the money and headed to see Kason to settle their tab. He told his fellow Marine it had been nice meeting him, and they'd see him soon.

On the way out the door, Laurel stepped in front of Andy. "You two are leaving early. Sure you don't want some company?"

"I'm sure, but thank you for the offer. There's plenty of other guys for you to snatch up tonight." Andy probably sounded rude, but he didn't care. He didn't like the woman. At all. He shouldn't be getting all high and mighty just because she liked to screw around, but he didn't want her anywhere near Bryan. He muttered, "Excuse me," and skirted around her out the door. When he reached the truck, Bryan was sitting in the passenger seat. Andy didn't hesitate to open the driver's side door and get in. "You okay?"

"I will be. It's been a while since I've been around that many people at one time. I'll get used to it." Bryan's hands were in tight fists, and he was breathing fast. Andy reached out and covered Bryan's hand with his. Bryan flattened his hand on his thigh, but Andy didn't let go. He wasn't coming on to Bryan; he was offering silent support. When Bryan's breathing returned to normal and his shoulders relaxed, Andy removed his hand and started the truck. He changed the radio to a rock station, knowing Bryan didn't care for country music.

"Thank you," Bryan said, barely above a whisper. If the music had been much louder, Andy wouldn't have heard it.

"You're welcome. I'm always here for you, B." As much as he wanted to be there in a different way, Andy meant his words. He intended to be Bryan's friend for as long as the man would have him in his life. Andy pulled out of the gravel parking lot and headed toward the farm. Neither one said anything on the drive home. *Home.* In just a couple of days, Andy had already started thinking of the farm as home.

When he stopped in the driveway, Bryan hopped out, opened the gate for Andy to drive on through, and then shut it behind them. He banged his hand on the side of the truck a couple of times, indicating Andy should go on. Bryan obviously wanted the alone time as he walked back to the house. Instead of going inside, Andy remained outside to make sure Bryan was okay. Moe and Curly danced around his feet as soon as he got out of the truck. Andy bent down, giving both dogs equal amounts of love while he waited for Bryan to make it up the driveway.

Bryan's hands were in his pockets, and his head was down. The closer he got, the more Andy wanted to reach out to him. He couldn't though. Friends didn't do that. Did they? If it had been Christy, he wouldn't have hesitated to wrap his arms around her, but this was Bryan. He probably wouldn't appreciate Andy being so touchy feely. "Want to check on the horses with me?" Andy wanted to get Bryan's thoughts on something besides being in the crowded bar.

"Sure."

90

Andy held the keys out for Bryan. When he reached for them, his fingers closed around Andy's for a brief moment. Surely, he hadn't meant to do that. Andy glanced sideways, but Bryan's focus was on his feet. When they reached the barn, Andy flipped on the overhead light before stepping inside. Both horses had their heads hanging over the stall doors like they'd been talking to each other. Their heads turned in sync at the approaching men. Andy laughed and began talking to the animals. Bryan hesitantly placed a hand on Callie's muzzle and rubbed.

"Sorry for freaking out on you," Bryan said softly. "I... The last time I went to a bar, a fight broke out, and I didn't handle it well."

"You weren't hurt, were you? I mean, not that I think you can't handle yourself, because look at you." Andy stopped rambling when Bryan cocked an eyebrow his way. Andy had no doubt Bryan could handle himself. The guy was built like a tank. He was just as broad as Andy was. Bryan had obviously continued to work out by the looks of his body.

"No. I ran like a girl." Bryan laughed, but it wasn't filled with amusement. It hurt to hear the sadness in Bryan's voice. "When the attacks kick in, I sort of lose focus. If I'd gotten in on the fight, I'd probably be in jail."

Andy hated fighting almost as much as he hated arguing. War was one thing, but when people used their fists or hateful words to prove a point, he found it exhausting. He was a lover, not a fighter. At least he had been before he signed on for the Marines. He'd found that most people who enlisted did so for honor and country. Most weren't a thin gay kid left with little choice once their parents kicked them to the curb. He had to lie to everyone about why he joined up. He had to put on a false sense of bravado. Put on an air of toughness he didn't feel. It didn't take Andy long to become the butt of jokes or the punching bag. It also didn't take him long to strike back. Even though he pretended to like women, he was still referred to as queer. He got his ass handed to him more than once, but he was bound and determined to not be the kid who got sand kicked in his face.

Andy hit the weights extra hard. When the others were enjoying any downtime they had, Andy was working on his body. The scars on his back were a constant reminder of his physical weakness. He vowed after the first fight he would become someone – some*thing* – nobody wanted to mess with, and he had succeeded. Over the last six months, Andy did his best to stay in shape, and he was ready to start really working out again. If they planned on staying in Arlo, he wanted to find a gym, or at the least, buy a set of weights to use.

"Hey, where'd you go?" Bryan asked.

"Oh, sorry. Just thinking about what you said. I hate fighting. Not because it triggers a panic attack, but I think people should be able to settle their differences like adults, not like kids on the playground."

"You look like you could hold your own in a fight, Lily. You're huge." Bryan play punched Andy's bicep.

Andy turned toward him and took up a fighter's stance, fists in the air. He threw a couple of jabs that he pulled right before they reached Bryan's chest. "Speaking of, what do you think about finding a gym or getting some equipment set up? There are a couple of empty stalls. Maybe Mal will let us use one."

"Honestly? I'd rather work out here. I don't see Arlo having a big gym that isn't filled with rednecks. I don't want to risk having people talk shit about the way I look. Like I said, I run from fights, and that just wouldn't do around here."

"I'd have your back, but then I'd be accused of sticking up for my boyfriend, and I'd probably blurt out something about them sucking my dick, and I'd be the one fighting," Andy said. Bryan burst out laughing, and Andy joined in. Damn it felt good to hear Bryan laughing.

"Then I'd have to turn around, because I'd have your back, too," Bryan said when he'd calmed down. His smile met his eyes, and Andy melted a little more.

Andy turned his focus back to Cochise so Bryan wouldn't see the longing there. He needed to talk to Mal and find out where to go for hookups outside of Arlo. Andy needed to get laid. He needed someone to take the edge off before he slipped up and did something stupid, like kiss his best friend. When had Bryan replaced Christy? The night of the baseball game. Andy knew then he and Bryan had something special.

"You up for a game of poker? I'm not ready to go to bed just yet."

"Sure, just don't whine when I take all your money."

Andy laughed. Not because he thought he'd win, but because Bryan was probably right. Andy had a shitty poker face, but if losing would keep Bryan smiling, he'd throw every game. They said goodnight to the horses, and the dogs followed them until they reached the back porch. Andy unlocked the door and punched in the security code. He didn't bother resetting the alarm since Mal would probably be along soon.

While Bryan grabbed a couple of beers, Andy set about making a plate of simple cheese nachos for them to snack on while they played cards. Instead of playing for a lot of money, Andy dumped out some change he'd been saving. He didn't know about Bryan's financial situation, but Andy couldn't afford to lose what little money he had playing poker. It would be another week before they got their first paycheck.

Bryan dealt the first hand, and the two of them got lost in the cards and the companionship. When Mal finally made it home, Bryan had raked in most of the change. "Who's winnin'?" Mal asked as he looked at Andy's hand first before walking around to peek at Bryan's.

93

Andy pointed at Bryan's pile of coins. "He is, but he's cheating," Andy told Mal with a wink. He knew he sucked at poker, but he enjoyed playing anyway. "Next time, instead of betting money, we're going to play strip poker. I'll be more focused then."

Mal barked out a laugh. "Yeah, you'll be more focused on his body. Bryan, don't do it, buddy."

It was the first time Mal had let loose, and Andy grinned at his boss. The more he was around Mal, the more he liked him. "How was your mom?"

"Good. She had the girls, well Mattie and Megan, anyway. I'd have been home sooner, but Mattie conned me into readin' her a couple of bedtime stories. Ma hinted around about me askin' her and Walt over for supper. I think she wants to get to know you two a little better. I told her I'd cook tomorrow night, if that's okay with y'all."

"I'm good with it. Your mom seems like a wonderful woman." Andy wasn't jealous of Mal and Suzette's relationship, but he often yearned for his own mom. Not the one who watched as he was kicked out of his home, but the one who'd shown him a semblance of love as a child.

"I... uh... I have a date tomorrow," Bryan reminded them.

"Oh, well. I'm sure Ma won't mind you catchin' up with her some other time."

"You want to sit in on the next hand?" Andy asked, changing the subject. He didn't want to think about Bryan and his date.

"Sure. I haven't played a lot of cards in my life, so you'll have to tell me the rules." Mal took the chair he normally sat in for meals, and Andy pointed to Bryan's pile of money.

"You'll have to borrow from the card shark. As you can see, I'm almost broke." Andy shuffled the cards while Bryan gave Mal half of the money on his side of the table.

"Five card draw, nickel ante with quarter maximum

bet." Andy dealt everyone five cards and when he saw he had three Aces, he squirmed in his chair.

Both Mal and Bryan glanced over at him, and Andy did his best to keep his face passive. When Mal and Bryan looked at each other, they both laid their cards down and said, "I fold," at the same time.

"What?" Andy huffed.

Grinning, Mal said, "I might not play a lot of cards, but I can see why he has all the money." Mal thumbed at Bryan who was biting his bottom lip to keep from laughing.

"What's so fucking funny, B?"

"Oh, Lily. You are. I shouldn't tell you this in case we ever play for real money, but you have these little tells. Like if you get a really good hand, you squirm in the chair. If you get a bad hand, you sigh. If you have an okay hand, you bite your bottom lip."

"You should be watching your cards instead of me," Andy huffed. But he was glad Bryan had been watching him. For more than one reason. The most important being that now he could concentrate on not doing those things when he was looking at his hand.

"Then I wouldn't know whether to bet or fold. Let's try again." Bryan took the cards from Andy, shuffled them, and dealt everyone a new hand.

Andy concentrated, and now that he knew what he'd been doing, he was able to win more hands. For the next couple of hours, they drank beer, ate nachos, and had a good time laughing with each other. When Mal's phone rang with Cade calling, he grinned and said, "I'm out. I'll see y'all in the mornin'."

Andy's eyes followed Mal as he hurried out of the kitchen and up the stairs where he could talk to Cade in private. As much fun as he'd had playing cards, Andy wished he had someone to talk to on the phone. Even though Cade lived in California, he came to visit Mal when he could. *You have Bryan.* He did, but only as a friend. At least Mal and Cade had sex a few times a year. All Andy had was his toys. They got the job done as far as getting him off, but he longed for the intimacy of kissing and holding someone after the sex was over. Not that he'd ever had that. Even with Patrick, there'd been no cuddling. Just rough sex that…

"You want another beer?" Bryan asked.

"Nah. I think I'm going to turn in, too." Andy scraped all the coins back into the jar he kept them in. At the end of the night, they'd all been pretty even in their winnings. "B, why did you let me in on what my telling signs are? You could have left me in the dark and took all the money."

"Because I like you. I never want to take advantage of you, and besides, it's more fun when you're competitive."

Because I like you.

"Well, thanks for that."

"You're welcome. I'll see you in the morning."

"Yeah, see ya." Andy double-checked all the locks and the alarm while he gave Bryan time to use the bathroom. He leaned against the back door, looking out into the dark night. He'd had fun with Bryan just like he always did, no matter what they ended up doing. Andy couldn't think of anywhere else he'd rather be or anyone he'd rather spend time with. His heart hurt knowing he could never have the one guy who was almost perfect for him.

Chapter Ten

Bryan

Other than the near panic attack Bryan almost had at the bar, the day had been perfect. He couldn't remember enjoying himself as much as he had, and it was all thanks to Andy. He imagined tomorrow being another great day until he thought about seeing Laurel. He'd been looking forward to his date, somewhat, until she'd flirted with Andy right in front of him. And asking for a threesome? While Bryan had thought about what it would be like to be with Andy, he wasn't lying when he told Laurel he didn't share. Not that Andy was his, but if Bryan was with someone, he couldn't see how bringing a third person into their bed would be a good thing. He knew people did that all the time, but that wasn't for him. He might not have ever been in a relationship, but when he thought of being with someone, he always thought it meant that person was loyal to you and you to them.

If what Mal said about Laurel was true, and by the way she acted at the bar, she wasn't the type of person Bryan wanted in his life. He knew he wasn't ready for a relationship, but he didn't want to hook up for the sake of hooking up, even if he wanted to test his theory about whether or not he was really into women. Plus, if he was going to go out with someone, he wanted it to possibly lead to something more. Bryan couldn't see there being anything more with Laurel. Instead of wasting his time and money on someone like her, Bryan decided to cancel their date. Besides, he didn't want to miss tomorrow's dinner with Suzette and Walt. It had been a long time since Bryan had eaten with family, and he was looking forward to it.

He was thankful to be using the bathroom before Andy had gone to bed. He couldn't stand another night like the last one. Bryan was ready for a good night's sleep. Hearing the sounds coming from Andy's room had done a number on Bryan. As soon as he got to his room, he stripped down to his boxer briefs and climbed under the covers. The floor outside his door creaked as Andy passed by. Bryan found himself smiling at the thought of Andy playing poker. If they'd been playing for real money, he wouldn't have let Andy in on what his tells were. Then again, he probably would have. It was no fun taking all of someone's money without a challenge. Bryan had a little bit of a competitive streak, but not one so big he would take advantage of his best friend. Bryan closed his eyes and drifted off to sleep with visions of Andy biting his full bottom lip running through his head.

Saturday morning began the way the others had with the exception of the cook. Andy was awake and making breakfast when Bryan hit the kitchen. "Morning," he said, staring at Andy's legs. He was wearing a pair of cut-off sweat pants that didn't quite reach his knees. The muscles in his thighs bunched underneath as he moved from one foot to the other.

"Oh, hey. I thought I'd tackle breakfast since we're supposed to take turns cooking. I can't make biscuits, but I'm not bad with pancakes. You wanna grab the plates and stuff for me?" Andy asked while flipping a pancake over, not bothering to turn around.

"Yeah, sure." Bryan had no trouble helping out other than keeping his eyes off Andy's legs. Instead of freaking out over it, Bryan chalked it up to hormones. Hormones he had no control over.

"Mal had to take a phone call, and he said not to wait on him." Andy put a stack of fluffy pancakes on a plate filled with sausage and handed it over to Bryan. The syrup was already on the table. "Don't wait on me either. Pancakes don't stay warm long," he instructed.

Bryan poured a cup of coffee as well as a tall glassful of milk. He poured one for Andy and set it at the seat next to him. "Thank you," Andy said, when he noticed the milk. Bryan loved pancakes but never had them much growing up. The few he'd had weren't nearly as good as the ones Andy made. The only sounds coming from the table were Bryan's moans each time he took a bite and Andy's chuckles. By the time they had cleaned their plates, Mal still wasn't out of his office. Andy had made enough for Mal and stuck his plate in the microwave.

Since he was already dressed to go outside, Bryan told Andy, "I'll clean up while you go get changed."

"Okay, thanks. I won't be long." Andy whistled some tune as he walked out of the kitchen, and Bryan watched him go. He stepped out onto the back porch and pulled out his cell phone, texting Laurel to cancel their date. He probably should have called, but he didn't see where he owed her an explanation other than he couldn't make it.

When Andy came outside, Bryan noticed his cammies were blue. "Marine, I know you like semen, but what are you doing dressed like a seaman?"

Andy blushed, shoving past Bryan as he headed to the barn. "I found them in a thrift store, and they were nice and broken in," Andy admitted.

Bryan hated the fact Andy had to shop in thrift stores. He'd said his money situation was tight, but now that he had a job, hopefully those days were over. Bryan knew all about having to wear second-hand clothes. Thinking back, the only time he'd seen Andy in anything other than jeans, cammies, and tees had been when they went to the bar. His button-up shirt had been nice and his jeans looked fairly new. As Bryan watched Andy disappear into the barn, he thought to himself, no matter what Andy wore, he wore it well.

The sun was already shining, and it was going to be a muggy day. The rain had seen to that. Andy fed the horses while Bryan filled their water. Mal had already mentioned he wanted them to check the fencing on the back part of the property before they turned some of the cattle loose back there. They loaded up the tools they would need if the fence needed mending and set off on the four wheelers.

It was close to noon before they saw Mal. He came riding up on Callie with Moe and Curly close behind. Mal apologized for taking so long, but he didn't elaborate on what the call was about. That didn't bother Bryan since Mal didn't seem upset about anything, and he was the boss. He didn't have to explain anything to them. "I brought your lunch to you so you don't have to go all the way back to the house to eat."

Mal placed the bag on the seat of Cade's four wheeler and looked at the fencing. "Y'all are doing a great job."

"Thanks. Once you showed us what to do, it wasn't that hard to continue on." Bryan had been pretty handy before he joined the Marines. Being the man of the house meant he was responsible for fixing the things the landlord always forgot about. He enjoyed working with his hands, and the fact his boss praised his work made him enjoy it even more. It was a far cry from being in the military, where you were yelled at all the time.

"Walt's meetin' me in the front pasture. We're goin' to vaccinate the heifers. Ma's gonna be in the den watchin' television. If you don't get finished out here, go ahead and stop so you have time to clean up by five."

"Will do, and thanks for the sandwiches," Andy replied for both of them. When they got to a good stopping place, they grabbed the bags and sat in the shade of a nearby oak. Leaning against the huge tree, Andy pulled the sandwiches out of the plastic bag and handed Bryan two of them. When Mal made a sandwich, he didn't kid around. It

100

was piled high with meat and cheese, just the way Bryan liked.

The two of them had worked together all morning, getting into a routine. Bryan was used to teamwork, but what he wasn't used to was being alone with Andy for hours on end. The man didn't make things uncomfortable. If anything, he did everything he could to make Bryan more relaxed around him. Gone was the flirting. There was no touching his arm unless it was accidentally when one of them had to pull on the wire while the other secured it to a post. Andy sang softly to himself instead of belting out whatever country song he was hearing in his head.

"Any idea where you're taking Laurel on your date?" Andy asked before taking a bite. He didn't look at Bryan while he waited for an answer. Instead, he chewed, swallowed, and took another bite.

"I'm not taking her anywhere," Bryan said.

"Oh, so you're staying at her place. Eating in," Andy said almost mockingly. If Bryan didn't know better, he'd think Andy was jealous, regardless of the way he'd been behaving all morning.

"No, smartass. I'm not going. I texted her earlier and canceled our date."

Andy turned his head so fast Bryan was sure the man got whiplash. "You did?"

"Yeah. After last night, I can't see me being around her and having a good time. I mean, she wanted me to bring you along with me. How crazy is that?"

Andy's face fell. Oh, shit. That came out wrong. "Not that her wanting you was crazy. That's not what I meant. I understand why she would want you. I meant it was crazy for her to want to fuck both of us. I wasn't kidding when I said I don't share. I'm not a prude, but I don't think I could be in a relationship with someone who couldn't be satisfied with just me."

"You've never fantasized about being a Bryan

101

sandwich?"

"No. Have you?" Andy coughed, choking on the bread he'd just swallowed, and Bryan rolled his eyes. "You know what I mean, asshole. Do you want to be an Andy sandwich, smashed between two big men who have their wicked way with you?"

Andy shivered, but from the look on his face, not in a good way. "No," he whispered.

Bryan had to wonder if the scars on Andy's back had anything to do with his answer. He didn't feel close enough to him to ask, though. Maybe one day Andy would feel comfortable enough with Bryan to tell him what happened. When he did, Bryan was afraid he'd travel to Texas, find the ex-boyfriend, and give him a scar or two of his own. No teenager deserved that kind of treatment, especially from someone who was supposed to be their boyfriend. They finished eating in silence, both their moods a little darker than when they started.

Once they were done, Bryan stood and held out a hand to help Andy up. It was a friendly gesture, but as soon as Andy clasped Bryan's hand, Bryan felt the same tingle he felt before. If Andy felt it, he ignored it. They tossed their trash in the back compartment of the ATV and got back to work. Even with the heaviness of the conversation, Andy lightened up and began singing. The next four hours passed quickly, and soon it was time to head indoors.

Bryan made his way to the den before taking his shower. He cleared his throat when he got close to Suzette.

"Bryan, is that you, sweetheart?" the older woman asked.

How in the hell did she know it was him and not Andy since Andy was standing right beside him? "Yes ma'am. I wanted to say hello before I got in the shower. How've you been?"

"Right as rain. Come over here and let me look at you both. How are you boys settling in? Everything going okay for you?" Suzette turned the volume down and held out her hands. Bryan closed the distance first and squatted in front of her. She didn't hesitate to place her hands on either side of his face. Unlike last time, she didn't explore the planes. Instead she held him there as if she were looking into his eyes. Bryan's heart hurt a little when thinking about his own mother. He was glad Mal had such an awesome mom to stand by him through the years.

"Everything's great so far. We went to the Dairy Barn last night and had one of their burgers."

"Oh, don't let Matilda hear you say that. She'll be begging for Friday night dates with the both of you," Suzette joked.

"If she's half as pretty as her grandmother, I wouldn't mind that at all," Andy said as he came up and stood next to Bryan.

"Aren't you the smooth one," Suzette said, smacking Andy on the leg. "You better watch this one, Bryan. He's a charmer." If she only knew how much he already watched his friend.

"I hear you have a date tonight," she said to Bryan, cocking her head to the side.

"No, ma'am. I canceled it."

"You did?" Suzette's face softened and she looked… happy.

"Yes, ma'am. I did. Now, I'm going to hop in the shower before Andy gets in there and doesn't leave me any hot water," Bryan said. Before he could stand, Suzette smiled and kissed him on the cheek. He didn't miss the grin on Andy's face when he turned his way.

"Something you want to say, Lily?" Bryan ghosted across Andy's ear.

Bryan didn't give Andy time to answer. As he stepped from the room, Suzette asked Andy, "Lily? What's that all about?"

When Bryan returned to the den less than ten

minutes later, Andy was still sitting with Suzette. She was holding his hand and patting it the way a mother would. Bryan didn't want to intrude on their conversation, but he couldn't make his feet move. Bryan leaned against the door frame and studied Andy while his attention was elsewhere. Andy sat tentatively while Suzette spoke softly. He probably felt the same pull to Mal's mom since his own mom had abandoned him as a teenager.

Bryan's life growing up was tough, but it was filled with love. He had no doubt his father loved him and his siblings in his own way. It had been months since Bryan had gone to see the man. He'd visited him right after he got out of the Marines but hadn't talked to him since. Bryan never bothered to ask his siblings if they ever heard from him or went to visit. Ever since Andy and Mal shared their stories of their own fathers, it got Bryan to really thinking about his. He might have had fucked up reasons for the bad shit he did, but he'd never turned his back on his kids. Not really.

"Are you okay?" Andy asked, standing in front of him. He'd been so lost in thought, he hadn't seen him get up and walk toward him.

"Yeah, fine. Bathroom's all yours."

Andy was standing close. Too close. Bryan had the crazy urge to lean in and see if Andy's lips were as soft as they looked. The urge was removed when Andy took a step back. "You sure about that, B?"

Bryan's cell phone rang in his pocket. He already knew who it was, but he couldn't stop staring at Andy. "You gonna get that?" Andy asked when it continued playing "Money" by Pink Floyd. It was the ringtone he'd chosen for his brother, the accountant. "I'm getting in the shower," Andy added and walked away. Bryan barely got his phone out of his pocket and swiped the answer icon before it went to voicemail.

"Hello, little brother," Bryan said as he stepped

outside onto the front porch where he could talk in private. As he sat down on the swing, he didn't miss the excitement in Brett's tone, so he asked him if it had anything to do with finding a surrogate.

"As a matter of fact, we've found the perfect person. She carried a baby a couple of years ago for her brother and his husband. Everything went well, and when she found out David and I were looking, she offered to do it for us."

"Which one of you is going to be the father?"

"We won't know, and that's the way we want it. The doctor is using both our sperm."

"What does the surrogate look like?" Bryan wasn't knowledgeable about genes and how they affected the way children looked. From his own experience, it made even less sense. He and Brianna were lighter skinned, more of a mixture of both parents, where Bryce and Brett were darker like their father. All of them had the funky-colored eyes, where their father's were almost black.

"Laci's blonde-haired, blue-eyed like Mom was. So the baby has a better chance of looking like David if it's his sperm that takes."

"I'm happy for you, Brett. I don't care who the baby looks like as long as he or she is healthy."

"Me, too, Bry. Now, tell me all about this new job."

Bryan closed his eyes and told Brett all about meeting Andy at the VA Center and Erik getting them the job. He didn't stop talking until he'd told his baby brother everything. Well, almost. He left out the part about his attraction to Andy.

"I'm happy for you, Bry. Sounds like you found somewhere that'll be healthy for you while you get adjusted to being back. Andy sounds hot, too."

"What?" Bryan hadn't described Andy to Brett. "I didn't say anything about his looks."

"Exactly. It's what you didn't say that spoke volumes. If I didn't know better, I'd think you like him."

"Of course I like him. He's perfect. As far as friends go," Bryan added the last part so Brett didn't get the wrong idea.

"David and I started out as best friends. That's a much better basis for a relationship than hot sex. The sex is a bonus."

Okay, so he already had the wrong idea. "I'll keep that in mind. Listen, I need to go. We're getting ready to eat. Mal's mom and her boyfriend are here, so I'm going to go help set the table. Keep me posted on the baby."

"Will do. Love you, big brother."

"Love you, too." Bryan disconnected and stared at the phone. Between the stirrings he got from looking at Andy and his brother's words, Bryan was more confused than he'd ever been in his life. Surely, if Bryan was gay, he would have known it before now. He wouldn't be attracted to women. He would be repulsed at thinking about them naked or having sex with them. *You could be bisexual.* Bryan had heard of people going for both men and women, but he'd never given it much thought. What if that's the way he was wired? Andy wasn't the first man to rev Bryan's motor. It didn't matter, though. They lived together, so it was probably a really bad idea to pursue his feelings. What if he was wrong and it was just a fluke? Andy might not want Bryan anyway. No, he needed to focus on the job he was hired to do and possibly continue looking for a nice girl to hang out with. With that decided, Bryan stood and headed to the kitchen to help out.

Chapter Eleven

Andy

With his chin against his chest, Andy let the hot water pelt down on his shoulders. The water swirled down the drain while his emotions swirled through his head and his heart. Between Suzette showing him love and tenderness and Bryan showing him... What exactly was Bryan showing him? Mixed signals for one thing. More than once he'd caught Bryan staring at his mouth. Andy was probably reading more into it than was really there. Pushing Bryan out of his mind, Andy let Suzette's compassion soothe him. He might not have his own mother doting on him, but now he did have a woman who he could count on to be a surrogate. Suzette had said as much. She'd also asked Andy for his parents' names and phone number so she could call them and give them a piece of her mind. Andy had laughed, but inside he was wishing his own mother could have loved him as fiercely as Suzette did Mal.

Andy smiled at the protectiveness Mal's mother showed over someone she'd just met. Wasn't that the way all mothers should be? Protective of their young? Andy wasn't that young now, but he had been when Hilary Holcomb stood idly by and allowed him to be tossed out when he was injured and bleeding. She didn't care that he could have been dying. She allowed her love for money and a place in the community to override any maternal instinct she had. If it hadn't been for Christy's parents, he might have died. He knew he was being dramatic, but at the time, Andy felt like he was on the brink of succumbing to the injuries his so-called boyfriend had inflicted.

Andy was thankful the scars from that night were on his back, where he couldn't see them. If he had to endure seeing the reminders every time he looked in the mirror, he would probably have gone back to Texas and taken revenge on the bastards as soon as he left the Marines six months ago. Now, the thought crossed his mind about once a week instead of every day. It was another reason he turned Christy down about coming back to Irving. Orange wasn't his color. Back when the shit went down with Patrick and his lover, the doctor who came to look at Andy had insisted he go to the police. Andy had been so scared he lied and said he didn't remember what happened. How he wished that were the case.

Grabbing the body wash, Andy pulled his mind out of the past and lathered up. As soon as the liquid turned to foam, Andy realized he'd picked up the wrong bottle. The scent was all Bryan. Andy rinsed the suds from his body and rewashed using his own stuff. Not that he was opposed to smelling like Bryan, but he enjoyed the scent so much he was afraid he'd be sniffing himself throughout supper. Once he was clean, Andy rinsed again and turned the water off, grabbing the towel he'd placed on the toilet tank.

When he was halfway dry, he stepped out of the tub and wiped the steam off the mirror. Andy wrapped the towel around his waist and took a look at his reflection. Andy knew he was handsome. Too many women commented about his looks for him not to know it. So why had he never had a partner? Someone to really care about him? He'd known guys to hook up in the Marines. They'd had to keep their relationship under wraps, but it still happened. Andy hadn't had sex with another man since Patrick. He'd never had a random hook-up. He was always too scared. He'd seen a club in Nashville that he wanted to visit, but there was always something that stopped him. One night, he had made it to the front door to Primus, but that was as far as he got. Going into the gay club alone with no one to have his back had him shaking. He'd turned around and gone back to his apartment where he drank himself to sleep. For the last eight years, Andy had nothing but his hand and toys to get him off.

Was that going to be his lot in life? Never finding someone to make love to before curling up and drifting off to sleep? He'd spent the last few years of his military career dreaming of getting out, finding a partner, and building a life. It seemed like fate had something else in mind for him. Andy closed his eyes and did something he hadn't done since he was a young boy – he prayed. He prayed that he wasn't going to grow old alone.

Not bothering with his hair, Andy dressed and headed to the kitchen where everyone was gathered. Since the table wasn't all that big, Mal left the food on the stove and everyone dished out their own plates. It was what Francine referred to as buffet style. Andy liked it better this way. You didn't have to wait for someone to pass the potatoes. When he sat down, he noticed there was already a glass of sweet tea in his spot. He didn't question who put it there. He was pretty sure he knew who it was.

Another problem with the table being small was that with the two extra chairs, everyone was seated pretty close. Bryan's thigh was pressed up against Andy's, and the heat from their legs touching was making Andy uncomfortable. Not that he wanted to move, he just didn't want to sport a raging hard-on with Suzette sitting on his other side. As bad as it sounded in his head, he was glad the woman couldn't see well at that moment.

Walt asked Andy and Bryan about their time in the Marines. Neither man offered up too much detail with Suzette present. They told what company they were in, what their basic duties had been, and a little about their teammates. With Walt being in the Army during Vietnam, Andy and Bryan didn't have to elaborate on their time in the Corps. The older man had seen as much death and destruction as they had. Maybe more. Walt might have been Army, but the comradery was still there. As often as Andy had heard Marines putting down some of the other branches of service, he knew those same Marines would have their fellow warriors back if it came down to it.

Walt explained how he took over his family farm when he got out. He didn't mention a wife and children, so Andy assumed there never had been a family for Walt other than Suzette and Mal. It was evident in the way he went on and on about Mal that he thought of Mal as a son and not just a friend. More than once, Walt touched Suzette's hand and her face would light up. Anyone could see these were two people madly in love. If they could find love at a later stage in their lives, maybe there was hope for Andy yet.

When Mal's brother, Curtis, was mentioned, Suzette changed the subject to Cade. Andy had seen the pictures Suzette kept on the mantle, but the younger brother had been declared MIA. That was tough. Not knowing if one of your loved ones was dead or alive. If he was alive, he probably wished he was dead. Andy had seen some horrific things over the last eight years, most of which he'd never be able to forget. He couldn't imagine being held and tortured.

Suzette gushed the praises of Cade Anderson, and even Bryan got in on the conversation. When Suzette mentioned Cade playing and singing for them, Bryan suggested Andy play for her. "Our Andy is pretty good on the piano, too."

Our Andy?

"Oh, Andy! Would you play something?" Suzette begged.

"For you, I sure will." Andy couldn't deny Suzette anything. Just one conversation with the woman and she'd put a suture in his tattered heart. They had a new friend in Walt with their military connection, and Andy felt like he had a new family the way everyone joked with each other. Mal was their boss, but he didn't make them feel like employees. He was more like a friend who was in charge during the day.

"Come on. We'll clean up the kitchen later." Mal pushed back from the table, and Andy's hands started sweating. It was one thing to play for Bryan, but another to play for Mal and Suzette when they'd had a rock star entertain them. He didn't want to disappoint them.

When he didn't get up, Bryan put a hand on his shoulder as if reading his mind. "Hey, don't be nervous. You're really good." Andy leaned into Bryan's hand, letting the comfort wash over him. Bryan gave a squeeze and pulled away. "Come on, Lily. Show 'em what you got."

Andy nodded and stood. He could do this. Andy played for almost an hour. Suzette requested country songs they all knew. Well, everyone except Bryan. Andy chanced a few glances at Bryan every now and then, afraid his friend was getting bored, but he was smiling. At one point, Walt swung Suzette around the room in a two-step. Mal had a decent singing voice that blended smoothly with Andy's. By the time Walt said he was taking his woman home, Andy's heart had another couple of stitches, mending the hurt from the past.

Before his mom left, Mal plated the extra food to send home with Suzette and Walt. Walt shook hands with the men, and Suzette gave them all tight hugs and kisses on their cheeks. When she got to Andy, she placed her hands on his face and whispered, "Thank you, my boy." And there it was – another stitch. If he hung around Suzette very long, she'd have his heart mended in no time.

While Mal was outside checking on the animals, Andy began washing dishes. Without asking, Bryan cleared off the table, bringing the dirties to Andy. When he'd done that, Bryan stepped next to Andy and began rinsing. The silence wasn't uncomfortable. The heat from Bryan was. Andy was glad he was facing the sink. Mal returned and asked, "Are y'all goin' out tonight? If not, I'm gonna lock up and hit the alarm."

"I'm not. Are you?" Andy asked Bryan.

"No, I'm good right here," Bryan replied, glancing at Andy.

"Okay, then. If y'all are good in here, I'm gonna head on up to bed. Got a hot rock star waitin' on my call. 'Night."

"Goodnight," Andy and Bryan said in unison.

Andy focused on the dishes. He scrubbed the plates a little longer than necessary. If Bryan was happy doing something as mundane as the dishes, who was Andy to hurry things along? Having his best friend want to spend time with him was a good feeling. Andy wasn't going to pretend he didn't want this – whatever *this* was.

After a few minutes, Andy asked, "I know we've only been here a few days, but how do you like it so far?"

"I like it. Mal's a good boss, and Walt and Suzette are great."

"Yeah, kind of like the parents I should've had," Andy muttered.

"I know what you mean. Not about the mother part, because mine was wonderful. But being around them feels like having a family again. I love my sister and brothers, but this is different. This feels like..."

"Home," Andy finished.

"Yeah. It does." Bryan's voice was wistful. Andy had to remember that he wasn't the only one who'd lost something. While Bryan had siblings, it wasn't like they were around to comfort him. Anyone looking at Bryan on the outside would see this muscled Marine. Tatted and tough. People probably thought the same thing of Andy. It was the pain on the inside folks couldn't see. Andy knew the pain. As he let the water empty down the drain, he had the sudden urge to hug Bryan. Not in a sexual way, but in a way that let him know he was there for him.

Wiping his hands on the dish towel, Andy turned to

Bryan who was lost in thought. "This might sound all kinds of wrong, but can I have a hug?" It was his way of offering support to his friend but making it seem like he was the one who needed comforting. It wasn't a lie. Other than Suzette, Andy couldn't remember the last time someone held him close.

Bryan didn't hesitate to open his massive arms. Andy stepped forward and wrapped his own arms around Bryan's waist as he cradled his face in Bryan's neck, inhaling the scent of his best friend's skin. Bryan leaned his cheek against Andy's hair and held on. As the two men stood together, just offering support, it felt right to Andy. The scent of Bryan's body wash invaded his senses. The broad expanse of Bryan's back tensed and relaxed under Andy's fingertips. Their lower bodies fit perfectly. Andy's dick must have thought so, too. When it began twitching, Andy knew it was time to pull back. He wanted this with Bryan. The friendship. The comfort. Before his dick got too hard and he scared Bryan away, Andy begrudgingly removed his face from the warmth of Bryan's neck and said, "Thank you."

Bryan didn't immediately remove his hands. When Andy pulled back, Bryan's hands remained on Andy's hips. Bryan's eyes searched every inch of Andy's face, landing on his lips. Andy held his breath. Just when he thought Bryan was going to kiss him, his friend closed his eyes and stepped back. "You're welcome." When Bryan opened his eyes, they were filled with so much emotion. Longing. Lust. Doubt. Andy wanted nothing more than to kiss Bryan, but not until he was ready. Andy wouldn't dare risk doing something to jeopardize the friendship they had.

"I'm going to turn in. I'll see you in the morning." Andy fisted his hands to keep from touching Bryan and made his way down the hall to his bedroom. He didn't bother brushing his teeth or taking a piss. He needed relief, and he needed it quick. With only the light of the moon shining into the room, Andy removed all his clothes including his underwear. Opening the bedside drawer, he didn't have to contemplate which toy he would use. He grabbed the dildo he liked to imagine was the same size as Bryan. The lube was already on the bed under the spare pillow. Andy found no sense in putting it in the drawer when he used it so often. Nobody came into his room, so what did it hurt to leave it out?

Andy was on his knees with his face to his pillow. Using his slicked-up fingers, he stretched his hole. His dick was already hard as fucking nails. By the time he got the toy to his entrance, Andy was ready to blow his load. He grabbed the base of his cock with one hand, stemming the flow of blood. With the other hand, he circled his ready hole with the dildo. The toy wasn't a monster. When Andy ordered his toys, he wanted something to make him feel good, not rip him apart like... Taking a deep breath, Andy slipped the life-like tip into his channel, inch by inch until it was as far in as it would go. Andy fucked his ass slowly at first, enjoying how the slight burn morphed into pleasure.

With his eyes squeezed shut, Andy imagined Bryan behind him, filling him up. Until he met Bryan, all Andy's fantasies had him on top, pounding into the tight ass of a twink. He was the one with the power. The control. Andy's massive size allowed him to toss around his lover. Never had he let someone have control over him in his fantasies. Now, all he could think about was Bryan taking control of his body. Sliding his dark cock in and out of Andy. Hitting his prostate the same way the dildo was. Remembering the smell of Bryan's neck from just a few minutes before, Andy grabbed his cock and stroked it in time with his thrusts. He needed the release. Andy welcomed the way his body tensed as his orgasm washed over him quickly. With thoughts of Bryan in his head, his release shot into his hand and onto the bed.

Andy removed the toy from his ass and eased over to his side so his sensitive cock wouldn't be pressed between the mattress and his body. A couple of aftershocks pulsed through his dick, and Andy sucked in a breath with each one. He lay there, spent. Andy pulled the spare pillow to his chest, hugging it close, pretending it was Bryan he was holding onto instead of a piece of material filled with foam. What he wouldn't give to lay his head on Bryan's massive shoulder and toss his leg over Bryan's thigh. Hell, if Bryan wanted to cover Andy instead, he wouldn't object. As long as they were entwined as they slept deeply together after making love.

If Andy ever had the chance to get with Bryan, he had no doubt it wouldn't be merely fucking. But Bryan wasn't going to fall into bed with Andy just because he was horny. The man was straight, even if he stared at Andy's lips. He had a gay brother, so he probably was wondering what it would be like to be with another man. Andy was certain that's all it was, though — curiosity.

Andy was curious, too. He had never been with another man in a way that counted. In a way that didn't end in pain. Maybe that was why he'd never allowed himself to find pleasure at the hands of any of the other gay Marines. He was too scared. Then why wasn't he scared of Bryan? *Because* he *would never hurt you.* Fuck! In less than two weeks, Andy was falling. Hard.

Flipping onto his back, Andy covered his eyes with his forearm. The snip of Bryan's bedroom door closing reached his ears. Had he just now gone to bed? Maybe he couldn't sleep either and had jacked off to thoughts of Andy. No, he'd probably jacked off to the image of the blonde bimbo with the big breasts. Andy didn't want to think about Bryan and Laurel together. He didn't want to think about Bryan with anyone else. Andy wanted to be the one filling Bryan's thoughts the way he did Andy's.

Chapter Twelve

Bryan

If Bryan thought listening to Andy jack off was hot, seeing him fucking his own ass with a toy had his dick so hard he thought he was going to pass out. There wasn't much light coming through the window from the full moon, but there was enough for Bryan to see Andy shoving a fake cock in and out of his ass. Bryan had never ventured to his hole when he masturbated. Brett had told him a long time ago if Bryan ever found someone to hit his prostate, they were a keeper.

As Andy moved the dildo in and out of his ass, Bryan's dick pulsed against his zipper. It became so painful he unbuttoned his pants and lowered the zipper, giving his cock some relief. It wasn't enough. Andy's breathing was jagged as he pumped in and out of his ass with one hand and stroked his dick with the other. Bryan didn't know where to look. Each movement was equally erotic. He palmed his own erection through his briefs, but it still wasn't enough, so he slid his hand underneath the waistband and grabbed hold of the base, staving off an orgasm. The toy Andy was using was bigger than Bryan's dick, but not by much. Being in the military, he'd seen all sizes when showering with his fellow Marines. Not that he'd really looked. But when men were naked and their junk was out there, it was inevitable to see them. Bryan's dick was above average.

He knew he should walk away. Should give Andy the privacy he thought he had. Or maybe Andy didn't care. Maybe he was into having someone watch him get off.

Bryan knew there were those who liked to watch and those who liked to be watched. Since he couldn't get his feet to move, he was obviously the former. The fact that Mal could come down the steps at any moment was also part of the thrill. Did Bryan want to be caught with his dick in his hand spying on his best friend? His dick pulsed in his hand, and Bryan had his answer.

When Andy asked him for a hug earlier, Bryan knew it was nothing more than his friend needing some comfort. But holding Andy in his arms, feeling his soft breath against his neck, tempted Bryan to pull back and kiss him. Taste his lips. Straddle Andy's thigh and rub his cock against the strong muscles to show him how Bryan was really feeling. Instead, he allowed Andy to use him for whatever it was he'd been seeking.

Keeping his eyes on Andy's ass being stretched, Bryan imagined it was his cock that was stretching Andy's hole. Bryan didn't understand his sudden infatuation with fucking another man. Yes, he'd thought about it before when he'd seen men in his platoon sneaking around, but it had never gotten him as hard as he was right then. Andy's thrusts faltered, and he did his best to stifle a groan as his body shuddered through his orgasm. Bryan slipped quietly into the bathroom and shot his own load into the toilet, barely making it in time. He bit down hard on his bottom lip to keep from calling out. *Goddamn*, that was intense. If he came that hard from thinking about fucking Andy, he couldn't imagine the real deal.

Bryan cleaned the jizz off his hand and the toilet seat where he'd missed. After washing his hands and brushing his teeth, Bryan walked as softly as possible back to his bedroom and eased the door closed. As much as being caught by Mal was a turn-on, the thought of Andy catching him wasn't as exciting. Bryan felt guilty about invading Andy's private moment, but the intensity of the orgasm was almost worth it. *Fuck me.*

Knowing sleep wouldn't come anytime soon, Bryan did something he hadn't done in months. He found the journal he'd started when he'd been out of the Corps for about a month. One of the counselors at the VA Center suggested writing. Not like a diary exactly, but just putting down whatever was going through his mind when sleep evaded him. He wasn't supposed to read the words he penned. The therapy was in getting his emotions out of his head and onto paper. Bryan propped up against the headboard with his pillows behind him, opened the journal to the first blank page, and started writing. When he couldn't hold his eyes open any longer, he saw that a couple of hours had passed, and he'd filled quite a few pages. Bryan closed the notebook and turned off the light. Sleep came easily at that point, and Bryan drifted off into an erotic dream involving a gorgeous blond built like a god.

Sunday was an easy work day. Mal and Andy saddled the horses, and Bryan loaded up on the four wheeler. He was glad to have the time to himself as well as the distance from Andy. Bryan was doing his best to think of anything except the scene that played out the night before and the dream that followed. Sporting a hard-on in front of Mal wasn't the way he wanted to spend his day. Luckily, Mal had them giving shots to the cattle, and it was a good distraction. Bryan did his best to keep his eyes averted from the object of his dreams.

By the time they broke for lunch, Walt, Suzette, and Mal's oldest niece were waiting at the house. Bryan had yet to meet Melanie, Mal's sister. From what Mal said, her husband was a homophobic dick. Suzette was holding on to Mattie's hand. If she let go, Bryan had no doubt the little girl would make a run for Mal. He could see the excitement on her face from where he was. Bryan parked the ATV beside the barn, while Andy and Mal tethered the horses to the fence. Mattie squealed, running toward Mal. The little girl launched herself at him, and he caught her, twirling her around.

"Uncle Mal! Yous really did get horses!"

"Hey, Munchkin, I really did."

"Can I ride?" Matilda asked, swinging her feet in excitement. Before she could kick Mal in the nuts, he wrapped a strong arm around her legs.

"Yep. First, I want you to meet my new friends. This is Andy, and this is Bryan."

"Andy looks like yous friend Cade. He's pretty."

Bryan laughed out loud until Andy put his hands on his hips and glared at him. That made him laugh louder. "Yeah, you's pretty, Lily," Bryan whispered.

Andy rolled his lips in to keep from laughing, but his bright eyes gave him away. When he was happy, they sparkled a lighter blue than normal. Bryan shouldn't know that little fact, but from the day he met Andy, he'd vowed to keep that brightness there. When Andy told him what happened to him as a teenager, Bryan had wanted to hurt someone the way they hurt Andy. He wanted to do everything he could to make Andy happy. Make him forget the shitty way he'd been treated. Maybe that was why he couldn't stop thinking about Andy in more than a platonic fashion.

Bryan turned back just in time to catch Matilda lunging toward him. He caught her and placed her on his hip the same way he'd done the twins so many times. "Hiya, beautiful."

"I like you eyes." Mattie traced her little finger over Bryan's eyebrow and down his cheek. Bryan's breath caught in his throat when she smiled at him. Even with a dickhead bigot for a father, this little girl didn't care that Bryan was a mutation of ethnicities or that Mal and Andy were gay. She saw people the way everyone should – beautiful. While the twins made him not want kids of his own, Mattie had reached into his heart and grabbed hold.

Clearing his throat, Bryan said, "Thank you. I like

119

yours, too."

"Is you gonna ride horses with me and Uncle Mal?"

"I better stick to the four wheeler."

"Okay." Mattie gave him a kiss on his cheek then turned back to Mal, holding her arms out. "Uncle Mal, can we ride now?" Bryan had seen Mal smile when talking about Cade, but his niece clearly was the bright spot in his life.

"I think you got yourself a girlfriend," Andy whispered.

"I'll take her," Bryan responded. If they could all be as sweet as this little girl, Bryan would have a houseful. The way she didn't speak plainly was cute. Bryan hoped he got to see her quite a bit.

Mal handed Matilda back to Bryan. "Here, Munchkin. Let Uncle Bryan hold you while I get Cochise ready."

"Is you really my uncle?" she asked Bryan while Mal mounted the Paint.

"If you want me to be. Andy can be your uncle, too."

"Gramma! Bryan's my uncle! So's Andy," Matilda yelled to Suzette, even though the woman was standing a few feet away. Suzette and Walt were laughing. Bryan looked at a grinning Andy and winked. When Mal was ready, Bryan lifted Matilda up to him and headed back to the four wheeler.

"We won't be gone too long, Ma."

"Don't you worry about us. Just take care of my girl." Suzette's smile was almost as big as Matilda's.

Andy grabbed Bryan's wrist and stopped him from getting on the ATV. "Since they'll be riding slow, why don't you try out Callie? I promise I won't let anything bad happen." Andy's hand was warm against Bryan's skin. It felt nice. Bryan was going to have to come to terms with his feelings sooner or later, but he couldn't do it right then with people watching.

Seeing the sincerity in Andy's eyes, he agreed, "Okay."

Andy smiled and released his arm. He untied Callie from the fence and walked her over to where Bryan was waiting. "Hold the reins, put your left foot in the stirrup, and grab the horn like this." Andy demonstrated slowly how to mount the animal. He just as easily slid off her back and handed the reins to Bryan. Andy held onto the bridle, making sure Callie stood still while Bryan mounted her for the first time.

When he was safely seated, Andy gave him instruction on how to hold and pull the reins, what gestures he could give with his legs, and how to stop. Andy let go, and Bryan gently nudged the horse with his heels. Callie began walking, and Andy directed Bryan to turn her left then right. When he had the hang of the basics, Bryan walked her farther away. He took deep breaths, doing his best to enjoy the ride. He'd never imagined riding a horse, but now that he was on one, he knew it was something he wanted to become proficient at. In the Marines, he'd commanded a team of men. His quiet disposition often fooled others into thinking he was laid back. He was for the most part, but Bryan could also be stern when the situation called for it.

He'd helped raise his brothers, so he knew how to take control of a situation with authority. That had gone a long way as a Marine in leading a platoon. Most of the time his orders had come from higher up, so he only had to pass the orders along. Rarely had he made ultimate decisions that could have cost his men their lives. That's not to say they never found themselves in dangerous situations. Quite the opposite.

"Uncle Bryan! Yous riding, too!" Mattie shouted from across the field. Mal said something to her, and she clamped both hands over her mouth. Bryan couldn't help but laugh. He turned Callie toward the other horse and met up with them.

"You sit a horse pretty good, Bryan. You sure you haven't done this before?" Mal asked.

"I'm sure, but I figure if I'm gonna work on a farm, I better learn."

"Callie there's a pretty sweet girl. I don't think she'll give you any trouble."

Bryan reached down and gave the horse a pat on her neck. She nodded her head as if she agreed. Mal turned Cochise back toward the barn, and Bryan followed along. He could already feel his thigh muscles tightening up. He would need to find some exercises to do to keep them from being too sore. An image of him lying on his back with his legs spread flashed through his mind. Andy was between Bryan's thighs, pushing on them as he gave Bryan head. And now his dick was getting hard. *Fuck.*

Once they got back to the barn, Walt helped Mattie down from the horse. Andy took Cochise from Mal. Turning to Bryan, he said, "Bring Callie in here, and we'll remove their tack." Mal thanked Andy and followed his mom and Walt inside where they could visit. Bryan did as Andy instructed. They had both watched and listened to Mal the first day, and between the two of them, they did a good job of taking care of the horses, if Bryan did say so himself. There was something therapeutic about brushing Callie's coat. Taking care of her. Bryan had taken care of his siblings, so it only made sense he'd be comfortable doing the same with an animal. Andy had horses when he was younger, but he'd had someone to do this part for him. Bryan shook his head when he thought of having someone to do the heavy lifting for you.

"What are you thinking so hard about over there?" Andy asked after he'd gotten Cochise inside the stall.

"I... it was nothing," Bryan muttered. He didn't want to tell Andy the truth.

"It had to be something; you were shaking your

head."

"I was thinking about you having servants and people to clean up after the horses, that's all."

"Does that bother you?" Andy asked, coming to take Callie from Bryan and moving her into her stall. Bryan was thankful for that. He didn't want to be in the wrong spot and have the big animal step on his foot. He did pay attention to the way Andy moved the horse in a circle, making sure to stay out of her way.

When Andy was closing the stall door, Bryan answered. "No, just trying to imagine it is all. I knew how to wash clothes and clean house by the time I was ten. If I'd been any good in the kitchen, I would have learned how to cook, too. Thankfully, Bree was decent in the kitchen, so we didn't starve. Brett and Bryce learned how to do all that stuff too, so when I joined the Marines, I knew it was okay to leave them."

Andy leaned his back against the wood, knee bent with his foot resting against the door. He crossed his arms over his chest, showing off the bulge of his biceps beneath the tight sleeves of his T-shirt. His blond hair was covered by a black patrol cap. It had surprised Bryan when Andy put it on the first day they were working outside. It shouldn't have, but Andy was so particular about his hair. Maybe that was only when he was going somewhere, or trying to impress someone. He'd taken his time primping before they went out to DWs on Friday, but he'd worn the military cap every day since they arrived at the farm. When Bryan looked up, he found Andy staring at him. Not his biceps or his mouth, but his eyes. He was frowning. *Shit.*

"I'd have given up the money and the servants to have the kind of mother you did. Just because we were rich didn't mean my mom had to be so distant. I always thought it was because my father and grandfather were grooming me to take over the company. When she stood by and watched as they tossed me out on my ass, I knew she just

123

didn't love me. Christy's parents had money, too, but her mom was like yours. She showed me more affection than my mother ever thought about."

"I'm sorry, Andy. I wish you could have had a good one, too. But we have Suzette now. I know it's not the same. She'll never take away what your mom did to you, and she can't replace mine, but I'm not going to push her away when she wants to show us affection. That would be like a hungry man throwing away a free hamburger."

Andy smiled, but it was sad. "I've written so many letters to my mother. So many times I've written the words, asking her how she could do it, but I've never had the guts to mail them. When we had to write our letters to our family in case something happened to us, I addressed mine to Christy. In it, I thanked her for always being there for me, and I asked her to thank her parents. They were the reason I lived after I was... after... I knew the Corps would tell my folks if something happened, but I couldn't find the words to tell them goodbye. They'd already told me goodbye the day they kicked me out."

Bryan couldn't stand the pain in Andy's voice. He closed the short distance between them. As much as he wanted to reach out and pull Andy into his arms, Bryan leaned back against the door next to him. Right next to him. Their shoulders were touching, and hopefully Andy would feel the support from the gesture. Andy surprised him when he put his head on Bryan's shoulder. Bryan leaned his head against Andy's and let him talk.

"You'd think I'd be over that shit, you know? It happened over eight years ago. How fucking long does it take for that kind of hurt to go away?" Andy asked in a broken voice.

"I don't know, Babe, I honestly don't. My mom's only been gone two years. The hurt has eased some, but I still miss her like crazy. I have to make myself remember she isn't suffering. What hurts the most is she didn't tell us. I didn't get to say goodbye until after she was already gone. She looked so frail in that casket. She'd lost so much weight I barely recognized her. I don't think there's a time limit on pain. Everyone deals with shit in their own way and in their own time. Maybe you need to send your mother one of those letters. See if she responds. At least you'll have tried. I'm no psychiatrist, but it doesn't sound like you've had any closure."

"You're right, I haven't. But what's worse? Thinking she didn't love me enough to stand up for me or *knowing* it? Because B, I don't think I'd be able to handle knowing she never loved me."

Bryan turned his face and kissed Andy over his cap. It was as natural as taking a breath. Oddly, his body wasn't reacting the way it normally did. His dick was behaving, but they were having a deep, emotion-filled conversation. This was Bryan being there for his best friend, offering support. Andy pulled away, looking at Bryan. The question was there in his eyes. Bryan didn't have the answer. Not yet anyway.

Matilda's laughter rent the air, and Andy took a step backwards. With haunted eyes, he whispered, "Thanks, B." Andy headed out of the barn, leaving Bryan to once again figure out what the fuck was going on in his head.

"You're welcome, Lily," Bryan said softly, watching Andy's retreating form. Callie stuck her head over the door and nipped at his shirt. Bryan turned around and gave the horse some love between her eyes. "Why does shit have to be so complicated?" he asked the animal. Callie shook her head, her mane tousling side to side. "You don't know either, huh?" Bryan felt at ease alone in the barn. The voices of his new family along with the occasional bird calling out or cow mooing in the pasture were the only sounds on the farm. Bryan closed his eyes and let the peacefulness wash over him.

Bryan wished there was some way he could take

125

away the pain Andy felt. Some way he could lessen the hurt from what his family had done to him. All he knew to do was be a good friend and offer a shoulder to lean on when Andy needed it. *You could give him a blowjob.* Bryan wouldn't know where to begin. He'd only been on the receiving end of head a couple of times back in high school, and he'd seen it done in the Marines, but that was the extent of his expertise. There was no way he could go down on Andy and make him forget his troubles. No, all he could do was what he was already doing, which wasn't much.

Taking a deep breath and adjusting his dick behind his jeans, Bryan pushed away from the door and went in search of the pint-sized smile that made *him* feel better.

Chapter Thirteen

Andy

As soon as he was outside the barn, Andy stopped and watched Mattie chasing the dogs and them her. What a joy that little girl was. She made Andy want kids someday. He already wanted that, but being around her was infectious. Her laugh was medicine to his heart. Where Suzette was putting stitches on the fractured organ, that little girl was an infusion of new blood of the purest kind. What if Bryan was right? Maybe if Andy sent a letter to his mother he could finally get some closure. As much as Patrick doing what he did hurt Andy's pride as well as his body, his mother turning her back on him was the one thing he couldn't let go of. Adding being a Marine for eight years and seeing the atrocities of the world on top of that, he should probably be in a mental hospital. Andy should at least have sought out psychiatric help when he returned from overseas.

Where Bryan's PTSD was triggered by loud noises, Andy's was more internal. Nightmares gripped him often. He'd suffered from them ever since he'd been thrown out of his home. Waking up screaming in the middle of the dessert wasn't unheard of, but most chalked it up to their surroundings and what they were required to do and see. The panic attacks hadn't started until after he'd come back home. Being alone with no friends to talk to other than the occasional hello to the neighbor across the hall in his apartment probably wasn't smart on Andy's part. He didn't feel like introducing anyone to his brand of crazy. Then he met Bryan, who understood what Andy was going through.

When Moe trotted over to where Andy was standing, he bent down and ran his hand through the dog's fur. A sense of peace washed over him, and the dog did nothing more than allow Andy to pet it. It was a win-win for them both, but in his heart, Andy knew he was getting more from it than Moe. Andy looked up when Matilda stepped right in front of him.

"Uncle Andy, is you okay?"

Uncle Andy. Pure blood. "I'm fine, sweetheart."

"Is this a happy tear?" Matilda placed her little hand on his cheek, wiping away the wetness. Andy looked up to see if the adults noticed he was crying. Mal was staring at him intently, but Walt and Suzette were nowhere to be seen.

"Yes, sweetheart. You make me happy, and so does Moe."

Andy felt the second Bryan walked up behind him. The man was lethally quiet. Andy had noticed that when they first met. Somehow, though, Andy knew when Bryan was near. As stupid as it sounded in his head, the air around him changed whenever Bryan was close. Not in a smothering way, but in a way that Andy wanted to breathe deeply and let the oxygen infuse his senses. Not only did Moe offer Andy a sense of peace, Bryan's presence had the same calming effect. Most of the time, anyway. When he wasn't giving Andy a hard-on.

"Can you handle supper?" Mal asked as he closed the distance. "I need to run Matilda home and stop off for a few things."

"Sure. I saw stuff to make spaghetti. Is that okay?"

"Fine by me," Mal said. "You ready to go, Munchkin?"

"I wants spaghetti," she answered instead.

"Maybe next time. Gramma's got some stuff she needs to take care of."

Andy had to bite his lip to keep from laughing at the pout on Mattie's face. If it had been him, he'd have given in

128

instantly. Maybe he shouldn't have kids. He doubted he'd be able to tell them no.

"I'll be back within an hour," Mal said as he lifted Matilda into his arms. "Say bye."

"Bye Uncle Andy. Bye Uncle Bryan."

Andy and Bryan both said goodbye. While Mal put his niece in the truck, Andy asked Bryan, "Want to help me cook supper?"

Bryan frowned then shrugged his shoulders. "I'll do what I can."

Once inside, Andy dug around in the pantry for the noodles and sauce. It was too late to make homemade sauce, so he'd have to make do with store-bought. He took a pack of meat out of the fridge along with some veggies he found in a chiller drawer. After washing their hands, Andy asked Bryan to wash and cut the peppers and onion.

"Thanks, Lily. I love getting the stinky job," Bryan grumbled.

"Then I'll cut the vegetables, and you can take care of the meat." Andy took the knife away from Bryan who stared at the meat like it was going to bite him. "Dump the hamburger into the skillet. Turn the eye on medium and stir it until it's brown."

Andy didn't mind cutting the vegetables. It was much less mundane than watching the ground chuck brown in a skillet. He kept his eye on Bryan, making sure he cooked the hamburger evenly. Once the veggies were chopped, he dumped them on top of the meat and told Bryan to stir. Andy washed his hands again and leaned against the counter next to where Bryan was standing. "Thank you."

"For what?" Bryan asked, keeping his eyes on his task. Andy had to smile at the concentration on Bryan's face.

"For letting me vent earlier."

"Well, it was kind of my fault. I brought up the subject of servants." Bryan looked at him then, and the regret was there in his eyes.

"No. This shit's been festering for a long time. It's something that's always at the back of my mind, so don't think you were the cause of it. It felt good having someone listen. Thank you for being my friend."

Bryan's frown deepened. "That I am," he muttered before turning back to the meat.

"We need to drain the grease off." Andy took the skillet from Bryan and showed him how to drain the meat into a bowl. When he put the skillet back on the stove, Andy took over. He added the sauce from the jar, but he also added extra spices he'd found in one of the cabinets. "This needs to simmer, and the veggies need to cook down some more. We'll wait until Mal gets back to put the noodles on." Andy put the lid on the skillet, turned the heat down, and washed his hands again.

"Can I ask you something personal?"

Andy hated that question. It usually never turned out to be something he wanted to talk about whenever someone wanted to get personal, but this was Bryan. If they were going to live together for the unforeseeable future, they needed to know more about each other.

"Sure."

"Why do you wash your hands so much?"

Okay, that was an easy one. "To keep from getting sick. Francine taught me when I was little to always keep my hands clean so the germs wouldn't stick. I think it was her way of making sure I didn't mess things up around the house, but I hated being sick when I was a kid. I was not a good patient when they'd try to pour that crappy tasting medicine down my throat. My parents got tired of the incessant whining but didn't offer up any solutions. Francine had the patience of a saint when it came to me. Not only was she our cook, but she was more of a mother to me than Hilary ever thought of being. When I complained about having to stay inside when I was running a fever, she explained that I had too many germs on my hands, and if I would keep them washed, the germs couldn't stick to them, thus I wouldn't have to be stuck inside. From then on, I washed my hands almost to compulsion."

"Does it work? The not getting sick part?"

"It seems to. I've had a few colds over the years, but nothing like what I had back then. It could be psychological, but it doesn't hurt anything, that's for sure. Tell me something about you I don't know." Andy went to the fridge and pulled out a beer. He held it up to Bryan who nodded.

As Andy twisted the cap off his longneck, Bryan took a long pull off his and swallowed it down. Wiping his mouth on the back of his hand, he said, "Well, let's see. When I was younger, I wanted to be a boxer. My dad often fought at one of the local gyms for money. From what my mom told me, he was pretty good at it. I never got to watch him in action, but he would come home all jazzed up from the fight, and he would show me some moves. I was only five at the time, but the bug stuck with me. Since he went to jail, I never got the chance to learn how to fight properly, but it didn't stop me from taking swings at punks."

"I did a little boxing in my time," Walt said from the doorway. Andy had been so caught up in listening to Bryan, he hadn't realized the man was in the house, much less the same room. "One of the guys I went to basic with wanted to be a professional boxer. James was his name. He was good, too, but due to every male in his family being in the Army, he agreed to do four years. While he was in, he learned about the Army Boxing Program. He could serve his country and still follow his passion. Before he started entering matches and winning, I sparred with him as often as I could."

"What happened to him?" Bryan asked.

"James went on to win the gold against the other military branches. He also fought in the Olympics one year.

He had a great career going when he got out of the Army. He sent me letters and newspaper clippings when he had big time fights. After a while, the letters stopped coming. By that time, I was back home working the farm. At first, I thought he'd either stopped fighting or didn't give two shits about a farmer he used to know. Then one day I got a call from his mother letting me know he'd passed. Heart attack, if you can believe that. Anyway, I need to get these boxes to the truck. I'm sure Suzette's wondering what's keeping me."

It wasn't until Walt mentioned boxes that Andy noticed the stack in the hallway. "You want some help?"

"I wouldn't turn it down," Walt said with a grin.

Andy stirred the sauce before going to help Bryan and Walt.

"Suzette's moving in with me now that you two are here to look after Mal. That woman's done a fine job taking care of that boy and this place ever since..." Walt's voice trailed off.

"Suzette's a wonderful mother. Mal sure is lucky to have her," Bryan said.

"So am I," Walt added. The love was evident in the older man's voice. Walt and Suzette weren't old, but they had a few years on Andy's parents, so he put them in their mid to late fifties. His parents had him before they turned twenty-one.

By the time Suzette had all the stuff she wanted to take with her packed up, Mal had returned from taking Matilda home and running his errands. Andy finished getting the spaghetti ready while Bryan buttered some bread and put it in the oven. The two of them worked like a well-oiled machine in the kitchen. Bryan might not be able to cook yet, but he was more than willing to do whatever Andy instructed. Once again, Walt and Suzette joined them for supper before heading home for the evening.

"I got you somethin', Andy," Mal said once the kitchen was cleaned up.

"A present, for moi?" Andy joked.

"I thought about what you said about the dogs." Mal handed Andy a box. A lump formed in Andy's throat when he realized it was a pet door. Mal was going to let the dogs come inside after all.

"Mal, I... Thank you," Andy choked out.

"I thought we'd bring 'em in for a trial run before cuttin' a hole in the door. See if they're gonna behave or tear the place apart. If they mind their manners, we can install this next week."

Mal went to the back door. When he opened it, he called the dogs. At first, they stood there staring at him like he was crazy. Andy bent down and called Moe to him. The dog tentatively stepped into the kitchen like it was a trick. He walked with his tail between his legs until he reached Andy. When Andy gave him love and praised him for being a good boy, the dog relaxed. Curly had no trouble with coming inside. He bypassed the humans and began sniffing every inch of the floor.

"I do have some rules," Mal said. "No feedin' 'em from the table, and no gettin' on the furniture. If they start chewin' shit up, they're goin' back out."

"Agreed," Andy said. "Thank you, Mal. I promise I'll clean up after them."

"I'm countin' on it. I've got some stuff I want to get outta Ma's room and put upstairs."

"You want help?" Bryan asked.

"Nah, it's not much. Since she's movin' in with Walt, if one of you wants to take her room, you can. Seein' as it's on the other side of the house, you'd have more privacy that way."

Andy didn't feel the need for privacy. It wasn't like they were bringing dates home to fuck. Besides, he liked knowing Bryan was right across the hall. Andy hadn't woken up screaming from a nightmare since he'd been there, but that didn't mean he wouldn't. "Bryan can take it if he wants. I'm good where I am."

"I'm good, too," Bryan said.

"Well, if you change your mind, it's there for the takin'." Mal disappeared down the hallway, and Andy leaned against the counter while the dogs surveyed their new surroundings.

Bryan pulled a beer out of the fridge. "I'm gonna catch the last few innings of the game. You coming?"

Andy remembered the fun he'd had the night before, pretending his toy was Bryan. He'd sure been *coming* then. "Yeah, I'll watch it with you." He took the longneck from Bryan and waited for him to go into the living room first so he could adjust his dick without Bryan seeing. Andy sat on what was becoming his end of the couch and placed the throw pillow in his lap. Hopefully, Bryan wouldn't think anything about it. Moe and Curly followed them and lay down on the floor at their feet. Andy twisted around so he was leaning against the arm. That way he could reach Moe's head to pet him. Bryan mirrored Andy's position, and before long, the four of them were enjoying the game.

When the game was over and it was time to go to bed, Andy thought it best to put the dogs back outside. They'd done well for their first few hours, but he didn't want to wake up to piles of shit everywhere. He and Bryan herded them both out the back door and locked up. When they reached their bedrooms, Andy stopped and put his hand on Bryan's arm. "Thanks again for earlier. Your friendship means a lot." He removed his hand before Bryan got the wrong idea.

"You're welcome, Lily. I appreciate you, too."

Andy retreated to his room. He closed the door, but it popped back open. He really needed to fix that. Unlike the night before, Andy wasn't in the mood to pull the toys out. As much enjoyment as he got out of them, trying to get them into the bathroom to clean them without anyone knowing what he was doing was a pain in the ass. Maybe he should take Suzette's room. It had a bathroom attached, and then he wouldn't have to worry about sneaking his toys around. When he thought of being that far away from Bryan, Andy decided he'd put up with trying to be discreet.

The next few days were pretty much all the same. The three men alternated cooking. On Bryan's days, Andy helped out, instructing as much as possible and helping out when he needed to. With Walt taking lead, Andy and Bryan rode around checking on the cattle and the fencing while Mal worked on the barn and house. The barn only needed a couple of cosmetic fixes, but the house needed quite a bit of work. Walt was a pleasure to be around. Like Mal, he wasn't bossy. He was quickly becoming a father figure, giving praise when they did something right and instruction when they were unsure. Andy knew he and Bryan both had fathers, but neither one of them were in the picture. While his father had been around when Andy was younger, Andy considered himself parentless. Hilary and Stanton Holcomb were dead to Andy as far as he was concerned.

When the mail arrived on Wednesday, Mal handed Andy and Bryan their first paychecks. "If you want to start gettin' your money sent direct deposit, we'll need to send the paperwork to Mr. Matheson. Normally we get paid on Fridays, but he thought y'all might want an advance, in case there's anything you need. Bryan, now you have a reason to stop off at the bank and check out Addison," Mal said with a wink.

Andy held his breath, hoping Bryan had gotten over wanting to meet a nice girl. Over the last few nights, Mal retreated to his room or office after supper, leaving Andy and Bryan to fend for themselves. Instead of sitting outside enjoying a fire, they'd both relaxed on the couch watching baseball while the dogs continued to get accustomed to being inside. There had been no more gestures of comfort giving off the feeling of intimacy. Then again, Andy hadn't needed comforting. Whatever vibes he'd gotten from Bryan when they first moved into Mal's home were now distant memories. Maybe he'd imagined them. The heated looks he was sure Bryan was sending his way were gone. In their place were nothing more than quick glances. Bryan was still nice to him. If anything, he was nicer than he had been since they met. But nice did not equate to longing. If there had been something there, it had dissipated. Bryan's next words solidified that notion.

"I'm looking forward to meeting her."

"Good. If you want to go ahead and go on down there, I'd appreciate if you'd stop off at the store. I've made a list of things we need, and y'all can get whatever you want to cook, too."

Andy was excited about branching out as far as the cooking went. He was not excited about Bryan meeting this Addison woman. If Mal thought she was pretty, Bryan would probably be ready to marry her and have babies with her next week. Mal gave Andy the list of groceries he wanted them to pick up and they headed out. Bryan hummed while heading to the truck, but Andy dragged his feet. Not literally. That would have been stupid. But he was in no hurry to watch Bryan flirt with someone else.

Their friendship was such that they didn't need to talk non-stop. The sounds of country music filled the cab. Normally, Andy thought it was sweet that Bryan let him listen to what he wanted to on the radio whenever they were together. Now, it was pissing him off. He pushed the button that changed it over to the rock station Bryan preferred and sat back against the seat. Looking out the window, Andy did his best not to think of the nights he'd be left alone at the house while Bryan was out on his dates. He'd been pissy with Bryan when he was supposed to go with Laurel. He would have to tamp down his jealousy when Bryan started going out with someone who was actually a nice girl.

When they got to the bank, Bryan turned the motor

off but didn't get out. He ran his hands down his massive thighs. Taking a few deep breaths, Bryan finally pushed the driver's side door open and slid to the ground. It didn't surprise him that Bryan was nervous. He was naturally quiet, and from what Andy had seen, shy as well. Andy had news for his friend; he wasn't going to make matters better. He would be Bryan's friend, but as for a wingman? Hell fucking no.

Chapter Fourteen

Bryan

Bryan should be happy. Life was good, for the most part. He and Andy were learning all about raising cattle. Seeing the calves being born had been an amazing experience. From what Mal said, it was the easiest season he'd ever seen. All the births had gone smoothly, and it had been a one-hundred-percent success. The hard part was done, and now they were spending most of their time with Walt. The man was becoming a daily fixture at the farm now that the calves were there. As much as Bryan liked being around Mal, Walt was much more talkative. Having been in the military himself, it gave them that extra something that bonded them even more than just working together. Over the last three days, Bryan had become the talkative one, and Andy had less to say than normal. Bryan didn't think there was anything wrong other than the stuff already plaguing his friend's heart.

Thankfully, there had been no more jacking off sessions that Bryan was aware of. He'd not waited outside Andy's door hoping to catch him. That would have been ten kinds of creepy. But lying alone in bed, Bryan's thoughts strayed to the room across the hall. His mind was becoming a strange place as Bryan imagined Andy naked. Andy giving Bryan a blowjob. Bryan giving Andy a blowjob. Bryan sliding his cock into Andy's hole instead of Andy using a toy. Bryan had gone so far as to pull up some gay porn on his phone to see if he was attracted to all men or if it was only Andy who did it for him. Some of the stuff he watched was entertaining at best. Some was educational.

Others he went back and watched more than once. When he realized he was stroking his cock while he watched one of the scenes, Bryan had to admit to himself he was at the very least bisexual, if not fully gay.

Now that Bryan knew his feelings for Andy were real and not some crazed part of his lonely mind playing tricks on him, Andy was keeping his distance. There had been no fun flirting. No innuendos. No mention of strip poker when they'd played cards the night before. Andy was barely looking at him, if truth be told. Bryan thought back to the last few days to figure out what could have happened to change things between them. He finally came to the conclusion it had been all in his head. Bryan only imagined Andy calling out his name the first night he'd listened to Andy jacking off. Was Bryan so hard up for attention he had to conjure up a false longing from his best friend? Well, fuck that. If Andy didn't want him that way, Bryan would settle for any attention he received from him.

Bryan held the door to the bank open, allowing the object of his obsession to walk through first. Andy's blue jeans were tucked inside his combat boots. His T-shirt stretched taut over his wide shoulders. His blond hair was hidden underneath his patrol cap. Remembering he was in public, Bryan kept his eyes locked to the back of Andy's head instead of traveling down to the round globes of his pert ass. Yep, Bryan had been noticing.

"Can I help you?" A lady asked from the desk in front of them. If this was Addison, Mal's definition of pretty was different than Bryan's. She wasn't bad looking, but she wasn't a knockout, either.

"He wants to open a checking account, and I want to cash my check," Andy answered for both of them.

"I can help with the account, and Addison would be happy to help with the check. If you'll step over to her window…" The woman was giving her best Vanna White impression like she had just introduced a new puzzle. Bryan

139

glanced over to where Addison was waiting. She smiled at Andy, and when she looked past him to Bryan, her smile faltered just a bit, but never went away. Nope. She didn't like what she saw. He forgot about her as he took a seat in front of the other woman. It took about twenty minutes, but Bryan had a new account opened. He should have already taken care of his banking once he got out of the Corps, but he'd not bothered with it. Most of the jobs Bryan had were paid in cash, so the need to have a checking account in Nashville had been moot. His savings account was with a bank in Chicago, and he saw no reason to move it. Yet.

Before he pushed the door open to walk outside, Bryan chanced another look at Addison. She was with a customer, but she glanced his way and smiled. Okay, maybe he'd misread the first look. He smiled back and went in search of Andy. He should have given him the keys so he didn't have to wait outside. Bryan found him leaning against the front fender, beefy arms crossed over his glorious chest. The scowl on his face made Bryan hesitant to say anything. He didn't have to, because Andy did the talking. "Here, I got you her number." Andy shoved a piece of paper toward Bryan. He grabbed it before it could float to the ground.

"Uh, thanks?" Bryan replied. "If you got her number for me, why are you pissed?"

"I'm not pissed; I'm hungry."

"Then by all means, let's get to the store and get you home so I can feed you," Bryan offered, trying to lighten the mood.

Bryan knew Andy well enough to know he was lying. Instead of arguing, he shoved the paper into his front pocket and got into the truck. While he drove the short distance to the grocery store, Bryan kept one eye on the road and the other on the volatile mountain of a man sitting next to him. When Andy was smiling and happy, he didn't seem much bigger than Bryan. But when his mood turned dark, it was like the Hulk was being let loose, only Andy didn't turn green. He kept his fury bottled inside, and Bryan was waiting for him to explode. He'd only seen Andy mad one other time and that was right after Bryan had met Laurel. Bryan was seeing a pattern. But if Andy didn't want Bryan going on dates, why did he get Addison's number, and why was he pissed?

"And what the fuck are you going to feed me? A jelly sandwich?"

Bryan barked out a laugh. It wasn't really funny, but he couldn't help it. "I'll at least put peanut butter on it. Damn, what do you take me for?" Andy didn't answer, but at least the hint of a smile edged his mouth.

Grocery shopping with Andy was a trip. Where Bryan didn't bother looking at the price tags, Andy stood and studied every purchase, making sure they were getting the cheapest price per unit. Most of the costs were already listed on the price tags, but when there was a sale, Andy calculated the new price in his head. Bryan was also used to buying whatever brand he wanted. Growing up, they'd been poor and always had to get the generic stuff. When he got out of the Corps and had money he didn't have to share, Bryan bought the name brands. Same with his clothes. Growing up, his clothes came from the thrift store or eBay. He didn't care, because they looked new, and he would never burden his hard-working mother with something so trivial. The jeans he'd worn to the bar the previous Friday were some fancy brand that cost a whack. He bought them because the sales clerk told him they made his ass look fine. And yes, the clerk had been a cute twink.

Thinking back on that shopping experience, Bryan knew the guy was flirting, but he thought it was so he'd get the commission. Now, he wasn't so sure. Had Bryan flirted back? Had the guy's gaydar gone off? No, he was sure the clerk only wanted the sale. That was too many months ago, and before Bryan had an inkling he might be into the rougher sex. Thinking of rougher sex, Bryan had seen some pretty rough shit when he was watching porn. There was no way a guy could fuck a woman that roughly and she not get hurt in the process. But the men who were being pounded had enjoyed it if their hard dicks and shooting orgasms were any indication. *Fuck.* Now his dick was coming to life. He grabbed the shopping cart away from Andy, hoping to hide his crotch from the other customers. "I'll push. You cipher," he said when Andy scowled at him.

"Do you like seafood?" Andy asked when he stopped in front of the counter directly past the lobster tank. It surprised Bryan that a town this small would have live lobster.

"Uh, yeah. Sure." Honestly, he'd not eaten any type of seafood other than the frozen fish sticks he and his siblings ate at least twice a week when they were growing up. Those and mac 'n cheese were staples in their kitchen.

"I haven't heard Mal mention eating seafood, and I didn't see any in the freezer. I'll get this for us to eat while he's off–"

"What can I get you?" An older man asked as he stepped up behind the counter. His apron was covered in blood, so Bryan figured he doubled as the butcher.

"I'll take all your crab legs."

Bryan glanced down at the counter and almost choked when he saw the amount of food Andy was getting. Andy didn't talk while the man was bagging the legs.

"Anything else?"

"That'll do it. Thanks."

The man mumbled under his breath, but Andy ignored him. Bryan, who was leaned over with his forearms on the cart handle, pulled up to his full height and gave the man a scowl of his own.

"I'll cook these while Mal's off fucking Cade in Nashville," Andy said, finishing his earlier thought once they were away from anyone else.

142

"Cade's coming to Nashville?" Now that was something to get excited about. Bryan wasn't star struck, but he couldn't wait to meet the famous drummer.

"Eventually. I overheard Mal on the phone. Not that I was eavesdropping. Mal was walking from his office to the kitchen. He obviously didn't care that I heard, because he didn't stop talking. It was weird, though."

"What was?"

"Well, it was like Mal almost didn't want to see him. He kept putting him off, telling him we were busy with calving season. We're not that busy. The mommas do all the work; all we have to do is keep an eye on them."

"Truth, and he's crazy about the man. I don't think Mal realizes how much he talks about him."

"I'm sure he has his reasons." Bryan couldn't imagine not wanting to be with the man you were dating especially when they rarely saw each other.

"Hey, do you like chicken in a biscuit?" Andy asked.

Bryan thought that was an odd question because Andy had seen him put a piece of fried chicken on a biscuit for breakfast. "Yeah, and I like sausage and bacon on biscuits, too."

Andy looked up from the box he was holding. "What?"

"You asked if I liked–"

"I know what I asked you. I meant these." He shook the box. "Crackers." Andy pointed at the name. *Chicken in a Biskit.*

"I've never had them, but if you like 'em, I'm sure I will."

"I haven't seen these since…" Andy tossed them in the cart and looked at the list again. They already had most of the things Mal wanted with the exception of milk and eggs, but those were on the other end of the store. Their cart was over halfway full with stuff Andy wanted.

"Hey, can you make some more nachos? Those were

great," Bryan asked. Andy had thrown together some cheese and leftover chicken on chips and nuked them in the microwave. Bryan loved nachos, and Andy's were better than any he'd ever had.

"Sure. We need to get some salsa and sour cream. Don't let me forget."

Bryan thoroughly enjoyed his shopping experience with Andy. It felt domesticated, and Bryan could envision them shopping together for many years to come. Right. Except Andy had gotten Addison's phone number for him. Maybe Bryan should go on a date with the girl. Maybe being around a female would change the way Bryan saw Andy. Addison Miller was definitely pretty. Her smile was sweet where Laurel's had been predatory. Bryan had no doubt if he'd gone to Laurel's, the woman would have expected sex. Maybe Addison would be okay with going to dinner and a movie. The thought of calling her and asking was as exciting as shoveling out Callie's stall. Still, he owed it to himself to at least try.

Now that he'd thoroughly depressed himself, he tagged along quietly as Andy filled their cart the rest of the way full. When they got back to the farm, Bryan helped Andy unload the bags and take them to the kitchen. On the way home, Andy had Bryan stop at the discount mart so he could get a small charcoal grill. The grocery store had their steaks on sale, and Andy couldn't pass them up.

"What the hell?" Mal asked when they walked into the kitchen loaded down with bags.

"Don't worry, Boss. I paid for all this. I don't expect you to feed us on your dime. Plus, I got a grill. I was wondering . . . What would you think about us building a small deck off the back porch? I'd pay for it, if you okay it." Andy had mentioned the idea to Bryan and asked if he was willing to help build it. Of course Bryan was on board with anything Andy wanted.

"It's not my house anymore, but I don't think the

company would be opposed. They'd consider it an improvement and probably pay for the materials. I'll give 'em a call and ask."

"Awesome," Andy beamed. It amazed Bryan how the man could go from pissed to happy in the span of a shopping trip. "Hey, B. Will you do me a favor?"

"Of course. What do you need?"

"Will you get the grill out of the truck and see what we need to put it together? I'll finish putting the groceries away and marinate the steaks for later."

"No problem." Bryan gladly left the two men to the food, because he really didn't know where shit went anyway. Since they'd gotten a charcoal grill and not a massive gas one, all that was needed was a screwdriver. Bryan found one in the barn, and before Andy came outside, Bryan was tightening the last screw. "Tada," he said, shaking it to make sure it was nice and sturdy.

"You didn't have to do that, B." The grin on Andy's face said he appreciated it.

"Didn't have to, but I wanted to. You do all the cooking, even though you pretend you're teaching me. Little stuff like this is the least I can do to repay you for your kindness." Bryan reached out and grabbed Andy's shoulder, giving it a little squeeze. Andy gasped and looked at Bryan's mouth. Okay, he was not imagining the way Andy was staring at him like he wanted to devour him. His cock twitched behind the zipper, warmth filling Bryan from his head to his toes. When Andy licked his lips, Bryan felt himself leaning in. The back door opened, and Bryan took a step back, letting his hand drop to his side. *Fuck!* Had he really been about to kiss Andy?

"Since y'all are in a buildin' shit mood, how 'bout we install that doggie door? I figure between the three of us we can't fuck it up too bad," Mal said.

"Yeah, sure," Andy said at the same time Bryan muttered, "No problem."

Bryan was an idiot. Andy had made it clear over the last few days he wasn't interested. If the lack of conversation and eye contact hadn't been enough of a clue, the phone number in his pocket was. But Andy had wanted to kiss, hadn't he? This shit was more confusing than trying to figure out how to cook without burning everything. Bryan couldn't look at Andy. He didn't want to see the rejection in his eyes. He was already embarrassed enough.

Mal returned with a jigsaw and the pet door. Andy was like a kid hopped up on Pop Rocks. Bryan enjoyed the dogs being inside, but having them around was good for Andy. Moe had become his constant companion whenever possible. Mal had joked about the dog being a traitor, but Bryan had seen the way Mal smiled at the two of them together. Mal might seem like a good-ole-boy cattle farmer, but the man was smart. When he and Walt were talking business, it never ceased to amaze Bryan how much Mal knew at such a young age. Hell, Mal was the same age as both Bryan and Andy, and here he was running a business. He'd been in charge of both the farm and the bar for such a long time. It almost made Bryan ashamed that he hadn't accomplished more in his twenty-six years.

Bryan remembered what his mom said to him when he told her he wanted to be a boxer like his daddy – "It doesn't matter what you do with your life as long as you do it to the best of your ability. The busboy and the dishwasher are just as important as the chef. If you don't have clean tables and clean dishes, it doesn't matter how good the food is."

His mom had been a hell of a waitress. Bryan had been a hell of a Marine. He'd given his country eight years, and he'd given them to the best of his ability, sometimes giving more than he thought he had. He could have given more if he'd gone on to MARSOC like his CO wanted him to. Bryan knew in his heart he couldn't give one hundred percent to the Special Forces team, so he opted out completely. Now, he could be one hell of a farmhand. It payed more than some white collar jobs. He'd read articles about folks graduating college with a degree only to be stuck without a job at all. So, Bryan was okay with what he was doing, and he was going to make sure he gave it his all so his mom would always be proud of him. If there came a time down the road when he figured out he'd rather do something else with his life, he'd worry about that then.

It didn't take all three men to put the pet door in. Since Andy was the one who asked for it, he offered to be the one to install it. Bryan read the instructions while Mal sat on the ground petting the two animals and keeping them out of the way. As soon as Andy was finished, he called the dogs to him and opened the flap. One after the other, they stuck their head past the vinyl covering and disappeared into the house. Less than thirty seconds later they both came back out. The three men laughed as the dogs ran in and out. It felt good to laugh. When Andy looked his way with that beautiful smile on his face, something hit Bryan hard. Being with Andy felt like home.

Chapter Fifteen

Andy

Andy couldn't breathe. The beautiful smile on Bryan's face had stolen his ability to move. To think. His head knew Bryan was straight and didn't really want him, but his heart was making him see things that weren't there. Like the fact that Bryan almost kissed him earlier. When Moe ran out the back door barking, the connection was lost, and Andy could breathe again. Curly was right behind his brother, and it looked like both dogs were enjoying their newfound entrance into the house. Neither one of them had caused chaos when they were inside. If anything, they were the picture of perfect animals. Andy had tempted Moe to jump up on the couch while he was watching television, but the dog had sat at his feet thumping his tail. The fact that Mal came down the stairs at that exact moment might have had something to do with it. As much as the dogs loved Andy and Bryan, Mal was the alpha.

"Are we eatin' steaks or what?" Mal asked.

"Yes, we're eating steaks. Let me put the potatoes in the oven so they can be cooking, then I'll fire up the grill."

"I'll handle the grilling," Bryan offered. "I might not be able to cook, but I can work a grill like nobody's business." There was that smile again.

I'd let you work my grill. Andy headed inside to wash potatoes before he made a fool of himself. When he came back outside, Mal had grabbed some hay bales and placed them in the area where Bryan had moved the grill. Andy made a mental note to pick up some lawn chairs next time he went to town. While they were waiting for the charcoal to burn down, Mal brought out a cooler and set it between them. They popped the tops on some longnecks and enjoyed the peacefulness the farm offered.

"I talked to Mr. Matheson, and he assured me the owner is fine with us buildin' a deck. Said for me to order the materials and put it on the company account. We just need to figure out how big we want it and go from there."

Andy had never built anything in his life. He didn't know where to start with figuring out how much wood they would need or the type of materials it would take. Bryan stood and walked over to the back of the house. Putting his back to the wall, he measured out the distance Mal suggested using his feet as a tape measure. When he was finished, he put a couple of empty bottles on the ground to show the corners. "That's roughly twelve by twenty. Plenty big enough for a grill and eventually a table and chairs. What do you think, Lily?"

Andy imagined the deck in his mind. He could see him and Bryan sitting on a patio set while the steaks cooked on their new gas grill. He pictured them enjoying a sky full of stars while the two of them sat outside together. "It's perfect."

"Mal?"

Mal nodded. "I agree. I'll order the materials tomorrow, and we can get started on it before it gets too hot."

Andy went inside to check on the potatoes. "Will you grab the steaks while you're inside?" Bryan asked.

Andy nodded and returned quickly with the marinated meat and some tongs he found in the utensil drawer. Bryan had already scattered the mound of white charcoal around in the bottom of the grill and was ready when Andy returned. The man hadn't been lying when he said he could grill. Andy was the one to marinate the beef, but Bryan cooked them to a medium rare perfection. He thought Mal was going to have a foodgasm.

"This is delicious, even for a store-bought piece of meat. I've never had a steak this tender," he praised.

"It's all in how you prepare it," Andy boasted. Bryan punched him gently in the arm, and Andy laughed. "Okay, maybe it has something to do with how it's cooked, too, but the secret is adding sugar to the marinade."

The past few nights had been a little awkward, leaving Andy out of sorts over his feelings for Bryan, but in that moment, he was comfortable and happy. After the dishes were washed, Andy asked, "How about a game of poker?" There wasn't a ball game on, and he wasn't in the mood for a movie. Besides, he was getting good at steeling his facial expressions when his cards were dealt.

"I'm in," Bryan said.

"Sure, I'll play." Mal usually opted out, but instead of hiding away in his bedroom or office, he joined the other two men. Since Andy and Bryan had gotten paid, they decided to play for actual money and not the coins from Andy's change jar. The winnings went back and forth for almost an hour before Mal lost almost two hundred dollars. He graciously bowed out, and that left Andy and Bryan. Feeling courageous, Andy said, "How about we change the stakes?" Andy had gone and done exactly what he vowed not to do – he got Addison's phone number for Bryan. He'd been pissed at himself afterwards, but then Bryan looked at the piece of paper like it would bite him, giving Andy had an idea. Whether or not it was a good one remained to be seen.

"What did you have in mind?"

Here we go. "Let's play strip poker." Andy kept his eyes on Bryan's face to gauge his reaction. He was glad he did, because Bryan let his gaze roam down Andy's body and back up. When he met Andy's eyes, Bryan was grinning.

"Okay."

Andy wondered if it was the alcohol talking, or if

Bryan was looking forward to seeing Andy without his shirt on. Not that they'd had that much to drink. Andy didn't even have a buzz, not after eating a huge steak and loaded potato. Thinking of buzzes, Andy said, "Hang on." He went to the kitchen and grabbed a bottle of Jack Daniels out of the pantry. He'd never seen Mal drinking liquor, but the seal had been broken, so someone drank the stuff. He probably should have asked permission, but he would replace the bottle next time he was out.

"Here are the rules. If you lose, you take off whatever piece of clothing the winner chooses, and the winner takes a swig of Jack."

Bryan's grin was cocky. His pile of money was significantly larger than Andy's. If Bryan kept his winning streak going, he would be clothed, but he'd also be more intoxicated than Andy. Andy had never seen a drunk Bryan, and he hoped this plan didn't backfire on him.

"Your deal," Bryan said.

Andy shuffled and dealt the first hand. When he saw the aces staring back at him, it was all he could do not to pump his fist in the air. Bryan asked for two cards, so his hand wasn't stacked. Andy only took one, but it didn't help his hand. Bidding went back and forth until Bryan said, "Call."

Andy laid down three aces, a seven and a nine. Bryan had two pair, but it didn't beat Andy's three of a kind. Andy took a swig out of the bottle. He wiped his hand on the back of his hand before saying, "Take your shirt off."

Bryan reached behind his head and gripped the neck of his T-shirt. Andy's eyes were glued to Bryan's chest, waiting for the reveal. He'd seen the other man's chest several times, but sitting like this, there was no way he'd be able to avert his eyes. Bryan tossed the shirt to the floor and rubbed a hand across his pecs, making them flex. When Andy looked up, Bryan was smirking. "Like what you see, Lily?" he whispered.

Andy couldn't speak, so he nodded and bit his bottom lip. Bryan gathered the cards and began shuffling. With nothing covering his arms, Andy got a good look at Bryan's biceps and forearm muscles in motion as he dealt the cards. When Bryan cleared his throat, Andy blushed and picked up the waiting hand. Okay, no fist pumping here. He didn't have shit, but he didn't want to ask for four cards, because that would be a dead giveaway he had nothing. He asked for three and prayed they were good ones. Nope. He could either bluff his way through and lose some cash, or fold. Either way, Bryan was going to win the hand, and Andy was going to lose some clothes. It was only a shirt, so he folded.

Bryan grinned, tossed back the whiskey, and said, "Pants."

"What?" Andy was already reaching for the hem of his shirt when Bryan surprised him.

"You heard me. I want you to take your pants off. Don't tell me you're shy, Lily. I've seen your briefs before. Unless…"

Unless he was commando, which he wasn't, thank God. "Shy? Have you met me?" Andy stood and went about removing his jeans. Facing Bryan, Andy slid the button out of its hole and slowly lowered the zipper. He hooked his thumbs between the denim and the cotton of his underwear and began pushing them down his hips. Grinning, he turned around and finished sliding his jeans down his thighs then his calves. He wiggled his ass slightly until he saw a problem. He still had his fucking boots on. What started off as a sexy tease turned into something much less erotic. Andy plopped down in the chair and struggled getting the tight legs over his boots. Before he could get them all the way off, they got stuck. "You've got to be shitting me," he mumbled.

"Trouble?" Bryan asked, still smirking.

"Yeah. A little help? You're the wiseass who wanted

the pants off before my boots. Come over here and tug." If that came out sounding sexual, so be it.

Bryan stood and rounded the table. Andy held his legs up and leaned back in the chair for balance. Bryan wiggled each pant leg until he was able to get them past Andy's black boots. He probably should have taken the boots off then put them back on, but this was much more fun. When Bryan had Andy's jeans free from his legs, he stared at the bare flesh longer than a straight man should.

"Like what you see?" Andy teased, running a hand over his semi-hard dick. Bryan blushed and returned to his side of the table. Andy never should have touched his cock. It had gone from somewhat erect to a full-blown hard-on in two point five seconds. It was his turn to deal, but his hands were shaking. He grabbed the Jack and took a deep pull, trying to calm his nerves. Whose fucking idea had this been anyway? Oh, right. His.

Andy won the next hand, and he graciously told Bryan to remove his boots. He couldn't see under the table anyway. Bryan won the hand after that, and Andy lost his shirt. Bryan won the next one as well, and Andy removed his boots. When they were down to nothing but their underwear, both men were slightly inebriated. Andy didn't know if he could handle the sight of a naked Bryan, so he thought long and hard about throwing the hand. *Long and hard.* Andy giggled like a girl at the thought, and Bryan raised his eyebrows.

"You okay over there, Lily?"

"Yep. Fine. Perfect." *Liar.* Andy was anything but fine. What happened when they were sitting there with nothing on? His dick was already impossibly painful. If he lost this hand, Bryan would have no doubt how he affected Andy. Would that be so bad? What would be worse was when Andy won and Bryan removed his briefs only for Andy to find a limp dick. But if that were the case, at least Andy would know for sure how Bryan felt about him. Every time he looked across the table, Bryan had been studying his hand and not Andy's body. He had a great body, almost as nice as Bryan's, but the other man wasn't staring like Andy was. He just had to play this out, and whatever happened, happened.

"If you like, we can call it a night," Bryan offered when Andy still hadn't dealt the cards. Bryan took another pull from the bottle that was almost empty.

"Scared, B?"

Bryan licked his lips and pointed at Andy while still holding the bottle. "Nope. Deal 'em." Bryan drank the whiskey down until there was only a small amount of liquid covering the bottom of the bottle. One last sip for the winner.

Andy shuffled. As he dealt out five cards each, he asked himself what he thought was going to happen after this hand. One of them would be naked, but they were in the middle of Mal's fucking kitchen. He'd just have to wait and find out if he was willing to make a move, or if Bryan ran and hid in his bedroom.

When Andy looked at his cards, he was torn. He had two pair. That wasn't a guaranteed win, but it wasn't bad. Did he want to throw the game so Bryan could see how hard he was for him? Or did he want to win so he could finally have a visual of the cock he'd been imagining for two weeks? He swapped out one card and let the outcome be whatever the poker fates decided. After going back and forth upping the pot, Andy finally called. They both had two pair, but Bryan had queens and kings where Andy had jacks and nines. Bryan won. Andy was about to show his junk to his best friend.

Bryan tipped the bottle back, emptying it. He set the bottle down with a thud and pointed. Andy bit his bottom lip. Was he really going to do this? "I think you should do the honors," he suggested. Bryan's beautiful eyes darkened and they traveled down Andy's chest. He couldn't see

Andy's crotch hidden behind the table, so could he be imagining what he was going to find?

Bryan pushed the chair back and stood, his hand rubbing down his chest and landing on his brief-covered dick. His dick that was hard. *Oh, fuck me.* Andy stood when Bryan reached his side. Bryan took his time looking Andy's body over. He placed his hands on Andy's chest and lowered his hands, skimming along Andy's abs, eliciting a full body shiver from Andy. Bryan kept his eyes locked on Andy's face as his fingers reached the waistband. He slid his hands between the band and Andy's flesh, closing his eyes as he lowered his fingertips to the globes of Andy's ass. As he breathed in and out, Andy inhaled the scent of Bryan's whiskey breath like it was pure oxygen.

Their faces were so close. If Andy leaned in a half an inch, their lips would be touching. He ached to taste Bryan's mouth, but he didn't want to ruin the moment. This was Bryan's win, and it was up to him to set the pace. Bryan opened his eyes, but instead of kissing Andy's lips, Bryan began moving his hands down Andy's legs while lowering his face. Bryan placed open mouth kisses on Andy's neck, his pecs, his abs, and finally the area just above the waist band that was precariously low at that point. When Bryan reached his knees, he pulled Andy's boxer briefs all the way over his ass, allowing Andy's cock to spring forward. It wasn't a huge dick, but Bryan was close enough it almost smacked him in the face.

Bryan continued lowering Andy's briefs until they pooled at his ankles. He stepped out of them and held still. Andy was completely bare in front of his best friend. The man he wanted more than his next breath. Bryan placed his hands on the back of Andy's ankles and made a slow pass up the backs of his legs, letting them settle below his cheeks. Bryan remained motionless, face to rock hard cock. Andy had no idea what Bryan was thinking, or if he was. Bryan's dick was straining against his underwear, and even though it was covered, Andy could tell that it was longer than his own and much thicker. Thinking about sucking on it had Andy moaning. Bryan snapped his head up at the sound.

It must have interrupted his thought process, because Bryan stood. Instead of keeping any distance between them, Bryan placed his feet on either side of Andy's, bringing their bodies together. Andy's cock was trapped between them, right alongside Bryan's underwear clad erection. Andy moved slightly, rubbing their dicks together. Bryan hissed, grabbing Andy's biceps and closing his eyes. Andy took that as permission to keep going, so he put his hands on Bryan's hips and pulled him closer, adding friction to their dicks. Bryan's breathing sped up, and Andy was about to blow. He wanted them to come at the same time. Before he could lower Bryan's briefs and stroke their cocks together, Andy came, his spunk shooting onto Bryan's stomach. Bryan's eyes shot open, and he pulled away so quickly Andy didn't have time to react. Bryan reached down, grabbing a handful of clothes, and disappeared down the hallway.

What in the ever-loving fuck? Talk about a waste of a good orgasm. One last drop of jizz leaked out of Andy's softening dick. He slumped down in the chair and cradled his head in his hands. What the fuck? How had something so right gone so incredibly wrong? When Andy raised his head, the first thing he saw was the empty bottle. Liquid courage had turned out to be the enemy. In one orgasmic moment, Bryan had sobered the fuck up, and now, Andy's throat burned with the sour taste of the alcohol. He threw open the back door and leaned over the porch railing, spewing half a bottle of whiskey and every bit of supper he'd enjoyed hours before.

With nothing but dry heaves left in his body, Andy straightened up and held onto the rail while his body calmed down. He should have cared that he was buck naked standing on the back porch, but he couldn't find a fuck to give. Not wanting Mal to come downstairs and get an eyeful of his white ass, Andy went inside. He closed the door and turned on the alarm. Moe and Curly sat at his feet, whining. "I'm okay, boys," he lied. Andy felt worse than when Patrick and his lover decided using Andy as their object of a little pain play was a good idea. Andy would rather have five more lashes with a whip than have to face Bryan the next morning. As he gathered the scattered clothes, Andy prayed Bryan was drunk enough he forgot what just happened.

When he got to his bedroom, Andy tossed the dirty clothes on the floor somewhere in the vicinity of the hamper. He didn't bother pulling underwear on. He crawled into bed and prayed for sleep to take him. Even though he'd thrown up, the light-headedness remained as he closed his eyes. The darkness surrounded Andy. That floating feeling was no longer there. It had been replaced with a weight on Andy's chest he didn't understand. He opened his eyes, but he still couldn't see. When he tried to touch his face, Andy found his wrists were bound. "Let me go," he begged. A deep chuckle sounded somewhere in the room. Andy was disoriented, so he didn't know who it was or how close they were.

Someone grabbed his cock and began stroking. "Oh, Andrew. Calm down. You said you wanted to play, so be a good boy and stay still. Clark is going to make it hurt so good."

"Patrick?"

"Who the fuck else would be touching your dick, Andrew? Who?" Patrick yelled.

"No... nobody."

"Fucking straight. This cock is mine," Patrick hissed into Andy's ear as he leaned over his back. "Nobody touches you but me." Patrick bit down on Andy's earlobe hard. "Well, maybe Clark."

Andy yelped and pulled harder on the ropes. "I

changed my mind. Please untie me."

"Don't you trust me, Baby? You need to trust me. Clark is going to make your orgasm so much better."

"I trust you, but I don't trust Clark." The name had no sooner left Andy's mouth than a sharp pain sliced across his back. "Owwww," he cried out. "What the fuck, Patrick? Untie me right fucking now, goddammit!"

Another crack of whatever Clark was using slashed on top of the other cut. Andy cried out again, tears streaming down his face. Patrick licked his face and said, "Shhh. Be a man, Andrew. Stop crying like the little bitch you are." Patrick grabbed Andy's flaccid cock, attempting to stroke it back into an erection. Andy could tell him it wasn't going to work.

"Get your hands off me!" Andy yelled at his boyfriend. Crack. Pain worse than the last two strikes tore through Andy. Would his back eventually get numb? He didn't know how much more he could handle.

"I'm going to fuck you now, Andrew. Then I'm going to give Clark a turn with your nice, tight hole."

"No! I don't want him to touch me! I don't want you to. Get away!"

Two more stripes landed on his back. "Stop! Get off me," Andy managed to strangle out before the pain of a cock slammed into his hole. No lube, no prep. "Please stop," he begged. At least he thought he did. Nothing but a huge cock stretching Andy. It had to be this Clark guy because Patrick wasn't that big. Wetness dripped out of Andy's ass. Clark had either orgasmed as soon as he breached Andy, or Andy was bleeding. A hand landed in the middle of Andy's back on top of the broken skin. Andy had lost all energy to fight. Had lost the will to live. He closed his eyes and prayed for God to take him.

Chapter Sixteen

Bryan

Bryan hadn't considered how hard it would be to walk and have an orgasm at the same time. How fucking embarrassing. If he'd stood still, he could have at least enjoyed getting off. Instead, he ran like a coward all because he was coming in his underwear like a teenager. He didn't know the proper etiquette for having an orgasm while still clothed, so he freaked. Freaked the fuck out, and now he'd never be able to look Andy in the eyes again. Bryan had blown his chance at moving forward with his best friend. *You blew it all right.*

Leaning against his bedroom door, Bryan could still taste Andy's skin. Feel the way his muscles bunched and released as Bryan ran his fingers over them. Andy's scent was imbedded in his nostrils. Bryan started to toss his clothes to the floor when he realized they weren't his clothes. Instead of picking his things up, he'd grabbed Andy's stuff in his hurry to get away before Andy knew what was happening. Bryan lifted the T-shirt to his nose and inhaled deeply. His traitorous cock started coming back to life. The scent was a mixture of Andy's body wash and his spunk. When the first ribbon of jizz hit Bryan's stomach, he'd lost control of his own orgasm. He'd been willing his balls to hang on until he could get behind closed doors, but the warmth of Andy's release had been too much.

What would have happened if he'd stayed in the kitchen? Would Andy have laughed at him for not holding off? Or would he have enjoyed the fact that Bryan couldn't wait? Andy was so fucking sexy. Bryan had seen the man in his underwear before, but never had he put his body on display on purpose. They both had ogled the other, not bothering to hide the fact they were staring. Bryan might not have been so brave if it hadn't been for the liquor, but in his drunken state, he'd enjoyed the hell out of Andy's body. The only thing better was when he actually got to put his hands on Andy.

Bryan had never touched another man in such an intimate way. If he hadn't been in such a hurry to kiss Andy, he might have stayed on his knees and licked the tip of Andy's leaking dick. He'd been tempted, but the need to taste Andy's lips overrode his curiosity about having another man's dick in his mouth. He cared about Andy. Deeper than he probably should after only two weeks, but Bryan knew how he felt. When he'd kissed his way down Andy's body, his cock wanted nothing more than to sink into Andy's hole. His body warred with his head. He planned on kissing Andy, but as soon as Andy began rubbing their cocks together, all thoughts of kissing flew out the window.

Bryan had to call on every ounce of strength he possessed to keep his orgasm at bay. He fully intended to get his own release, but not in his underwear. He wanted Andy's hands touching him. His mouth sucking him. His ass surrounding him. *Best laid plans.* Now, he'd probably never get the chance. The buzz from the alcohol was beginning to turn from that fuzzy, warm feeling to the slow ache spreading through his head. He was going to have one helluva hangover the next day. Bryan had sworn off liquor for that very reason. He hated the next day blahs he got from drinking too much. Beer he could handle in large quantities. Liquor he could not. Not only was he going to be hungover, he was going to have to face Andy.

Their mixed come was already drying on his stomach, but he didn't have the energy or the guts to take a shower. Running into Andy now would be the nail in the coffin. Bryan pulled Andy's shirt over his head and let the other items fall to the floor. Normally, he didn't sleep in a shirt, but he wanted Andy's scent with him in the bed. If he couldn't have the man, his shirt would have to do. He could have balled it up and hugged it to his chest, but that screamed stalker. This way, he could pretend he didn't realize it was the other man's shirt he was wearing.

Bryan popped open the bottle of anxiety pills and swallowed one dry. When he crawled underneath the covers, he wished he had a bottle of aspirin. He needed to buy some to keep in his room for the next time. *There won't be a next time, fool.* No, probably not. Not with Andy, anyway. There definitely wouldn't be a next time of drinking half a bottle of Jack Daniels. What the hell had he been thinking? And on a work night, no less. Tomorrow was going to be one shitty-ass day.

Praying for sleep so his mind could shut off for at least a few hours, Bryan closed his eyes and waited for the sound of Andy coming down the hall. Bryan snorted. *You're the fool who came down the hall.* If he hadn't been so mortified, he would have stopped walking and enjoyed the release as best he could. Instead, he jizzed in his underwear and didn't enjoy it one bit. As an afterthought, Bryan removed the ruined briefs and tossed them on the floor. Trying to pry the sticky material off his pubic hair wouldn't be fun in the morning. Maybe he'd just shave all that shit off. It served no purpose anyway.

Bryan was in the place between being awake and drifting off when the floor creaked outside his door. Andy was probably laughing to himself as he passed by. The shower turned on, and Bryan had never been so jealous of water in his life. He wanted to be the water cascading over Andy's magnificent body. The droplets touching every inch of his skin. Caressing him like a lover. Bryan wanted to rewind the clock and spend more time ghosting his fingers over more than just the backs of Andy's legs or his chest and stomach. He wanted to touch his tongue to that place between Andy's neck and shoulders right before he bit down, marking his skin so everyone would know Andy was his. The sound of the shower and the haze from the alcohol pulled Bryan under.

Bryan awoke to a piss hard-on. Dammit to hell. When he rolled from the bed, he saw that it wasn't much later than when he'd lain down He didn't realize until he was standing in the bathroom that he wasn't wearing his briefs. *Fucking great.* After peeing and making a half-assed attempt at washing his hands, he headed back to his room. As he passed by Andy's door, he heard Andy crying. Bryan pulled the T-shirt down over his junk and pushed open the door to check on his friend. "Andy, you okay?"

Andy's cries turned into sobs. "Andy?" Bryan sat down on the side of the bed and touched Andy's arm to get his attention.

"Get off me!"

Bryan pulled his hand back and stood back up. Andy already hated him. Bryan didn't blame him. He didn't want to leave Andy alone, but the man made it clear he didn't want him. Bryan returned to his room, his heart shredded.

"Bryan?" Andy's voice was calling him, but it was far away. Muffled.

"Bryan, wake up." The pain was unbearable. What was happening? Had someone hit him over the head? Why couldn't he see Andy?

"B, wake up." Andy's voice was closer now. His hand warm against Bryan's cold face. Why… Bryan forced his eyes to open. Bright blue eyes stared back at him. A frown marred Andy's beautiful face.

"There you are. I was worried about you." Andy's breath was a mixture of mint and whiskey. *Whiskey.* The previous night came crashing back, the ache in his head not as strong as the pain in his heart. Andy removed his hand

162

and stood from his kneeling position on the floor. "Breakfast is ready. I'll keep your plate warm while you shower."

Bryan pulled the spare pillow back down over his face and groaned. Obviously, nobody had ever died from embarrassment, because if they had, Bryan wouldn't still be on this side of the stratosphere. As much as he'd love to hide the rest of the day, Bryan made himself get up. When he sat up, there was a bottle of ibuprofen and a glass of water on the nightstand. He downed four of them and drank all the water. About two more gallons to flush his system and he'd be good to go.

When Bryan stood, he searched the room for his dirty clothes. The floor was bare except for the rug. Where were his fucking clothes? He scratched his stomach only to find Andy's T-shirt covering his chest. His ass was bare, and when the previous night bounced around in his memory bank, Bryan dipped his chin to his chest, giving himself a minute to silently curse his behavior. Grabbing clean clothes, he opened the door and made sure the coast was clear before he walked mostly naked down the short hallway to the bathroom. While the water was heating, Bryan brushed his teeth to remove the funk. He brushed them again for good measure. Once inside the shower, he washed quickly until he got to his groin. Lathering as gently as he could, Bryan cleaned the dried jizz off his skin and then washed again to be sure he'd removed any remnants of the night before.

By the time he'd garnered enough courage to show his face, Andy and Mal were no longer in the kitchen. It was already past eight, so he had some apologizing to do. True to his word, Andy put a plate of food in the microwave. Why the fuck was Andy being so nice to him? Bryan nuked his breakfast and poured a cup of coffee while he waited. He wasn't sure he could keep the food down, but he had to try. Hungover on an empty stomach was worse than having a head that pounded from both too much alcohol and too little food.

He downed one cup of coffee and poured another before he tried to eat. Bryan managed half his breakfast before his stomach began to protest. He dumped the scraps into the trash, washed his plate, and put it away. When he made his way to the barn, Andy and Mal were nowhere to be found. The horses weren't in their stalls, so Bryan straddled Cade's four wheeler and set out in search of them.

When he found them, neither Andy nor Mal made comment of the fact he was late. He opened his mouth to apologize, but Mal held up a hand. "Don't, Bryan. You're not the first to drink too much when you aren't used to it."

Bryan had yet to look at Andy, but after hearing the excuse he'd obviously given their boss, he couldn't not look. Andy gave him a small nod. Bryan stifled a groan and pulled on his big boy briefs. The ones that weren't stained with come.

The day flew by with the three of them tag-teaming the cattle. It probably would have gone faster if Andy didn't have to ooh and ahh over every calf in the pasture. When noon came around, Andy left Mal and Bryan alone to go make lunch for them all, and Bryan took the time to apologize. "Mal, I'm real sorry about this morning."

"Like I said earlier, we've all drank too much when we didn't mean to. Just tell me this – was it worth it?" Mal was grinning. Did he know what they'd been doing? "I mean, Andy's a handsome fella. If I wasn't in love with Cade, I might not mind playin' strip poker with the man."

"So, if you weren't dating Cade, you'd be interested in Andy?" Bryan had never been jealous before, but he was feeling it now.

"Would that bother you?" Mal answered with a question of his own.

"Why should it? I'm straight." *Liar.*

"Just checkin'." Mal went back to the heifer at his feet.

Andy returned with sandwiches for them all. Instead of eating in the pasture, Mal led them to the pond. A spot had been cleared off where they could sit on the ground while eating. The three of them enjoyed their lunch in silence. It wasn't uncomfortable. It never was between them. Mal and Bryan were quiet by nature, and Andy seemed more at ease now than he had when Bryan first met him. They returned to the task of giving the heifers their shots, and the rest of the day went by as quickly as the morning had.

Bryan refused to look at Andy, but he could feel the other man's eyes boring holes through him all day long. Bryan had skipped supper. He used the excuse that he wasn't feeling well, but the truth was he didn't feel like being that close to Andy. Bryan's head was a jumbled mess and not just from the alcohol. Now that they were sitting on the sofa together watching a game, it was easier to ignore him. That was until Andy stood from his spot and walked in front of him, blocking the TV. "I'm sorry about last night. It won't happen again."

Bryan couldn't stop the pain from ripping through his chest. Andy might have wanted him, but not anymore. Bryan couldn't blame him. As badly as he wanted to, he couldn't watch Andy walking away. Bryan tried to focus on the game, but it was useless. All he could think about was what was going on with Andy. Or what wasn't going on. There had been too many conflicting looks, touches, and words. There's no way Andy hadn't been turned on. Not with the way he rubbed against Bryan, unless he'd only been using him to get off. Andy had been drunk, but then again, so had Bryan. Maybe his whiskey-addled brain had him seeing signs that weren't there. Maybe he was remembering everything all wrong, and he'd been the one to rub their erections together. *But he shot his load all over your stomach.*

Bryan thought about Andy getting Addison's phone

number. He'd tried to push Bryan away, but Bryan had foolishly made himself believe his best friend wanted him, too. He thought about the folded piece of paper in his bedroom that had Addison's number on it. He'd meant to throw it away. Maybe it was a good thing he hadn't. His heart wasn't ready to date, not when it wanted someone it couldn't have.

Bryan woke up on the couch. All the lights were off, and the dogs were asleep on the floor beside him. Padding to the kitchen, he made sure the house was secure before heading to his bedroom. He flipped on the light and closed the door. There on the bed were not only his clothes from the night before, but everything he'd had in his hamper was washed and folded. Andy had done his laundry. Even if he didn't want a relationship with Bryan, Andy was still being a good friend. Bryan had to suck up his feelings and realize what a good thing they had together, even without the intimacy. He would take what he could get where Andy was concerned.

Friday was like being in the twilight zone. If Bryan hadn't lived through the last couple of days, he would swear they never happened. Andy was more chipper than he'd been in a week. "We going back to the Dairy Barn tonight?" Andy asked as they were untacking the horses. Mal had sent them out on their own all day, so Bryan took advantage of the time to practice riding Callie.

"If you want," Bryan answered. He wanted nothing more than to go eat with Andy and spend more time with him, even as friends.

"Great. I thought afterwards we could go say hello to Kason, if you're feeling up to it."

"Yeah, I'd like that, but I'm sticking to beer."

"I hear you there. I'm not ready to puke my guts up again."

Did that mean Andy had thrown up Wednesday night? No wonder he was able to get up on time. Bryan should have made himself throw up, but that would have meant going into the bathroom and possibly facing Andy after what happened. Nope, dealing with a hangover had been the lesser of two evils. *But you did face Andy afterwards.* Yeah, that rejection was something he didn't ever want to think about.

After they finished taking care of the horses, they took turns in the shower, and while Andy was primping, Bryan called his sister and checked in. When Andy walked into the living room, Bryan could only stare. Andy had on a dark pair of jeans over his new cowboy boots. He had a button-up shirt tucked in and the sleeves rolled up. Damn, he looked good. Bryan hadn't made any special attempt at looking nice. What was the point? He wasn't going out to impress anyone. The one he wanted to impress had already shot him down.

The Dairy Barn was crowded when they arrived, but they were able to find a table in the back. Andy grabbed their ketchup and drinks while Bryan waited on their food. They really were in tune with each other when it came to most things. Andy smiled at everyone, putting them at as much ease as he could while Bryan looked on in awe. Bryan didn't smile. He'd tried it the last time they were there only to be scowled at. He always felt people were judging him for the way he looked, and now was no exception. At least in the projects he'd been around people of color and different ethnicities. Here, Bryan ignored everyone. Everyone except the blond sitting across from him.

When they arrived at DWs, it was a little later than the last week, and several tables were already filled. Instead of making Kason come to them, they took a couple of empty seats at the bar. Their fellow Marine smiled when he saw them.

"I was wondering if I'd see you two tonight. How's it going?" Kason had already poured the same beer they'd ordered the week before.

Since Bryan didn't know how things were going, he let Andy do the talking. Bryan enjoyed listening to Andy's voice, so he saw no reason to speak up. Andy told Kason all about the farm. He sang Bryan's praises of grilling steak. He gushed on and on about Matilda. He even talked about the cattle. Kason laughed when Andy admitted stepping in a pile of cow shit. That had been funny watching Andy hopping on one foot while trying to sling the dung off his boot. Kason kept their glasses full, and it was much easier to talk to him sitting at the bar. Bryan was oblivious to his surroundings which was unusual for him. Normally, he liked to sit where he could see all the action, but having another Marine on the other side of the bar put him at ease. Kason would warn them if something bad was going to happen.

After a few beers, Bryan switched to water so he'd be okay to drive home. Andy wasn't drunk, but he was feeling good. All night, he'd kept his thigh pressed up against Bryan's. Andy had touched his arm or his shoulder whenever he got up to pee. It was enough to have Bryan ready to take him home and try getting naked again, embarrassment be damned.

Several women had tried to get them both to dance. Bryan graciously declined, but after a while, Andy had taken them up on their offer. Bryan turned his stool sideways so he could still talk to Kason while keeping an eye on his best friend. Not that way. He wanted to make sure none of the men started anything. *Right.* Andy was a good dancer. He moved with the music like it was part of him. Bryan guessed it was. Andy was musically inclined, so it only made sense he'd have rhythm as well. When a country song came on the juke box, Andy and the girl he was with joined several others in doing the same dance around the floor. While most people just shuffled their feet, Andy twirled his partner like they'd been dancing together forever.

When a slow song came on, Andy looked over at Bryan with a funny expression. Bryan held his breath as couples began swaying with their bodies plastered together. Andy said something to the girl he was with. She smiled and waved. Andy returned to his seat and chugged the fresh beer Bryan hadn't noticed Kason set down. Bryan didn't know how to dance, but if it would have Andy holding him in his arms, he'd be willing to learn. "Maybe you should have been a stripper, Lily. You sure do know how to move." The words were out of Bryan's mouth before he could stop them.

Andy's face lit up. He leaned close so no one else could hear him. "Were you watching my ass, B?" Andy winked before signaling to Kason. Bryan knew he was blushing, but damn, Andy's warm breath was doing a number on his cock, and his attitude was giving Bryan emotional whiplash.

When Kason got a free minute, he came to their end of the bar. "You ready for another?"

"Nah, we're ready to tab out. I'm ready to take this 'un home," Andy said with a wink.

What the fuck? Bryan put some cash on the bar to cover his tab and a big tip. When they got to the truck, he asked Andy, "Are you trying to out yourself or just staking your claim on me?" He was halfway joking, but when Andy pressed him against the door of the truck, Bryan sucked in a breath.

"Maybe both, B." They had parked in the lot across from the bar, and nobody else was around as far as Bryan could see. Andy noticed Bryan scanning the area, and he looked around, too. "Nobody but us. And even if there was, I wouldn't give a shit." Andy leaned in, and just when Bryan thought he was going to kiss him, Andy said, "I've been thinking."

"Yeah?" Bryan whispered, licking his lips.

"I think we should invite Kason over for the Fourth

of July."

"What?" Bryan clenched his fists. Here he was ready to humiliate himself again, and Andy was thinking about another man. If that wasn't a kick to the nuts.

Chapter Seventeen

Andy

Andy enjoyed dancing, and the woman he was dancing with was good at the two-step. It was hard to grow up in Texas and not learn how to dance. Every time he looked at the bar, Bryan was staring at him. He might have been looking at his dance partner, but the way his eyes were hooded, Andy knew better. He'd spent all day Thursday trying to figure out what the hell happened between them that would have made Bryan run. If the man had ever jerked off, he had to have gotten spunk on his stomach. Having Andy's jizz on him shouldn't be any different. It wasn't like he'd asked him to lick it off his fingers or anything. Thinking of licking Bryan's jizz was getting Andy horny, and that wouldn't do while dancing with a woman. He would hate for her to get the wrong idea.

When Andy had grabbed Bryan's clothes to add to his own so he'd have a full load, he'd found some of his things mixed in with Bryan's. He'd also found the wet underwear Bryan had been wearing that night. The only conclusion Andy could come to was that Bryan had come in his briefs and was embarrassed. Andy thought it was hot as fuck. He couldn't come right out and ask if that's what happened without causing further embarrassment, so he decided to play things down. He would go back to his flirty ways, and if Bryan took the bait, so be it. What he didn't count on was being so turned on that he couldn't stop himself from thinking about kissing his best friend. It was something Andy had wanted to do since he met the man. But when he got close enough to do so, Andy feared the rejection and changed tactics. Besides, he wanted to get to know Kason better, and he figured the Marine wouldn't mind hiding out on the farm to stay away from the fireworks.

Seeing as they were in the parking lot of a small town, redneck bar, he didn't think pushing his luck any further was wise in both regards. Andy didn't want to get in a fight and go to jail. Not when they could go home and pursue whatever he was feeling in private. When Bryan just stared at him like he'd punched him in the gut, Andy leaned away and said, "Let's go home, B." By the hurt on Bryan's face, he'd been expecting something totally different.

On the drive home, Andy had to sit on his hands to keep from touching Bryan in ways sure to make him wreck. Andy was ready to say 'fuck it' and throw caution to the wind. If Bryan turned him down sober, it would hurt more, but at this point, Andy was ready to take that chance. When they pulled in the driveway, Bryan said, "What the fuck?" There were two strange cars parked by the house. "Was Mal having a party and didn't invite us?"

"I don't think so," Andy answered. One of the cars was an older sedan. The other was a brand-new Camaro. *One of these things doesn't belong.* When they got out of the truck, the first thing Andy noticed was the dogs weren't outside waiting on them. The second thing was the fire in the pit had dwindled down like it hadn't been tended in a while. The third thing was the alarm was already set when they entered the back door. The house was quiet except for the clicking of Moe's toenails when he met them in the kitchen. Curly was not with him.

As soon as they turned the corner, they found Curly. He was lying on the floor next to the couch. The couch where someone was snoring loudly. Andy tiptoed over, and Curly thumped his tail on the floor. As he knelt down to give the dog some loving, Andy studied the person asleep. Bryan stepped behind him, and Andy looked up at him, shrugging. Bryan gestured toward the bedroom with his head, so Andy stood and followed him down the hallway. When they got to Bryan's room, Andy stepped inside and closed the door for some privacy.

"I would be worried about a stranger sleeping on the couch, but the dogs were calm, so I guess he's a friend of Mal's, whoever he is," Bryan said.

Andy had been ready to finally taste Bryan's lips, but now he wasn't sure it was a good idea. What if the stranger got up in the middle of the night, or Mal came downstairs to check on him? "There were two cars. Who do you think the other one belongs to?" Before Bryan could answer, there was a thump upstairs followed by footsteps. "Cade," they answered together.

Now that Andy had time to think about things, he decided to go for it. What did he have to lose? Andy pushed away from the door and said, "I think we should. . ." at the same time Bryan said "I don't think we should. . ."

Andy stepped back and held up his hands. "Yeah, you're right. We shouldn't. Goodnight, B," Andy stammered and rushed to his room. That didn't go as planned. He'd been hopeful Bryan was past what happened when they played poker. Obviously, he wasn't. When Andy had grabbed Bryan's clothes to wash for him, he'd seen Addison's phone number on the nightstand. Instead of throwing it away like Andy hoped, Bryan still had it. Why couldn't it have been in his jeans where Andy could "accidentally" wash it? No, he wouldn't do that. Hell, he was the idiot who'd gotten the girl's number in the first place. No wonder Bryan was confused. Or against being with Andy. Or whatever the fuck he was. Andy needed to find a way to go get laid, or at least get a blow job so he could get his mind off fucking his best friend. Maybe he'd borrow the truck and head off to Nashville.

Instead of grabbing a toy or jacking off, Andy went to bed and kept his hands under the pillow. He forced

173

himself to think of things that would keep his dick from getting hard. Things like Patrick. That was a stupid thing to do, because it was only inviting the nightmares to join him in his sleep. He didn't know which was worse – dreams of what Patrick had done or dreams of Bryan rejecting him.

When Andy awoke from a dreamless night, he thanked anyone who was listening for that small favor. He'd all but given up on there really being a God when Patrick hurt him and his family turned their backs on him. As he opened the door to his room and headed to the bathroom, he heard someone in the kitchen opening and closing cabinets. Andy hurried and did his business in the bathroom before seeing what the commotion was. The man from the couch was obviously looking for something.

"Can I help you?" Andy asked.

The man yelped and turned around holding his chest.

"Jesus, fuck, you scared me."

"Sorry about that. If you don't mind me asking, who are you?"

"Oh, I'm Tyler."

The name sounded familiar, but Andy couldn't place it. "I'm Andy," he said. Not that it explained who either one of them were.

"Nice to meet you, Andy. You got any aspirin? My head's fucking killing me."

"Sure, but if you have a hangover, I have the perfect cure. It works better and faster than pills."

"Whatever, man, just give me something." Tyler plopped down at the table and held his head in his hands. Andy started a pot of coffee before mixing together a smoothie that was nasty but killed a hangover quickly. He should have made one for Bryan after their poker night, but he didn't think his friend would have appreciated it.

"Here, drink this. I suggest you down it all at once instead of sipping." Andy poured himself a cup of coffee and sat down next to Tyler.

Tyler sniffed the smoothie and jerked back.

"Good mornin'," Mal said as he entered the kitchen. Andy hadn't heard his boss come down the steps. When he looked down, he noticed Mal was barefooted. He'd never seen Mal without his old boots on.

"Morning," Andy replied. Tyler didn't respond verbally. He might have grunted, but he could have been trying not to throw up.

"What are you drinkin'?" Mal asked Tyler, pointing at the smoothie.

"Some nasty shit your friend here thinks is the wonder cure for what ails me."

Mal poured his own coffee and told Tyler, "If Andy said it'll work, it'll work."

"Then you drink it," Tyler whined.

"How does your wife put up with three kids?" A tall, blond god asked from the doorway. He wasn't as thick as Andy, but the man was stunning. His chest was adorned with tattoos. He had the same nautical stars Andy did and a compass in the middle of his chest. And were those… Andy almost salivated at the sight of the barbells running through his nipples. Damn, Mal had done well for himself.

When Andy caught Mal's gaze, he ducked his head and mumbled, "Sorry, Boss."

"I thought you'd be gone by now," Mal said, looking at Tyler.

"I wanted to apologize to Cade, for, you know…"

Dammit, what had he missed? Andy and Bryan should have stayed home last night instead of going to the bar. Not one to be left out of a conversation, Andy asked, "What happened?"

Cade stepped into the kitchen and leaned against the counter, crossing his arms over his perfectly sculpted chest. If he were Andy's boyfriend, Andy would want the man to put a shirt on instead of showing off the goods. Andy did his best to look at Tyler and not the man making his dick hard. When an image of Bryan flashed in his mind, Andy felt guilty.

The blond said, "Tyler had a little trouble with his zipper. And his dick. I can't remember getting so drunk I couldn't put my own junk in my pants."

"You didn't…" Andy must have heard him wrong. There's no way he would have helped the man put his dick in his pants.

"He did," Mal seethed. Oh, shit. That was the first time Andy had seen his boss anything less than calm. Normally, Mal was across the board laid back. He was nowhere near happy with Cade nor Tyler.

When Andy looked over at Tyler, the man's face couldn't have been any redder. It didn't help that he was light-complected. It made the embarrassment that much more pronounced. Andy couldn't help the laughter that burst out of his chest. He would love to have seen that little scenario play out. "Drink up, Tyler. It'll help with the nausea you're probably feeling right about now." Andy chuckled again. He knew he was being an ass, but he couldn't help himself. Taking it a step further, Andy asked, "Mal, since you have company, are you going to cook us some biscuits?" Mal had taught Andy how to make biscuits, but they weren't as good as Mal's. Andy glanced over at Tyler, who was glaring at him.

"It's Bryan's day to cook," Mal reminded him.

Seeing Bryan out of the corner of his eye, Andy groaned, "Ah, man. You know he can burn water. Why you wanna do us that way?"

"I heard that, asswipe. Next time, you can burn your own damn water," Bryan growled as he entered the kitchen. Instead of making a fool of himself and ogling the boss's boyfriend, Bryan tipped his chin in an unspoken *hello* to Cade before turning his attention to Tyler.

Tyler took a deep drink of the smoothie and let out a

belch. "Damn, that shit's nasty. And you complain about someone else's cooking?" he asked Andy.

"That's okay, limp dick. Call me and apologize later when you feel better," Andy snapped back, grinning. Bryan frowned at Andy, oblivious to why he'd be calling a virtual stranger "limp dick."

Tyler pushed back from the table. "On that note, I'm going home. Mal, I'll call you if I hear anything else." He didn't look at the others, just headed toward the back door. As Cade followed Tyler, Mal's eyes tracked them, scowling. Andy really wanted to know all the details of the night before.

As soon as Tyler was safely out the back door, Cade stopped right next to Mal, leaving no room between their bodies. He leaned over and pretended to whisper, "I really don't want burnt water. Will you please make biscuits? I'll repay you later." Cade turned to Bryan, offering an apology, "No offense."

"None taken. I'm Bryan, by the way." Bryan held out his hand to Cade, and they shook. Cade reached across the table, and he introduced himself to Andy. He didn't miss the fact that Mal was watching them closely. After they shook hands, Cade excused himself and ran up the stairs. He returned less than a minute later sporting a Motley Crüe T-shirt.

Even though it was Bryan's morning to fix breakfast, Mal agreed to cook. Andy had been exaggerating when he accused Bryan of burning water. They had been tag-teaming all the meals on Bryan's day. He was getting the hang of the simple things like bacon and sausage. Once Andy told him to cook it slow so he didn't burn it, he was getting better. Bryan was obviously a fan of Cade's band. Instead of acting like an awestruck groupie, he asked intelligent questions about the music process as well as the new band Cade had recently joined. Andy was completely out of the loop since he didn't listen to hard rock, but when Cade explained what all went into cutting an album, Andy sat up and listened. Cade Anderson was a down-to-earth man. He didn't put on airs, and he definitely didn't act like his shit didn't stink. He also didn't try to hide the fact he was completely in love with Mal. Andy doubted the two men had admitted their feelings to each other, but it was evident in the way they couldn't keep their eyes off the other how they felt. One thing Andy noticed about Cade was that he loved sweet tea. He drank almost all that was in the jug before they ever sat down to eat.

During breakfast, Mal explained to Andy and Bryan who Tyler was and why he had come to visit. "I guess I have some explainin' to do. I told you both a little about my past and how Dwight found me and my boyfriend." Mal rubbed a hand over his chest before continuing. Andy had seen the scar that cut a mean path down the middle of Mal's body. "Tyler was that boyfriend. I haven't talked to him in a long time, but last night he came to warn me." Cade reached over and took Mal's hand in his. He knew what was coming, and he was giving his man his strength. Jealousy eased its way into Andy's mind. Not over Mal and Cade specifically, but because they were there for each other.

"Tyler's been gettin' threats from Dwight. Even though he was sentenced to forty years, he's up for parole after ten. He told Tyler he's got men watchin', and if Tyler goes to the cops, the men will go after his family. Dwight gave Tyler a message for me. Said when he gets out, he's gonna finish what he started."

"Holy shit. What are you going to do?" Andy asked.

Cade answered for Mal, "We are going to be prepared. I want both of you to carry weapons at all times while you're on the farm." Cade sounded more like their boss than Mal did, and he wasn't finished. "I'd prefer if you didn't leave Mal alone until the threat is over."

Mal tried to interrupt, but Cade stopped him. "No, Babe. This shit's serious. I know you have your shotgun, but

Andy and Bryan are trained with weapons, so there's no reason they shouldn't both carry their pistols as well as rifles or shotguns. When it comes to your safety, I won't take this lightly. Dwight may be all talk, and since his threat was he was going to finish what he started, that gives us until the day of his parole to figure out a plan. I'm going to get on that today. Now, I want to see these baby cows you've been bragging about," Cade said, changing the subject.

Andy offered to do the dishes so Mal and Cade could go calf watching. If he was truthful, it was one of Andy's favorite things about his days. He'd never given much thought to birth since he'd never had an animal of his own, but seeing those little fellas being born had been like a miracle. What was even more astounding was how quickly they began walking around. Now that he was alone with Bryan, things felt pretty awkward, but they had the issue with keeping Mal safe to talk about.

"That's crazy about Mal's dad," Andy said while he filled the sink up with soapy water. He and Bryan had fallen into a routine where Andy washed and Bryan rinsed and dried. As comfortable as it usually was, something about doing it that morning hurt Andy's heart when Bryan stood next to him at the sink. Bryan wasn't relaxed, that was for certain.

"Yeah. I can't believe he's being paroled so soon. I have to admit, I'm not opposed to carrying my pistol. It'll feel natural having it on my hip again."

"I feel you," Andy said. He wished he could feel Bryan, but that ship had sailed.

"Can I ask you something?"

"Of course."

"You wanna tell me what was going on when you called Tyler 'limp dick'?" Bryan asked.

Andy burst out laughing. "You are *not* going to believe this shit. Tyler was so drunk last night he couldn't get his dick back in his pants after he took a piss. Cade did the honors."

"Cade stuck Tyler's dick back in his pants? Where was Mal?"

"From the glare he was giving them both, I would say he was standing right beside them. He was not too happy about it either."

"I imagine so. I couldn't do it."

"What, touch another man's dick?" Andy asked before he thought of how it sounded.

"No, disrespect my boyfriend that way," Bryan snapped. Now that Andy thought about it, he could see where Mal and Bryan were coming from.

They finished the dishes in silence, and once Andy had dried his hands, he headed into the living room to watch the game. Bryan sat at the other end of the couch, and Andy did his best to concentrate. It didn't work. When Mal and Cade came back inside, the game was over and another one had started. Andy had relived the previous night over and over, but every time he moved to kiss Bryan, he'd not pulled away. More than once, Andy had to put the pillow over his lap so Bryan wouldn't see the hard-on. Yeah, Andy definitely needed to go find someone to take the edge off.

When he thought about doing that, though, it scared him. The last time a stranger touched him, things hadn't gone so well. Andy would have to make sure whoever he found to help with his release was small enough he wouldn't get the upper hand if he tried.

Chapter Eighteen

Bryan

Bryan couldn't believe *the* Cade Anderson was upstairs taking a shower with Mal. Other than him tucking Tyler's dick in his jeans for him, Cade was cool. Down-to-earth. Bryan still found it crazy that a world-famous rock star had fallen in love with a small-time cowboy. And the way he'd gone all alpha when talking about keeping Mal safe had added to his awesomeness. Bryan hadn't missed the way Andy couldn't keep his eyes off Cade, but Bryan could understand why. Cade was a good-looking guy. And his nipple piercings? Those had Bryan's attention. That shit had to hurt. When he watched porn, Bryan had been intrigued with the guys licking and sucking on each other's nipples. He knew women liked it, but he had no idea men did too. Next time he jerked off, he was going to play with his and see what it felt like.

The first ballgame ended, and Bryan stood to stretch. Andy had been unusually quiet throughout the entire game. Every once in a while, he'd shift in his seat, but he never said a word. Bryan wondered if it had anything to do with their awkward moment in Bryan's bedroom. Whatever it was, Andy needed to work through it. He'd wanted to kiss Andy, but he didn't want to do it with so many people in the house. When he finally gave in to being with Andy, he wanted to do it the right way. "You want something to drink?" he asked as he headed to the kitchen.

"No, I'm good."

Bryan inhaled the aroma of something heavenly. Mal's crockpot was on the counter, and if Bryan's nose wasn't failing him, it was a roast. Bryan could go for some meat. *Are you sure about that?* Why did his inner voice have to be such a doubter? For Andy, yeah, he could do it. Bryan pulled the sweet tea out of the fridge and poured what was left in a glass. The jug was almost empty, thanks to Cade, so he found some tea bags in the pantry and put them on to boil. He was learning his way around the kitchen, thanks to Andy, and sweet tea was one thing he was able to make without screwing it up.

While waiting for the tea to steep, Cade ran down the stairs like his ass was on fire. "Everything okay?" Bryan asked on alert. By that time, Andy was standing in the kitchen, too.

"My mom's had a heart attack. I have to go. Please take care of Mal for me," Cade begged.

"You have my word," Bryan promised.

Cade hurried out the door, and Andy said, "That sucks."

"Yeah, it does. I hope she's gonna be okay. At least Cade can be there with her."

Mal came down the stairs with a funny look on his face. Instead of following Cade outside, Mal headed straight for the office. Maybe he was going to book a flight and go after his boyfriend. That's what Bryan would do if it were him.

After finishing making the tea, Bryan returned to the ballgame. After a while, Mal still hadn't come out of the office. "Do you think we should check on him?" he asked Andy. When the office door opened, they both watched Mal storm down the hall and into the kitchen. Bryan and Andy looked at each other, jumped up from the couch, and followed their boss. Andy stopped quickly, and Bryan ran into his back, grabbing onto him to keep them both from falling. It would have probably been comical if Mal wasn't on a tear about whatever was bothering him. Without a word, he filled a cooler full of beer and stormed outside.

"Holy shit!" Andy declared. "I wonder what that's about?"

"No idea, but we should probably keep an eye on him. I've not seen him drunk, but as much beer as he put in the cooler, I'd say he will be before too long."

While Andy took the lid off the crockpot and peered inside, Bryan looked out the window. Instead of going back to the ballgame, they stayed in the kitchen where they could keep an eye on Mal. He had started a fire and sat down against a hay bale, opening one beer after another. Bryan peeled potatoes and carrots, adding them to the roast. Neither one of them wanted to bother Mal, but they both wanted to know what was going on. At what point did they say "to hell with it" and intrude on his business?

Since Mal was tossing his empties in the fire, they had no idea how much he'd had to drink. When he stood to take a leak and stumbled a little, Bryan decided it was time to go talk to the man. Not getting too close, he asked, "You hungry, Mal? The roast is ready."

"Nope." Mal managed to sit back down without falling into the pit. He opened another beer, tossing the cap into the fire.

"You wanna talk about it?"

"Nope."

"Fair enough." Bryan left Mal to his misery. What the fuck could be so bad?

When it was dark and Mal still hadn't come inside, Bryan and Andy agreed to sit outside and watch him together. They'd spent the last few hours taking guesses at what could have happened from the time Cade left until Mal came downstairs and hid out in his office. They walked out the back door to Mal's drunken laughter. Bryan looked at Andy and raised his eyebrows. Could Mal have worked through his problems? When Mal began talking, Bryan saw he was on the phone.

Mal slurred as he said, "I'm goin' to call my pilot...

Oh, god… Do you know how ridiculous this all is? You and your fancy jet, and your fancy mansion in the hills, and your fancy red sports car. Ain't a goddamn thing fancy 'bout me. Just a worthless redneck you saw as a challenge. I tell you what, Rock Star – I'm gonna make you some more money. I'm gonna bust my fuckin' ass to make you enough money to buy another fancy car. I'm gonna make a go of the farm so when you finally retire from tourin', you can find a nice *fancy* man to settle down with, and I'll still be here, tendin' the cattle on *your* goddamn fancy farm. Goodbye, Cade." It took several tries, but Mal found the off button. The phone rang, but Mal tossed the phone behind him, landing at Bryan's feet.

Mal took a drink of his beer but spit it back out. He flung the bottle into the fire before pulling another out of the cooler. Bryan couldn't believe how much Mal was drinking without passing out. His phone continued to ring, but neither Bryan nor Andy answered it.

About an hour later, Mal finally slumped over on the ground. Moe and Curly whined, concerned about their master. Bryan and Andy picked him up and carried him upstairs. They pulled off his boots, but left his clothes on. Bryan glanced around the bedroom. It was quite a bit larger than his, but other than that, it wasn't anything special. Andy pulled the covers up around Mal's chest and stared down at the man. When Andy turned, he was frowning. He didn't say anything, just pointed to the hallway. Andy turned the light off and closed the door behind them.

When they got downstairs, Mal's phone rang for the nine millionth time. Of course, that was an exaggeration, but it sure felt like Cade had called that many times. As soon as it stopped ringing, Bryan's phone rang. He pulled it out of his pocket. It showed an unknown number, but he had a feeling he knew who it was.

"Hello?"

"Bryan, thank god. Is he okay?"

"If by okay you mean passed out from drinking, then yes."

"Jesus fucking Christ. I screwed up."

"You wanna talk about it?" Bryan asked as he sat on his end of the couch. He cradled the phone between his ear and shoulder while he unlaced his boots. If Cade wanted to talk, Bryan wanted to be comfortable.

"I didn't tell him I'm the one who bought the farm. I wanted to give him time to get things going really well before I sprang that on him."

"I can see where that might not have been such a good idea. What are you going to do now?"

"All I can do — give him time. Bryan, I want you to program my number into your phone. I'm not asking you to betray Mal's trust, but I want you to call if you feel there's anything I should know. Like if someone comes snooping around that doesn't belong."

"You got it. Andy and I both have Mal's back."

"Thank you. I. . . I better go. I'll talk to you later."

"Bye, Cade."

Andy was sitting on the other end of the sofa waiting to hear Cade's side of the conversation. Bryan told him that Cade owned the corporation that bought the farm. Neither one of them had seen that coming. Instead of hashing it out between themselves, they knew it was up to Mal to either forgive Cade for not telling him, or tell the man things between them were over. Bryan knew which one he'd do. Love was too fucking hard to come by. Yeah, Cade should have been honest, but keeping Mal from losing the only home he'd ever known was worth forgiving in his opinion. He and Andy said goodnight and retreated to their rooms.

Bryan closed his eyes, thinking about Mal and Cade's situation. Bryan had saved almost all the money he made in the Marines over the last couple of years. It wasn't a lot, but it was more than he'd ever had in his life. He thought paying cash for his truck had been something. He couldn't fathom having so much money you could buy a farm just because you wanted to. Andy probably knew what having that kind of money felt like growing up. It had technically been his parents' money, but Andy hadn't wanted for anything. Well, materialistic, anyway. Bryan almost felt sorry for Mal. Almost. The man had everything he could want, yet it still wasn't perfect. There was the threat of his father hanging over his head. But Cade said he was working on that, too. Bryan's father was also in prison, but at least he loved his son and didn't want him dead. Switching his thoughts to something more pleasant, like Andy's naked body, Bryan drifted off to sleep.

When Mal made his way down the stairs the next morning, Bryan and Andy were already eating breakfast.

"Mornin'."

"Good morning," they both answered at the same time.

"Whoever put me in bed, thank you." After Mal poured a cup of coffee, he sat down at the table and grabbed one of the biscuits Andy made.

"It was both of us. You were pretty out of it, Boss," Andy told him.

"I'm sorry. I shouldn't have got like that, but sometimes…" Mal didn't finish his thought.

"Your phone's on the charger. You've had several calls and texts from Cade. When you didn't answer, he called me, and I told him you were already asleep," Bryan said. "It hasn't stopped him from calling back this morning, though."

"Thanks. He and I had a disagreement." Mal shoved the rest of the biscuit in his mouth.

"I know you probably don't want my opinion, Boss, but I'm gonna give it anyway." Bryan took a sip of coffee giving Mal time to tell him to mind his own fucking business. When he sat there chewing, Bryan continued, "I know all about Cade's past. You can't be a fan of rock music and not read about 7's Mistress. The guy in the tabloids is not the same guy who comes here to visit you. The one that comes here loves you. I don't know what it is you're upset about, but he's just as upset. I finally turned the ringer off on your phone because I was tired of hearing it go off all night."

"All night?" Mal looked around the kitchen. He stood from the table and went to his phone. "Jesus," he muttered. After sliding the phone in his pocket, he said, "He bought the farm."

"So, you have an issue being in love with your boss? Like a conflict of interest thing?" Bryan asked. He didn't tell Mal they already knew this.

Mal shook his head. "No, I have an issue with the fact he bought it and didn't tell me. Why lie about it?"

"How would you have reacted if he told you the truth? You already give him shit about his money," Andy said.

"No, I don't," Mal argued.

"Boss, you do. You threw it up in his face pretty harsh last night, talking about all his fancy shit. I wasn't eavesdropping. You were yelling, and I was worried," Andy added.

"I think it's more because he lied, you know? If he'd come clean about it when he first bought it, I would've had time to digest it. He never once let on that he bought the place, or that he was responsible for the new equipment or the horses. He has been behind everything that's gone on around here and kept quiet. That's what bothers me."

"I'm not saying he was right to keep the truth from you, but I do see where he might not want you to know. Andy's right, Boss. You take issue with Cade's money, whether you admit it or not. He can't be all bad if he bought the farm to keep you from losing it. Sure, it's technically his now, but doesn't he let you make all the decisions?"

Mal nodded and rubbed his temples with his fingers.

"He's goin' on tour next month, so it won't matter anyway. He'll be on the road, and I'll be here by myself. It was a short-term thing."

Andy and Bryan cut their eyes at each other. Bryan didn't believe it was short term. Not the way they'd been with each other.

Changing the subject, Mal asked, "Do either of you know where the aspirin is?"

Bryan went to retrieve the aspirin while Andy heated up some biscuits for Mal. They had all planned on going fishing together, but Mal told them to go ahead without him. He was going to take Matilda to get an ice cream. Bryan hated to see the man so torn up, but there was nothing more he could say or do. Forgiving Cade was all up to Mal.

Hanging out at the pond alone with Andy turned out to be more fun than Bryan expected. He didn't worry about the sexual tension he'd been feeling. He forgot about all the things that had gone wrong and focused on what the two of them did best. The two of them spent the day being nothing more than friends having a good time. They laughed when one would catch a fish that wasn't big enough for bait or the other caught a big one only to lose it on the reel-in. Their plan had been to catch enough fish for supper to go with the crab legs Andy bought at the store. Bryan had never fished a day in his life and he sure as hell had never cleaned one. When he asked Andy if he knew how, his friend burst out laughing.

"Uh, no?"

After they figured out they couldn't eat the fish, they began tossing them back into the pond as soon as they caught them. Before they headed back to the house, they rode the four wheelers around checking on some of the calves.

"I can't get over how cute these little guys are," Andy gushed as they watched a baby suckle from his mother. Bryan thought they were cute too, but that wouldn't stop him from eating steak whenever possible. They had been blessed with an easy calving season so far. Mal had been a ball of nerves before the births, saying if he failed the company, he could still lose everything. Now that he knew Cade was the owner, Mal had nothing to worry about, but Mal probably didn't see it that way.

Bryan would give anything to have someone love him enough to buy his failing farm so he and his mom wouldn't be put out on their asses with nothing but their clothes. Sure, Cade probably should have been up front with Mal from the start, but Mal had grumbled several times about their differences. He probably didn't realize he did it. One breath he was singing Cade's praises, and in the next, he was saying how they shouldn't be together.

When they got back to the house, Andy set about boiling the crab legs while Bryan checked on the horses. He was enjoying learning to ride. He and Callie were becoming accustomed to each other, and she loved nipping at him. After giving equal attention to both Callie and Cochise, Bryan closed up the barn and stood outside alone. The sky was moving past twilight into dusk. He didn't think he would ever get tired of being able to see all the stars. It was one of the few things he missed about being in the Marines. When he moved back into an apartment, the lights were too bright to ever see the glory of the sparkling heavens. Bryan saw a shooting star, and like a silly little girl, he made a wish on it.

His phone vibrated in his pocket. He wasn't surprised to see it was Cade.

"Hello."

"Bryan, it's Cade. Can you talk?"

"Yeah, Mal's not here. Took his mom and Matilda out for ice cream earlier. He's probably still hanging out at Walt's."

"I've called Gerard, and he's going to look into more

189

security. I'll be going out on the road soon, and I need you to promise me you'll take care of Mal."

"You have my word, Cade. Not only is he my foreman, but he's a friend. I like the guy, and I like working here. For what it's worth, he's hurting. He misses you, and he loves you. Give him time." Bryan hoped like hell he wasn't lying to Cade. He hadn't seen a lot of couples in love, but he thought back to his parents. Even though his father committed some awful crimes, he did it out of love for Bryan's mom. Somehow, she forgave him and stood by him until the day she died. If that wasn't love, Bryan didn't know what was.

"That's all I can do at this point. Please, if anything comes up I need to know about, call me. Unless I'm in the middle of a show or rehearsal, I'll answer. No matter what time it is."

"You got it. Can't wait to see your show in Nashville later this year. I can't believe I know Cade Anderson," Bryan said, laughing. Cade was a down-to-earth man, but it was still a little surreal to be having a friendly conversation with him like they were best buds.

"Yeah, not that exciting, is it?" Cade laughed, too, but Bryan could tell Mal wasn't the only one hurting.

"I don't know about that. I bet I've seen a side of you a lot of people don't get the chance to." The 'standing in the kitchen with no shirt on staring lovingly at your boyfriend' side."

"You're right there, but don't go letting people know I'm not always the cool rock star. If you want, I'll get you backstage passes. That way you can hang out side stage during the show."

"Hell yeah! Thanks, Cade. And don't worry about Mal. I'll take care of him until you two are back together."

"Thanks. I'll talk to you later."

"Later." Bryan disconnected and once again turned his gaze skyward. Why did shit have to be so complicated?

Speaking of complicated, Andy's silhouette crossed the kitchen window. Bryan was figuring out the cattle and the horses. Now, if he could only figure out his best friend.

Chapter Nineteen

Andy

As well as things had been going, they slowly turned to shit. Ever since Mal found out Cade owned the farm, their boss became a surly ass. They had put off building the deck because neither Andy nor Bryan wanted to finish it only to have Mal say it wasn't done properly. One of the rare occasions he was civil was when they were sitting around the fire on the Fourth. Kason had declined their offer to join them, saying he was fine with fireworks. He was on shift at the bar, anyway. They still cooked hamburgers on the grill and had a bonfire afterwards.

After he lost his temper over the tractor needing repaired, Mal retreated to his office where he had been staying more often than not, leaving Andy and Bryan to tend the cattle. It wasn't that Andy didn't like his job, because he did. With Mal staying closed up, Andy and Bryan divided and conquered the outside chores. Alone. When they set out on the horses, they went their separate ways and didn't see each other until they were back at the end of the day.

This should have made their friendship stronger, but to Andy, it felt as if they were slowly drifting apart. Bryan had called Addison and taken her on a couple of dates. He wouldn't talk about it afterwards, so Andy didn't know if the date hadn't gone well, or if Bryan didn't want to rub it in Andy's face. Neither one was acceptable as far as Andy was concerned. They should be able to talk to each other. All Andy knew was, after the second one, Bryan had come home with some weights in the back of the truck. He'd put them in one of the spare stalls and spent a good amount of time burning energy.

Bryan had also installed a chin-up bar in the barn, and Andy often found Bryan doing pull-ups when he was supposed to have gone to bed. One night, Andy had been restless and decided to go talk to the horses. The light in the barn was already on, and when he looked through the open door, he'd about jizzed in his jeans. Bryan was hanging by his knees doing upside down sit-ups without a shirt on. The flexing of his sweat-glistening muscles was more than Andy could handle, so he did the only thing he could – he returned to his bedroom and jacked off.

The two of them continued to cook together on Bryan's night, and he was actually getting pretty good. Granted, it wasn't gourmet, but it was more than edible. They were preparing supper when Mal made one of his rare appearances. "What's for supper?" he asked.

"Chicken pot pie," Bryan answered.

Bryan was rolling out homemade pie crust Andy had mixed up. They didn't discuss who was going to do what. They naturally had an unspoken routine. They worked well together, and it did crazy things to Andy's heart. He wanted their friendship back on track, but more than that, he wanted something more. Something Bryan wasn't willing to give him.

"Say, do you know when Cade's band is comin' through Nashville?" Mal asked. Since Andy had his back to his boss, he didn't know which one of them he was asking. Andy talked to Cade on occasion, but Bryan was the one the man reached out to most often. They talked at least every other day.

Bryan halted the rolling pin and turned toward Mal. "Yeah, you wanna go with?"

"You're goin'?" Mal asked almost accusingly. He shouldn't be surprised, though. Bryan was a fan of Cade's music. The little bit of time they spent together that one morning had been filled with talk of albums and touring.

"Yeah, Cade's getting me a backstage pass. I'm sure he'd get you one, too."

"I'd appreciate it if you'd talk to him about it."

"Why don't you ask him yourself, Boss? I know he'd rather talk to you than me."

"You talk to Cade a lot?"

"Not a lot," Bryan fudged. If Mal knew how much they talked, he would probably toss Bryan out. Andy picked up the rolling pin and turned his back on Mal. This was not a conversation conducive to keeping their jobs. Jealousy was a righteous bitch.

"And what about you, Andy? You talk to Cade, too?"

"Not a lot," he said, keeping his back to Mal. When he heard an almost imperceptible growl, he knew he had to do damage control. "Boss, Cade isn't my type."

"Oh, really? And what is your type?" Mal grumbled

"I like twinks," he lied. There was no way Andy could admit that he preferred his men to be built like Bryan. Even though he had been hurt, that was because he was much smaller at the time and had trusted his boyfriend to protect him. His older, larger, stronger boyfriend. There was nothing sexier to him than someone who took great care of their body. Someone like Bryan.

"What the fuck's a Twinkie?" Mal asked. If their conversation wasn't so serious, Andy would have laughed. Gay men had so many names for the different types of bodies, but Mal wasn't out and proud. He didn't go to gay clubs. Hell, he probably didn't watch gay porn if he didn't know what a twink was.

"Even I know this one," Bryan said. "It's a man who looks young, almost like a boy still." The look he was giving Andy wasn't a friendly one.

"Why would you want a boy when you can have a big man to toss you around and manhandle you?" Andy looked at Bryan at the thought of him tossing Andy around. He grinned to hide his true feelings as well as hoping to remove the scowl from his friend's face.

Mal huffed, "Oh, shut up. Seriously, why would you want a boy?"

Dammit. Now Andy had to continue the lie. He needed to make it sound convincing. "I don't want a boy per se, but I like my men a little less hairy and masculine looking. I also like to be in control. I like to do the manhandling, if you get my drift." While he wouldn't mind handling Bryan, Andy didn't know if he would be willing to hand over control in the bedroom to his best friend. He knew in his heart Bryan would never hurt him, but the thought of having someone that large behind him scared the shit out of him.

Mal must have accepted his explanation, because he changed the subject. "We've got two new guys startin' tomorrow. They're gonna be watchin' over the place since my fuckhead father is up for parole next week."

"Good," Bryan said over his shoulder while he shredded the chicken. "Andy and I do our best to watch things, but eleven hundred acres is a lot of land to cover. If Dwight decides to come after you, it's gonna take more than the two of us to watch your six."

"Mr. Matheson sent me pictures of the men so we know what they look like. Their names are Cole and Toby. They're former Marines like you."

When Andy got a look at the photos, he whistled. "Holy shit, they're hot." The angry look Bryan flashed him confused Andy. Was he jealous?

Mal frowned and asked, "I thought you liked 'em little?"

Oh fuck. That right there was why lying was bad. You had to continue piling shit on top of shit. Eventually you'd step in the shit when it got too deep. "I do, but I can appreciate a fine piece of man when I see one, and those two are finer than frog hair."

Mal laughed, and Bryan rolled his eyes. "As long as you keep the frog hair outta my pie, I'll be happy. I'm gonna go for a drive. I'll be back in a bit." With that, Mal left them alone. Again.

Cole and Toby arrived the next morning. Cole was built a lot like Mal – tall and muscular, but in a lean way. He would be one of those sneaky bastards who could take you down with his quickness. His dark hair and eyes gave him a mysterious air. Toby was even more massive than Andy was. They had the same coloring, but where Andy's blond hair was spiky and styled, Toby's was still military perfection. You could balance a plate on his flat top. His eyes were a darker blue than Andy's, but they were more haunted, if that was possible. This man had seen things even Andy hadn't. As tough as Toby appeared, his deep voice was friendly.

After a while, Mal left the four Marines to talk amongst themselves. He said he trusted them to do whatever it was they needed to do to look after things. After chatting briefly about their time served, talk turned serious. Cole took point and asked Andy and Bryan to show them around the farm. It took most of the day, but Cole came up with a game plan that allowed for the most coverage. Until Dwight got out of prison, the four of them would take a quadrant to watch over during the day. Cole and Toby agreed to split the night shift, just in case. Andy and Bryan both offered to take turns, but Cole insisted he and Toby could handle it. Besides, they needed to be well-rested to continue doing their day job well.

On the morning of August 3rd, Mr. Matheson called with the news that Dwight's parole hearing was the following day. He had come up with a plan, and he needed Cole and Toby to accompany him to the prison. The four men spent the day going over the best way to keep Mal safe in case things went awry. Mal wouldn't like being babysat, but his safety was more important than his attitude. Curing the day, Mal was still sulking about this thing with Cade, but when it came time for supper, he joined the four Marines and actually participated in their conversations. The five of them were more like a brotherhood than boss and employees. Andy enjoyed having the other two men around. It gave him something to focus on other than his best friend.

Cole and Toby left before daylight to meet Mr. Matheson at the prison. They didn't elaborate on the plan, but Andy figured if Cade was behind it, he was going to pay off Dwight Wilson to stay away from his son. That or kill the bastard. Toby had broken down his rifle, cleaned it, and put it back together faster than anyone Andy had ever seen. The man and his weapon were one. Andy didn't want to imagine being a sniper. Being in charge of killing people with little to no intel had to be a mind fuck. He knew from those snipers in his platoon it took a special kind of mentality to do what they did.

Cole had insisted Mal remain in the house where Andy and Bryan would be able to keep him safest. He hadn't complained about it, but he did shut himself in his office. Andy had a feeling he was doing something other than paperwork, but who was he to question his boss? He and Bryan both had tried countless times to get Mal to talk to Cade and try to work things out. Andy had tried making Mal mad and jealous by telling him if he didn't want Cade, Andy would be more than happy to take him off his hands. That riled Mal up, but as far as Andy knew, Mal still hadn't called Cade.

A few hours later when Mal got a call from Mr. Matheson, who they now knew was Cade's uncle, the look on his face offered no clue as to how things went when Gerard and the two bodyguards met with Mal's dad. His side of the conversation consisted of a lot of uh huhs and yeahs. Before he hung up, Mal said, "Why. . . Why would he do that?" He listened for a few more seconds then disconnected the call. Mal looked at them and, with no emotion in his voice, said, "It's over. Gerard convinced my father to leave town and never come back."

Andy and Bryan both gave loud cheers congratulating Mal, but he seemed to be in a daze.

"We should go celebrate!" Andy suggested, thinking that no longer having his life threatened should make Mal happy.

"We'll do that tonight. Right now, I want to tell Ma the news."

Andy knew where he wanted to go. He had been planning on testing a theory or two, and he knew just how to do it. He was going to suggest they go to the gay club in Nashville, and if things went as planned, Mal would realize how much he missed Cade, and Andy would know how Bryan really felt, one way or the other. When Mal returned, he gave them a little more detail about the "deal" Gerard had made with Dwight. He also informed them Toby was the one driving Dwight to Florida. Now that Mal's life was no longer in danger, Cole and Toby wouldn't be hanging around.

Andy suggested going to Primus, and Mal reluctantly agreed. They had to tell Bryan what kind of club it was, but he also agreed, saying he was secure in his manhood. Andy shut himself in the bathroom to get dressed. It took Bryan about ten minutes total to shower, shave, and dress. Andy? He could linger an hour if he set his mind to it. He wanted his hair to be perfect. He wanted everything to be perfect. Now that he'd taken a shower and was almost ready to go, he felt like he was going to throw up. He didn't know if he could go through with his plan to find out Bryan's feelings once and for all.

Andy closed the toilet lid and sat down, sticking his head between his knees. It took several minutes, but he finally felt well enough to leave. The three men piled into the cab of Mal's truck and headed toward Nashville. Mal had the radio tuned to a rock station, and since it was really his night to celebrate, Andy didn't mind. He'd started listening to some of Cade's music so he wouldn't feel left out if Cade came back one day. Andy prayed tonight proved to Mal he wanted Cade in his life. Cade was a good man who loved Mal with everything he had, even if everything included a shit ton of money.

Primus wasn't as busy as Andy figured it would be, but it was a weeknight, and it was relatively early. According to Mal, who admitted to coming there in the past, the place didn't start getting packed until around ten or eleven. They should have gone to eat beforehand, but they'd agreed to drinks first. Since they were there before nine, there was no cover charge. They walked in after showing their IDs and found a high-top table close to the dance floor. It was the perfect arrangement for what Andy had in mind.

Andy ordered a whiskey and soda. He downed it before leaving the bar and ordered a second one he took back to the table with Mal's and Bryan's beers. Andy sipped his drink while looking for the perfect dance partner. "Mal, see anybody you want to... dance with?" Mal frowned at him, but Bryan glared. "I mean, if you aren't with Cade anymore, you can at least dance. Nobody says you have to take a trip to the men's room."

"Primus is a little classier than havin' to get blown in the bathroom. There are private alcoves along the back hallway where you can duck in for a little privacy."

"Good to know. See anyone who strikes your fancy?" That little tidbit of information worked nicely with his plan.

Mal took a swig of beer and glanced around the room at the men who were trickling in. There were all kinds to choose from, including several twinks Andy hoped to get up close and sweaty with the dance floor. When Mal stopped looking around, Andy pushed a little more. "Come on, Boss. This is your night to celebrate. If this isn't getting it for you, we can go somewhere else."

"No, I'm good here."

Andy nodded and turned away before Bryan came across the table. Andy didn't want Mal to hook up, but Bryan didn't know that. He was a romantic at heart, and he knew Mal and Cade belonged together. Maybe the first part of his plan wasn't working, but he wasn't going to give up on the second part.

The music was some techno junk that Andy didn't care for, but he was in a club, and he was ready to shake his ass. He noticed one of the twinks staring his way. When he made eye contact, Andy winked at the man. He used the term man loosely. The guy had to barely be legal. He smiled even larger and made his way toward Andy. Andy remained seated and let the guy come to him. He spread his legs, and the guy stepped between them, getting much more intimate than Andy would have liked, but it was all part of the plan.

"Hey, Sugar. You wanna dance?" Twink asked, running his finger down Andy's chest beneath his shirt.

"Sure." Andy downed his drink and let the guy grab his hand. When the man wanted to wade deeper into the sea of bodies, Andy pulled back. "This is far enough." Twink must have liked Andy's authoritative tone, because he practically swooned. The music was fast, and the man was good with his body. He didn't hesitate to shove his tight ass into Andy's crotch. Andy put his hands on the guy's hips and ground against him, praying his dick would get on board with what was happening. Andy closed his eyes and imagined it was Bryan he was grinding against, and his erection came to life. Twink had to think it was for him.

With all the bodies swarming around them, it was hard to remain close to the edge of the floor, but when Andy turned, the look on Bryan's face said Andy's plan was working. Someone approached the table. Bryan scowled, and Mal said something to the man, who walked off alone. The same guy came back to the table for Mal, and on the third try, Bryan got in the man's face. Damn, that was hot. Now, to drive the final nail home. Andy told his dance partner he was going to find the restroom and wiggled his eyebrows for good measure. He wasn't stupid enough to ask the man for a blowjob and then turn him down once they were out of Bryan's sight. He didn't want to be accused of being a cock tease even if that's exactly what he was.

When he passed by the table, Mal gave him a smirk. Andy smiled, but he didn't look at Bryan. That would have also been too cruel. Andy pushed open the door to the restroom and stepped up to the trough with a couple of other men. When his dick was soft enough to get it out of his jeans without being painful, Andy took a leak, making sure to keep his eyes on his own dick. The bathroom door opened, and his dance partner stepped inside. He leaned against the wall waiting for Andy to finish his business. Andy grinned, but didn't speak, escorting the man out into the hallway. "I'm Stefano. What's your name?" Stefano? Andy doubted that was the kid's real name. Probably something boring like Steve.

"I don't think we should exchange names. I only wanted to dance tonight, not hook-up with anyone."

"You sure could have fooled me the way you rubbed your fat cock all over my ass," Stefano purred, running his finger down Andy's chest. He kept going lower, but Andy grabbed his hand before the guy could grab his dick.

"You're a hot guy, what can I say? You sure did turn me on, Stefano." There was no need in making the guy feel like shit just because Andy had used him.

"Then let me blow you. I can suck a baseball through a tailpipe."

Andy laughed. "I'm sure you can. Maybe next time?"

Stefano pouted then smiled. "If you promise there'll

be a next time."

Andy hated lying almost as much as cheating, but for the sake of his mission, he made an exception. "There'll be a next time." Stefano smiled and returned to the bathroom, leaving Andy to walk back to the table alone. He put on his best "I just got blown" smile and yelled, "I can die happy now." Bryan and Mal still had beer, and Andy wasn't going to rush them.

Bryan wouldn't look at him, but Mal joked, "You ready to go find something to eat besides Twinkies?"

"Yeah, I'm ready."

Chapter Twenty

Bryan

When Bryan got the message that Andy only wanted to be friends, he figured he didn't have anything to lose by calling Addison and asking her out. When he picked her up, her mother was working in the yard. Yep, she lived with her parents. There was nothing wrong with that, but if they were going to see each other, they would have to get creative in being alone. The first date, however, didn't go exactly as Bryan planned.

Once Addison was in the truck, she asked if they could go to a restaurant in the next town over. Bryan didn't think too much about it since Franklin was larger than Arlo and had more places to choose from. He tried to hold her hand as they were walking inside, but she pulled away. He chalked that up to her being shy. When they were seated and she started asking questions about Andy, he began seeing the truth of why she'd agreed to the date. She didn't want Bryan; she'd only agreed to go out with him so she could get the scoop on his best friend. It had pissed him off so much, he threw Andy under the bus and told Addison Andy was gay. That conversation hadn't gone well, either.

"So, the guy you were with at the bank... Andy?"

"What about him?"

"Well, it just surprised me when you called instead of him."

"Did he not tell you he was getting your number for me?"

"Yeah, but I thought he was being shy." Addison's whole demeanor changed when she mentioned Andy. He knew he shouldn't, but he told Addison the truth.

"He's not shy; he's gay."

"But wasn't he a soldier, too?"

"No, he's a Marine."

"He's still enlisted?"

"No, but once a Marine, always a Marine."

"But he's so big and muscular."

Bryan was getting pissed. "You think gay men have to be what? Small? Feminine? Weak? Let me tell you something about being gay. It takes a strong man or woman to be true to their nature. There are too many bigots in the world putting people down just because they don't fit what society sees as normal. Gay people who are out and proud are some of the most courageous people there are."

"I didn't mean. . . Never mind. I can see I hit a sore spot with you. It's just unusual to see a gay man somewhere like Arlo."

The date had gone downhill afterwards. He drove her home and walked her to the door, not bothering to thank her for a nice evening. Bryan did his best not to tell lies. When he arrived at the farm, Andy was waiting for him. Bryan hadn't been in the mood to talk about his failed date or to tell Andy he was the one Addison had been interested in, so he mumbled hello and kept going to his bedroom. It was still early for a Saturday night, but Bryan preferred hiding out the rest of the night instead of facing Andy.

Things after that were strained. Mal was being a complete ass. Andy was acting like there had never been any sexual tension between the two of them. He even went as far as telling Mal he preferred twinks over someone like Bryan. His friend's message was loud and fucking clear, so Bryan did the only thing he could think of to counter Andy's declaration. He went on another date. At least that's what he told Andy. In truth, Bryan rode around the back roads listening to the radio until he decided to find another way to expel his pent-up aggression. He found the local gym, and even though he preferred to work out at the farm, he decided to at least check the place out. Once he got inside, Bryan turned around and left. The good old boys of Arlo had made it clear his kind wasn't welcomed.

Bryan got back in his truck and drove to Franklin. Being quite a bit larger than Arlo, he found a sporting goods store and bought a basic weight set he could put in the barn. When he got back, Andy looked at him funny but didn't mention anything about his date. Instead, he helped Bryan get the weights out of the truck and set them up in an empty stall. The one good thing about Mal being in a shitty mood because of Cade was that Andy and Bryan split the duties on the farm. They still had breakfast together most mornings, but after that they went their separate ways. Andy was back to his jovial self, and Bryan had retreated into his quiet.

Bryan also installed a bar over the door where he could do pull-ups. He spent as much spare time working out as he could, getting his body back to where it had been when he arrived on the farm. All the home-cooked meals had softened him up a bit. Working out also wore him out, and he didn't have the energy for nightly jerkoff sessions.

When Cole and Toby arrived, everything but the threat to Mal's life was all but forgotten. With that threat cloaking the farm, everyone's priorities changed. Bryan was happy to have something else to focus on other than Andy or Addison. On the day of Dwight's parole hearing, Cole and Toby left early to accompany Cade's uncle to the prison. Mal's father agreed the amount of money being offered was worth more than finding his son and finishing the job he started ten years before. Toby and his sniper rifle might have added to the incentive.

Mal and his mother were safe. Mal still wasn't convinced he should let Cade back into his life, but Bryan could see his boss softening each time Bryan mentioned Cade's name. Bryan might not have someone in his life to love, but he wanted Mal and Cade together. He knew Cade was about ready to give up on Mal, and Bryan needed to help push them in the right direction. When Andy suggested they go to Primus to celebrate, Bryan had been furious. Being around other gay men was the last thing Mal needed, but when Mal agreed to going, Bryan went along with the plan.

When they arrived at Primus, Mal didn't seem interested in being there, so Bryan took it as a good sign. When the same man hit on Mal three times, Bryan lost his cool. He point-blank asked Mal if he had broken up with Cade, and Mal said he hadn't. Bryan was still hopeful, at least for his boss. When Andy all but fucked a twink on the dance floor, Bryan almost lost his grip on his jealousy. Knowing Andy didn't want him was one thing, but seeing him blatantly rub it in his face was something else. And when he took the twink to the back for a blowjob? Bryan was ready to kill someone, namely a kid who probably never shaved a day in his life.

Afterwards, they left the club and went in search of something to eat. When neither Bryan nor Andy would make a decision, Mal chose Hooters. It was the safest place for two gay guys to go, and Bryan figured Mal had done it for his benefit. None of them enjoyed their supper if the amount of food left on their plates was any indication.

When Mal got up to go to the bathroom, Bryan lit into Andy. "What the fuck was that back there at the club? I thought you were on Mal and Cade's side! Why would you try to get Mal to cheat on Cade?"

Andy leaned over and narrowed his eyes. "You idiot, I wasn't. I wanted to fucking test him. Show him he had something so much better waiting on him than some fucking piece of meat at a gay bar."

Bryan wanted to yell back that Andy also had something better waiting. He hadn't told Andy how he felt, so how would he know? Fuck! What if he let down his guard and Andy didn't want to be with him? Could he handle the rejection again? Mal returned to the table, and they decided they'd all had enough excitement for one day.

The ride home was tense. Bryan was ready to jump out of the truck and take a taxi back to Arlo. Sitting next to Andy, being able to smell a strange cologne on his skin, was torture. Knowing Andy had either had his mouth on that kid's dick or vice versa was on a constant loop in his brain. As soon as Mal parked the truck in the driveway, Bryan threw open the door and stalked into the barn. He needed to hit something. Since he didn't have a punching bag, he did the next best thing. Bryan ripped his shirt off and began working out.

When his arms would no longer support the weight he was lifting, Bryan dropped the bar with a loud clang and stood from the bench. He was still so fucking angry. He threw his head back and yelled at the top of his lungs, fisting his hands at his sides. When he turned to make his way to the pull-up bar, he saw Andy standing at the stall doors petting both horses. Bryan's chest was heaving, and while he should have been embarrassed that Andy saw his outburst, he was even more pissed.

"Haven't you tormented me enough for one night?" Andy crossed his arms over his massive chest. "How did *I* torment *you*?" Andy's face was furious. Why the fuck was he mad?

"You all but fucked that guy on the dance floor. Then you disappeared so you could suck his dick!"

"And what business is that of yours? You've been going out on dates, but I'm not allowed to have one night of fun? Fuck you, Bryan."

Bryan strode to where Andy was standing, leaving little room between them. "Addison didn't want me. She fucking wanted you! She was so goddamn embarrassed to be seen with me, she had me take her to Franklin where I wouldn't stick out like the mutt I am!"

Andy closed the distance and bumped Bryan with his chest. "So what? Because you didn't get any action, I'm not allowed? I'm supposed to continue to jack off every night while I think about —"

Bryan didn't let Andy finish. If he was thinking about someone besides Bryan, it would kill him. He grabbed Andy behind the neck and slammed their mouths together. It wasn't soft or filled with love like Bryan dreamed it would be. It was painful when his teeth cut into the back of his lips. He didn't give a shit. Andy grabbed Bryan's biceps and pushed him away.

Bryan touched his lips to see if he was bleeding. His mouth wasn't, but his heart was. Now he knew. He'd taken the chance and it backfired. Andy was fuming. When Andy's hand came toward Bryan, he braced for Andy to hit him. Andy growled, "It's about goddamn time." Instead of punching him, Andy pulled Bryan forward. Andy's kiss was forceful but much less painful than Bryan's had been. Andy slid his tongue over Bryan's lips, and Bryan opened for him. As soon as Andy's tongue touched his own, Bryan thought he was going to cry. Andy was dominating his senses to the point Bryan couldn't think. Their tongues swirled together as naturally as if they'd kissed each other hundreds of times. Andy tasted like whiskey and hot wing sauce. Bryan wanted to know what Andy tasted like every moment of the day. Coffee and biscuits. Fried chicken and sweet tea. Steak and beer. Bryan wanted to know what Andy tasted like when he came. He had tasted his own spunk out of curiosity, and now he wanted to taste his best friend's.

Andy slid his free hand around Bryan's back and pulled their bodies together. Andy's erection was hard against Bryan's, and he was afraid if they didn't stop, he'd embarrass himself all over again.

"Andy, stop," he begged, breaking the kiss.

"You have got to fucking be shitting me right now!"

"No, I'm not saying I don't want this. I do. God knows I want this more than I want my next breath. I just don't want to come in my pants again."

"What's wrong with that?" Andy asked, frowning.

"What's wrong. . .? It's fucking embarrassing."

"Is that why you ran off? You were embarrassed?"

"Well, yeah."

"God, B. I thought you freaked out because I shot jizz on your stomach."

Bryan mentally slapped himself. He was such a fool. "No. That was hot."

Andy's eyes darkened, and he licked his lips. "Don't you fucking move," he commanded. Bryan froze in place, obeying Andy's directive. Dominant Andy was fucking sexy. Andy took his time gazing at Bryan's body. When his eyes landed on Bryan's hard dick, Andy reached out and unbuttoned Bryan's jeans before lowering the zipper, allowing his fingers to caress Bryan's length as he did. Bryan couldn't help the moan that escaped his throat.

"I'm not going to last if you touch me," Bryan admitted.

"I'm counting on it." Andy dropped to his knees, and Bryan tensed. Not because he wasn't ready for what was going to happen next, but his mind flashed back to earlier in Primus. Andy looked up at him, and as he pulled Bryan's jeans and briefs down his thighs, he said, "Nothing happened. Earlier tonight? I went to the bathroom alone and took a piss. I turned the guy down and came back to the table." Andy fisted Bryan's cock. "I was trying to make you jealous, B." Andy slid his tongue across the leaking tip of Bryan's throbbing head. Keeping his eyes on Bryan, he said, "I've wanted you since the first day we met." He ran his tongue from the base of Bryan's cock up the vein that stopped just below the tip. "I've jacked off to thoughts of this almost every night." Andy sucked the head into his mouth, mimicking kissing him earlier. Bryan drew in a sharp breath at the sensation. "I've fucked myself with toys pretending it was you doing the fucking." With that, he swallowed Bryan's cock down as far as he could, gagging a little before pulling off.

Bryan had been on the receiving end of a couple of blowjobs. He'd enjoyed having his dick sucked, and even though the girls had been somewhat enthusiastic, they were nowhere near as skilled as Andy was. His mouth was hot and his hand firm. Andy pulled on Bryan's balls with just enough force to be both pleasurable and painful. Bryan couldn't tear his eyes away from the sight of his cock sliding in and out of Andy's mouth. That alone was enough to make him come.

Andy kept his hand stroking up and down the length while he said, "I want you to come in my mouth, B. I want to see if my imagination is anywhere close to how good you really taste." All Bryan could do was nod. And groan. Andy took him all the way down again and began bobbing his head up and down. Bryan grabbed hold of Andy's hair, pulling tighter than he probably should. Andy moaned around Bryan's hard-on, so Bryan pulled again. Andy moaned again, and the vibration shot up Bryan's dick. He had been right when he said he wasn't going to last, but Andy's mouth felt too good to hold back.

"Fuck, I can't… I'm gonna…" Bryan squeezed his eyes shut as his balls tightened and he shot spirt after spirt of come into Andy's mouth. His hands held Andy in place so he could thrust into his mouth harder. "Jesus Christ." When the last aftershock subsided, Bryan opened his eyes. Andy was grinning and licking his lips. He had a drop of Bryan's jizz at the corner of his mouth, and it was the hottest thing Bryan had ever seen next to Andy fucking his ass with a toy. Bryan dropped to his knees, not caring how bad it hurt. He licked the corner of Andy's lips, tasting his own spunk. It wasn't enough. Bryan angled his head, eagerly sucking Andy's tongue into his mouth so he could taste the two of them mixed together.

Bryan was so turned on, his dick was already getting

hard again, and Andy had to be in pain by now. He tried to deepen the kiss, but Andy pulled back. "Was that okay?" Andy asked, his face full of worry.

"Okay? God, Lily, that was beyond amazing," Bryan whispered. "I don't want to think about how you got so good at it." And he didn't. Bryan didn't want to know about anyone who had come before him. No pun intended.

Andy seemed to accept his answer. He leaned back in, bringing their lips together once again. This time it wasn't as urgent or needy. It was softer. Sweeter. The kiss was filled with so much emotion that the backs of Bryan's eyes started to burn. It had been a long time since Bryan had cried, and he didn't want to then. This was a tender moment, and he didn't want to ruin it with stupid tears.

"I've never given a blowjob before," Andy admitted when they came up for air, his eyes imploring Bryan to believe him.

"Could've fooled me." Bryan's heart skipped a happy beat knowing he was Andy's first. Andy would be his first blowjob. His first at a lot of things if things continued as he hoped they would. His mind was still muddled at the thought of being gay, but he decided to not worry about the label and focus on his feelings. Holding Andy, kissing him, being with his best friend intimately felt right. Andy turned him on, and Bryan wanted to go with whatever was happening with them and find out how far they could go together.

"I've thought about it enough, though." Andy stood and helped Bryan to his feet. Bryan pulled his jeans up, tucking his dick in.

"Then I guess you'll be okay with it being my first time, too." Bryan reached for Andy's button, but Andy pulled his hands away. "You don't want me to?"

"Of course I do, but I think we need to talk first."

"Okay," Bryan agreed, even if he was scared to talk. He was still confused over his feelings for Andy and why

Andy pushed him away if he truly wanted him. "Can I ask you something?"

"Anything," Andy said, reaching for Bryan's hand. He led him over to a stack of hay bales and pulled him down beside him.

"Why did you push me away that night?"

"What night?" Andy asked, frowning.

"The night I . . . the night we played poker. I came to your room when you were crying. Was it because you didn't want me to see you so upset?"

"B, I have no idea what you're talking about. The last thing I remember is throwing up outside after you disappeared to your room."

"I had already gone to bed, but I had to take a piss. When I came out of the bathroom I heard you crying. When I went to you, you were telling me to get off you and to please stop."

Andy turned his face away and propped his elbows on his thighs. "I was having a nightmare."

"About me?"

"What? Of course not. Like I told you, I've wanted you since day one. No, my nightmares are always about…"

Bryan slid his hand underneath Andy's shirt, skimming his fingers up his back. When he touched each scar and raised his eyebrows, Andy nodded but didn't explain what happened that day with his ex-boyfriend. "Before I tell you about those, I need to ask you… are you sure, you know, about this? About us?" Andy turned his head so he was looking at Bryan.

"Yeah, I'm sure. I don't understand it, but I want you."

"Why? I mean, you're straight, so why do you want me?" Andy was frowning, and there was a mist covering his blue eyes. "Is it because I'm convenient?"

Bryan wanted to pull Andy to him. Wrap him so tight he never doubted the sincerity of how Bryan felt.

Instead, he propped himself on his forearms so he was mimicking Andy. He at least wanted to be face to face when he explained it. Or tried to, anyway. "When I was in the Corps, I saw guys together, and it would get me hard. I attributed it to the fact I hadn't been laid in years and was horny. I'd go to jack off and try to think of one of the girls I'd been with back home. My dick wouldn't stay hard. I'd remember the guys sucking each other, and my dick would perk back up. Maybe I've been gay my whole life and didn't realize it. I was so busy working and taking care of my family that I didn't have time to date. The few girls I fucked had hit on me; I never sought them out. I thought it was what young guys were supposed to do, so I went along with it, but I didn't really enjoy it.

"I never once asked a girl out. I thought since the sex I had back then wasn't very satisfying, it would only be exciting if I was with the one person I was meant to spend my life with. The few times I had sex, the girl did the pursuing, and I didn't turn them down. The first time I saw you without a shirt on, my dick got so hard I thought I was going to pass out. You were so fucking sexy, and it scared the shit out of me. I wasn't supposed to want you that way. I did my best to ignore it, but then I heard you... I went to the bathroom and, well, your door doesn't latch. I heard you jacking off, so I listened. I'm sorry. I know that was invading your private time, but I couldn't move. Then I thought I heard you call my name, so I went to the bathroom to give my dick some relief. I thought of Laurel, and when my dick started going soft, I thought about you. My dick hardened, and I came because I was thinking about you."

"I really need to fix that door," Andy deadpanned.

"I know I'm —"

Andy didn't let him finish. He leaned over and pressed their lips together. When he pulled back, he asked, "Is that the only time you've spied on me?" Andy wiggled his eyebrows, and Bryan moaned.

"Honestly?" Bryan asked. When Andy nodded, Bryan felt the heat rushing up his neck and onto his cheeks. He hated lying, but did he really want Andy to know?

"Why, Mr. Moore, I didn't realize you were such a voyeur. Tell me, what did you see?" Instead of Andy being angry, his eyes hooded with lust. Bryan's dick jumped in his jeans at the thought of the toy breaching Andy's hole.

"You had a toy... You were... oh, God. It was so fucking hot, Lily. You were fucking yourself with a dildo. I didn't understand why, but I wanted to be on the bed behind you, shoving my cock in your tight hole."

Andy went from turned on to tense. He stood and strode over to the horses, petting Callie. Bryan had been around Andy enough to know that it was one of his anxiety attack deterrents. Bryan couldn't stand the haunted look on his friend's face. He went to him but didn't touch him. "I'm sorry. I assumed since you like toys and said you imagined it was me fucking you that you would be okay with me... We can..." Bryan stopped talking when Andy met his eyes.

Andy whispered, "I need to tell you a story. When I'm done, you'll probably change your mind about wanting to be with me."

Chapter Twenty-One

Andy

Andy walked over to where Bryan had ripped his shirt off and picked it up. "Can you put this on, please? You distract me enough as it is without being half-dressed." Bryan took the shirt from him, allowing their fingers to touch. As much as Andy wanted to grab hold of Bryan's hand, he knew in his heart he had to tell his best friend the truth of his past. The whole truth. He was excited at the thought of being with Bryan on an intimate level. He was also scared to death. This is what he'd been wanting ever since he met his fellow Marine. This is what he'd been waiting for ever since he figured out he was gay. That one person to complete him. Telling Bryan the truth could go either way, but he had a right to know what kind of person Andy was.

They had been together enough that Andy knew Bryan's body language. Bryan was normally quiet, but now he was tense as he waited on Andy to talk. Bryan slid his shirt over his shoulders. The buttons were gone, so the shirt gaped open, showing off his massive chest. It would have to do.

After Andy told Bryan the truth about Patrick, he might walk away and never give them a chance at a relationship. Andy couldn't stand the thought of never having another taste of Bryan, so he closed the distance between them, wrapped his arms around Bryan's shoulders, and poured his love into Bryan's mouth through a sweet, sensual kiss.

Andy had no doubt what he felt for Bryan was love.

What had started out as friendship had grown into something so much stronger. Andy's every waking thought was about his best friend, whether they were together or not. When Bryan was upset, Andy wanted to soothe him. When he was happy, Andy wanted to join in that happiness. Andy wanted the intimate times as well as just hanging out. He wanted to make love to Bryan and fall asleep in his arms. He wanted it all with his best friend. When Andy broke the kiss, he pressed his forehead to Bryan's and took a deep breath.

"It's okay, Andy. Whatever you have to say won't change how I feel about you."

Andy hoped that was true. "How *do* you feel about me? Before I tell you my darkest secrets, I need to know what you want, B. I need for us to be on the same page."

"I care for you a great deal on a level that's more than friendship. I want to see what this is between us. I'm tired of pussyfooting around each other when we can be like this all the time. Well, maybe not all the time. I don't think Mal would appreciate if we slacked off on the job. But I don't see him having a problem with us being together as long as we're doing our jobs well."

"What if it doesn't work, though? What if we try this and you find out you really do like women? What if you want to have sex and I can't let you be the one on top? Are you willing to let me make love to you, B? Because I honestly don't know if I'll ever be able to let anyone have that control over me again."

"I'm not going to make promises I can't keep. I try my best to always be honest. Do I think I'll go back to women? No. I wasn't that attracted to them in the first place. Am I willing to let you make love to me? Yes. Will I be upset that I'm not the one on top? Not upset, but I'll be disappointed that I won't get to show you the same tenderness I know you'll show me. Does thinking about you fucking me scare me? Absolutely. I've never even had a toy in my ass, so yeah, it's a big deal. But I'm willing to do that for you. My feelings for you run deep. You and I are best friends. We like the same things. We know each other's moods. Most of the time we know when to back off or when to step in. The only thing we don't have that people in a relationship do is the intimacy. I want it."

Bryan touched his fingertip to one of Andy's eyebrows, smoothing it down. He traced the contour of Andy's face so gently Andy barely felt it. Bryan cradled Andy's face in his palm and continued, "I hate going to sleep across the hall from you. I want to lie down with you at night. Hold you while you drift off to sleep. Kiss you when you wake up. I want to be able to hold your hand while we're watching TV. It's the little things we don't have now that I want. I'm probably getting ahead of myself, but I want someone to spend the rest of my life with."

Andy's heart filled to the brim hearing Bryan describe how Andy was feeling. He pulled Bryan's hand away from his face and led him from the barn. "Let's take a walk." It would be easier telling about his past if he didn't have to look at Bryan while he was talking. Moe and Curly ran out the back door and trotted alongside them. Mal's bedroom light was on, but Andy wasn't worried about Mal. He'd already asked Andy if there was something going on between them the morning after they played strip poker. Andy had asked Mal if he'd be okay if there was, and he said he thought they would be good for each other.

Andy laced their fingers together as they walked down the driveway toward the road. There was a security light on the barn as well as one close to the mailbox. Between the two, the driveway was lit up most of the way. Andy took a deep breath and said, "I knew early on I was gay. Christy and I grew up together. We spent the night at each other's houses and slept in the same room until we were old enough that our parents put a stop to it. I always thought of her as the sister I never had. When I reached puberty, I was like every other boy my age. I figured out I liked jacking off, and I did it often, much to our housekeeper's dismay.

"When I accidentally saw Christy naked, I didn't think anything about it, but like I said, she felt more like a sister than a best friend. At school, I began to notice how one of the boys in my class smelled. I'm pretty sure it was his father's cologne. Or it could have been aftershave. All I know is my dick thought he was delicious. It bothered me at first. I'd not thought too much about my sexuality, but I began paying attention. I stared at the girls' boobs. I got close enough to smell their perfume. I even kissed a girl after school as a test. I felt nothing. I didn't have to test myself around guys. I was naturally drawn to them, and I accepted I was gay."

When they reached the gate, they turned and headed back. Andy led them to the front porch where they could sit on the swing together. He remained quiet until they were side by side. Bryan reached for his hand again, keeping them connected. "My grandfather is old money and old values. He never held his tongue when it came to gays or people of color."

"He'd fucking love me," Bryan muttered.

Andy laughed and gently nudged Bryan with his shoulder. "From the day I was born, I was groomed to take over the family business as well as the family name. I didn't rock the boat. I snuck around with a boy who was also gay. We didn't really like each other, but it was convenient for both of us to make out or jerk each other off. Then one day, I met Patrick. He was in college and seemed like he had his shit together. I couldn't believe he was giving me the time of day, let alone flirting with me. One thing led to another, and we started seeing each other. It wasn't hard to hide it from my family. Patrick had his own apartment, and I would meet him there when I was supposed to go to the library. I made good grades, so not studying when I was supposed to didn't hurt anything.

"This went on for about six months. Things got intense. I thought I was in love, and I thought he loved me back. We never went out on dates, but I was okay with that. I was glad to hide in the closet, because I knew how my family felt about gays. Anyway, one day when I got to the apartment, another guy was there. Patrick introduced him as a fellow classmate and said they were studying. A few days later, I went to the apartment, and Clark, that guy, was there again. When Patrick was out of the room, Clark pressed me against the door, started rubbing my dick, and tried to kiss me. Patrick came in the room but didn't say anything. Instead, he stood there watching and rubbing his dick. When I protested hard enough, Clark let me up and he left.

"Patrick pouted, saying I'd ruined the fun. I was too stupid and naïve to believe they'd never done anything without me there. When Patrick and I started fucking later, he got a little rougher than usual. He tried to convince me it was what couples did — they explored in the bedroom. Since he was my first and he was older, I believed him. The next time I went to see him, Patrick said he had a surprise for me. Told me to get undressed and wait for him on the bed." Andy stopped and looked at Bryan. "Are you sure you want to hear this?"

"Only if you're ready to tell me, Babe. I'm here for you, either way."

Andy nodded. He'd never told anyone the whole story. Not even Christy. Maybe it was time to let the demons out. "I need for you to know this before we go any further." Andy took a deep breath, closed his eyes, and told Bryan what he'd never told anyone. "I did as he said, and when he came into the room, he had me lie on my stomach. He put a blindfold over my eyes and tied my arms to the headboard. I struggled and decided I didn't want to play his game. He reached between my legs and started stroking.

The more I begged to be untied, the tighter his fist got. Before I knew what was happening, I felt a sting on my back. It was painful, and I yelled, demanding to be turned loose."

Andy swallowed hard. "He... I... There were four more strikes across my back with a whip. Not a crop. Not a flogger. A goddamn whip. Each strike harder and deeper than the one before. During this time, Patrick thought it would be a good idea to have sex. There was nothing I could do to stop him since I was tied up. After he finished with me, Clark decided to fuck me raw. No condom, no lube, no warning. He ripped my ass open. When Patrick untied me, I lost it. I threw myself at him, but he was so much larger than me. He punched me several times. By the time he was finished, I had passed out. I woke up being dragged from a car and tossed onto my parent's front porch. You know the rest."

Andy couldn't look at Bryan. The man was already about to break his hand from squeezing so hard. He dropped his chin to his chest and let the tears he'd been holding in fall to his lap. His silent crying turned into sobs, and Bryan pulled him into his arms. Bryan didn't say anything while Andy purged the memories from his mind through his tears. Bryan held him close, pressing kisses to his temple and rubbing small circles on his back. When the last of the tears left his eyes, Andy wiped his face. "I'm sorry."

Bryan gently tugged on Andy's chin and forced him to look up. Andy had never seen his best friend this mad. "Don't. Don't you fucking apologize for what those motherfuckers did to you. They raped you, Andy. They raped you and beat you when you told them no."

"But I willingly laid down on the bed," he whispered.

"Then you changed your mind. That is rape. Did the doctor not file a report?"

Andy shook his head. "I didn't tell him that part. He only treated my back."

"Why the fuck didn't you get checked out?"

"Because I was scared! I had already been kicked out of one home. If Christy's parents knew I'd been sneaking around having sex, they'd have kicked me out too!" Andy yelled. He shot to his feet and stalked to the other side of the porch. Moe and Curly followed him, whining. Bryan was at Andy's back immediately, wrapping his arms around Andy, pulling him into his body.

"I'm sorry. I'm just pissed at what happened to you. I understand now."

Andy shook his head, the tears falling again. "I'm damaged goods, B. You don't want someone like me."

"Don't tell me what I want. Me not wanting you because of your past is like you not wanting me for mine. My father's a murderer, and I am nothing more than a mutt who has absolutely nothing to offer you."

"You're *everything* to me," Andy protested as he turned to face Bryan.

"And *you* are everything to *me*. I hate what happened to you, but it doesn't define who you are. You put that shit behind you and became a Marine. I happen to know how tough that is. You were already broken, and you joined the one group who strives on breaking a person down even further. You are the strongest person I know, Andy Holcomb." Bryan cupped Andy's face and kissed him gently, returning the love Andy had given earlier.

When he pulled away, Bryan's face returned to furious. "But I *am* going to kill the motherfuckers."

Andy probably shouldn't have laughed, but he couldn't help it. His heart swelled with Bryan's protectiveness. Christy had been the only person in his life to get mad on his behalf, and she didn't know the whole story. He needed to call her and talk to her. He had talked to her briefly a few times over the last couple of months, but he

221

needed to really talk to her. Maybe one day they could plan a trip and meet somewhere in the middle of Texas and Kentucky. He wanted his two best friends to get to know each other. "I want you to meet Christy," he said causing Bryan to frown.

"Uh, okay?" Bryan had been talking murder, and Andy switched topics on him.

"I was just thinking that you and her are the only two people who've ever been pissed *for* me not *at* me."

"Don't forget Suzette. I think she'd probably give your mom what for if they ever got in the same room."

"She would, wouldn't she? Mal's lucky."

"That he is. But so am I." Bryan settled his hands on Andy's hips, pushing him against the porch rail. "Are there any more secrets you care to divulge while we're purging? I want everything out there now so we can put it all to rest and move forward."

"Nope. No more secrets. You know about my panic attacks and nightmares. You now know how I got the scars. That's the worst of me. You still want the rest of me?"

"I want all of you, Andy. The good and the bad. I might not have the scars on the outside, but I'm flawed, too. I bet there's a shrink out there that would tell us we shouldn't do this, but I think we're good together."

"So where do we go from here?" Andy asked.

"My bedroom. The door actually locks."

Andy laughed and shoved Bryan back. "I meant long term."

Bryan grinned and pulled Andy back to him. Not that Andy minded. Ever since Bryan put his shirt on, Andy had been dying to touch him. Something about his shirt hanging open and showing only a tease of his chest was so fucking hot. Andy placed his palms on Bryan's pecs. Hard muscle was covered by soft skin. Bryan's chest was dusted with dark hair that Andy wanted to rub his cheek on. Andy pushed the shirt open farther then down his arms so he had an unimpeded view of Bryan's upper body. Andy had not had the pleasure of seeing Bryan's ink up close and personal. Andy's tattoos were minimal – nautical stars on his chest, Marine tats on each upper arm, and one tribal band circling his right bicep.

Bryan's Marine ink was crazy intricate, and it spanned his upper back across his shoulders. Andy couldn't wait to get Bryan in bed on his stomach so he could go over every inch of it. That wasn't the only reason Andy wanted to get Bryan on his stomach. He wanted to explore Bryan's sculpted ass cheeks, too. Andy had seen plenty of naked bodies over the years, but none were as perfect as Bryan's. Andy's cock had softened while talking about Patrick, but thinking about Bryan's ass had him erect and pressing against his zipper. Andy ghosted his thumbs across Bryan's tiny nubs. Bryan hissed, so Andy went a step further. He bit one then licked the pain away.

Bryan growled and reached between them, cupping Andy's erection. "B. . ." Andy pushed his hips into Bryan's hand, wanting more friction. Bryan had offered to blow him earlier, and Andy was ready to take him up on it. He'd told Bryan everything, and Bryan still wanted him. Andy wanted everything with his friend, and he wanted it right then.

Bryan must have read his mind. He put his lips against Andy's ear and hissed, "Like I said, my bedroom." Andy followed a stalking Bryan inside. Bryan stopped long enough to lock the door. "I'm going to make sure the house is secure. When I get to my room, I want you waiting for me, and Lily, I want you naked." A shiver ran down Andy's spine at the authoritative tone. It should have scared the shit out of him, but this was Bryan, his best friend. He knew B would never hurt him. He was counting on him to make him feel good in a way he'd never felt.

Andy did as he was told and was waiting on the bed. He was propped against the headboard with his legs stretched out in front of him. He felt stupid, not knowing if he should pose for Bryan, spread his legs and offer up his hole, or get under the covers and hide. He'd only ever stripped for Patrick, and then he was always on his knees with his ass in the air. He shouldn't be nervous; this was Bryan. His best friend and now soon to be lover. Still, Andy bit his bottom lip and worried about doing something to scare Bryan off.

Bryan entered the room and locked the door before turning his gaze to Andy. The hunger in Bryan's eyes had Andy's dick getting harder. He subconsciously ran his hand down his body until he fisted his cock. If Bryan didn't hurry and get on the bed, Andy would be the one embarrassed. He was ready to come from the way Bryan was eyeing him. His body language left no doubt Bryan was the predator and Andy was the prey. Bryan made quick work of his clothes and crawled between Andy's legs. Bryan glanced up at Andy, and without preamble, he sucked Andy's cock all the way down.

Chapter Twenty-Two

Bryan

Bryan should be nervous about giving his first blowjob, but he wasn't. He was eager to taste Andy. To show him what it meant to be with someone who wanted to please him and not use him. Someone who loved him. Andy's cock wasn't so long that it gagged him when he sucked him all the way down, but it was beautiful, nonetheless. Bryan recalled how Andy had alternated between sucking on the tip and sliding along his shaft, so that's what he did. Andy's pubic area was cropped close, and when he bottomed out on Andy's dick, his nose touched the hair. Bryan breathed in, relishing the scent of Andy. It was a mixture of body wash, musk, and man. He'd never envisioned being turned on by the way a man would smell, but this wasn't any man – this was Andy.

Bryan's mouth was getting tired, so he pulled off and licked Andy's nut sac. Bryan was encountering so many firsts that his head should be spinning. It wasn't. It was filled with the knowledge that he was giving Andy something no one else had. They were each other's firsts in so many ways. He only wished he would be the first one to make love to Andy so his memories would be good ones. Bryan vowed silently to work Andy's body over in a way that erased the bad and filled him with nothing but good.

When he sucked Andy back into his mouth, Andy tried to grab onto Bryan's hair, but it wasn't long enough to pull. Andy grabbed his ears instead and pushed his dick farther into Bryan's mouth. "Fuck, B, that feels so good. I'm not going to last." Andy pumped his hips harder, and Bryan let him take over. "I'm… ahhh, fuck… You need to pull off, B. I can't hold back." There was no way Bryan was going to pull off. He wanted to taste Andy. To swallow him down the way he had Bryan earlier. Bryan wrapped his arms around Andy's thighs and held on tighter, his fingers digging into Andy's skin. The first stream of jizz hit the back of his throat, and he did his best to swallow with Andy's dick in his mouth. It was an odd experience but not unpleasant. Andy continued surging inside until he was spent. Bryan swallowed again and licked the tip of Andy's dick for good measure. He placed open mouth kisses along Andy's inner thighs, on the area above his pubic hair, up his abs, and finally on his lips. Andy sucked on Bryan's tongue, tasting his own spunk.

Bryan was dizzy. He'd given his first blowjob, and he loved it. Having Andy's dick in his mouth along with the enticing way he smelled was a heady combination. If he had any doubt before whether or not he was gay, he had none then. His dick was hard again, and it was because he'd *given* this part of himself to Andy. His erection was pressed between their bodies, and Bryan wanted to be buried inside Andy's hole. He knew that wasn't a possibility. Not yet anyway. Maybe once Andy was more comfortable being together, once Bryan showed him he'd never hurt him, maybe then. Until then, he'd have to be content with what Andy could give him.

It was like a dam had burst, and Bryan craved everything to do with sex with Andy. Andy spread his legs wider, wrapping them around Bryan's thighs. It didn't take long for Andy to get hard again. Andy deepened the kiss and grabbed onto Bryan's ass, thrusting their cocks together. Bryan thought about asking Andy to fuck him but decided he wasn't quite ready. This was their first night together, and they had all the time in the world to explore things between them. Bryan pulled back from the kiss and pressed their foreheads together. "I love the way you taste, Lily. The way you smell. And fuck me, the way you feel in my arms? This is perfect. *We're* perfect."

Bryan rutted against Andy's cock, not worrying if he seemed needy. He was. Bryan needed this connection with Andy. Andy pushed on his chest and said, "Turn over." Bryan didn't hesitate to do as Andy requested. He knew his best friend wouldn't hurt him. "Do you have any lube?" Andy asked, kneeling on the bed between Bryan's knees.

"In the drawer," he said, pointing to the bedside table. Andy opened the drawer and grabbed the bottle of slick. He poured a generous amount in his hand and held himself up with the other hand. When he fisted their erections together, Bryan thought he would come immediately. He propped up on his elbows so he could watch what Andy was doing. Most of the friction was on Bryan's cock, so he reached down and added a hand to Andy's so they both had equal attention. Andy grinned at him, and together, they stroked. The slower pace Andy had set seemed more erotic somehow.

Andy kept his eyes on Bryan's face, his bottom lip caught between his teeth. Bryan wanted to be the one biting his lip, so he said, "Kiss me." Andy obliged, and Bryan sucked Andy's lip into his mouth. Sucking, licking, biting.

Andy jerked back, his eyes darkening. Bryan pushed up so he had access to Andy's skin. He sucked the area between Andy's neck and shoulder. When Andy moaned at the pressure, Bryan sucked harder. He'd never given a hickey before, but fuck if he didn't want to mark Andy. The harder he sucked the faster Andy's hand was on their cocks.

"Oh, god, harder B," Andy begged. Bryan sucked Andy's neck until he thought his lips were going to bruise. "I'm gonna come . . . unh." Andy thrust his hips into their joined hands, his seed hitting Bryan's chest. Bryan's own release followed almost immediately, and both men were writhing through their releases. Andy fell onto Bryan's chest, the creamy liquid squishing between them. Bryan enjoyed Andy's weight. It felt right. In that moment, Bryan knew without a doubt he'd found the person – the man – he wanted to spend the rest of his life with.

Andy rolled to his side and looked at Bryan with so much love in his eyes that Bryan knew Andy felt it too. Their lips met in a soft connection. Bryan loved how they could go from passionate to sweet so quickly. He'd never encountered either before, and he liked them both equally. "Stay here, and I'll get us a washcloth." Andy kissed him again before rolling off the bed. He opened the door and listened before easing his way to the bathroom. Bryan looked at the ceiling like it would help him hear better. There was no movement coming from overhead, and he prayed Mal stayed asleep until they could get cleaned up.

Bryan wasn't ready for Andy to go to his own room, but he also didn't know how Mal would feel if they slept together. Andy returned and gently cleaned off Bryan's chest. He'd closed the door and locked it when he came back. "Let's get under the covers; I want to hold you." Bryan pulled the bedding over them, and Andy settled next to him with his head on Bryan's chest and his arm around his waist. "God, this feels good," he whispered. Bryan tightened his arm around Andy's shoulder, agreeing silently.

There was so much going through Bryan's head that he didn't know how to put voice to it. His body was sated, and his heart was full. At the same time, his mind was still trying to come to terms with everything that had happened in the last twenty-four hours. Instead of dwelling on it and trying to make sense of it all, he did his best to relax and enjoy the feel of his man in his arms. *His man.* Bryan kissed the top of Andy's head before pressing his cheek there. Their bodies fit together perfectly, and Bryan closed his eyes to enjoy the moment. Andy's breathing had evened out, and soon he was softly snoring. Bryan hadn't planned on sleeping together, but he didn't have the heart to wake Andy up. He allowed himself to follow Andy into unconsciousness.

When Bryan woke the next morning, he noticed two things. One, Andy was no longer in bed, and two, Bryan didn't like it. It wasn't quite time to get up, but Bryan was filled with too much emotion to stay in bed and not go in search of Andy. He feared Andy had woken, and after realizing what they did was a mistake, had returned to his own room. On the way to the bathroom, Bryan peered into Andy's bedroom, finding it empty. After Bryan peed, brushed his teeth, and washed his hands, he headed to the kitchen, where Andy was leaning against the counter drinking coffee. As soon as he saw Bryan, his face lit up with his beautiful, straight, white teeth smile. Bryan had always been self-conscious about his own smile because his mom couldn't afford to get him braces. It was another one of those things he couldn't help, like the color of his skin.

"Morning," Andy purred, setting his coffee down. He didn't wait for Bryan to come to him. Andy met him at the door and slid his arms around Bryan's waist. He buried his face in the crook of Bryan's neck and placed kisses there. Bryan's arms automatically circled Andy, and they stood there quietly for several minutes, just being. In that moment, Bryan realized it was the first time in his life he felt at peace. He let out a long, contented sigh, and Andy searched his face.

"I don't think I've ever slept as soundly as I did last night," Bryan whispered. There was no one else in the kitchen, but he wanted his words to be for Andy only. "It felt good having you in my bed, but I hated waking up alone. I know we're new – *this* is new. But do you think it's possible to sleep together every night? Now that I've had you with me, I don't want to ever sleep without you."

Andy's eyes held his answer; still, he said, "Yes, I think it's possible." He pressed their lips together, keeping it chaste. Andy pulled away and poured Bryan a cup of coffee, adding the right amount of sugar. When he handed it over, he said, "I've been thinking…" He had a look on his face like a mischievous little boy.

"Oh yeah?" Bryan sipped his coffee, eager to hear what Andy was contemplating.

"After we get Mal and Cade back together, I think you and I should move into Suzette's old room. It's bigger, and it has the bathroom attached."

"I like that idea. But why wait until Mal and Cade are back together?"

"Then Mal will be happy. He will be getting laid and won't have time to worry about what the two of us are getting up to," Andy said, wiggling his eyebrows. Bryan laughed at his lover, but he had to agree it made sense.

"You have a point."

Mal's footsteps coming down the stairs had them separating to opposite sides of the room like two teens hiding from their parents. Andy grinned and headed to the fridge. Bryan took a sip of his coffee doing his best not to look guilty. Even though they hadn't been doing anything wrong, Bryan didn't want Mal to have any reason to get mad at them.

"Mornin'."

Andy and Bryan responded in kind, and as Andy prepared to make breakfast, Mal poured his coffee and said, "The supplies for the deck are comin' in today. Walt's gonna come over and help set the posts in concrete. He's willin' to help with the rest of it, unless the two of you want to tackle it on your own. Up to you."

Bryan had never taken on building something as large as a deck, but he was confident he and Andy could figure it out together. "I think Andy and I can handle it. If we get started and I'm wrong, we'll ask for help."

"Sounds good to me," Andy agreed, then added, "Mal, I've been thinking. I really like having your mom and Walt around. Is it okay if we invite them over for dinner on Sundays?"

The offer didn't surprise Bryan. He knew how much Andy was hurt by his mother's betrayal, and Bryan missed being able to talk to his own mother.

"I'd like that. I miss havin' her around all the time."

"Excellent. I'll mention it to Walt when he gets here." Andy clapped his hands together and got busy cooking the bacon.

Over the next few days, Bryan, Andy, and Walt built the deck. Walt was an excellent carpenter, and Bryan could tell he enjoyed working with his hands. Instead of leaving the two of them to build it like they'd planned, Walt asked if he could help with the rest of it once the posts were set. They didn't have to discuss whether or not they would accept his help. One look between them was all they needed, and Andy clapped Walt on the shoulder telling him they'd be glad to have his help. Suzette came with Walt, and since Mal was holed up in his office, Suzette sat in a new lounge chair enjoying the fresh air while the men worked together. When Andy invited them for Sunday dinner, Suzette got misty-eyed and gladly accepted.

The days were spent as friends and co-workers, and Bryan had no problem with that. Now that they had decided to be together as a couple, they were back to the easy-going relationship they'd started off with. They kept their hands to themselves, but they never went long without giving the other a smile or a knowing look. At night, they watched television together, but they weren't comfortable being affectionate in front of Mal. Not yet. They waited until he went to bed before going to Bryan's room and spending the night exploring each other. They kept it to blowjobs and hand jobs, but they always fell asleep with Andy snuggled against Bryan's side. They both rose well before Mal did to ensure he didn't catch them in bed.

Walt had some work to do at his place, so Bryan and Andy worked together to put the finishing touches on the deck. They hadn't been outside long when Mal joined them.

He admired their handiwork and complimented them on a job well done. Then he said he was going to take Cochise out and look over the cattle. Both Andy and Bryan had made the rounds each evening after Walt and Suzette left, ensuring all the animals were safe and well. By the time they were finished with the deck, it was going on five o'clock. Mal still wasn't back, but it wasn't odd for him to stay out all day, especially if he was checking all the pastures. Eleven hundred acres was a lot for one person to cover.

Andy had just pulled stuff out of the fridge to start supper when Mal came inside. He stopped when his phone pinged with an incoming text. He pulled his phone out of his pocket, looking at the screen briefly. "I'm gonna head up and take my shower," he muttered before rushing out of the room, taking the stairs two at a time.

"I wonder what that's about," Andy said. Cade's calls to them both had come less and less. Bryan had tried talking to Mal, but he shut him down every time. Cade's lack of communication with them both had Bryan feeling that Cade had given up on Mal. Now that he and Andy had admitted how they truly felt, Bryan wanted Mal and Cade to find their way back to one another more than ever. It would really suck if they'd found their happiness only for Mal to have lost his.

Bryan was taking the casserole out of the oven when an excited Mal flew down the steps and slid to a stop in his sock feet. Bryan and Andy gave each other a "what the fuck" look before turning their attention back to their boss.

"Can either one of you draw?" Mal asked, looking between them. Obviously, the text had been a good one, because Mal was practically bouncing.

"My stick figures don't even look normal," Bryan admitted. He had no artistic abilities whatsoever.

"I can draw a little. Why? What do you need?" Andy asked.

232

"I have an idea. I want to get a tattoo, and I want it to look specifically like the one on Cade's chest with a few exceptions." Mal's excitement was palpable, and Bryan felt hope for Mal and Cade for the first time since Mal found out the truth about the farm.

"So, you talked to Cade?" Bryan asked, making sure he wasn't misreading the situation.

"Not exactly. I texted him earlier, but he must be busy." Mal shrugged. "I want to have this done soon so it has time to heal before the show in a few weeks. That's enough time, right?"

Bryan lost a little of that hopefulness. Mal hadn't talked to Cade, so this idea might backfire on him. Still, if Mal wanted ink, who was Bryan to stop him? "If you can find a good artist that isn't booked. This is an important piece, and you'll want an experienced tattooist, not an apprentice." Bryan had dealt with enough tattoo shops to know that they often hired people who were trying to get established. His first tattoo had to be redone because the person who did the original work wasn't as experienced as he let on. Luckily, it wasn't a big piece, and Bryan was able to have it fixed with little trouble.

"Will you help me find someone while Andy draws it out?" Mal asked Bryan.

"Yeah, sure. Let's eat first then we'll get to work on it."

Mal ate faster than Bryan had ever seen. When Mal took his dish to the sink, Andy caught Bryan's eyes, grinning, and Bryan just shrugged. He had a good mind to call Cade and make sure everything was still okay on his end before Mal made a big mistake. Declaring your love was one thing, but doing it in such a permanent way was another. Since Mal was sitting right there, Bryan didn't want to chance calling Cade in front of him. Instead, he looked up tattoo shops in Nashville, studied several artists and their portfolios, and read reviews on the ones who specialized in the type of tattoo Mal wanted. He was able to get Mal an appointment with one of the better-known artists who just happened to have a spot open after a cancellation.

Andy drew the design Mal wanted. Instead of simply getting the same nautical compass like the one Cade had, Mal had Andy change the letters. In place of the N, E, S, and W, Andy drew the letters of Cade's name at the four points.

While Andy was putting the finishing touches on the drawing, Mal said, "I know I've been an ass, but I realized it was my own insecurities puttin' the wedge between us and not how much money Cade has. He's been nothin' but givin' and supportive, and I've been nothin' but a dick. I want to do this for him, to show him how much he means to me. Cade is my compass. Wherever he is points me home." Bryan had to admit it was an excellent idea for a tattoo once Mal explained the meaning behind it. It got him to thinking about making a permanent declaration of his own for Andy.

The change in Mal was like night and day. He no longer hid out in his office. He spent his days riding the land with Bryan and Andy. On the nights he wasn't visiting his mom and Walt, Mal stayed downstairs and watched movies. That Sunday, Walt and Suzette came for dinner, and they brought two of Mal's nieces with them. Matilda was still her talkative, cute self, and Bryan thoroughly enjoyed being around her. It was Megan, the three-year-old, who stole his heart. As soon as Mal brought her in the house, she reached for Bryan and didn't turn loose until it was time to go.

Bryan caught Andy staring at the two of them together. They had talked briefly about having families when they first moved to the farm. Now, though, things were completely different. Their relationship was fresh, and they didn't need to be considering kids yet, but if Bryan was honest with himself, he'd love nothing more than for him and Andy to raise a child or two together. Until then, he would enjoy every minute spent with his new "nieces."

Mal's tattoo turned out really well. Both Bryan and Andy had taken the trip to Nashville with him. Afterwards, they'd walked up and down Broadway, stopping in several of the honkytonks and having a beer while listening to live music. It was the first time they'd been back since the night at Primus, and Bryan had to grin when he thought about Andy's ploy to make him jealous. When they got in the truck to head home, Mal asked, "Sure y'all don't wanna check out Primus before we head home?"

"*No*," they both groaned at the same time. Mal grinned at them. "That's what I thought." He didn't elaborate, and neither one of them asked if he knew. Bryan did put his arm across the back of the seat, and Andy leaned a little closer on the ride home.

Chapter Twenty-Three

Andy

Andy and Bryan began to get worried as Mal's mood slipped a little more each day into the broody man he'd been. One night while they were sitting outside on the front porch together, Bryan called Cade. When they first met the rock star, both Bryan and Andy talked to Cade usually once a week about every day stuff like his tour, the band members, cattle, the horses, and the girls. When he didn't answer, Bryan left a message stating he just wanted to say hi since they hadn't talked in a few days. Cade didn't return his call, and their unease increased.

Mal wasn't as talkative as he'd been after getting his ink, but he wasn't hiding away in the house. That morning before they'd gotten out of bed, Bryan told Andy he was ready to ride Cochise. It was the first time he'd even mentioned getting on the Paint, but he'd ridden Callie enough, and Andy felt he was ready. If he didn't, he would tell Bryan the truth, because there was no way he would let Bryan do anything to endanger himself. When they said something to Mal about it at breakfast, he was on board.

Mal and Bryan saddled the horses and walked them out the barn. Andy was just about to fire up Cade's four wheeler when a UPS truck stopped at the end of the driveway.

"You want me to get it?" Andy asked.

Mal waved him off. "Nah, I got it." He climbed atop Callie's back and trotted down to retrieve the package.

When he came back, he slid off the side of the horse, handed the reins over to Bryan, and mumbled, "Here, please watch her." Mal ripped the cardboard packaging open as he walked into the house.

Andy got off the ATV and took Cochise's reins from Bryan. He led the horse into the small enclosure on the far side of the barn. Bryan followed with Callie. The horses were able to graze while waiting on Mal to come out of the house. The two of them stood propped against the rails talking about going to look for patio furniture, and that led to them discussing a new bedroom suite. They still hadn't moved into Suzette's bedroom, but the more Andy thought about it, the more it made sense. The two of them still wanted Mal and Cade to have made up before approaching him, even though he more than likely had figured out they were together.

When an hour passed, Bryan said, "I'm going to check on him." Andy followed him, and when they entered the kitchen, music was floating through the house from Mal's office. Andy waited in the hall while Bryan pushed open the door and asked, "Hey, Boss. You okay in here?"

Since Andy was outside the door, he couldn't see Mal. When he didn't answer, Andy took the opportunity to listen to the song. Andy didn't recognize the song, but the voice sounded familiar. When he began listening to the lyrics, it dawned on him who was singing – Cade. The words coming from the speaker of the laptop were so sad, Andy's heart hurt for Mal.

When the song was over, Bryan grumbled, "Aw hell, Mal. I thought you talked to him."

"He wouldn't call me back," Mal whispered, but it was loud enough for Andy to hear. Both men were silent, and Andy wondered if they were just staring at each other.

Andy was just about to make his presence known when Bryan said, "Holy shit!" Andy entered the room and went to Bryan when he held out some papers for Andy to read.

"Holy shit," Andy echoed Bryan's sentiment after

237

reading enough of the document to see that Cade had signed over the farm to Mal. "Why would he do this? I thought things were good between you." He handed the papers back to Bryan.

Mal removed his cap and resettled it on his head. "He never called me back. I just assumed he was busy. I guess he was, gettin' on with his life."

"What are you going to do?" Bryan asked, handing the deed back to Mal.

"There's nothin' I can do. It's clear he doesn't want anything to do with me. I waited too long. I shoulda called. Texted. Somethin'. This is all my fault. I waited too long, and now he's movin' on."

Bryan's demeanor changed. Andy knew the look well. Bryan was getting pissed. "I'll ask you again, what are you going to do? The Malcolm Wilson I know isn't a quitter."

"But he's —"

Bryan slapped his hands down on the desk in front of Mal, startling him and Andy. "But nothing. You love him? You want him? You gotta fight for him."

Mal pressed a button on his laptop, turning the music off. With tears in his eyes, he said, "Yeah, I love him. I just hope it's enough."

"Isn't the concert tomorrow?" Andy asked.

"Yes," Bryan said as he pushed away from the desk, frustrated. He had come to think of Cade as a friend, and Andy knew his heart was hurting for both men.

"Mal can settle things between them after the show. Mal, I know Cade loves you, and once you explain how you should have accepted his generosity instead of throwing it in his face, he'll forgive you for being an ass, and y'all can kiss and make up."

Mal didn't respond. He leaned his head back and closed his eyes.

"Come on, B. Let's give Mal some space." Andy

didn't worry about Mal seeing when he put his hand to the small of Bryan's back as they walked out of the room. He needed the connection between them after seeing Mal so upset. He waited until he was outside to say, "Goddamn, that was a sad song."

Bryan ran a hand down his face and sighed. "Yeah, it was. Dammit, why didn't Mal respond to him sooner? All the silence had to be killing Cade. I'm going to text him and see if I get a response."

Andy walked over to the fence to wait. The first few days after their trip to Nashville had been fun. Their time spent with Walt, Suzette, and the girls had filled Andy's heart with something he'd needed for a long time. Family. It was one of the reasons he asked Mal about having them over every week. Bryan gave so much to Andy that it should be enough to make him whole, but it wasn't until he watched Megan cling to Bryan that he felt complete. Seeing the two of them together had Andy wishing for things he knew were better left to the future.

Being around Walt and Suzette, and them accepting Andy for who he was, went a long way in mending that place inside that had been destroyed when his grandfather disowned him and his mother stood by and watched it happen. When he first met Suzette, she began putting him back together, one stitch at a time. When she recently stood in front of him with his face in her hands and told him she loved him, well, it was all Andy could do not to break down in front of everyone. He'd waited until he and Bryan were in bed together before he let the tears go. Instead of being mortified that Andy was a big, badass Marine crying like a little bitch, Bryan shed his own tears right along with Andy's. Andy felt that much more love for his best friend. He could be himself with Bryan.

When Bryan rejoined him, he said, "Let's go for a ride." Bryan opened the gate and mounted Cochise while Andy pulled himself atop Callie. The two set off at an easy pace, giving Bryan and Cochise time to get used to each other.

While they were riding, they made the rounds. "Does it bother you that we get paid to spend all day together?" Andy asked.

Bryan grinned. "All day *and* all night. Fuck! I was ready to talk to Mal about us sharing a room together, and then this. He really is our boss now. Do you think things will change?"

"I can't imagine they will other than who signs the paycheck. I don't see Mal letting us go, not when things are so good. Not that he can't find others to do what we do, but he likes us and has no reason to let us go. He's not like that."

"True, but now that the farm's his again, he gets all the responsibility that goes with it. Dammit. Let's just hope when they see each other tomorrow it's not too late. I can't imagine loving someone so much only to lose them over miscommunication."

Andy knew the feeling. He and Bryan had almost done the same thing. Only instead of miscommunication, there had been none. But they were together, and he intended to keep it that way. He had yet to tell Bryan he loved him. They were still feeling each other out and hadn't taken things in the bedroom to the next level. They had planned on talking to Mal about moving bedrooms so he'd have no doubt they were together. If things went the way he hoped they did, Mal and Cade would make up after the concert, Mal would stay downtown with Cade afterwards, and Bryan would come home to him where they could finally make love.

"I want you, B," Andy blurted out.

"You have me, Babe."

"I mean I want to make love to you."

Bryan pulled back on the reins, and Cochise stopped. "Now?"

Andy shook his head. "No, but soon. If Mal ends up

staying with Cade tomorrow, I want you to come home to me. We'll have the house to ourselves, and I want to be with you."

"And if things don't go well with them?"

"Then we should go get a hotel room somewhere. I want a night with you where we can be as loud as we want. Naked all night without worrying about who's gonna see us. Tell me you want that, too."

"I want that, too." Bryan stretched out his hand, and Andy took it. He wanted so badly to kiss Bryan, but he didn't want to take a chance on spooking Cochise by getting too close. The need to be skin to skin with his man threatened to smother him. Andy took several deep breaths, and Bryan gripped his hand tighter. "Breathe, Babe," Bryan urged, frowning.

Andy tried. He breathed in deeply, trying to control his emotions. Normally, he didn't have to be touching Bryan twenty-four seven, but the sadness with Cade and Mal mixed with the thought of finally making love to Bryan was overwhelming.

"Talk to me, Andy."

"I just..." He blew out a deep breath. "I'm scared, but at the same time, I'm overjoyed, you know? It's hard to explain."

"I get it, Baby. Every time I look at you, I can't believe you're mine. It scares me to think one day you're going to wake up and figure out you could do so much better than me. Not that you'd ever find someone to love you more than I do, but someone with more of the other stuff to offer."

Andy's breath caught again. "What's more important than love, B? I don't have anything to offer you, either. We're a lot alike, you and me. We have the same job; I'm figuring we make the same amount of money, not that it matters. We're both Marines. We're the same age; we like the same things. We love each other. Unless you get bored of the job we have, I don't see life getting much better except for maybe throwing in some kids down the line."

"Kids, huh?"

"I saw the way you were with Megan. You'd make a great father."

"So would you, Lily. So would you. I really want to kiss you right now. Follow me." Bryan turned loose of Andy's hand, and with the touch of his heels, got Cochise moving toward the barn. Both men slid off the side of their horse and tethered them to the fence post. Bryan grabbed Andy's hand and pulled him inside where they could have a bit of privacy. Bryan didn't attack Andy like he expected. His movements were slow and gentle. His kiss was so tender, Andy never wanted it to end. Without coming right out and saying it, they'd both declared their love.

"I will make sure Mal and Cade find their way back to one another tomorrow night. Then, I'm coming home to you, and we will spend all night making love," Bryan promised.

"I can't wait." And he couldn't. Andy was ready to strip Bryan bare right there in the barn and worship his body.

"Let's get the horses put up and go check on Mal." Obviously, Bryan could wait, but Andy knew he was right. They only had one more day to wait until they were finally together completely. Once they had the horses back in their stalls with feed and water, they headed inside the house. They had already planned on grilling out, so Bryan got the charcoal ready while Andy headed upstairs to talk to Mal.

Andy knocked on Mal's door and waited for a response. "Come in." When Andy eased the door open, Mal was leaning against the headboard looking through a notebook.

"Hey, Boss, we're gonna put the steaks on. You want a baked potato or fries?"

"I'm not hungry."

"Maybe not, but you need to eat anyway. I'll fix you a potato, that way you can heat it up. Rewarmed fries suck."

Mal looked up from whatever he was reading and gave Andy a smile that didn't reach his eyes. "Thanks, Andy. You and Bryan have been good friends to me, puttin' up with my bullshit these last few weeks."

"It's what friends do." Andy closed the door and made his way downstairs. He washed and wrapped three potatoes before putting them in the oven. Once that was done, he took the steaks out to Bryan. The small grill was the only thing on the deck besides a couple of chairs Suzette had brought over. Andy sat back and enjoyed the view of Bryan manning the grill. Bryan had said he couldn't believe Andy was his, but Andy was the lucky one. Bryan Moore was a hell of a man, even if he didn't realize it.

Mal surprised them when he came out of his room and joined them for supper. He even sat around watching a baseball game afterwards.

During a commercial, he said, "I've been thinkin' about remodelin' the den and turning it into a dining room. Now that Ma and Walt are comin' around more often, we need a bigger table. What do y'all think?"

Andy thought it was a wonderful idea. He loved having his new family around. "I'm all for it, just please don't get rid of the piano." Andy had played it several times while he and Bryan had been avoiding each other. He had forgotten how much music meant to him and how therapeutic it was to get lost in playing. Now that he and Bryan were together, he wanted to write a song for his love. He'd never tried to write one, but he had a tune floating around in his head, and if things went the way they all hoped, Andy was going to get Cade to help him.

"Will you play somethin' now?" Mal asked.

"Sure." Andy led the others to the den and sat down at the bench. Mal sat in the chair close by, but Bryan stayed by the door, leaning against the frame the same way he did the first night Andy played for him. "What do you want to hear?"

"Somethin' happy," Mal answered.

Andy played the intro to Bob Seger's "Old Time Rock and Roll" and waited to see if Mal approved. When he smiled and nodded, Andy played it again and began belting out the lyrics. Mal joined in, and by the second verse, Bryan was singing with them. Andy played several songs they all knew, and when he was finished, Mal had a genuine smile on his face. "You can give Cade a run for his money. The two of you should get together and jam."

Andy blushed at Mal's compliment. It felt good to let loose with something he enjoyed so much. On that high note, they all said goodnight. Mal headed upstairs while Andy and Bryan got ready for bed. They had gotten into a routine of taking turns in the bathroom before meeting in Bryan's room. Andy hadn't slept in his bed since the night they'd gone to Primus.

Maybe it was because they'd had such an emotional day, or it could have been the anticipation of making love the next night, but neither one moved to get naked. Andy curled up against Bryan's body as he did every night and ran his fingertips across Bryan's chest hair. Bryan stroked Andy's arm slowly and placed random kisses on his temple. Andy had never felt so secure. Content. Loved. As he felt himself being pulled under, Andy whispered, "I love you, B."

Bryan's arm tightened around him as he said, "I love you, too, Lily."

Andy was a ball of nerves as he went about his morning. He knew Mal had to be even more nervous because his love life was on the line. Still, Andy wanted everything about that night to be perfect. He'd woken up with silly ideas running through his head. Ideas that wouldn't quieten in his brain, so he decided they weren't silly after all. When Mal and Bryan finally headed to

Nashville for the concert, Andy called Christy to catch up. He told her all about Bryan and listened while she talked about her last failed romance. Andy hated that his best girl friend couldn't find a good man. She was a beautiful, smart, kind woman. Andy asked about her parents and told her about Walt and Suzette. When they had caught each other up without talking about his family, they promised to meet up soon, somewhere besides Texas. When he hung up, Andy borrowed Bryan's truck and drove into town. He stopped by the bar to say hello to Kason since he had some time to kill. The two men shot the shit while Andy had a couple of beers. The place filled up, and several women asked Andy to dance. He turned them down, though. Now that he and Bryan were together, Andy didn't want to have anyone else in his arms.

Kason kept asking him what had him so wound up, but Andy couldn't tell him. He wasn't ashamed of being gay, but considering where they were, there was no way Andy would think about breathing the word gay in DWs. He wanted to be able to visit the bar on Friday nights without the threat of getting into a fight. Instead, he blamed his mood on the full moon, and when he couldn't sit still any longer, Andy paid his tab and headed to the store. When he got back to the farm, he still had a lot of time to kill before Bryan would return. And if he didn't return alone? Andy's plans would be fubar.

Bryan had promised him in bed that morning, right after he'd woken Andy with a blowjob, he would not leave Nashville until Mal and Cade reconciled. The blowjob had been a surprise, but a nice one. Smiling, Andy looked at the clock. God, he couldn't believe in a few short hours, the two of them would consummate their relationship.

Chapter Twenty-Four

Bryan

Bryan had been crawling out of his skin all day. Andy had been a ball of live wire while at the same time his thoughts would take him somewhere else. Bryan had to call his name several times to get his attention, but he laughed at his lover when Andy would finally look up, grinning. Leaving Mal to his own planning and thoughts, Bryan and Andy set out on the horses and went their separate ways. That was probably for the best, because if they'd been together, Bryan would have wanted to get naked. Ever since they admitted they loved each other, Bryan couldn't think about anything other than Andy and how to keep him. Bryan wasn't a catch. He wasn't good-looking. He wasn't talented. But he loved Andy with everything he had, and he prayed it would be enough.

He was nervous about having sex. He had researched about anal on the internet, reading article after article on what to do to prepare and what to expect. Bryan wasn't afraid of the pain, because everything he read said the pain quickly turned to pleasure. He was afraid Andy would find him lacking in some way and decide they shouldn't be together. So far, that hadn't happened when they were intimate, but they hadn't had full out sex either.

Shaking off his nerves, Bryan turned his thoughts to the concert. Cade had left backstage passes at will call so they could stand at the side of the stage during the show, but Mal wanted to be in the audience and get the full effect. He'd never seen Cade play, and he wanted to watch his man in his element. It was probably better for Cade that way, as well. He could focus on his drums without wanting to look over at Mal every few minutes.

By the time they were ready to go, Andy was practically pushing them out the door. Andy grabbed Bryan's arm before he could make his way outside and said, "Text me when you're on your way and let me know if you're alone."

"Why? So you can rush your boyfriend out the door?" Bryan joked.

"No, so I can get ready to rush my boyfriend *in* the door when he comes home to me." Andy brushed his lips across Bryan's with a promise of what was to come later.

Bryan touched a finger to Andy's cheek and gave him a smile. God, he loved his man. They'd only said the words the night before as they were falling asleep, but they didn't need the words. They had the looks, the touches, the quiet moments alone. And in a few hours, they would have each other in a way no one else had.

After getting their passes at the will call window, Bryan and Mal headed into Bridgestone Arena with thousands of other concert goers. It made Bryan proud to know that they were two of the select few who knew someone in the band and would get to go backstage afterwards. Bryan had seen Cade play before, but that was before he'd become friends with the drummer. It was still surreal to know Cade considered him a friend as well. After getting a beer, they made their way down to the general admission area on the floor. "You sure you don't want to go stand on the stage? We'll have more elbow room."

Mal grinned, but it was filled with trepidation. "I'm sure. I've never been to a rock concert, and I really want to see Cade from this viewpoint." On the outside, Mal looked like any other fan with his Divining the Dark T-shirt. He'd left his ball cap at home, but he'd styled his hair away from his face. On the inside, Bryan knew Mal was scared shitless. In just a couple of hours he'd come face-to-face with the man he loved, and they were either making up or breaking up.

The two of them hadn't rushed the stage like a lot of people, so they were standing about fifty feet away from the front of the crowd. The Neurotic Prophets were the only opening band. It surprised Bryan that there wasn't more than one opener. Usually there were at least two lesser known groups to play before the headliner. The lights went down, and the crowd got rowdy. Bryan was glad to be standing farther away from the stage. After a couple of songs, a mosh pit formed toward the front, and he wasn't a fan of pushing and shoving. Their set lasted forty-five minutes, and that included an encore. When the lights came back up for set change, Bryan asked Mal if he wanted another beer.

"No, I'm good. I'm too nervous to drink any more. I'm already about to throw up," he admitted.

"Okay, I'll be right back." Bryan wedged his way through the crowd and up the steps to the concourse. While he waited in line for the restroom, he sent Andy a quick text telling him he couldn't wait to get back home. Bryan had thought about home and what it meant to him quite a bit. He had called his siblings and chatted with each one, but when he and Brett spoke, Bryan admitted he was in love with Andy. If anyone would understand, it was his baby brother. Brett asked all the same questions that were running through Bryan's head, and Bryan had been completely honest. Brett told him to follow his heart and he supported his big brother one hundred percent. Before they hung up, Brett promised to visit, stating he and David had some vacation time coming up, and Chicago wasn't that far from Arlo.

After speaking with Brett, Bryan had also confided in his other siblings about Andy. Brianna had been ecstatic that he was in love, and Bryce had actually admitted to being gay as well. It hurt Bryan that his middle brother hadn't told him before, but he could also understand it, too. Now that Bryan was with Andy, all four Moore siblings were happy with a partner. He knew it was what his mom had wanted for them all, and he could smile a little easier when thinking about her. He had a feeling she had something to do with Bryan being at the VA the day Erik came around. Why else would he end up with the perfect job, a surrogate mom, and a man who loved him for who he was?

The lights were going down just as Bryan reached Mal. The pounding of the bass drum reverberated through his chest, and he knew Mal had to feel it, too. Mal looked at him and said, "That's Cade!" Bryan grinned and nodded. That indeed was Cade. When the spotlights came up, there he was in all his glory. Cade's was one of the largest drum kits Bryan had ever seen. After he'd met Cade at the farm, Bryan did a little research on Cade's time with 7's Mistress as well as the tour for Divining the Dark. He didn't bother to read the tabloid shit, because he knew the real man, not the one the trash mags made him out to be. Mal had told them how Cade had been in love with his former bandmate, Taggart Lee, and how he'd tried to sabotage Tag's relationship with Erik. Bryan didn't think badly of him for it. He'd apologized and made amends with both men.

Bryan shouldn't have been surprised that Mal knew the words to all the songs. If his boyfriend was a rock star, he'd listen to their music nonstop as well. Hell, he did listen to Cade's bands more than any others, and they were just friends. He already knew how badass Cade was, but when the other guys left the stage for Cade to do his solo, Bryan couldn't help but smile at Mal's face as he experienced Cade in all his glory. It truly was a sight to behold.

Before the show started, he and Mal had agreed to stay on the floor until the band left the stage between the final song and their first encore. Bryan figured it would take a while to get through the crowd. He pulled out his phone and texted Carl, Cade's bodyguard and friend. When they reached the side of the stage, Carl ushered them past the barricade.

"Mal, Bryan, it's a pleasure to meet you both. Do you want to see some of the encore before I escort you to the dressing room?" Carl asked after introducing himself. Bryan had heard all about Carl, and he immediately liked the man.

When Mal nodded, Carl led them to the side of the stage opposite from where Cade came and went. Mal's nerves were palpable as he fisted his hands at his sides. Bryan put his hand on Mal's shoulder and squeezed. "You've got this, Boss. Everything's gonna be fine, you'll see."

Mal nodded, but his eyes were still wide. After Divining the Dark played two songs, Carl led them down a long hallway to a private room where they could wait. "I'm really glad you're here, Mal. Our guy's not been the same lately, and I'm tired of dealing with his mopey ass. I'm going to go get him. I'll be back in a few." Carl closed the door to the spacious room. It had a sofa and a couple of comfortable looking chairs, as well as a long table in front of a mirror that had hand towels stacked on top. There was a cooler on the floor by the sofa. Mal began pacing back and forth, but when the door opened, Bryan rushed Cade.

"Man, what a fucking show! You were phenomenal. And your drum solo? Oh my god! How do you play for that long without needing a break? Seriously, that was the shit!"

Cade's face was cheek-to-cheek smile. He had to still be on an adrenaline high. He grabbed one of the towels and wiped the sweat from his forehead and neck. "Practice, my man. Lots of practice and gym time. How are you?" Cade asked. Before Bryan could answer, Cade saw Mal leaning against the far wall, his arms crossed over his chest. Bryan was immediately forgotten.

The two men stood and stared at each other for what seemed like an eternity but was only a few seconds before

Mal said, "Hi."

"Hi," Cade replied, his voice cracking. He cleared his throat and tried again. "Hi, Mal. You look good."

Mal pushed off the wall and quickly had Cade in a tight grip, devouring his mouth. As badly as Bryan wanted to know how things went after that, he turned to leave the room and give them some privacy. Carl followed him out into the hallway and closed the door.

"I hope like hell your boy can talk some sense into mine," Carl said, clearly exasperated. "Cade's a handful on a good day, but you get him in a pissy mood? Jesus, Mary, and Joseph. I'm too old for this shit."

Bryan grinned. Carl didn't look that old, but looks could be deceiving. "Yeah, well living with Mal hasn't been sunshine and rainbows, either. He was a complete ass when he found out Cade owned the farm, but after what Cade did with Dwight, Mal had time to re-think things. I tried to get him to call Cade and make amends, but by that time, Cade had shut down. Let's hope the face-to-face reminds them of why they fell in love in the first place."

The two men swapped stories of the last few months while they waited. After about thirty minutes, Roarke Fowler, the guitarist for the band, came down the hallway whistling. When he stopped in front of them, he introduced himself to Bryan. The man was larger than life and just as loud. "Are they duking it out in there or fucking like bunnies?" he asked, thumbing at the closed door.

"We've not heard any yelling or loud noises, so hopefully they're discussing things like adults," Carl said.

"Where's the fucking fun in that?" Roarke didn't bother knocking before he slung open the door to the dressing room. As soon as he was inside, he shouted, "Whoowee, let me get my camera!"

Bryan looked at Carl and they both went to the door and looked in. Cade was on his knees in front of a shirtless Mal. At first, Bryan thought they'd walked in on a blowjob, but when Cade stood, he pulled Mal to his side. Grinning at Roarke, Cade said, "Shut up, you sick fucker, and get over here and meet my fiancé."

"Fiancé? I thought… Never mind. Roarke Fowler," he introduced himself to Mal.

Shaking his outstretched hand, he responded, "Mal Wilson. Pleasure."

Roarke was bouncing on his toes. "I just came to tell you we're all headed out to the hotel. Your buddy Bryan's waiting with Carl for you two to come up for air."

"Thanks. Please tell them we'll be right there."

Carl and Bryan stepped out of the doorway as Roarke stalked toward them. "You got it." When Roarke got to the door, he stopped and twisted back toward Cade. "How cute . . . matching tattoos." Laughing like a maniac, the man ran out the door past Bryan and Carl. When he got to the end of the hallway, he turned back. "They're all yours."

Carl led Bryan farther down the hallway to wait. "Don't want him to think we've been eavesdropping," Carl said with a wink, even though that's exactly what they'd been doing.

A few minutes later, Cade and Mal emerged from the room hand in hand. Bryan breathed a huge sigh of relief for more than one reason. Cade asked Bryan, "You want a room at the hotel?"

No way in hell. "Nah, I better get back home to Andy. He's been feeling kinda sick," Bryan said. Mal gave him an odd look, because he'd seen Andy feeling just fine when they left.

Mal handed Bryan the keys to the truck. "Here you go. I'll catch a ride back with Cade tomorrow."

Bryan looked between the two of them and asked, "We're all good now?"

"Yeah, we're all good," Cade assured him. He put his hand on Bryan's shoulder and squeezed. "Thank you for watching over my man while I'm gone."

Bryan smiled and said, "It's my pleasure." Looking around, he asked Carl, "How do I get out of here?" After Carl directed him to the nearest door, Bryan said his goodnights and quickly made his way to the exit. He waited until he was in Mal's big truck to text Andy.

Cade and Mal made up. On my way home. Alone.

He put the key in the ignition and fired up the engine. He waited before leaving the parking lot for Andy to text him back.

Be careful, but hurry.

Bryan planned to do both. As he headed toward the interstate, his nerves began taking over. Normally, his panic attacks were brought on by loud noises, but he'd had enough of them to recognize the signs. He rolled down the window, hoping the fresh air would do him some good. Bryan didn't want to have to pull over to the shoulder and get out. Turning the radio down helped some. He continued driving north as he did his best to get his breathing under control. Bryan had no idea why he was reacting this way. Andy loved him, and he loved Andy. They'd already been intimate. He'd sucked Andy's cock and swallowed his come, for Christ's sake. He let his mind remember what Brett told him – yes, his baby brother had gone there – this wasn't just anal with a random hookup. This was making love between two people who loved each other. There was nothing more special than offering your body up to the other person.

When he let that mantra run through his head, he calmed down. He knew this was special, and after tonight, neither one of them would be the same. Bryan could do this.

253

He would feel better being the one on top for his first time, but he couldn't ask that of Andy. Not after what had been done to him all those years ago. Bryan wanted Andy to talk to someone about that day as well as what happened afterward with his family. PTSD wasn't just for men and women in the military. Andy admitted his nightmares were more often about Patrick's abuse and rape than what Andy had seen overseas. Bryan had kept his mouth shut before when they were only friends. Once the made love, they would truly be bound to one another, and Bryan would make sure Andy did whatever it took to become whole again.

The gate was open when Bryan pulled into the driveway. He closed and locked it before parking the truck. He didn't want there to be any surprise visitors interrupting their night alone. He noticed his truck wasn't parked where he'd left it, so Andy must have gone to town. Bryan didn't mind Andy borrowing his vehicle. He'd left him the keys for that purpose. He was curious to know where he'd gone and how he'd spent his night alone.

When he walked into the kitchen, the first thing Bryan noticed was almost all the lights in the house were off. The second thing he noticed were rose petals strewn across the floor. Bryan's heart fluttered at the romantic gesture. He'd never been in a relationship, but more than that, he'd never had anyone care enough about him to do something so special. Bryan followed the path. Instead of it leading to his bedroom like he suspected, it led to the other side of the house. When he reached the door to Suzette's old room, Bryan stopped and took in everything Andy had done.

Dozens of white candles lit the room, casting shadows over the walls. On the table beside the bed, a bottle of what Bryan assumed to be champagne was chilling in an ice bucket. A platter of strawberries sat next to that. But the best part of the room was the sight of Andy leaned back against the headboard wearing nothing but some skimpy underwear. Bryan's mouth watered, ready to have a taste of what was waiting for him. Andy didn't speak, but he did adjust his cock. Bryan clocked the movement before meeting Andy's eyes.

Bryan took one step into the room giving himself space to remove his clothes. He untucked his T-shirt from his jeans and pulled it over his head dropping it to the floor. He took another step. Andy's eyes were on Bryan's chest, so he rubbed a hand across it from one nipple to the other. Andy loved to tease the little nubs, and the sensation was something that sent fire to Bryan's dick every time. He moved his hand lower, letting it rest against the band of his jeans. As nervous as he'd been on the way home, Bryan was having a hard time not ripping his clothes off and putting his ass in the air for Andy to have his way with. Where this sexy bravado was coming from, he didn't know until he caught the heat in Andy's eyes. His man loved his body and had told him so every time they removed their clothes. Bryan would work hard to keep fit if it turned Andy on that much.

Working the button loose, Bryan hesitated before lowering the zipper. Andy licked his lips in anticipation, and Bryan didn't make him wait. Hooking his thumbs beneath the denim, Bryan eased his jeans over his hips only far enough to free his dick. His cock sprang loose and hit him in the stomach, pre-come coating his skin. He'd worn his cowboy boots on purpose. Toeing off one boot then the other, Bryan bent at the waist and pushed his jeans the rest of the way off. He'd not thought about buying some skimpy piece of fabric to cover his cock, but Andy would have probably ripped it off by now if he had. Andy had the comforter fisted in both hands. Lastly, Bryan pulled his socks off and took one more step closer to where his lover waited.

Andy scooted off the bed and stood less than an

arm's length away. When he met Bryan's eyes, he said, "Hi."

"Hi," Bryan whispered back. He wanted Andy. Needed to touch him. Taste him. Feel their bodies together. He took the final step that left no distance between them and placed his hands on Andy's hips. His fingertips brushed bare skin, and Bryan figured out Andy was wearing a thong. "Fuck, Lily. That right there has me ready to blow. You know I love your ass." Bryan moved his hands until they were holding onto Andy's tight globes. Bryan had only gone so far as to kiss Andy's cheeks, making sure to stay away from his hole. Until Andy gave him permission to play there, Bryan wasn't going to risk it.

"And I love yours, B. I can't wait to have your tight hole surrounding me. Squeezing me better than your fist does." He put his arms around Bryan's back and pressed their mouths together. Their tongues did a slow dance, neither one seeking dominance. Tonight was about making love, not fucking. When Andy pulled away, he asked, "Would you like a glass of champagne now or later?"

Bryan could probably use the liquid courage, but he was also afraid to drink anything until after. His stomach was already in a knot. "Everything looks wonderful, and I appreciate you going to all this trouble for me, but let's save it until after. Right now, I want to taste *you*," Bryan said against Andy's ear. Andy shivered, and goosebumps formed on his skin. Bryan kissed Andy's neck and shoulder. He kneaded the muscles of his ass. He drew Andy closer so his aching cock was rubbing against Andy's erection. The silk material added an extra sensation to the friction. Andy moaned in Bryan's ear, and Bryan kissed his way back to where the vein was pulsing in Andy's neck. The previous mark he'd put on his lover had faded, and Bryan decided it was time to rectify the situation.

With their lower bodies melded together, dicks rubbing back and forth, Bryan sucked on Andy's neck,

256

pulling the blood to the surface, once again marking his man. Andy waited until Bryan dragged his mouth away before he put his hands on Bryan's hips, halting their movements.

"I need you, Bryan. I need to be one with you, but you have to promise me you want this, too."

"I promise," Bryan vowed. "I'm ready, Baby. Make love to me." He was scared shitless, but he was ready to give himself over to Andy. Let Andy mark Bryan in a different way.

Chapter Twenty-Five

Andy

Andy wanted their first time to be special, and Bryan said he appreciated the champagne and berries. He wasn't sure if Bryan would want the opportunity to ease into things before they made love for the first time, so Andy gave him the option. When Bryan opted to forgo the refreshments, Andy was glad. Nervous, but glad. This had to be scary for Bryan. He'd never had sex with a man, much less be on bottom for his first time. Andy was going to do his best to make it pleasurable for both of them.

"How do you want me?" Bryan asked.

"I'd love to have you on your back so I can see your face, but on your knees might be easier on you the first time. Your choice." Andy didn't know that for a fact because he'd only ever been fucked from behind.

Bryan crawled to the middle of the bed and remained on his hands and knees. Andy had already placed the lube and condom on the foot of the bed, so he climbed on and situated himself between Bryan's legs. "Spread your legs for me, B." Andy smoothed his hand over Bryan's shoulders, caressing the ink. He traced a path over Bryan's spine until he got to his ass. Andy rubbed both cheeks, getting Bryan used to having attention close to his hole. He allowed his thumbs to dip in the crease, getting near his pucker. When Bryan's arms began to tremble, Andy pushed on his upper back. "You can relax onto your chest if you want."

Andy knew Bryan was a strong man, but under the circumstances, Andy's arms would probably be ready to give out as well. When Bryan was situated with his head resting on a pillow, Andy resumed getting Bryan ready. Other than what he'd read about online, he honestly had no idea what he was doing. He'd never had anyone get him ready to have sex other than slap some lube over his hole before they pushed their way in. Andy was doing what he would want done if their positions were reversed. The closer he got to Bryan's hole, the more he desired to lick it. Andy had never rimmed anyone or had it done to him, but he wanted everything with his man.

"Your hole looks delicious, B. It's so tight and pink. I want so bad to lick it. I want to taste you there. Is that weird?"

"Fuck, no. It's... No, it's not weird," Bryan said, breathing harder.

Andy decided to save that for another time. Right now, he wanted to bury his cock deep in his lover's ass. He wanted them to be connected in the most perfect way. Wanted them to become one. Reaching behind him for the bottle of lube, he explained, "This is gonna be cold, but I'm going to warm you up quickly. I need to get you ready for me, B. Is that still what you want?"

"Yes, Baby. I want it. I want you," Bryan assured him. Andy didn't miss the fact that Bryan was stroking his cock.

Andy poured a generous amount of lube on his fingers. He tested Bryan's hole with the tip of one, circling the entrance and letting Bryan get used to it. When Bryan pushed back, Andy slid the digit in up to his first knuckle. He slid it in and out, deeper each time. He added a second and continued working Bryan's hole open a little at a time. Bryan began thrusting against his hand. "That feels... more, Andy. I want more."

Andy added more lube. It was probably overkill, but since he'd never had enough when Patrick fucked him, he was going to make sure he used plenty. It was a tight fit when he added another finger, but he continued until Bryan was loose. Feeling adventurous, Andy twisted his hand and searched for Bryan's prostate. He knew the second he found it, because Bryan jerked, moaning. "Holy fuck, what did you do?"

"I found your prostate. Did you like that?"

"God, yes. You can do that all day long. Well, not all day, because that was... intense." His breathing was erratic, but Andy figured that was a good thing.

Andy ran his free hand over Bryan's back as he continued getting Bryan good and stretched. Andy was more than ready. His cock was pulsing and the tip was leaking. He was waiting on Bryan to tell him he was ready.

"Andy, I need you. I'm never going to be more ready than I am right now."

Andy removed his fingers and found the condom. He was clean. He'd not had sex in over eight years, but he wasn't going to breech Bryan without a condom. Not until they talked it over. He rolled the latex over his cock and took a deep breath. He coated the sheath with lube and scooted on his knees as close as he could get and still have room to move his cock over Bryan's hole. Andy teased the ready pucker, rubbing up and down. Andy placed the tip at Bryan's entrance and began pushing.

Bryan tensed but didn't say anything. "Take a deep breath, exhale, and push against me." Andy had read up on how to have sex without hurting someone. He continued rubbing his free hand over Bryan's lower back, hoping to soothe his nerves. When Bryan pushed back against him, Andy eased his cock in a little more. "Fuck, B, you are so goddamn tight. I think I'm going to nut before I get all the way in." Andy squeezed the base of his dick to keep from ruining their first time.

"Just do it, Babe. It's going to hurt, but I can take it."

Andy didn't want it to hurt. "I don't think. . ." Bryan pushed back, impaling himself on Andy. "Shit, B!"

"It's fine, just give me a second." Bryan's breathing was heavy. His fists were gripping the bedding. "Ok, yeah. That's good. Now, move, Baby. Please."

Andy prayed Bryan wasn't lying just so Andy could enjoy himself. He eased out, leaving the tip inside, and slowly inched his way back inside. God, it felt so much better than he imagined it would. "Feel's good, B. Better than good. It's... perfect." Andy never wanted to be anywhere else than where he was at that moment. Moving his hips a little faster with each thrust, Andy asked, "You okay?"

"Fuck yeah. I feel full, but god, Babe, this is... like you said, perfect." Andy leaned over Bryan's back and kissed him several times on his shoulders. Bryan reached one hand around and grabbed hold of the back of Andy's thigh. "Come on, Lily. Let me see what you got," Bryan taunted. Andy didn't want to hurt him, but he wouldn't mind moving faster. He had both hands on Bryan's hips and pulled back as his hips thrust forward. Bryan wasn't making any sounds, and Andy didn't know if that was a good thing or not. Andy filled the silent house with his grunts and the sound of his skin slapping Bryan's.

"I can't hold out, B." Andy had held his orgasm off as long as possible, giving Bryan time to come with him. "I want you to come with me." Andy leaned over and grabbed hold of Bryan's cock to jack him off. Bryan's limp cock.

"What. . .?"

"Don't stop, Andy."

"What's wrong?" Andy asked, his hips faltering at the thought of Bryan not enjoying what they were doing.

"Don't you fucking stop!" Bryan growled and thrust his hips back, encouraging Andy to finish.

Andy's throat threatened to close up, and he grunted through his release. Tears pricked the backs of his eyes. He squeezed them tightly as he caught his breath. Andy grabbed the edge of the condom and pulled out of what had

261

started off as heaven. "Oh, god, B," he choked out.

Bryan flipped over and immediately pulled Andy into his arms. "Hey, shhh. It's okay. Everything is fine." Bryan kissed his neck and shoulder. When his lips met Andy's wet face, he placed his hands on Andy's cheeks. "Babe, what is it? Did I do something wrong?" Now Bryan's eyes were misty.

Andy shook his head, but a sob caught in his throat, keeping him from speaking. It was supposed to be perfect. Bryan pulled the condom off Andy's limp cock and tossed it in the garbage can. "Come here," he said, pulling Andy down on top of him. With one arm around his back and the other on his face, Bryan did his best to soothe Andy.

"Babe, please, tell me what's wrong."

Andy couldn't look at Bryan. "I wanted it to be perfect."

"I'm sorry I ruined it," Bryan whispered.

Andy jerked his head up. "You? You didn't ruin it. I did."

"How did you ruin anything? That was so much better than I imagined. I was scared at first, but then you hit my prostate, and I couldn't hold back."

"You mean you —"

"Shot my load before you even got your dick anywhere near me? Yeah. If you want proof, I'm laying in it."

"I thought. . . Oh, Bryan, I thought you didn't enjoy it." Andy dropped his head to Bryan's chest and laughed. It wasn't really funny, but he couldn't help it.

"I wanted to come with you, but I gotta tell you, that prostate thing is something else. You kept hitting it with your dick, but I guess I needed more recovery time." Bryan shrugged one shoulder. "So, other than worrying about me, how was it for you? Was it as good as you hoped?"

"Better. God, B. Being inside you is pure heaven. You fit so tight around my dick, squeezing it in a way our hands can't. It's like you were made just for me."

"Kiss me, Andy."

Andy rose up and kissed his man. Bryan rolled them over and settled between Andy's legs. "I *was* made for you." Bryan peppered kisses all along Andy's cheeks, down his chin, on his neck. He pulled back and touched the mark he'd made earlier. "This means you're mine, Andy Holcomb. You get that?"

"Yeah, I get it." And he did. Andy never felt as wanted or loved as he did when he was with Bryan.

"Let's open the champagne. I'd like to make a toast. We'll sample the strawberries, and then, we're going to do it all over again. Only this time, you're going to keep your fingers away from my sweet spot so we can come together. Deal?"

"Deal."

Bryan rolled off Andy, propped the pillows against the headboard, and scooted back against them. Andy poured them both a glass of champagne and put the berries on the bed where they could reach them. Settling in next to his man, Andy waited to hear what Bryan had to say. Bryan laced their free hands together and kissed Andy's knuckles.

"I never thought I would have what other people have. When my father got sent away, I knew then my life would be different. I never expected to find someone and fall in love. I never expected to fall in love with a man. But I have, and I realized that part doesn't matter. You and I are what matter. I don't know what the future holds, but I do know I want to face it all with you by my side. Like I told you before, the only thing I have to offer is my love. I will love you until the day I die. I will stand by you through thick and thin. I'll support you no matter what choices you make, as long as you allow me to be part of your life when you're making them. If you want to find another job and move, if you want to live here and help raise cattle, if you want to pursue a business degree and take over management of the farm, or if you and Cade decide to form a band and tour the world — whatever you decide, I want to be there with you.

"Here's to a life together." Bryan held his glass up, and Andy touched his to it. They sipped the bubbly liquid, and Bryan licked his top lip. "That shit's good," he raved.

Andy laughed at his expression, but he should have already realized Bryan might not have had a reason to celebrate in the past. Andy had been allowed to drink champagne at his parents' parties, but he couldn't remember one thing they'd celebrated that was more important than him and Bryan. "I love you, Bryan Moore. I want everything you mentioned, but I want something else. You said you'd love me 'til you die, and that sounds like you're willing to make a commitment to me. I'm not asking for this now, but one day in the future, I'd really like to become Andy Moore."

Bryan blinked several times, his mouth hanging open. "You want to marry me?"

"Of course I do. That's what loving someone until death should be about. Right?"

"Sure, but wouldn't you rather I take your last name?"

Andy shook his head. "No. I haven't been a Holcomb for over eight years. Your family is about love and acceptance, and I want to be part of that family."

Bryan kissed Andy, smiling. "Andrew Theodore Moore does have a nice ring to it."

Andy set his glass down and picked up a strawberry. "I just realized I don't know your middle name. Why is that?"

"You've never asked."

"Well?" Andy asked, holding the berry out for Bryan to take a bite. He did, and the juice ran down his chin. Andy leaned over and licked at Bryan's jaw, tasting both the sweet of the fruit and the salt of his man.

Bryan made a big production of chewing. Andy laughed. "Oh, no. You don't get off that easy."

"Obviously, I do," he said pointing at the wet spot between his legs.

Andy laughed. "We're going to remedy that. But first, if you want this..." Andy grabbed his dick and stroked, "you're gonna have to give me your name."

Bryan sat up, took a strawberry in his mouth, and bit into it, letting the juice fall onto Andy's hard-on. He placed the other half onto Andy's waiting tongue. Before Andy finished chewing, Bryan kissed him, muttering "Harrison" against his lips.

"Like George Harrison? I know your mom liked her music."

Bryan rolled his eyes as he eased his body down between Andy's legs. He licked the strawberry juice off Andy's cock. "Harrison Ford. She also loved the Indiana Jones movies."

"That's cool. At least you aren't named after two dead presidents." Andy moved the strawberries back to the bedside table for later.

Bryan dragged his tongue up the length of Andy's dick, sucking it down when he got to the tip. "Mmm. You taste so good." Andy spread his legs farther apart, letting Bryan have at him. He was really good at giving head, and Andy had no problem with being on the receiving end. Bryan worked his cock up and down while fondling Andy's balls. He pulled off Andy's erection and sucked on each nut, pulling them up and licking underneath. Bryan's tongue got precariously close to Andy's hole, but he didn't flinch. He'd thought a lot about whether or not he could ever let anyone fuck him after what Patrick and Clark did. He decided the answer was no. But Bryan wasn't anyone, and what they would do together wasn't fucking. Andy wanted to let Bryan make love to him. To make him forget the bad and replace it with good.

The longer Bryan sucked, the more he made Andy forget everything. But he didn't want to come in Bryan's mouth. Not this time. "B, stop. I want to make love to you again. That is, if you aren't too sore."

"I'll worry about that tomorrow, and if I'm walking funny, I'll blame it on Cochise." Bryan crawled up Andy's body and straddled his thighs. His cock was hard and leaking. Andy slid his fingertip through the moisture and placed it on his tongue. Bryan hissed, "So fucking sexy, Lily."

Bryan pushed up on his hands and stretched out until their erections were touching. "I want you to make love to me bare." Bryan slid down then back up. "I want to feel you. Nothing between us, and instead of you coming down my throat, I want you to come in my ass. Fill me up with your seed." He slid down again. On the way back up, Andy grabbed his ass and held him still.

"On one condition." Andy licked at Bryan's lips, teasing.

"What's that?" Bryan licked back.

"You let me see your face." Andy teased, the tip of his tongue barely touching Bryan's lips.

Bryan circled his hips, the movement erotic. Seductive. He held still for a moment then circled his hips again. For someone who had little experience, Andy's lover knew how to move. How to kiss. How to suck. Bryan dipped his head, taking one of Andy's nipples into his mouth, sucking the flesh all around it before biting the tip. The jolt from the bite went directly to Andy's cock, and he was ready for round two.

"I need you, B. Can I have you?"

Bryan rose up on his knees and spread Andy's legs like he was going to fuck him. He pushed his hard cock down until it rested against Andy's ass. Bryan's aqua eyes were darker than Andy had ever seen. Rubbing his erection along Andy's crack, he growled, "Yeah, Baby. You can have

266

me. But one day, you're gonna let me have you. I'm gonna show you how good it feels to have this cock fill you up."

Andy shivered at the promise. He had no doubt Bryan would make him feel good. Bryan took his length in his hand and stroked. When his thumb lapped up the moisture, Bryan stuck it in Andy's mouth, pressing on his tongue. Andy swirled his tongue around, sucking Bryan's thumb in and out like it was his dick. When Bryan pulled away, he rolled to his back, spreading his legs.

Andy didn't make him wait. He opened the bottle of lube and poured it over Bryan's hole, working enough inside to loosen him a little. He spread the rest of the slick over his cock and eased inside his lover. When he was fully seated, he stilled, giving Bryan time to adjust to being filled again. "I can't believe the difference. You feel fucking amazing," Andy purred.

"I need you to move." Bryan pulled his knees back farther, opening himself wide for Andy. Holding the backs of Bryan's legs for leverage, Andy set a pace that was faster than their first time.

"God, you're beautiful, Lily. The way you move above me . . . fuck."

This time was different. No longer was Andy worried about hurting Bryan. He rolled his hips until he hit Bryan's prostate with the tip of his dick. Once he found the perfect angle, he kept at it, pegging it over and over, driving his lover crazy. Bryan fisted his cock and began stroking in time with Andy's thrusts, moaning. "God, that's... harder. I need it . . . harder," Bryan grunted.

Andy increased his thrusts, pulling out and slamming in. He kept his eyes on Bryan, making sure he wasn't hurting him, but goddamn, it felt good to let loose. Too good. "Please tell me you're close, B."

"I'm close. Come inside my ass, Baby. Fill me up."

Bryan's words sent Andy over the edge. Yelling out Bryan's name, Andy pumped back and forth, each time sending more of his release inside Bryan's body. Bryan flattened his feet to the bed, and his ass clenched around Andy's dick, making the aftershocks more powerful. Ribbons of creamy liquid landed on Bryan's chest and even his chin. Keeping his softening cock buried as deep as possible, Andy bent his elbows so he could lick the jizz off Bryan's chest. He loved the way Bryan tasted. Loved the way his body shivered with each swipe of his tongue. When he had most of it lapped up, Andy pressed their chests together. "God, I fucking love you."

"I love you, too, Baby. As cheesy as it sounds, you complete me. I hate the shit we've both been through to get where we are, but I'd do it all over again if it meant spending the rest of my life with you."

Andy rolled to his side, his spent dick easing out of Bryan's leaking hole. Instead of getting up to get a washcloth, Andy hitched his leg over Bryan's muscular thighs and ran his fingers over his chest. They stayed like that for a while, neither one talking, just being.

Chapter Twenty-Six

Bryan

Fully sated and wrapped around each other, Bryan told Andy about the concert and how Cade introduced Mal as his fiancé. Not only had they made up, but they'd also agreed to take things to the next level. After a quick shower to clean the spunk off their bodies, they spent the next couple of hours finishing off the berries and drinking champagne while talking about nothing in particular. When they woke the next morning, they decided a longer shower was in order.

Bryan poured shampoo in his hand and lathered Andy's short hair. The longer he massaged his lover's scalp, the more Andy moaned and the harder his cock became. Since they had already bathed one another, Bryan got on his knees to worship Andy's dick again. Making love had been so much more than he ever expected. Now he knew why he didn't feel anything with the girls he'd slept with. His body was meant for Andy. It didn't really surprise him when Andy mentioned marriage. They were completely committed to one another, and that was the natural next step. It did surprise him when Andy suggested taking Bryan's last name, but he understood. Andy no longer felt part of his family and hadn't in a long time.

When Bryan felt Andy's body tense, instead of sucking harder, he pulled off Andy's dick and stroked it until he was shooting across Bryan's chest and chin. As much as he loved the way Andy's salty release tasted, he liked being marked by his man even more. Bryan knew it wouldn't be long before he added Andy's name in ink somewhere on his body. Some people considered that the mark of death for a relationship, but Bryan had no doubt Andy was it for him. He'd promised to love him until the day he died, and Bryan didn't make promises he couldn't keep.

After Bryan washed again, they dried off and slipped into sweat pants and T-shirts. Together, they stripped the sheets on Suzette's bed and added fresh ones. Bryan straightened the room and put the sheets in the wash while Andy started breakfast. They really did make a great team. After they ate, Bryan led Andy to the front porch swing where they finished their coffee. "We really need to get a patio set for the deck," Andy said.

"You don't like swinging with me?"

"Of course I do, but we could have enjoyed our breakfast outside."

"True. If you want, we can go over to Franklin later today and look around."

Andy put his hand in Bryan's and laced their fingers together. "I'd like that. Listen, I wanted to ask you something. Last night you mentioned me going to school for a business degree. Why did you say that?"

"Before the shit went down with your family, that had been your plan. I just thought if it was something that interested you, you could still do it. Instead of running an oil company you could take over the business end for Mal. I'm not saying you should, I was just throwing it out there as a possibility."

"I hadn't really thought about it."

Bryan had thought about it. He had thought about it a lot. He had no doubt Andy loved him. He also had no doubt Andy would stay on the farm for Bryan because it was probably the only job he was going to be able to get with his PTSD. He didn't want to hold Andy back. He was too selfish to let him go, but he wanted Andy to be happy with his job, whatever it was.

"You wouldn't mind if I went back to school?" Now, Andy was thinking about it. "Not that I am, but if I did?"

"Not at all. I want you to be happy, Babe. I'll follow you to the ends of the earth if that's what it takes."

"You're such a good man."

"I don't know about that, but I am a man who loves you."

"I wish I could have met your mom."

Bryan smiled. "Me, too. She'd have loved you."

Moe and Curly, who were lazing at the tops of the steps, sat up, ears perked. "I bet that's Mal and Cade," Bryan said. When Andy started to pull his hand away, Bryan wouldn't let him. "They're gonna find out sooner or later. I'd rather it be sooner so we can be ourselves around everyone."

Andy leaned over and kissed him just as a blacked out SUV rolled down the driveway.

"Stop that shit," Cade yelled out the driver's window, grinning.

"Sooner it is," Bryan said before deepening the kiss. He could sit there kissing his man all day, but they had to face the music. "Come on, Lily. Let's get this over with." Bryan pulled Andy to his feet and linked their fingers together as they made their way to the back of the house. Cade angled out of the vehicle and pulled both of them into a bear hug.

"I can't thank you both enough for everything."

Mal came around the SUV wearing the biggest smile Bryan had ever seen on the man. "We couldn't be the only ones happy around here," Bryan joked.

"Andy, I see you made a quick recovery," Mal said.

"Huh?" Andy asked, frowning at Bryan.

"I might have told him you didn't feel well. I had to tell him something so I could get back home to you last night."

Andy's face lit up. "Yeah, I'm feeling *much* better."

271

"How long's this shit been goin' on?" Mal asked, still smiling.

"Since for-fucking-ever," Andy said at the same time Bryan said, "Not long."

Cade and Mal both laughed, and Cade pulled Mal into his side, wrapping his arm around his shoulder. "I'm glad there isn't a 'no fraternization' rule for the hired help."

"You and me both," Bryan agreed, pulling Andy to him the same way Cade held Mal. "We're gonna head over to Franklin and do a little patio furniture shopping."

Mal pulled out his wallet. "Here, take the company credit card."

Bryan held up his hand and protested, "No, Mal. Andy and I live here, too. It's not fair for you to pay for something we want."

"You're not the only ones gonna sit on it, are ya? Besides, I'm the one wantin' a new dining table. Why don't y'all look for one of those while you're out?"

"Why don't we all go?" Cade said. When Mal shot him a nasty look, Cade laughed. "We have the rest of our lives to fuck like bunnies, Cowboy. Besides, if we're gonna build our own house, we can look at the other furniture and get an idea of what you want."

"Y'all are building a house?" Andy asked.

"Yep. Somewhere out in the north forty. Or south forty. Hell, out there," Cade pointed behind them. "So, you two will have that whole big house to yourselves."

"Speaking of that. Mal, I've decided I do want to move into your mom's old room after all," Andy told him.

"And leave Bryan on the other side of the house all alone?"

"Nah, I'm bringing him with me. If that's okay."

Mal grinned. "Fine by me. That'll open up the other rooms for when we hire on more men."

"More men?" Bryan asked. He wasn't sure how he felt about sharing the house with strangers. Then again, he'd done it with Andy and Mal, and things had turned out pretty good.

"Yeah, we're gonna be buyin' up as much land around us as we can. You two won't be able to do it all on your own, so eventually we'll hire a couple new men to help out. Now, let's go furniture shoppin'." Bryan was glad to know Mal and Cade were planning on staying in Arlo. He'd worried that Cade would try to get Mal to head off to California, leaving him and Andy behind. Not that they couldn't handle the farm, but it was a lot of responsibility.

Andy and Bryan closed up the house and piled in the backseat of Cade's rental. The trip to the next town over turned out to be a lot of fun. Bryan and Mal remained quiet for the most part, while Cade and Andy cut up and joked with everyone they met. When they didn't find exactly what they were looking for in Franklin, they ended up south of Nashville at a huge furniture mall. They picked out a large patio set as well as a matching high top with stools for the deck. Cade insisted on buying a gas grill, even though Bryan refused to cook on it. Mal chose the perfect table to put in the den turned dining room for the time being. Once he and Cade built their own home, they'd be inviting everyone to their house to eat.

Bryan pulled Andy to the bedroom section of the store. "I was thinking... Since we're going to be sharing a room, what do you think about a king-sized bed?"

"I was thinking the same thing," Andy wiggled his eyebrows. "I want to be able to roll around without falling off the bed."

They walked around, followed by a sales clerk, looking at different styles, and they both pointed at a large sleigh bed at the same time. Next, they tried out different mattresses. "You know you'll get in trouble if you try these out, don't you?" Cade asked when he and Mal found them lying side by side on one of the displays. The woman who was writing down the items they were choosing gasped then giggled.

"Sorry, I. . . Is this the mattress you want?" she asked, recovering.

Bryan turned his head to Andy. "What do you say, Lily?"

"I say let's get it."

Cade went behind their backs and paid for everything. Bryan waited for Mal to lose his shit, but when they were all back in the SUV, he leaned over and kissed Cade. "Thanks, Rock Star."

"My pleasure. Just think of it as a thank you to Bryan and Andy for keeping my man safe."

"You really didn't have to do that, Cade. We have money," Bryan told him.

"I know, but I want to do this for you."

Bryan and Andy both thanked him and settled back for the ride home. Bryan wanted to protest, but if he did, he would be no better than Mal when he'd been pouting. Cade had plenty of money, so Bryan let it go. Cade had paid extra to have all the new furniture delivered the next day. When they got back to the farm, the four of them worked to get most of the old furniture out of the house to make room for the new. The only thing they didn't move was Suzette's old bed, since Bryan and Andy would need it that night. Until they could figure out what to do with everything, they put it in the barn. Mal suggested asking his mom if she wanted any of it, but Cade told him he'd buy her all new stuff. Mal rolled his eyes, and Cade kissed him.

"What about the piano?" Cade asked.

"It's stayin'. Andy likes to play it, and I enjoy listenin' to both of you," Mal told him.

"That's right. I hear you're better on the keys than I am," Cade said to Andy.

Andy tried to make light of his talent, but Bryan spoke up, "I've never heard you play piano, but Andy's seriously talented. Maybe we can get you both to play later?"

Andy's phone rang before he could argue. Frowning, he answered, "Hello?" After a second he said, "Here? At the farm? Hang on, and I'll let you in."

"Who's that?" Bryan asked.

Andy was still frowning as he headed toward the door. "Christy. She's down at the gate."

"Who's Christy?" Cade asked.

"His best friend from back home. Something must be up for her to show up out of the blue." Bryan went to the door and watched Andy jogging toward the road. A few minutes later, a small car came rolling up the driveway. Christy was driving, and Andy was in the passenger side. Bryan waited for them to come in the house, but they continued to sit in the car talking.

"I'm going to go straighten my room. I have a feeling she's going to need somewhere to sleep tonight." Bryan went to his bedroom and stripped the bed, adding clean sheets. Now that Mal had okayed it, he and Andy would move into Suzette's room. *Their* room. He cleaned out the bedside drawer, tucking his pistol into the back of his jeans while taking the condoms and lube he'd stashed to their new room. He even went as far as swapping their toiletries to their new bathroom. By the time he was finished, Andy and Christy were in the living room talking to Cade and Mal.

Bryan stopped at the doorway and watched the two of them together. Christy was a beautiful girl, and Andy was holding her hand. A spark of jealousy hit Bryan square in the chest until Andy caught his eye and smiled. "There you are." Andy stood and held out his hand for Bryan. The jealousy subsided, and when he reached Andy's side, Andy pulled him close. "B, this is Christy. Christy, my fiancé, Bryan."

Bryan held out his hand, but Christy threw her arms around Bryan, hugging him tight. He looked over at Andy

275

who was smiling, but something about it wasn't right. There was a sadness behind his eyes. As Bryan hugged the woman back, she sniffled into his chest. "Thank you, Bryan. You have made me the happiest girl in the world." When she finally pulled back, she wiped under her eyes, making sure her mascara wasn't running down her face. "I've been so worried about this guy for so long. Now I don't have to worry anymore."

"No, you don't. I'm gonna take good care of him."

"Can we all sit down? I have something to tell Andy," Christy said, sniffling.

Mal said, "We'll just leave you alone." He and Cade headed upstairs.

The three of them sat on the couch with Andy sitting in the middle. He reached out for Bryan's hand, threading their fingers together. Christy smiled at the gesture. "I could have just called, but I really have missed you. And I wasn't sure how you'd take the news, so I decided I would take a chance and come visit."

"Stop, Chris. You don't have to have a reason to come see me. Now what is it you need to tell me?"

"It's… your grandfather passed away last week."

Andy's hand tightened around Bryan's. "And? I'm glad you wanted me to know, but he's not my grandfather. None of them are my family, not since they tossed me out."

Christy tried to smile. "That's not all. Your mom came to visit after the funeral, asking me if I knew where you were. I lied and told her no. I figured if you wanted her to know, you'd have told her yourself."

"I can't see why she'd want to see me now. She didn't give a rat's ass about me when I needed her the most, so why would she want to talk now?"

"I think it has something to do with the company. Andy, I think they want you to come home."

Bryan's heart skipped a beat. What if Andy decided running his family business was what he wanted now?

Where would that leave Bryan? What would happen to them? Bryan knew he wouldn't be welcome as Andy's partner.

"I *am* home," Andy seethed. "Here, with Bryan, is home. I have a new family now, and the Holcombs can all rot in hell as far as I'm concerned."

Christy coughed out a laugh through her tears. "Come here," she said, pulling Andy into her arms. She looked over his shoulder at Bryan and mouthed, "thank you." Bryan placed his hand in the middle of Andy's back, rubbing small circles.

"Now, that's settled. How long are you going to be here? Can you stay a few days?" Andy asked. He leaned back against Bryan. Andy was still tense, so Bryan grabbed Andy by the nape and massaged his neck while he and Christy talked.

"Uh, actually. . . I'm. . ."

"What? Christy, just spit it out."

"I miss you," she admitted. "I'm thinking about relocating to Kentucky."

"Really?" Andy's body relaxed a little.

"You should stay here for now. I've already got a room ready for you," Bryan told her. Andy turned his body so he was facing Bryan.

"When did you do that?"

"When you two were in the car. You were outside for quite a while."

"We were talking about... you," Andy lied. Bryan knew his lover well enough to know there was something he was hiding. That didn't sit well with him, but he wasn't going to call Andy out in front of Christy. Whatever it was had caused the haunted look Bryan noticed earlier. Bryan touched Andy's face with his fingertip. God his man was gorgeous. He just wished he could take the pain away. Andy was trying to put on a good show for Christy, but Bryan knew him. Knew when he was truly happy his blue eyes sparkled. There was no sparkle in them now. He wanted to drag Andy to their room and make love until the ghosts of Andy's pasts were finally locked up tight.

"I couldn't impose," Christy said, breaking their moment.

"We have two extra bedrooms. Besides, Andy has missed you, too. So why don't you stay with us while you figure out if Kentucky is really the place for you?" Bryan wanted his lover to be happy, and maybe having a little bit of home would help ease the ache of everything he'd lost all those years ago.

Christy looked at Andy, and he nodded. "I think it's a wonderful idea."

"If you're sure."

"We're sure."

Bryan was still unsettled with the news that Andy's mother was looking for him. He wanted to believe Andy wouldn't go back to Texas, but his family was beyond rich. While Andy helped Christy get settled in his old room, Bryan decided to go for a walk, but ended up in the barn lifting weights. The pain from overexerting his arms matched the pain in his chest. If Andy decided he wanted to run the family business after all, Bryan wouldn't be able to stop him. He had nothing to offer that could stack up against all that money.

"You sure are sexy when you're sweaty," Andy said from the door. Bryan didn't put the weights down. He couldn't look at Andy and see the truth on his face. "What's got you in a tizzy, B? You don't work out this hard unless something's on your mind. So why don't you put the weights down and talk to me." Andy grabbed the bar as Bryan pushed the weights off his chest. "Bryan," Andy said with more force. Bryan settled the weights into the supports and sat up, wiping the sweat from his face with the hem of his T-shirt.

Andy sat down on the bench facing him, their knees

touching. "Talk to me, B."

"I was thinking about what Christy said, about the possibility of you going back."

"It's not a possibility, B. Let me tell you something, in case you've forgotten already." Andy paused. His breathing increased, and his eyes flashed with an anger Bryan hadn't seen since the night they went to Primus. "I love you. You," – he poked Bryan in the chest – "are my family. This is my life now. I would rather live in a one-bedroom trailer with a dirt yard than to go back to Texas, as long as I have you by my side. Do you think so little of me, of my love for you, that you believe for one second I'd choose that over you?"

"I just –"

Andy put his fingers over Bryan's lips. "You just don't give yourself enough credit. You never have, but let me tell you something. You are the best man I know. You gave up your childhood, your formative years, to take care of your family. You joined the Marines to help your family. I joined because I was a scared kid running from my ghosts. I didn't have an honorable reason, not like you. Bryan, I don't give a shit about the money. I could have all the money in the world, but if you aren't there to spend it with me, it's worthless. I like my life. *Our* life. I want to build on the life we have together."

"I'm sorry," Bryan whispered. Andy's words went a long way to ease his worries.

"It's okay. Now kiss me," Andy demanded, grabbing Bryan's T-shirt and pulling their faces together. When they separated, Andy said, "What do you say we show Christy the Dairy Barn and then head to DW's? That'll give Cade and Mal some alone time while we show Christy where she's thinking about relocating to. It'll also help get her mind off her troubles."

So, the lie Andy told earlier must have something to do with her troubles, not Andy. That he could abide by.

"What about her job?"

"She's a graphic designer and can work from anywhere. I think moving to Arlo could be good for her, at least temporarily. She wants to be near me, and I wouldn't mind that. I've missed her. But don't worry, B. You're still my number one." Andy kissed him quickly before sliding off the bench and holding out his hand. "I told you I want to marry you, Bryan, and I meant it. I want you for the rest of my life."

How could Bryan argue with that?

Chapter Twenty-Seven

Andy

Andy had missed Christy more than he realized, but having her around didn't take away from his time with Bryan. Having both his best friends in his life went a long way to healing the old ache Andy felt. He'd been pissed off that Bryan would even think for one second Andy would choose his old world over the new one they were building together. It reiterated Bryan's lack of self-esteem, and Andy was going to work on that.

They had taken Christy to DW's, where they sat at the bar talking to Kason. Christy let loose, drinking more than Andy had ever seen; but then again, he'd not spent any real time with her since high school. During the course of the evening, she dragged both him and Bryan on the dance floor. While Andy sat and enjoyed his two best friends dancing together, Kason asked about her. "She's my best friend from back home. She's thinking about moving here."

"Really?" Kason's voice had more than a passing interest.

"Yeah." Andy leaned closer. "You like what you see?"

"What? No, I. . ." he huffed, visibly flustered.

"She's a great girl, but she's been hurt. A lot. So, go easy with her, okay?" Andy couldn't think of a better man for Christy than the Marine behind the bar, and Christy was kind and caring. Just the sort of woman to help ease the troubles of a man like Kason.

They'd been there a few hours, and Andy was ready to get Bryan home so he could hold his lover, but Christy and Kason were talking, and he didn't want to ruin something for her. He waited another half hour, and when he suggested they go home, Kason asked Christy if she'd like to stay a while longer. The bar was practically empty, and he was closing up early. "I'll get her home, if that's okay."

Christy put her hand on Andy's arm, and smiled, nodding.

"You kids have fun," Andy said. Bryan paid their tab, and they left Christy and Kason grinning like teenagers.

"You think she'll be okay?" Bryan asked as they were walking to the truck.

"Yeah. He's a good guy. Besides, she's a grown woman, and she needs someone good to make her forget." Andy didn't elaborate. He would eventually tell Bryan what Christy had confided to him in the car, but not yet.

Cade and Mal were already upstairs by the time they got home. Andy took Bryan to the bedroom, and once they were undressed, Andy stepped up to Bryan until there was no room between them – bare skin touching from their chests down their legs. Andy pressed his lips to Bryan's, inhaling his breath in, using Bryan's oxygen as a lifeline. Andy wanted Bryan to know how deep his feelings were. He could say he loved him all day long, but unless he showed him… "I want you to make love to me," Andy said into Bryan's ear, kissing the shell, licking his way down Bryan's jaw.

"Andy—"

"No, B. I need you to do this for me. I need you to love me completely."

"Are you sure?"

"Absolutely. I want to lie on my back with my legs spread open for you so I can watch you make love to me. I want to see your face when you fill me up with your seed. I want to watch your beautiful eyes change colors from love to lust. I want you in the most special way I can have you."

282

Bryan held Andy's face in his hands, searching his eyes. When he saw the truth there, Bryan kissed him more tenderly than ever before. Keeping one hand on Andy's hip, Bryan turned the covers back and urged Andy to lie down. He opened the bedside drawer, retrieving the lube before crawling between Andy's open legs. His moves were slow, yet sensual, as he ran his fingertips from Andy's knees all the way down the insides of his thighs until they met at his cock. "So beautiful," Bryan cooed. He took his time rubbing Andy's legs, stroking his erection, playing with his balls. Andy didn't rush him. He let his lover take his time exploring, since this was his first time making love to a man. If Bryan was nervous, he didn't show it.

Bryan poured the slick onto his palm and rubbed his hands together. He fisted his cock, stroking his length a few times, while stroking Andy's in the same rhythm. Bryan continued rubbing Andy with one hand while teasing his hole with the other. Andy focused on Bryan's gorgeous face as he breached his pucker. He had to remind himself this was Bryan, the man who loved him. The man who was going to be his husband one day. This man would never hurt him. Bryan poured more lube over Andy's hole and continued to stretch him open. Andy wished he'd thought to put in a butt plug earlier so he'd already be stretched, but he hadn't planned on asking Bryan to make love to him until he saw the fear in Bryan's eyes earlier. Realized Bryan needed this as much as he did. And having Bryan stretch him gave him the chance to get used to Bryan's touch. When Bryan hit his prostate, Andy bit his lip and moaned, arching off the bed.

"I'm ready, B. Please. . ." If Bryan didn't enter him soon, he was going to blow.

Bryan teased Andy's hole with the leaking head of his cock, rubbing it up and down as the pucker quivered. Taking a deep breath, he pushed through the tight ring and stopped, giving Andy time to get acclimated to having a dick in his ass. "More," Andy begged, taking a deep breath and blowing it out. Bryan eased the rest of the way in, stopping when he couldn't go any farther. God, he'd never felt anything like being inside Andy's hot, tight channel. It was so much better than he could have imagined. It was like Andy had been designed specifically for him.

"So beautiful, Lily. You feel so good wrapped around me, loving me like only you can."

"I've never…" Andy cleared his throat. "Love me, B. Make love to me."

Bryan placed Andy's legs over his shoulders then settled his hands on the bed, keeping his eyes locked with Andy's. He eased in and out at first, the same way Andy had done the first time he made love to Bryan. Being with Bryan this way freed something in Andy. With Bryan filling him up with his cock and with his love, the final piece of his past broke free from the shackles. No longer was he burdened with the pain. Instead, he was filled with so much love, so much emotion, so much Bryan, he couldn't hold back the tears.

Bryan froze, but Andy shook his head. "No, Baby. It's all good. I promise. So goddamn good," he whimpered as he grabbed onto his cock and began stroking. "So fucking good, B. I want you to fill me up with your release."

Bryan's eyes darkened as they did when he was turned on. He quickened the pace of his hips, thrusting harder with each stroke. He pushed Andy's legs off his shoulders, placing his hands on the backs of Andy's calves, holding his legs farther apart. "I wish you could see this, Andy. See my cock filling you up. *My* cock, Babe, filling *my* hole. Mine, Andy."

"Yours," Andy grunted as he pulled harder and faster on his dick. "Gonna come so hard, B."

Bryan pegged his prostate over and over, and Andy closed his eyes when his orgasm took over. "Oh, god, Bryan. . ." Andy's cock pulsed, shooting streams of come over his hand and onto his stomach. His ass clenched around Bryan's hard length, and Bryan growled as he thrust harder and harder through his own climax, filling Andy like he'd wanted. When the last of Bryan's pulses faded, he lowered his chest to Andy's, kissing him with an urgency Andy didn't understand. Bryan pressed their foreheads together, eyes closed tightly.

"I'm so sorry. I got carried away."

"Bryan, look at me. Look at me," Andy said more forcefully when Bryan wouldn't open his eyes.

"That was perfect. You took away the pain of my past while giving me your love in return. I've waited over eight years to have that pain removed, and you did it. You."

Bryan rolled to his side, his spent dick slipping out of Andy's body. This time, it was Andy who pulled Bryan to him, allowing him to rest his head on Andy's chest. If felt good to hold his man. His future husband. "I want to get married, B. I don't want to wait."

"Tell me what you want, and I'll give it to you. Just the two of us at the courthouse? Small affair with our family with us? You wanna go to a beach somewhere and dig your toes in the sand?" Bryan asked, as he placed kisses on Andy's chest.

"Do you want your family there? Christy would kick my ass if I didn't include her."

"I think Brett would want to be there. Brianna might be able to get away without the twins, but she'd probably be okay just knowing about it."

"What about Bryce?"

"I doubt he'd want to be there. Don't get me wrong, I love my brother, but there's something there that won't let him get close to me."

"When's the last time you saw him?"

"The day I left for the Marines. I think sometimes he resents me for taking off, leaving him with the responsibility of looking after Brett. He's never come out and said it, but

285

Brett hinted at it a couple of times in his letters."

"I'm sorry."

"I'm not. I shouldered the responsibility for years. There's no reason he couldn't step up and be the man of the house for a little while. If truth be told, I think it was Brett who looked after Bryce."

Andy's phone rang somewhere in the room. "Shit, I forgot about Christy. She's probably sitting at the gate," Andy said as he scrambled off the bed. "Hello?"

"Hey, I wanted to let you know I won't be back tonight."

"Everything okay?"

"Great."

"You sure that's a good idea?" Andy asked. She'd just met Kason.

"Yes, Dad. I'm sure. I'll see you in the morning."

"I love you, Chris. Call me if you need me."

"I will, and I love you, too."

Andy disconnected the phone and stared at it.

"Christy and Kason hitting it off, I take it?" Bryan asked.

Andy nodded and placed his phone on the nightstand. He slid back in bed and pulled the covers up over them. Taking his place against Bryan, he got comfortable. "Seems that way."

Bryan kissed him on the temple. "Maybe we can talk to Cade and Mal in the morning about getting married. We can find out together if there's a minister willing to perform a same sex marriage in Kentucky."

"Sounds good," Andy said, yawning. He'd had a long day filled with both good and bad emotions. Bryan had as well, especially when a car backfired earlier and his PTSD kicked in. Luckily, they'd been in Cade's SUV, and Andy had been there to comfort him. "Thank you, for everything."

"I do what I do because I love you. No thanks is needed."

"I know, but still. . ." Andy closed his eyes and let the strength of Bryan's arms and eventually his soft snores lull Andy to sleep. It was the best night of sleep Andy had in over eight years.

The house was complete chaos the next morning. Christy arrived just in time for breakfast, and Andy invited Kason to stay and join them. Cole and Toby surprised them, showing up soon after Christy and Kason had come in, stating they'd missed everyone, but Toby admitted they were there for Mal's biscuits and gravy.

Christy looked around the room, laughing and fanning herself. "How'd I get so lucky? I'm surrounded by five Marines, a rock star, and a cowboy."

Andy popped her on the butt as he walked by. "Yes, but only one of the aforementioned is straight."

Christy's eyes widened when she looked at Cole and Toby. "You two are. . ."

Toby grinned, and confirmed it to be so with, "Yep." Cole just nodded and shrugged.

"It's a good thing *you* like me," she joked with Kason, giving him a wink. The smile he gave her in return warmed Andy's heart. He had worried about Christy just as much as she had him. She'd chosen some really shitty men in the past. Kason was kind, funny, nice-looking, and a hard-worker. Plus, he was a Marine. He was also looking at Christy like she was the last good woman left on Earth. Maybe she was.

The furniture truck arrived, and with the extra help, they had everything unloaded, put together, and set up by lunch time. The rest of the day was spent hanging out, drinking beer, and just having fun. Mal called his mom and invited her and Walt to come over for supper. When they showed up with all three of Mal's nieces, the full house felt even more like a home. Megan couldn't make up her mind if she wanted Bryan or Cade to hold her. It was apparent she was smitten with them both. Matilda kept them all laughing with her funny ways. When she started singing a country song Andy recognized, he took her to the new dining room and sat her down at the piano with him. He played while she sang her heart out. Pretty soon, the room was crowded with everyone listening in. Other than Matilda, no one was having more fun than Suzette. The smile on her face was worth a million dollars.

"You want to take over?" Andy asked Cade.

"Nope. You've got this covered. Besides, I have my hands full." He was snuggling with Megan who was asleep on his shoulder. Andy had no idea how the child could sleep amid all the noise, but she was out.

"What do you want to sing now?" Andy asked.

"Stuck Like Glue!" Mattie yelled excitedly.

"I'm not sure I know that one," he admitted. He had heard the song but had never played it.

"Sure you does," she said, and started singing it from the beginning. It didn't take Andy long to pick up the tune, and soon he was playing right along with her cute voice.

During the middle of the song, the dogs started barking when there was a knock on the door. They took off running outside to see who the guest was on the front porch. It wasn't anyone who knew them, or they'd have come to the back door. Everyone was quiet until a voice from Andy's past asked, "What are you doing here?"

"What am *I* doing here? What the hell are *you* doing here?" Christy practically yelled.

"I came to talk to my son." Andy tensed up. What the fuck was his mother doing at the farm, and why did she have to ruin such a perfect day?

"I'll be right back," Andy told Matilda. He grabbed Bryan's hand as he went to confront the one person he'd never expected to see again. Hilary had pushed her way inside and was looking around at all the people. Andy stopped, leaving several feet between them, and Bryan stood directly behind him, pressing his chest to Andy's back for support.

"How did you find me?"

His mother scoffed like it was a stupid question. "No thanks to her," she said, pointing at Christy. "I hired someone. Now get these mutts off me."

"What do you want, Hilary?" Andy ignored Moe and Curly, who were doing nothing more than sniffing her shoes.

"Hilary? That's no way to address your mother. I... can we talk in private? There are some things we need to discuss, as a family."

Suzette was now standing next to Andy, the fury coming off the woman in waves. "No, we can't talk in private. If you want to discuss something as a 'family' then you're in the right place, because these people, every single one of them, are my family."

"Andrew, I know you think —"

"You have no idea what I think," he said, cutting her off. "What I think is I needed a mother when my life turned to shit, and you weren't there."

"You don't understand," Hilary butted in.

Suzette stepped in front of Andy, getting right in his mother's face. "*He* doesn't understand? I don't think *you* understand, lady, and I use that term loosely. Your child, your *only* child came home beaten up, bleeding, in need of medical attention! What did you do? You handed him forty dollars and a few clothes and shoved him out the door, not caring that he could have died from his injuries."

"What do you know about it? You weren't there. You don't know what I went through. I would have lost everything. Andy was smart. I knew he'd find a way to be okay."

Suzette took a step closer, and Walt was right behind her. Andy wanted to stop Suzette, but she was on a roll. "What do *I* know about it? I'll tell you. That boy was *not*

289

okay. And he *did* lose everything. He lost so much more than his family that day, but you wouldn't know that because you're a selfish, money-hungry bitch. I know all about it, because like Andy, my son accidentally outed himself to his homophobic father. But instead of him kicking Mal to the curb, he took a knife to him. Cut a path from his chest to his hip and left him for dead. But that wasn't enough. He came after me next, accusing me of birthing a faggot. He hit me over and over in the face until he thought I was dead, too. I didn't die, though. I woke up having lost most of my eyesight.

"It's *you* who doesn't understand what being a mother is. You don't toss your child out like the trash just because someone thinks you should. You stand by them. You protect them as best you can. You sure as shit don't turn your back on them and show up eight years later acting like nothing happened!"

"I'm still his mother," Hilary argued.

"No, you're not. You gave up that right when you chose money over your child. He doesn't need you. I'm his mother now. Walt, here, is his father, and everyone else you see in this room is his family. So, unless you want me to call the law and have you arrested for trespassing, you'll take your fancy ass back to Texas and stay there." And with that, Suzette put the last stitch in place, completely mending Andy.

Hilary gasped and stuttered, "Andrew . . . please . . . Your grandfather . . . The company . . ."

Andy pulled Bryan's arms around him tighter and glared at her. "Those things mean nothing to me. This is my home; this is my family. The man behind me is going to be my husband, and this woman right here?" Andy put his arm around Suzette. "This amazing woman is my mom. There's nothing left for you to say, so I suggest before one of the big ass Marines in this room gets hold of you, you leave of your own accord. Goodbye, Hilary."

Andy pulled Suzette into his body, hugging her with everything he had, while Toby and Cole created a barrier between them and his mother. No, not his mother. Hilary Holcomb. Andy's mother was in his arms. The room was silent, letting Andy and Suzette have their moment, shedding cleansing tears, until Mattie yelled, "Gramma, yous called her a bitch!"

Suzette, along with everyone else in the room, burst out laughing. Walt put his hand on the side of Andy's neck and smiled. Mal surprised Andy when he stepped next to him and said, "Looks like we're brothers." Andy nodded, and they did a quick man hug.

Matilda wormed her way between the adults. "Uncle Andy! Uncle Andy!"

"What, squirt?"

"Let's sing!" she yelled, jumping up and down.

"You got it." Andy returned to the piano, where he and Mattie sang several more songs with most everyone joining in. His new family had filled his heart to overflowing, and now the music was filling his soul. Only one thing left to do to make his life complete, and that was to make the man standing next to him his husband.

Epilogue

Bryan

Bryan twisted the titanium band on his left hand while he waited on Andy to finish in the bathroom. "Come on, Lily. The wind's blowing. Your hair's just gonna get messed up as soon as you step outside."

"You know this is a special day, B. I want to look good."

"Baby, you always look good." And he did. It had been over a year since Bryan met Andy, and he still couldn't believe the man was his. It was one of the reasons Bryan constantly touched his wedding ring. When Bryan told his siblings he was getting married, all of them insisted on being there, even Bryce. Seeing his brother had done wonders for Bryan. They had a chance to talk privately, and Bryce apologized for being so distant. He'd felt like Bryan abandoned him much the same way their father had. It took a lot of soul searching on Bryce's part, but he finally figured out Bryan had left out of love and familial obligation.

Their wedding had been small but beautiful. Cade rented a lodge in northern Kentucky and had flown all of Bryan's family in. Everyone in Mal's family now considered Andy theirs, so they were in attendance as well, including Mal's sister, Melanie. Andy had his closure. He and Suzette had formed a special bond after the day she let Hilary Holcomb have a piece of her mind. Cole and Toby, who'd been hanging around the farm often, had joined them at the lodge. Christy and Kason, who'd never stopped seeing each other past their first night together, were there as well. A few months after Christy arrived, Andy confided to Bryan

292

that Christy had a miscarriage right before coming to Arlo. It was the main reason she wanted to put Texas behind her.

It had been nothing short of magical, and to Bryan, it had been perfect because it's what Andy wanted. Bryan didn't need the sparkling lights and fancy champagne flutes. He just needed his man. The one thing he wouldn't change about their wedding was when Andy sat down at the piano and sang Elton John's "Your Song" to Bryan.

Bryan had visited his mother's grave before going to see his father. This time, Bryan spent more than five minutes on the other side of the glass partition talking through a phone. He sat by his father's hospital bed as he begged Bryan's forgiveness. Bryan held his father's hand as he took his final breath. None of his siblings were there, but it was the way his father wanted it. Calvin Moore was buried next to his wife in a small cemetery in Chicago. With his husband by his side, Bryan and his siblings said goodbye to the dad who loved them almost as much as he loved their mother. In a way, Bryan had the closure he needed.

Now they were getting ready for another wedding — Suzette's. She was in the kitchen with Melanie and Matilda, waiting to walk out the front door and marry the man she'd fallen in love with in high school. It was almost time, and Bryan reminded Andy of the fact.

"Lily, your mom is going to walk out the front door in less than five minutes."

"I'm ready," Andy said coming out of the bathroom. Bryan sucked in his breath. Andy Moore was a handsome man, but Andy Moore in a suit was something Bryan would never get used to.

"Fuck, Lily. You need to walk out of this room right now, or neither one of us is going to make the wedding."

Andy tilted his head to the side and bit his bottom lip. Goddamn, he was too much.

"Andy, you ready?" Mal asked from the hallway.

"Yep." Andy held out his hand and pulled Bryan

from the bed. "Let's go get my parents hitched," he whispered.

Suzette's eye surgeries had been a success for the most part. She looked stunning in her stylish glasses and her pretty, cream-colored dress. Chairs were set up in the front yard facing away from the house. Cade had hired a florist out of Nashville to turn the area into something simple yet spectacular. A string trio softly played while Andy and Bryan made their way to the front where they stood by Walt as his best men. Melanie was next, taking her place as Matron of Honor. Matilda tossed flower petals into the air before taking her seat next to Cade, who was holding Megan. Mollie, the baby, was sleeping peacefully in Christy's arms. Mal escorted his mom, and it was one of the most beautiful moments Bryan had ever seen. When Mal handed Suzette off to Walt, he hugged them both before standing next to his sister. It didn't matter who stood where, Suzette had explained. They were all family.

The words Suzette and Walt spoke to each other were heartfelt yet simple. The ceremony was short and sweet, and soon after, everyone was on the deck or in the yard, enjoying themselves as they usually did. The only difference was Cade had catered the food in so those who usually cooked — Mal and Andy — could enjoy the day without the hassle of feeding everyone.

Talk surrounded the new house being built toward the south end of the property where Cade and Mal would eventually live. The two of them had been scarce with Cade showing Mal parts of the US he'd never seen. Andy had started taking a few classes online with plans to eventually handle the business side of running the farm. Mal had been more than thrilled at the idea. In his opinion, he was a better cowboy than he was a paper pusher.

Bryan and Andy had settled into married life, and so far, there hadn't been any bumps in their road. Hilary stayed away, but one day, an official letter showed up at the house. After reading it, Andy handed it to Bryan. Andy stood by the window of their bedroom, looking out at nothing while Bryan took in the words. After Andy's grandfather passed, his grandmother had adjusted her own will, reinstating Andy into the family. None of that mattered since his father would inherit everything anyway, but Bryan saw it as an olive branch from an old woman trying to mend the pieces of a broken family. Once Bryan had read the letter, Andy put it in the fireplace, not bothering to watch it burn.

Cade and Andy had been huddled together in secret quite a bit, and Bryan had a feeling he knew what they were up to. More than once, the two of them had gotten together with Cade playing guitar and Andy on the piano. The two men were phenomenal together, their voices harmonizing perfectly. Bryan could listen to Andy sing all day and all night. Well, maybe not all night. He preferred to use that time making love. Once Andy let Bryan make love to him the first time, more often than not, he asked to be on the receiving end of their lovemaking. Bryan had no problem with that. Nor did he mind when Andy was in an aggressive mood and pounded him into the mattress. It didn't take them long to figure out they could still make love while getting as rough as the other wanted.

Andy pressed a tender kiss against Bryan's mouth. "I love you, B." The way he said it let Bryan know something big was going to happen. Andy turned and whistled, getting everyone's attention. When everyone gathered around, Cade stepped next to Andy with his guitar. "We have something we've been working on for a few months now. While I wrote this for Bryan, we thought it was perfect for today, as well," Andy said, never taking his eyes off his husband. "It's called "Finding Me." Cade began strumming, and Andy closed his eyes and sang the most beautiful words Bryan had ever heard. When he got to the chorus, Cade blended his voice with Andy's.

Found myself in hell
With nowhere else to go
Beaten and broken on the floor
There's nothing left inside

Years I spent searching
For a way out of my own head
Looking for a small glimpse
Of the boy I used to be

Then one day there you are
Sitting across from me
A kindred spirit full of life
A wish upon a star come true
A beautiful soul is all I see

In your eyes I see the truth
In your arms I find my strength
In your love I find myself
In finding you, I've found me

Found myself in heaven
Nowhere else I want to go
Healing and happy for the first time
I'm filling up inside

Years I spent searching
For the love inside of me
Looking for a small glimpse
Of the man I want to be

Then one day there you are
Standing next to me
A beautiful face lit up by your smile
You're so much more than you know
Your love is all I see

In your eyes I see the truth
In your arms I find my strength
In your love I find myself
In finding you, I've found me

Then one day there you are
Lying in bed with me
My very own heaven
I can't believe you're mine
Our future is all I see

In your eyes I see the truth
In your arms I find my strength
In your love I find myself
In finding you, I've found me

By the time Andy sang the last word, Bryan could barely see. He blinked several times, clearing the tears from his eyes. He was on Andy before the last note left Cade's guitar. Not caring that it was Walt and Suzette's day, Bryan crashed his body to his husband's. Bryan also didn't care that three other Marines were witnessing him fall apart. Andy held him and placed kisses along his cheeks and forehead until Bryan had his emotions under control.

When they broke apart, Suzette was right there to take Andy's place. "I'm sorry, Suzette," Bryan choked out.

"Oh, my sweet boy, you have nothing to be sorry for. And how many times do I have to ask you to call me Mom?"

"Mom. . ." Bryan tried it out. He'd not wanted to take anything away from Andy and Suzette, but the way Andy beamed at them both let Bryan know there was enough love to go around. When there was a commotion behind them, Bryan turned to see Toby with this phone in his hand. Everyone was watching the huge bodyguard pacing back and forth, his free hand raking through his hair.

"You're completely sure?" Toby asked whoever he was talking to. Cole was standing close by his best friend as he usually was. Bryan had never seen the two men look at each other in a way that would indicate they were a couple. They fussed and carried on like two brothers instead. When Toby disconnected his phone, he looked at Cole and nodded. One side of Cole's mouth turned up in an almost smile.

"Mal, I need to talk to you and your mom."

Suzette's knees almost buckled, but Bryan was still holding on to her. She shook her head and said, "No."

"Suzette, please," Toby pled.

"No, Toby. We're all family here. Whatever you have to say, just say it. If you don't, I'll turn around and tell everyone anyway." Mal and Walt had made their way to where Suzette was. Bryan backed away giving the two men room to surround her.

Toby looked at Cole again. When he nodded, Toby said, "When we first found out about Curtis, I made a few phone calls. I have some contacts in pretty high places, and... they've located Curtis. Suzette, your son is alive."

Suzette's knees did give way, but Mal and Walt caught her. Andy placed a chair behind her and sat her down. "I'm fine, I'm fine," she fussed. Toby closed the distance between them, and everyone gathered around. "When can I go see him? When can I bring my boy home?"

"That's the thing. . . We know where he is, we just have to go rescue him first."

"We?" Mal asked.

"Yes. Cole and I are going to join a team of men who were Special Forces before they opted out. I'm not sure how long it will take, but we won't stop until we have Curtis. Suzette, I probably shouldn't have told you yet, but since today was a day for celebrating, I wanted to give you my own wedding present."

"This is the best news I've had in a long time, Toby.

Thank you. Just knowing Curtis is alive gives me hope, and I know you'll do your best."

"Yes ma'am, I will."

"*We* will," Cole added. He knelt down in front of Suzette and pulled her hands to his lips, kissing her knuckles. "You are such a special woman, making all of us feel like your family. Many of us don't have mothers of our own, and you've shown us the love we've been missing. We want to give something back to you. We promise to do our best to bring Curtis home alive."

Suzette wiped her eyes beneath her glasses. "Thank you. Thank you both," she whispered.

"We need to go," Toby said. "We'll be radio silent for a while, but as soon as we have word for you, I'll call." Toby and Cole strode down the deck toward their car. Bryan, Andy, and Kason met them before they could leave. The five of them stood in a circle, arms wrapped over the shoulders of the Marine next to him. "Semper Fi," Bryan said. Four deep voices responded with, "Semper Fi."

The rest of the day was less of a party and more of a quiet celebration of love. Of family. And now, of hope. Toby and Cole would find Curtis. They would bring him home, and, surrounded by his family, Curtis would be showered with love and begin the healing process. Bryan had no doubt things would be okay in the end. Theirs was a family who had to go through hell to find their heaven.

When Bryan went to bed that night with Andy tucked safely at his side, he knew he'd found his own little slice of heaven in a little country town in Arlo, Kentucky.

About the Author

Faith Gibson lives outside Nashville, Tennessee with the love of her life, and her four-legged best friends. She began writing in high school and over the years, penned many stories and poems. When her dreams continued to get crazier than the one before, she decided to keep a dream journal. Many of these night-time escapades have led to a line, a chapter, and even a complete story.

When asked what her purpose in life is, she will say to entertain the masses. Even if it's one person at a time. When Faith isn't hard at work on her next story, she can be found having her own concert in the shower (or car, or wherever music is playing), playing trivia while enjoying craft beer, reading, or riding her Harley.

Connect with Faith via the following social media sites:

https://www.facebook.com/faithgibsonauthor

https://www.twitter.com/authorfgibson

Sign up for her newsletter:

http://www.faithgibsonauthor.com/newsletter.html

Send her an email: faithgibsonauthor@gmail.com

Other Works by Faith Gibson

The Music Within Series

Deliver Me

Release Me

The Stone Society Series - Paranormal

Rafael

Gregor

Dante

Frey

Nikolas

Jasper

Sixx

Sin

Jonas

The Samuel Dexter Stories

The Ghost in the Desert – Novella

The Ghost in the Mirror

The Sweet Things Series

Candy Hearts – A MM Short Story

Troubled Hearts – Contemporary Romance

Made in the USA
San Bernardino, CA
29 April 2017